THE UNIFORM

A Novel

GUERNICA WORLD EDITIONS 74

THE UNIFORM

A Novel

GEORGE GUIDA

GUERNICA
World
EDITIONS

TORONTO–CHICAGO–BUFFALO–LANCASTER (U.K.)
2024

Guernica Editions Founder: Antonio D'Alfonso

Michael Mirolla, general editor
Scott Walker, editor
Cover design: Allen Jomoc, Jr.
Interior design: Jill Ronsley, suneditwrite.com

Guernica Editions Inc.
287 Templemead Drive, Hamilton (ON), Canada L8W 2W4
2250 Military Road, Tonawanda, N.Y. 14150-6000 U.S.A.
www.guernicaeditions.com

Distributors:
Independent Publishers Group (IPG)
600 North Pulaski Road, Chicago IL 60624
University of Toronto Press Distribution (UTP)
5201 Dufferin Street, Toronto (ON), Canada M3H 5T8

First edition.

Legal Deposit—First Quarter
Library of Congress Catalog Card Number: 2023943805
Library and Archives Canada Cataloguing in Publication
Title: The uniform : a novel / George Guida.
Names: Guida, George, 1967- author.
Series: Guernica world editions (Series) ; 74.
Description: Series statement: Guernica world editions ; 74
Identifiers: Canadiana (print) 20230522904 | Canadiana (ebook)
20230522939 | ISBN 9781771838818 (softcover) | ISBN 9781771838825 (EPUB)
Classification: LCC PS3607.U4935 U55 2024 | DDC 813/.6—dc23

"The dead grow larger each day until sometimes
they become quite too big for their uniforms."

—Ernest Hemingway, *Death in the Afternoon*

"Though we travel the world over to find the beautiful,
we must carry it with us or we find it not."

—Ralph Waldo Emerson, "Art"

(1968)

The battalion mustered at 116th Street and Broadway, the wrought iron university gate looming behind them. Alfie looked down the line of cops in full riot gear. Night sticks smacking palms were the chirrups of upstate heat bugs, growing louder as the sun sank. If only he could be there now, on his cousin's land, next to his father, watching the tree line for game.

Alfie looked down the line again. Still as beagles with a scent, the detail listened to the lieutenant-in-charge give final instructions: Enter through the tunnels, eject the occupiers, secure the buildings, get back to their precinct houses a couple of hours later, home in time for the Carson show. The briefing room that day had been all ears open, mouths shut. The brass didn't feature the operation. NYPD could only look bad tangling with a bunch of eggheads, but it was a job more than a few cops couldn't wait to do. Ever since they killed King, most patrolmen had been living with double shifts and assaults from the black bastards whose neighborhoods they should've let burn. Alfie hadn't had a night home with his kids in two weeks. He was annoyed, tired of the *mulies* and tired of all the bleeding-heart shit from these spoiled brats. "Bust their fuckin' college holes," was the way Sweeney put it, lowering Monday's *Daily News*.

"Right," Alfie answered. "Bunch of rich communists. Part of the big slide."

He'd seen a photo of Somers, the ringleader. Typical: shaggy hair, thin, face like a rat. The little prick liked to hold up pictures of all the

1

so-called leaders: King and the one they killed in Harlem. How could his father have been that close with Joe Jefferson up Rome? Nothing but big smiles, the old preacher. And his old man trusted him, on instinct. The same old man who was always telling his sons not to trust the shirts on their backs. Alfie had proven his father's point, the way he'd turned on him, on the other people he was supposed to love.

Which is why he had to respect Somers a little. The snotty fuck had gone to a faculty meeting and told the professors that unless they backed the student strike a hundred and ten per cent, everything else they did would be bullshit. The kid had balls and really seemed to believe in something, even if he was arrogant and more-or-less wrong. If you asked Alfie what he himself believed in, he would say maybe order, or, a bigger maybe, his family. Or the biggest maybe of all, what he still felt for Adeline.

He'd become one of the cops the Department sent out to keep the *mulies* in line. Six-foot-three and solid muscle, from hurdler's legs to slim waist to weightlifter's chest and shoulders. Hair military short. Face angular, rugged, most often stubbled. A face that could go from wide smile to hollow stare in the second it took Alfie to catch a whiff of trouble. He walked with a forward-leaning swagger that promised a beating to any fool who got in his way. He whispered to Sweeney, his partner, a shorter man, but just as solid, who was grinning as if the lieutenant were up there telling stories about the latest broad he'd nailed after work.

"Their fuckin' college holes."

Sweeney's grin widened, reminding Alfie of the bastard who'd nearly done the preacher in. Alfie always did what he had to do, but fellas like Sweeney enjoyed the sound of bone on bone. Officially, of course, it was hands off the students, but the warning came with a gleam in the sergeant's eye. Making an example or two usually broke up the party. If he were to ask how to handle himself, the commandants would tell him what his father would have said: Just don't lose control. Nothing would happen until after the six o'clock news. And the reward for a job well done would be a step closer to a desk, a little peace.

Alfie had done his homework and made a plan. He and Sweeney would lead the charge into Low Library. Once they got inside, they would cuff the punks, who would go limp. Then they'd drag them onto the campus steps and down to paddy wagons parked along the brick walk. The job would be all strength, like lifting forms into place on one of his grandfather's construction sites. No question Somers and his two goons, Lundstrem and Wiesniewski, would be inside the library building. Somers physically was nothing, but Lundstrem and Wiesniewski had been linebackers on the Columbia football team before they went over to the dark side. The last couple of weeks, whenever things had gotten a little hairy, these two had pulled their captain out before any shit hit the fan. Today would be different. Alfie felt the anger rising in his throat.

The lieutenant's voice filled the quad.

"Brooklyn, Six-Eight, Seven-Five, Seven-Three, line up!"

Brooklyn. He used to feel at least a little proud of it. In the Army, allegiance to the borough was his own Confederate flag to wave back at the rednecks in his regiment. Now even the name of the place bothered Alfie. Most of these fellas around him had grown up in one of the boroughs, and most of them, like him, were dying to get out. His old neighborhood was still safe, but you could see it was changing. Every day the sight of the 61st Street train ditch made him a little sicker. The chain link fence that lined the ditch was rusting away. Years ago, the street had been like an estate the whole block owned. It was groomed, guarded, sacred. Now people drove up in cars and threw garbage right over the top of the fence. The slopes of the ditch looked like an exploded landfill. Across the way, the old 62nd Street Guinea gardens were almost empty, a lot of the Italians too old to tend them. At the 65th Street station, the first ugly red graffiti had shown up a few months before. Probably the Puerto Ricans, who were taking over the far side of Borough Park, or the *mulies* down in Coney Island. It all made Alfie sick.

Living in the old house made things even worse. When Alfie was a kid, after his family moved down from Rome, they'd lived in the upstairs apartment, which was at least a decent size. A few years back, he and Michelle had decided to move back from Queens and into the apartment below. They were broke, and moving in with Michelle's mother wasn't an option, since she was crazier than her daughter, who had always wanted kids but couldn't handle them. His grandfather let them rent the first floor for practically nothing. Now the four of them were all living in three rooms. His parents had never been thrilled about the arrangement or about his wife. His mother felt free to tell Michelle exactly what she thought of her and of the way she was raising her grandchildren. Then Alfie had to hear all about it all night long. Going to work was a relief. But this last month, the outside world had become such a headache that he almost looked forward to getting home and sitting on the couch with the kids, watching television, and eating whatever piss-poor dinner Michelle put in front of him. She was still a hell of a lot better in the bedroom than in the kitchen, enough so that at least once or twice a week he got the kids off to sleep in time to do to her what had gotten him jammed up in the first place. Sometimes it was worth it. Most of the time it wasn't. Nothing changed the fact that his wife was like a grounded partridge, running through the house and squawking back over her shoulder at him or at the kids, who most of the time were quiet, doing whatever they did. Thank God they'd taken after him that way. In a house out on Long Island, Michelle might calm down, and he might have a little shop or studio where he could hide. If he could score some points with the honchos, get the detective's salary, they might hold it together long enough for the kids to have a normal childhood.

The detail marched toward the library, between two rows of flowering cherry trees. The dying blossoms looked sickly pink in the late afternoon light. Fallen petals carpeted the walk. Alfie remembered the story of Palm Sunday. When the troop halted, he picked up a blossom and sniffed it. Rotten sweet. Up ahead he could see the lieutenant waving the men forward. He slipped the flower into his pocket.

Near the library steps the squad found themselves surrounded by protestors. Most were students with their fists in the air. Their shouts came in waves, like cheers at a football game. On the lower plaza in front of the library, one group of clean-cut kids, most of them tall, good builds, tough-looking, stood inside police barricades, pointing their fingers at the field of long-haired heads that stretched like fuzzy weeds to every corner of the quad. Alfie nudged Sweeney. The two of them scanned the crowd of smooth-skinned faces.

Fifteen years ago, with a little push from his family, different timing, he could've been a student here. But where would he have fit in? Would he have been one of the athletes? One of these sport-coat types? If they'd had demonstrations then, would he have been an Army/Navy store rebel or just a spectator on the lawn? More than likely, he would've been sitting in his dormitory room, practicing guitar, maybe rehearsing with a band in the student lounge, following the action from a window. But then his grandfather had the business and wanted him to take over. And he had his music, Sammy and the group. He'd spent all his time listening to Django Reinhardt, Doc Watson, Chuck Berry. Then there were motorcycles. And the Army. And Michelle. And Adeline. In the end it came down to picking a uniform, holding up one sign or another.

A few of the students in the pen were holding up a banner: The Majority Coalition. Most of the protestors wore buttons. Alfie walked closer to the nearest barricade, where he could read them:

Columbia SDS
STRIKE!
"I Have a Dream"
If You're Not Part of the Solution, You're Part of the Problem
IWW
Feed the Hungry!

Every button screamed so loud that you couldn't think for yourself. One had a picture of two *mulies* wearing berets, Panthers, with the caption: "*Political Prisoners of U. S. A. Fascism.*" Who were they kidding? LBJ was an asshole, but he was no Mussolini. Alfie did see one button that he liked: An old, bearded man in a fur hat, staring into the distance. No caption. A few of the plainclothes cops wore buttons of their own: little red circles that they used to identify one another in the crowd. Plainclothes, he'd heard, had infiltrated the occupied buildings. He pointed out the red buttons to Sweeney, who squinted his psycho eyes, grinned, and asked,"Where's *my* button?"

A different kind of grin, Sweeney's, but just as intense as the preacher's that morning up Delta Lake. Old Joe Jefferson had a smile that could ease your mind. It was the preacher had talked his father into taking Alfie on his first hunting trip. How could he forgive him? Or his father? Or himself? They hadn't been an hour out on that trip when he'd stopped and pointed to a line of men standing on the ridge of a wooded hill ahead of them. The sun sat low, so the men were dark giants in its red rays.

"Baliato!" the biggest of the bunch shouted, striding forward like a movie cowboy. He was Bob Bronson, red and black hunting cap pulled low, round face half-hidden in shadow. Alfie recognized the voice and knew why he was there. Bronson pointed to Jefferson.

"Who's that you got there witcha?"

A few paces to his right, Alfie's father stopped dead, resting his arms on the barrel end of his upright shotgun. He spat tobacco juice in front of him.

"Friend of mine," he answered. "How's it business a yours?"

In a flash the other men surrounded them. Before Alfie could move, one of them grabbed his arm and pulled him to the side. Instead of gunfire—he'd always known his father would never shoot a man—he heard the sixteen-gauge fall in dry leaves. His father charged at Bronson's chest. Barely five foot eight, but hard as granite, the old man, maybe forty then, hit the taller man so hard that he knocked him backwards three feet.

"Sonofabitch," his father yelled, hammering punches into Bronson's face.

Then hell started raining fists. His father disappeared in a tangle of arms, legs and torsos, the oranges, blacks, reds, browns of the hunting clothes most men of Rome wore that time of year.

When he looked the preacher's way, Alfie saw a different sight: Lou Quattrochi, a bar back at Bronson's place, the Paradise, the competition for his uncle's Romohawk. Quattrochi was maybe twenty and already had a reputation for fighting at every bar in East Rome. This *cidrul* and a man Alfie didn't recognize were pulling the preacher's arms back around a big maple tree, tying a rope around his wrists, binding him to the trunk. Once they had him strung, Quattrochi took out a pair of brass knuckles, pounding them into his palm. The preacher's eyes lit up like campfires stoked by the wind. A second later Alfie heard a crack and saw blood explode from the bridge of the preacher's nose. Then another, as fragments of the preacher's teeth peppered Alfie's jacket like buckshot. The third blow was an uppercut to the jaw.

The man holding Alfie's fourteen-year-old arms pushed him to his knees.

"This what you was waitin' to see, son? Take a look. Here's what happens to the ones think they're like white folks."

Another roundhouse from Lou tore a hole in Jefferson's cheek. At least the preacher was unconscious by then.

Alfie wished he'd had then what he had a little piece of now: the power to put people right. He and Sweeney led their battalion along a narrow, barricaded path, past a gauntlet of protestors whose clothes and songs said they had no place in a brawl. Their faces said something else. Snarling. Like animals. They didn't know what it was to feel a club bust your gut or a gun butt smash your nose, to bleed like you'd never stop. Leaving most of the crowd behind, the detail jogged up a side staircase, toward Lewisohn Hall, cutting a wide berth around the spillover crowd, then reaching Earl Hall, an unoccupied building where the college prayer groups held their meetings. Earl was inconspicuous, but it had an entrance to the system of tunnels connecting most of the other buildings on campus. The one from Lewisohn to Low was the shortest, and if they were lucky, it would take them straight to Somers. Years of footsteps had worn depressions in the marble stairs leading down. Under the light from its caged bulbs, the place felt familiar. The walls were thick concrete painted battleship gray. This could have been the basement of any big New York apartment house, but it smelled of sour dirt from deep in the ground. Alfie knew the smell from days playing along the Erie Canal, from excavation sites, from the Brooklyn cellar where his band had rehearsed.

In those days it was mostly rhythm and blues with a little Elvis and Buddy Holly thrown in, what they thought people would want to hear, but the night always ended with deeper tunes, with loneliness he felt in his father's Brooklyn exile: Hank Williams, the Stanley Brothers, Leadbelly, "Goodnight, Irene." Every time the group played it, he imagined Irene, what could have happened to her, how this singer's world could have fallen apart so fast. Now he understood. Every sustained note tore through him. A melody like that could kill whatever was left of his heart.

He walked on, Sweeney right behind him. In the distance a red light marked the entrance to Low. The protestors had thought far enough ahead to lock it, but a pick gun got the battalion in. They tip-toed forward. Stepping up the first flight, Alfie could make out tinny voices and music, the echoes of a party heard from a child's bedroom. He thought of family dinners, of Adeline in her Sunday dress.

Sweeney snapped him out of it.

"No lookout."

"What?"

"At the door."

"They're too busy smoking dope."

Before he was on the job, Alfie had tried the stuff. With a girl he'd met at a bar after work, when he was supposed to be staying late at the office. Easy to get. And now it was easier still. Drugs were everywhere. In the old neighborhood, the skells sold them at night in front of the closed-up side-street five-and-dimes. Here, with the money these brats had, with the nooks and crannies, with all the deviants and rabble-rousers at the gates, the dealers probably walked around the campus like they owned it. If these kids were smoking, they might be using something harder. One of them on LSD might come flying down the stairs any second. The lieutenant had told them the occupiers were unarmed, but what if they had rifles from the Panthers? Was he supposed to get shot so some Ivy League delinquents could make a political statement? Word was they'd taken over the President's office, destroyed the furniture, burned files, slashed the Rembrandt painting over the boss's desk. Alfie had seen a few Rembrandts and liked them. The little fucks were going down. They picked up the pace. Sweeney flew past him.

The sound from above was cover. Alfie could hear individual guitar chords now, distorted, rough. And laughter over the music. Occasional bull-horned messages:

"You don't need a weatherman to know which way the wind blows. Yeeee-haaah!"

"Down with capitalism!"

"No class rank lists!"

"Fight for our brothers and sisters in the ghetto!"

"Don't trust anyone over 30!"

After each exclamation, Alfie heard a muffled cheer from the crowd on the ground.

Then one voice and a line all the cops knew:

"Up against the wall, Motherfucker!"

Alfie caught up with Sweeney and grabbed his shoulder.

"Somers."

They flew up the stairs like superheroes in a comic book, legs blue blurs, body armor heavy, nightsticks, blackjacks, walkies, cuffs, everything jangling like castanets and wood blocks, their own music competing with the crunch of chords louder and louder, the wails of solos, a Black man's raspy voice. At the bottom of the last flight, they surprised a kid in dungarees and polo shirt. The moron was just sitting there, smoking a cigarette. He tried to turn and run up the stairs, but as Alfie got close enough to hear him wheeze, he saw the dark flash of Sweeney's billy club and heard the thud on the kid's skull. Like a scarecrow the poor fuck dropped straight down, rolled a few steps to the landing, and was out. Sweeney was right. It was important to maintain the element of surprise.

Their batons rose again as they approached the door of the President's office. Two lines of demonstrators, most of them dressed for a night of drinking, locked arms across the threshold. Alfie rammed one in the belly with his nightstick, blackjacked another on the shoulder, and only had to hear the loud snap to know that Sweeney had broken one of their arms with his club. Alfie remembered his accident. That kind of pain was indescribable. A guitar solo blared from behind the door. He thought about how his grandmother had been right when she'd told him, with the old Italian sense of fate, "You'll never be the same."

Sweeney's target was thrashing around on the marble floor, pawing at his shattered arm with his one useful hand. You hated to hurt a dumb kid, but in a case like this you had to take out the weak link. Anyway, it was Somers and his bunch had brought this on. Alfie wanted nothing more than to grab the little jackass and personally drag him screaming to the wagon, preferably in front of at least two or three of the commandants. As the detail put the rest of the student guards on the ground, Alfie felt a hand on his foot. It belonged to the injured kid, his face twisted like a raisin, head raised.

"Fucking hired thug," he spat between coughs.

Thug. The word his father had used after the attack in the woods. The old man lay in a hospital bed, recuperating from two broken ribs and a ruptured spleen.

"Bronson's thugs," he said. "*Vigliacchi*, cowards, every one of 'em. Fair fight, I'd a broken Bronson in half."

Fair fight? God rest his father's soul.

"He got off easy. He grabs my son, I pull out one of his eyes."

He'd almost killed Bronson. But the preacher wasn't so tough or so lucky. By the time the thugs took off and Alfie was able to crawl over to the big maple tree, Jefferson's face was red pulp. Only his rolling white eyes said he was still on earth. And whose fault was it? Was the old man so high and mighty that he thought he could violate the code of Rome without paying a price?

Now Alfie could feel the kid's fingers at the top of his boot. Blood surged through his legs. Staying grounded took all his strength. His chest was burning for action, anything. His foot shook. As the kid tightened his grip, Alfie ground his teeth. The tendons in his neck were steel strings. All around voices shouted, so that words were twigs snapping in the woods, gunshots in the air. The kid at his feet was what? Nineteen? Twenty? At that age, maybe a little younger, Alfie too had been trouble, always trying to find a use for the muscles he'd built in his basement like a science project, to be the tough guy people expected him to be. His instinct was to raise his leg and stomp the kid's hand, crush his fingers. Instead, he reached down and grabbed him by his broken arm. The kid screamed like a sick baby. Sweeney glanced over, giving him the thumbs up. Alfie threw the boy's good arm around his shoulder, dragged him to the closest wall, and let him crumple to the ground.

"This is where you stay, you hear me?"

With a slow movement of his head, the kid signaled Alfie to come closer. His mouth just an inch or two from Alfie's ear, he groaned, "No matter what, we're taking the university down."

Alfie took the kid's head in both hands, slapped his cheek, and spoke slowly.

"And then what? … Jerk-off."

The kid closed his eyes and swooned.

The battle was all about proving who had the biggest balls, and Alfie wasn't about to lose his. Feeling another rush, he jumped in again. Butterflies in his stomach lifted him through the office door and inside. Bodies were flying everywhere. Some flying toward the oak-paneled walls, some flying at him and Sweeney. The partners stood back-to-back, weapons up, the way his father had taught him to do whenever wild dogs came sniffing through the woods. Other cops did the same, taking swings, connecting with the punks who came at them in their dungarees, turtle-neck sweaters, monkey dress shirts, tennis shoes. Blood streaked the floor and spattered the walls. The smell of it drove Alfie ahead.

"Anything you see, hit," he shouted.

And he and Sweeney swung like a single four-armed monster, cracking arms, pounding backs, bashing skulls, whatever body parts had the bad fortune of getting in the way. To anyone with a camera, the scene would've looked brutal, just what the bosses didn't want. But Alfie had a method.

"The back," he yelled to Sweeney. "Let's go."

They were almost to the door behind the President's desk, next to the Rembrandt that somehow was still in one piece, when Alfie spotted Somers's unmistakable head. His hair was curly, his nose straight and long—a Pinocchio nose—and he wore a green fatigue jacket. He was motioning to someone in the adjoining room, until he spotted the two cops behind him. Sweeney was almost at the door when Somers skipped through a storm of bodies and disappeared.

A shoulder drove Alfie into the wall. He got to his feet. Then another shot, this one banging his head into a chair rail. He came back up swinging.

"Ahhhh, fuck."

Sweeney tugged his arm.

"C'mon, no time for that shit, Baliato."

The room was tilting sideways, but Alfie kept moving, steadying himself against the wall, then a chair, then propelling himself off one of the pukes. Through the door he spotted Sweeney again, club up, a mob whirling around him.

"Out of my way, you spoiled little fuck."

Club. Blackjack. Club. Elbow. Alfie wished he'd brought brass knuckles, but the only thing brass in the room was the handle of a stand-up ashtray near a big brown leather chair. A student nursing a head wound sat there, holding his glasses in one hand, rubbing his bloody temple with the other. Above the chair Alfie saw a framed diploma, the President's: University of Wisconsin, and some Latin, … *scientia civilis* … *MDCCCXXX*. Numbers always looked better that way, stronger, like counting meant something. Next to the chair was a side table with a book on it: Erasmus. *The Praise of Folly*. All of sudden Alfie felt as though he could sleep. He could sit right down here in the middle of all this shit and read and doze off. His father, a man he'd never seen read a book, had told him once, as they were walking past a shelf in his uncle's library, "Anything you wanna learn, you can find in one of these." And the world let kids like Somers just sit in libraries and take it all in. It was books had taken Adeline away. And drugs. And Alfie. His choices. His family. He wished he could erase it all.

Time to go. The second door of the office led to another stairwell and a lower hallway. A few at a time, the students were finding their way down, trying to keep ahead of the men in blue.

"Baliato, c'mon," Sweeney's voice called from down the hall.

Alfie pushed his way through the exodus. Footfalls on the marble floor echoed around a corner. He jogged as best he could toward a faint sound like bongo drums. When he made the turn, he caught sight of Sweeney, loping along and turning around to wave Alfie on. Alfie's head felt full of spiders. He shook it as clear as he could and took off running.

Sweeney again. "Where you goin', Asshole?"

A group of students appeared at the next corner, running toward Alfie. They'd been holed up in another office. Were they supposed to be the cavalry? Sweeney was giving them all the hell he could, which slowed him down enough for Alfie to catch up. As he reached Sweeney's side, the two cops jostled with this rear guard, doling out whacks as the *cidruls* pushed past. Sweeney's uniform was torn at the shoulder. His face was full of marks, but he smiled as he spoke.

"He's right up there. Time he gets through the doors, we'll nail him."

Alfie followed Sweeney in a sprint to the next stairwell. They could hear Somers's voice, deep chipmunk, cackling, taunting.

"Up against the wall, Motherfucker!"

A few seconds behind, the partners burst into the lobby. One of the goons was pushing Somers through a side window. Alfie thought of drawing his .38, then thought better. It took him years to get up the nerve to shoot a deer; it would take more than a day like this for him to blast a rich kid. The goon hopped through before Sweeney's dive could catch his leg. Alfie followed his partner out the window, crouching down, trying not to hit his already pounding head on the sash. He emerged on the side of the library near the campus chapel, and hit the pavement running. Sweeney flashed in front of the chapel, chasing shadows through the twilight.

From one direction came a chant: "Kirk must go! Kirk must go!"

The President. Sonofabitch had a living room in his office, but still, it was disrespectful. He wasn't Hitler, this guy. Hell, he probably liked the students.

From another direction somebody yelled, "Free Huey!"

Fuckin' Panthers. He wouldn't mind collaring a Panther. That would be a successful hunting trip.

By the time Alfie reached the Thinker statue, Sweeney was gone. He sat down on the statue's base, needing to clear his head. In front of him, on the library steps, the crowd was pushing against barricades, as the demonstrators in the office, some hanging out of windows, called down.

"Pigs go home!"

"No police state!"

Even most of the *mulies* treated cops with more respect.

The last straw was a banner that a group of students were draping over the big statue in front of Low, the woman with open arms: "Alma Mater, Raped by Cops."

Alfie turned away from the action. It was a cool night, but inside the uniform he was burning up. He took off his helmet and wiped the sweat from his forehead. In front of him Philosophy Hall rose up like a symmetrical mountain. People were running everywhere as if the whole city were burning. He looked up to see the expression on the Thinker's face. Depressing. Depressed. Maybe like he didn't care or couldn't really do anything about anything. Alfie wished he had stayed in school. Up Rome he'd loved studying history. All the empires. Who was Octavian? Where did Genghis Khan come from? What made him such a sonofabitch? If his family had stayed there, sure, he never would have met Adeline, but maybe it would've been better that way. And they would have stayed if it weren't for him. Or, he could say, if it weren't for his father. But was that fair?

He remembered the day Johnny Bronson called him a dago, told him his father was no better than a nigger. He'd gone right back to the old man and put it to him.

"Why do you gotta go around with a nigger, Pop?"

"A who? I don't know that word." He turned to his wife. "Pen, you ever hear that word?"

Alfie's mother looked daggers at her husband.

"Tell your friends to mind their own fathers' problems ... and keep their minds on something other than you. Books, maybe. Or how about girls?"

Back at school Johnny and the other kids wouldn't let up.

"My father says your father needs a good lesson, sitting with a nigger in public."

"My father says there's no such thing as a nigger."

"Maybe your father's a nigger, then."

Johnny touched Alfie's hair: curly, dark.

"You a nigger?"

Alfie shoved him into a wall. They were standing outside the lunchroom, right near the monitor, or Johnny would've been picking up his teeth. On the way home from school Alfie picked up a tree branch from the woods and bashed a mailbox on the American side of town. Back at the house, he found his father underneath their old black Chevrolet.

"Pop?"

The old man groaned, sliding himself out from under his boat of a car.

"What's the story, Son?

"Kids in school today asked me was I a nig...you know, was I colored, like Joe Jefferson."

His father sighed and wiped his hands on a rag.

"Pop, why do you gotta take Joe out in public? Can't you just be hunting friends?"

His father got to his feet, a full inch shorter than his lanky first-born.

"Alfie, I don't like to repeat myself," he said, "but I'll say this now and that's it: I love you, and I wish I could save you from all the stupid people that's in the world, but, boy, sometimes you gotta pick a side and do what you think is right. Matter of fact, I'm goin' hunting with Joe next weekend. Up Delta Lake. And you're invited. Joe's idea."

He patted Alfie's shoulder, and knelt down next to the sideboard of the car.

"Go tell the rascals at school if they got a problem with that, they can come out to see me in the woods."

Then he disappeared under the car again.

Alfie dropped his books on the front lawn and headed toward Dominick Street. His life would be hell from here on out. Johnny Bronson wouldn't let up. And enough kids felt about colored people just the way Johnny did. Alfie hated his father sometimes. Stubborn, and then some nights he'd stay out so late that the next day his mother would be nasty as a witch. But what could you do?

The crackle of his walkie brought Alfie back to a chorus of 10-13s, all over the place officers in need of assistance. There were 1-4-5s, even a likely 1-8-7. The whole operation was going off the rails. A blare of electric guitar filled the quad. This time he knew the work: Jimi Hendrix. Wild stuff. When Alfie stood up, his head felt like the Thinker was sitting on it. He lurched ahead, putting into his walk all the authority he could manage, straightening his shoulders and clenching his fists, pretending to be what he needed to be. At Kent Hall the music hit him like a train. Something in three-four time, crashing symbols, bass that rattled the classroom windows, guitar like a switchblade. He searched the walk for Sweeney. Here and there he spotted a cop, but not much action. Most of the crowd had come to a standstill, watching the show. Then from the direction of Hamilton Hall, over the music he heard someone yell: "Hey, Pig. Hey, White Boy, whatchu lookin' for?"

Where the fuck was Sweeney?

Again, to him.

"Yo, you lose somebody, Officer?"

Standing under one of the Hamilton Hall ledges were two Panthers. The caps, the fatigues, everything but the rifles, though if you frisked them, it was even money you'd find pistols in their pants. He drew his revolver.

"Stay where you are, hands in the air."

The pair raised their hands in slow motion. Bodies without faces flew past, screaming, shouting. Alfie could barely think, but it hit him that this was no time for an arrest. He re-holstered the weapon.

"All right. Move."

The taller of the two stepped close to him and spoke.

"We was just tryin' to help you out, Brotherman."

He took another step forward, and put an arm on Alfie's shoulder.

More of his father's words: "One day a hand on the arm, the next day they're slappin' your face."

Alfie smacked the hand away. The Panther immediately shoved him.

"We stand our ground, Pig."

His friend drew up behind him.

"We ain't afraid a ya crackah ass."

Then, quick, to his side, Sweeney, tearing for the entrance of Hamilton.

"C'mon, Baliato! We got a situation."

His revolver again. Almost out of the holster before another hand smacked it away. The gun behind him on the ground.

The guitar, slicing.

Where?

The Panthers bolted.

There, by the kids with their arms in the air. Shout after shout. Alfie squatted. Ankles, feet, out of the fuckin' way.

"... KNOW WHAT I WANT, BUT I JUST DON'T KNOW ... HOW TO GO ABOUT GETTIN' IT."

Got it. Get up. Fuck the helmet, fuck the uniform. The kids would cry. Even his wife. Fuckin' holster. Fuckin' job.

Alfie finally found the revolver and tucked it in, took off his helmet, ran fingers through his matted hair. When he looked up, there, in his face, was Wiesniewski, the stringy shag of his overgrown head. Then knuckles hissing through the air. Nose, suddenly feeling it, off-kilter, numb, warm, wet. Falling backward. Another body. Thick legs coming toward him. Another shot to the temple. The pavement. Head. Heavy damp in his hair, on his cheek. Alfie's father lying on the ground. Dry leaves blood-stuck to his forehead. Eyes purple, swollen shut. "Joe," said his father, pointing to the tree. The sound of men running off through dead leaves, then in the distance car doors slamming, engines roaring away. Sirens: cruisers, wagons, fire trucks. A herd's worth of footsteps, one ear, the other. Pop in the leaves, bleeding, ooze on his sleeve, arm extended. "Joe." Sky, pink. Cuffs, denim. Sandals. Gravel. Stink of dirt, feet. Roll, roll over, cover up.

"... MAKE LOVE, YOU BREAK LOVE, IT'S ALL THE SAME ... WHEN IT'S OH-VAH."

A boot in the ribs. Motherfucker. Not dying here. The night stick. Fence. Take a hold. Half-punch on his neck. Up. Shouldn't a missed, Punk. Stick. Crack.

Wiesniewski staggering. Around him too many kids, like some outdoor dance, shoulders bouncing up and down. Red lights flashing. Riot squad on its way. Whistles. Wiesniewski back at him.

"Up against the wall, Pig."

"Here's the wall, Asshole."

Alfie swung the baton with all he had into the ex-jock's side. He groaned, doubled over. Alfie brought it down, double-fisted, full-force on the middle of the kid's back, heard the breath shoot out of him. Wiesniewski tried to turn and run, still bent, stumbling, half-sideways, another berserk dance. What difference did it make? The whole world was going berserk. Alfie slammed another shot into the back of his right knee, and Wiesniewski went down against the side of Hamilton. Could've happened to him during some football game nobody would remember, and he'd have been a gimp for life anyway. At least he could tell his grandkids it was for some cause. The *cidrul* somehow got to his feet, a painful, slow climb, leaned back against the wall, looking up. Staring at the sky, a six-foot baby. Then, like a dying flame's last surge, he leapt at Alfie, a roundhouse blocked with the baton. A return straight right to the kid's chops brought blood from his mouth as he slumped again against the wall.

"Joe," his father had moaned to Alfie, pointing to the preacher. "Cut him down."

Alfie shuffled to the big maple. The preacher's face was ruined, but the real horror was his body, curved and bent almost at ninety degrees to his hips, ankle snapped under one leg. Alfie got out his pocket knife and sawed at the ropes until first one arm, then the other came free and shot forward. Jefferson fell to the ground with a weak cry. Alfie dragged him out in time to save him. Joe would spend weeks in the hospital before a relative, a brother or cousin, came to take him away for good. A few hours later Alfie was home, shaken, a few cuts on him, but mostly in one piece, under his mother's protective wing. Sitting there, patting her boy's head, she must have seemed to the old man the picture of satisfaction, like she'd won a battle.

"Soon as your father's out of the hospital," she told Alfie, "we're leaving for Brooklyn. Grandma and Grandpa have an apartment all made up. Your father'll meet us there."

Brooklyn. New York City. Everything and nothing. Here was this kid, probably some businessman's or doctor's son, crippled and on his way to jail, and for what? Was he helping the *mulies*? Was he stopping the war?

It had taken Alfie a long time to see what his father had always seemed to know and accept. Nobody was free. Whoever had built these buildings would still run things. You could work for them or kid yourself you were working against them. You could stay in the city or you could leave. Where were you gonna find peace? Wiesniewski would have kids, and then he'd live just like Alfie, maybe in a little bigger of a house, in a neighborhood or town with not so many skells. Maybe the only difference was how far you had to travel to reach the woods. The old man dealt with the whole mess by spending as much time as he could in bars or out hunting when he had the chance, or hopping from job to job. Alfie had done a lot of the same, but he could never accept it. He'd blamed a dozen people and God for building him this cell. He'd had a better plan, but just too much bad luck. The truth was he'd fallen back on a second plan, easier and just as impossible.

As he watched Wiesniewski lying there, he wanted to tell him to get the fuck up. Nobody would ever really help him. He felt the kind of rage that drove him into the Army and into Michelle's arms. He grabbed Wiesniewski's wrists and cuffed him. The kids around them noticed and turned on Alfie.

"Fascists!"

"Police brutality!"

"Cop thugs, go home!"

Suddenly water was dripping on Alfie's head. He pulled Wiesniewski a step away from the wall and looked up. He spotted Somers and Lundstrem leaning out of a second-story window, mid-spit. Down the building a little way, in the next window, he spotted Sweeney.

"Can't get at 'em over there. Door's blocked," his partner yelled. "You all right?"

Alfie raised an open palm, to signal everything was under control. In the meantime, he saw Lundstrem climbing out on the ledge. The mob below cheered as the dumb kid stood up with his hands in the air.

"Your baton," Sweeney called, pointing to a spot on the ground in front of where Alfie stood, "you're gonna need it."

Carefully, carefully, Alfie moved forward again. One hand still on Wiesniewski, he bent over to pick up his weapon.

"Yeeee-haaah!" someone yelled, the sound Dopplering.

Then Alfie felt the weight of a hundred trees fall on his back. His legs shot out from under him. His face slammed against the concrete. For a minute, black swirls and distant chords behind his eyelids, then red, then almost light, then a body next to his: Lundstrem, limbs dancing in pain, hands grabbing at the bone protruding from his leg. Alfie tried to reach him, but couldn't move. Not an arm, not a muscle. All around was chaos. A swarm of uniforms yanked students from the scene, clubbing the ones who didn't move fast enough. They formed a circle around Alfie and the kamikaze. One of the cops got down on the ground and tried to comfort him.

"Don't move. Ambulance is almost here. The boys are breaking down the door right now. Gonna ream those pieces of shit a new one. And don't worry, this is your collar, Baliato."

Alfie blinked, then closed his eyes, listening to a strange quiet, the shouting and fighting fading far as the horizon. Even the cops had gone mute, standing vigil. Minutes. He remembered the petals in his pocket, springtime, walking with Adeline. He felt himself fading again, and tried to picture his kids. Weren't they the reason he was here? Were they? Their features escaped him, lost as the preacher's. The best he could do was imagine a house, with faceless children standing in front of it, waving, and then himself, at a distance he couldn't cover, sighting them through the old binoculars his father had used for the hunt.

(1950)

Alfie practiced "Sweet Adeline" until his fingers could follow every note of the Mills Brothers record. He lifted his father's guitar, strumming and humming, picking when he could, over and over, while the Victrola spun the thick black disc in the dark back bedroom. After the needle slid to the center and brushed the label like it was sharpening itself, he kept the melody running until the scraping sound rubbed him raw. Now and then he set himself free to play a solo, sing a line when the feeling hit him, and think of her. Every note meant he'd make up for what he'd done and what he couldn't yet do.

From time to time, Alfie's father would poke his head in.

"That one there's a dandy," he'd say, pointing to the fabric panel that hid the Victrola's speaker.

Alfie played the song every day, all winter, so often that his old man's face went from smiles to frowns, and he started making remarks like couldn't Alfie find something else to play. On those days, Alfie didn't feel so sorry for what he'd done to him, but most days he loved his father for being like an older brother who watched over him. If he didn't exactly want his father's life—working different jobs, drinking a lot, ignoring the bad things people said about him—he hoped he could learn his secret for not letting what people said eat at him.

"Mills Brothers are something, boy, but you shoulda heard your uncles and me back when."

Some days Frankie burst in, doing his best Al Jolson, stretching out his arms to steal the air. A wisenheimer, his kid brother, though to their mother he was Christ Almighty.

Some days she heard Alfie playing and came stomping in like an army.

"They can hear you in New Jersey!"

And who was she to talk? She played fiddle full volume, at least a few times a week. Could she play? Sure. But it was classical music, and who wanted to hear it? Neighborhood dogs would whine when she hit the high notes. So when she showed up in the doorway with a puss on, he ignored her until she slammed the door shut again.

When he needed a break, Alfie lay on his stomach, across the bed that took up half the room. The disc's grooves spun him to a place he'd never been. He felt older than sixteen, his and Adeline's age. And didn't a lot of famous people marry their cousins? He'd tried to look it up in the library, but you couldn't exactly ask the librarian for that kind of list. He did learn that four Presidents, including Jefferson and FDR, married their cousins, and one Vice-President too. Einstein married his cousin. A first cousin. And he was Einstein. And you knew at least a couple of musicians did. No one ever said you couldn't. Except Aunt Cecelia, who nobody cared for. She carried on about incest and damnation, which Alfie didn't exactly believe. But God did scare him. If it was just thirty percent God didn't want you to do something, maybe you shouldn't take the chance. Still, when it came to Adeline, he would. So most likely they could get married. Some people might not like it, but at least her mother and father would know the husband.

At their wedding, Adeline's straight black hair is pulled up into a pin-neat tiara. Her shoulders are smooth and white as Ivory Soap. Her back curves like an almond crescent when she bends to blow out candles. She smiles with that little gap between her front teeth and crinkles the dimples that make her look like the porcelain doll on his mother's chest of drawers. She pushes the wide knife through the pink and white wedding cake icing, wipes icing from the blade with her middle finger, and slides the finger between her lips.

Alfie flipped on his back and stroked the bedspread. She was the flower of his heart.

One cool April day, straight from this fantasy, Alfie wandered to the kitchen, where his mother was opening mail while his Aunt Milly stirred gravy.

"She's getting married in two months. Here's the card," his mother announced, waving a pink envelope.

She should've been a schoolteacher, the way she loved to read out loud, to pronounce words.

"*Mister and Missus Pasquale Pace request the pleasure of your company at the marriage of their daughter, Anna Maria, to Mister Stanley Papeleo ...*"

"Stanley?" Aunt Milly asked.

"The mother's Polish. He's a nice boy. You met him."

"Oh."

"*... to Mister Stanley Papeleo, son of Mister and Missus Giuseppe Papeleo, on Saturday, the Third of June, Nineteen Hundred and Fifty, at eleven o'clock ...*"

"Penny, eleven o'clock? Who ever heard?"

"The hall costs less in the afternoon."

"Oh."

"*... at eleven o' clock in the morning, at Saint Francis de Chantal Church, with a reception following at two o' clock, at the Rex Manor.*"

His aunt turned back to the stove, stirring the gravy faster.

"At least it's the Rex," she said, then stopped her stirring and put a finger to her lips. "I wonder why our invitation didn't come."

"You should be happy it didn't. This means we have to buy suits for the boys."

Aunt Milly spotted Alfie in the doorway, smiling at him.

"Oh, look, here's the big brother."

"Good, you're out of my room. You can be the first to know. Your cousin Anna Maria's getting married. We're all going."

"The whole family? All the cousins?"

His mother slapped the invitation against her apron and looked sideways at Aunt Milly.

"I would say so."

"So Dominick, Vince, Bernadette, Ralph, Adeline?"

"For starters. So you'll need a new suit. At the rate you're growing, it won't last two months. I'll ask Old Man Tufariello to sew some extra fabric inside the lining."

Alfie couldn't stand wearing a suit. It made him feel caged. But he didn't want to look like Billy the Boob while Adeline was wearing a fancy dress.

"Can I get pinstripes?"

Aunt Milly rolled her eyes. His mother twisted her mouth.

"We'll see."

Brooklyn Day meant no school. Alfie spent the free morning trying on his new get-up, a double-breasted gray number with wide shoulders and razor-thin pinstripes. He stood in front of the full-length mirror. Turned sideways he looked too skinny, so he faced forward. His hands disappeared inside the sleeves. It was a jail suit. No matter what you did, you were trapped. It wasn't natural. At least the tie was all right, but when he pulled it up, the way his father showed him, he was hanging himself. Every now and then he snuck a look out the front window. Frankie and his friends were playing stickball in the street. If they hit a Spaldeen into the train ditch, they'd have to stop until one of the kids ran to get another ball. If that happened, his brother might come upstairs for a drink and give Alfie a good razzing. Still, if you ignored the sleeves, the suit looked sharp. Alfie ran his palm over his slicked-back hair. By the time he was old enough to marry Adeline, he'd look even better.

He was sweating, already tired when they got to the church. He
hadn't slept more than two hours. And why? It wasn't like he never
saw her. Adeline lived right near the El, not a mile away. The families got together every couple of weeks. It was true he was always
afraid to talk to her and usually just stared across the table. But
couldn't he visit his aunt and uncle any time he wanted? He could
walk to their house, though he'd have to keep clear of the Rampers
and the other gangs. Aunt Lena wouldn't mind. It was Uncle Enzo
you had to worry about. He'd make things miserable. A real Italian,
and older than Aunt Lena, and from money. He owned a store in
the city and went to work when he wanted, thought who he was.
He started in with Alfie whenever he had the chance.

"Don't be like-a you fadda. Ina school you pay *attenzione*."

And he'd point his index finger at his eye.

"You see, I get my degree—*ingegnere!*—and I have-a nice-a
live-a like-a dis."

He liked to tell them about the books he read, all about the history of Italy. Tons of battles. What Alfie knew about Italians, they
weren't too good in battles. And what did the old pain-in-the-ass
know about fighting? His stores sold dresses and skirts. Now he
was standing by the back door of the church, greeting people like it
was *his* daughter's wedding.

"My wife, my daughter, they come from-a cah."

Alfie's father waved his sons to their pew, where their mother
was talking with her brothers and sisters.

"Sheesh, the whole family's here," Frankie whispered in Alfie's
ear as the two brothers walked up the side aisle.

"You're not supposed to take the Lord's name in vain," Alfie answered, trying to live up to the idea that he should set an example.

"I didn't. The Lord's name ain't 'Sheesh.'"

Alfie gave his little brother a shove, so that Frankie had to grab
the end of a pew to keep from falling onto a woman's lap, before
sitting down, quiet as a mouse, looking all around like he'd never
seen the place before. Which Alfie didn't get. The little bastard had
just gotten confirmed.

"What's eatin' you?" Alfie asked.

"I'm just looking at the windows. Monsignor said the glass comes from Italy."

"So what?"

"I don't know. I like the colors better than American glass, I guess."

Alfie shrugged. His brother was one of those Arista kids, head in the clouds and mouth always going. If you spent most of your time thinking, should you be thinking about glass? It was better to be almost sixteen.

And what about Adeline? He looked over his shoulder to see if she'd come in yet. Nope. It was still just his father and Uncle Enzo, who was making Italian hand gestures like they were going out of style. Alfie's father once told them that their uncle had melted down his wife's rings and sent the metal to Mussolini. So Alfie's cousin Paulie could've been shot with a bullet that his uncle helped pay for. Was every family this way? But then finally here was Adeline, wearing a light pink dress, satin underneath, with one big piece of chiffon laid across the satin and her bare shoulders, giving Alfie a good view of the skin he wanted to touch so badly he could cry. Her hair was done up like Ava Gardner's, with a pink flower. He imagined her looking at herself in the mirror while her mother fussed with her bobby pins. She hugged her father and walked with her head down to the Holy Water bowl, dabbed her fingers, and made the Sign of the Cross. Alfie eyed her figure as she sauntered up the center aisle. When she stopped suddenly at Alfie's row, he knelt down quick as he could on the Communion bench and pretended to pray. He peeked through his clasped hands, to watch her squeeze into the pew. Aunt Lena caught his eye and waved, tapping Adeline, making her do the same. He smiled a weak smile and bowed his head as if he were praying.

The mass felt like it would never end. When it finally reached the part where the priest started the actual marriage, Alfie watched Adeline for a reaction. Her profile was perfect: a straight little Irish-looking nose, even though she was full-blooded Italian like him, and a chin that was strong but not sharp. Her slanty eyes almost made her look like a girl you'd see in a harem or even a Chink girl, which he wouldn't say to her, even though he was sweet on Chink girls. When the bride and groom knelt down in front of the priest, Adeline didn't smile or blush or anything like you'd expect a girl to do. Instead she did something amazing. She looked at the giant crucifix above the altar, folded her hands, and while she bent her head down to pray—Alfie could swear to it—she looked his way and puckered her lips.

What could he do?

He lost his breath and wanted to pucker back, but her father was right there next to her, watching his daughter like a hawk. Meanwhile Frankie's knee was banging against his. The kid had a bad habit of bouncing his legs up and down, in and out. Alfie rapped his arm again when nobody was looking. Anna Maria and Stanley stood up now, holding hands, looking into each other's eyes, while the Father made them say their vows. Then they kissed. A good long one like Alfie would have with Adeline. He tried to imagine the softness, better than a pillow against your cheek when you were tired. Thinking about her, he'd kissed his pillow a thousand times, and now he was in his own room again, puckering, with his eyes completely closed. The applause snapped him out of it. At the end of the row, Uncle Enzo was clapping like he was at a show. Aunt Lena was crying. Adeline was patting her hair and straightening her skirt. When the time came for their row to file out, Alfie watched her glide all the way down the aisle. This time he paid attention to the shape of her calves as she headed again for the Holy Water. He felt a hand on his shoulder. His father's.

"Son, I don't know about you, but I'm hungry as a starved bear."

Up Rome, Alfie had only gone to one reception, and that was at a firehouse. This place, the Rex, looked bigger than Grand Central Station, and had the same kind of ceiling with stars painted on it. The curved walls were lined with gold-inlaid wood paneling.

Against that background Alfie was swimming in an ocean of dark
suits, light dresses, and flowered hats. The waiters who circled the
edges of the crowd wore tuxedos as fancy as the groom's. A small
stage rose in front of the huge dance floor. To the side was a long
table for the wedding party. If Adeline were a little older, she would
be sitting up there with Anna Maria's sisters, and Alfie would be
out of luck. Luck was on his side, though, because here she was
sitting at the next table, just a few feet away.

His mother straightened Frankie's collar.

"You boys look very handsome. Like movie stars."

With his mouth full of hors d'oeuvres, Alfie's father winked
at his sons, nodded his head, and smiled through tight lips. Alfie
hoped he was making the old man proud. It was the least he could
do. When the band started playing a quiet song with a lot of flute
lines, Alfie's mother gave her boys instructions.

"When the time comes for dancing, don't be shy. Ask your
cousins to show you how."

Alfie had been trying to practice the Lindy, but something
slower would take the pressure off.

"Oh, look, here's your cousin now. Look at those beautiful
shoes, Adeline."

"Thank you, Aunt Penny. I got them at Miles."

"You're a lucky girl."

Adeline stood with her head bowed. She didn't notice—or at
least Alfie thought she didn't notice—him taking all of her in while
his mother bent her ear.

"I was just telling the boys they shouldn't be shy about dancing."

"Sure," Adeline said, standing between Alfie's chair and his
mother's. "I just wanted to tell Alfie that if he wants to, he can
dance with me."

"Isn't that nice? Your hear that, Alfie? You have a partner."

Alfie's heart pounded against his ribs. He tried not to face
Adeline, whose chest was a magnet for his eyes.

"Thank you, Adeline. That's very sweet. Thank Adeline, son."

He could feel the heat in his cheeks.

"Thank you."

Sometimes he wished his mother spoke Italian instead of English.

When Adeline went back to her seat, he turned on her.

"C'mon, Mom."

"C'mon, Mom, what? You should learn how to dance."

She did this a lot, his mother, setting things up for him before he had the chance to do it himself. Sometimes she thought she knew everything, like some kind of witch. Not to say that she was setting him up with Adeline. She wouldn't do that. Or would she? Maybe she didn't care. She was like that. Whatever the other women in the family did, she seemed to do the opposite. She danced with anybody who asked her. She played music better than the men in the family. And she even went to church only when she felt like it. A mind of her own, his father liked to say.

So, if Alfie had to dance with Adeline, he'd do it. He was bracing himself. But the first song after dessert stumped him.

"Benny Goodman, Matty. Let's get up."

And there they went, all the grown-ups, like dogs who heard a whistle. Frankie fidgeted in his seat, primed to complain.

"You want my cake? I don't like the middle."

"There's rum in it, that's why. Maybe you'll like it when you're older."

"I don't think so. Why couldn't they have something good, like sfugliadells?"

Alfie smiled as he conjured the flaky pastry.

"That would be good. Tell you what. You leave me alone the rest of the night, and tomorrow I'll go down to Savarese and get you a couple. Whaddya say?"

"Sounds all right to me."

"Good. It's a deal."

Adeline's sweet voice.

"What's a deal?"

Alfie liked that she said what she thought. He could talk to a girl like that.

"Nothing. Just my kid brother."

"Oh. Maybe he can go sit next to Cousin Sammy. I think he brought some baseball cards. Said he has a lot of the Dodgers."

Frankie perked up.

"Which ones? Campanella? Furillo? Where is he?"

Adeline pointed across the immense ballroom.

"Better go now, before the other boys get the good ones."

She watched Frankie dodge waiters and skirt tables until he reached the promised land. Alfie watched her watching, how she craned her neck and giggled. Some kind of miracle.

"He loves playing ball," she said, still watching Frankie. "Any time we come to visit Grandma, I see him out there."

Alfie suddenly felt easy as a breeze.

"Are you gonna show me how to dance?"

She studied him.

"If you want. But I just said that so I wouldn't have to dance with the older boys. Whenever there's a wedding or a party, they throw me around like a rag doll. If you don't do something about it, being a girl can be that way."

Alfie loosened his tie, so the collar stopped pinching his neck.

"What do you want to do, then?"

"Well, why don't we just talk? We're cousins, and I hardly know you."

Alfie looked into her black eyes. They glowed like the darkness around a campfire, the kind that made you comfortable and scared at the same time. Like you could walk off into the woods and disappear, or an animal could leap out and tear you to shreds.

"We should be close friends."

No girl ever wanted to be his friend before. Why did Adeline have to be the first? He dropped his eyes. Still, it was true that he didn't have so many friends in Brooklyn. For one thing, he liked to practice and didn't go out as much as the other kids. For another, they told him he talked funny, like someone was holding his mouth open. There was Sebby Paone, who he knew from school, but who worked with his father most of the time; and there was Snooky, his best pal here, except lately he'd got himself a girl, some dish from Bath Beach, who never left him alone.

"So you wanna talk?"

Adeline nodded.

"I think there's a hallway outside those doors over there. Probably quiet."

Their whole family and the Polack's family filled the dance floor. The young kids played games by the far wall. She led him away. Slipping past her, Alfie held open one of the double doors leading out to the hallway and took a deep whiff of her perfume as she walked through. If she just wanted to be his friend, she didn't have to smell so good and smile so much.

"There's a bench by the telephone booth."

Adeline sat him down, then sat as close as she could, facing but not touching him. Through the wall Alfie could hear the band crucifying Duke Ellington.

"That's better," she said. "Now, ask me a question. Any question you want?"

In his head Alfie ran through the kinds of question you could ask a person you didn't really know. If he asked what was her favorite anything, he'd sound like a dope. What else? He already knew where she lived and what she was. Oh, here was a good one:

"Why don't I ever see you in school?"

Adeline's face lit up, then hardened into a serious expression, so that Alfie noticed the worry lines in her forehead. They made her look older, like someone had written secrets on her skin.

"That's a very good question," she said, giving him a quick pat on the hand. "The reason is simple. It's my father. He's from Italy."

"I noticed."

She play-swatted his hand.

"I mean he has strange ideas about girls. All he wants me to do is study, study, study, yet he thinks girls only have a certain place."

Did Alfie disagree?

"Like what?"

"Like being secretaries."

"Is there something wrong with being a secretary?"

Adeline stared at him for a few seconds, which made Alfie feel something he didn't often feel and didn't like to feel: stupid.

"No, there's nothing wrong with it, I suppose. It's just not what I want to do."

How could he get her to smile again?

"So don't do it."

"I don't want to, but he sent me to Girls' Commercial, because that's what girls learn there. And that's why you never see me at school."

Alfie was disappearing into her. He could feel her breath on his cheek. She was so close he could count her eyelashes. He asked low, almost whispering, without caring about the answer, "Can't you talk to your father?"

"Did you ever try to talk to my father?"

Those dark eyes.

"What do you really want to do?"

"I don't know. Maybe something where I could travel around. I know I don't want to be at Commercial, or even here—in Brooklyn, I mean. And I know you know what it's like to be someplace else. Did you like it upstate?"

The question surprised him. Wait. Think. Say something smart.

"It was okay. I liked how quiet it was."

No response. Was she expecting more?

"You could just walk around town and nobody worried about you."

Smirk meant what?

"Do you ever want to leave Brooklyn?" she asked.

Through the wall now Alfie could hear music. They were playing some Italian song he didn't know, and every once in a while the crowd yelled, "AAY!" If he married Adeline, they'd pick better music for the reception.

"I just got here."

She frowned. He should clear things up.

"I guess I'd leave when the time was right. Like the time was right for us to come here."

"What do you mean?"

If he told her his wedding plans, she'd think he was a nut. But then.

"Up Rome I had some things happen."

Adeline rested her hand on top of his as he spoke.

"I don't really know if I could tell anybody. Do you mind if I don't talk about it?"

He tried his best to look sad, which worked. After checking to make sure they were still alone, she leaned in and gave Alfie a hug that made him feel like he was floating. He felt her hands lightly massaging his back. He was fox trotting with her across the waves, doing the tango as they drifted around the world. When he started moving his hands over her shoulders, she pulled away but kept hold of his fingers.

"It's all right. We'll be friends for a long time."

The words "I know" came from his mouth before he could stop them.

"So what do *you* want to do?"

Alfie showed her the palms of his hands.

"Play guitar."

He looked at his fingers as though each one could explain.

"All kinds of guitar: bluegrass, country, blues, race music, even some jazz. Back in Rome my folks didn't care much about school, but here all of a sudden it's a big deal. And when I'm in school, all I think about is playing."

He exhaled.

"And some other things too."

He squeezed her hand, and her eyes glowed.

"When I get a D on my report card, Pop tells Mom it's for 'Dandy.' But she's afraid I'm gonna flunk out of 10th grade. And then what?"

"Then you'll play the guitar."

He wanted to hug her again, but instead tried to do what he really wanted to do. He held her shoulders and pulled her closer. This time she pulled away.

"What's the matter?"

Adeline's pout put her eyes' fire out.

"I'm not one of those girls from *The Amboy Dukes*, Alfie. And besides, you know why not. What would people say?"

He wanted to tell her about the Presidents and their cousins, but instead a wave of shame broke over him, a cold shower, except that he was sweating.

She stroked his arm.

"I like you. And we'll both leave. You'll see. But we'll still be close like this."

Like this.

She squeezed his hand one more time.

"Wait."

Her dress whispered as she walked back toward the hall, making a final swoosh as she struggled with the door. When she finally got it open far enough, she looked back at him and screwed up her face, then disappeared.

The music was still going. It was "Angelina," the Louis Prima number. Alfie sat listening to the rest of it.

He got up from the bench and pulled open the door. Back inside the hall, the band started something slow and probably older than him. He spotted his mother and father among the few couples left on the dance floor. He tried to imagine them keeping company, what they'd had in common. His father's hair was almost gray, slicked back, so that he looked natural in a suit, even though you knew he'd rather be in shirt sleeves. His arms were around his mother's waist, while hers were over his shoulders. They swayed back and forth in front of the bandstand. His mother looked bored, but his father smiled like she was singing him a love song.

(1952)

Alfie lived with his family on the second floor of a house on 61st Street, across from a train ditch where three different subway lines ran all day and all night. His Grandpa Ruggiero, his mother's father, owned the house. The Castronovos lived downstairs. Mr. Castronovo worked for his grandfather, who lived with Alfie's grandmother two doors down, in a brick house his grandfather had built.

When Alfie got home from school every day, his mother would either be standing at the stove, cooking, or else sitting at the kitchen table, reading a book. He'd kiss her on the cheek, put his book bag down on a chair, pour himself a glass of milk and, if there was gravy on, tear off a piece of semolina bread and dip it in the pot, then head to the front bedroom, to practice. If he looked out the window a half-hour later, he'd see his father walking back from the subway station, whistling and gawking at the train ditch like he was searching for somebody on the other side.

Alfie listened for the old man's footsteps on the creaky hallway stairs, and every day tried to play a different melody to their rhythm. The way his father walked, it usually turned out to be a country riff, but on days his father had a little energy, Alfie managed a bluegrass run or a jump blues. The old man also worked for Alfie's grandfather, half the time as a laborer and half the time as somebody the old grouch could complain to or complain about. His father never groused to his mother about Grandpa Ruggiero, but once in a while he'd admit that he wasn't crazy about the situation, which made Alfie feel guilty. Alfie's life might be all right, but his father's was rough, and it was Alfie's fault. If you could say anything about the old man, it was that he tried to keep the peace. And when he made it to the top of the stairs every day after work, he tried to give his wife a hug. Sometimes she hugged back, sometimes she didn't. Alfie could tell they still watched over each other, but something was off. Each one argued like the other had put them both in prison. His grandparents were the same way. Chickie's parents too, and Bobby's, and Adeline's. Maybe he could be with Adeline without marrying her.

Once his father got past his mother, the two of them would stay quiet in different rooms, so Alfie could strum and pick until it was time for him to get the bread. No way they could count on Frankie to do it. He'd be outside, playing stickball or stoopball or Johnny-on-the-pony, and he was so good in school that nobody said boo about it. Still, Alfie didn't mind. When he finally left the house, he might jump into a stickball game and show Frankie up. He could hit the Spaldeen three sewers and throw so hard that the other kids were afraid to catch it. And Johnny-on-the-pony? Forget about it. He'd break their backs. But other boys didn't care, because Alfie was the law. When he stepped onto the street, any kid who might be about to yank the handle on a fire-alarm box or pick on a much younger kid seemed to stop in his tracks and shove his hands in his pockets. Not that Alfie wanted to be a tough guy. The way his father taught him, and what he'd seen, being a tough guy meant trouble. Sure, he loved watching boxing matches, studying how a guy like Robinson or Marciano did it, and he would box with Frankie, but why fight for real? Anyway, who'd fight him? Between his size and his grandfather being boss of the block, nobody would dare. So he was the cop. Even the vendors treated him that way. The ones with the horse carts especially. They always stopped when they saw him. The fruit man might hand him a free apple. The ice man might chip his mother off a little extra. The grinder man would keep his bell quiet as he passed Alfie's house. To them, he'd earned it. He kept the other kids from stealing, and he made the girls on the block run out a little faster to get their scissors sharpened.

Once Alfie got back from the bakery and got Frankie inside, if there was any time left before dinner, the brothers would go to the basement, where they'd hung a heavy punching bag and a chinning bar from the ceiling joists. Next to the bag was a weight bench, next to that some dumbbells, and in the corner a mat for sit-ups. After a day of school and guitar practice, it felt good to use your muscles, to feel the energy rush through your arms and chest when you finished a set. Later, you'd feel sore and tired, and that made sleeping easy, no matter how much snoring came from the other bedroom. And, of course, it helped the brothers look good. One Sunday when they were walking down 65th Street after church, one of the wise guys stopped them at the corner.

"Ay, fellas. Look at youse two. The builts on ya. You do the Italians proud. You ever need a little work, you come talk to me."

Working out could get you respect and girls, but it was torture. Mostly because of Frankie. Alfie tried to get his brother to pace himself, but it was impossible. Frankie was a nice kid, except when he was playing ball or working out. Then he wanted to kill you. He was smaller than Alfie, but if Alfie did ten reps, Frankie had to do twelve. If Alfie bench pressed 175 pounds, Frankie had to go for 180, even though Alfie almost always had to save him from crushing his own neck with the bar. When they boxed, things got worse. One shot from Alfie could knock his brother across the room, but Frankie never let up. He'd run at Alfie, throw a dozen punches in the air before he reached him. A little tornado. And when he landed a punch, it sounded like rain on a roof. Alfie hated to think about his brother this way, but the kid hit like a girl. In fact one girl he knew, Carmella Foppiano, hit a hell of a lot harder, as he'd found that out when he tried to kiss her under the El. But Frankie never gave up. Alfie would have to whack his brother one, just to buy a few seconds to breathe. If that didn't work, he'd have to make himself mad enough to really pound him. He'd think about the worst things in the world, things that should never happen. One time he'd thought about his little cousin Ann Marie, who almost burned to death when her mother knocked over a candle and lit her communion dress on fire. You could see how pretty she would have been without the scars and how sad she was now, and it made you want to beat the world to death or run up to God and throw a right cross. Picturing her face, Alfie hit Frankie with such a body shot that he went flying into the wall and doubled over. He might've cracked his brother's rib, but Frankie never let on. Once he got his breath back, the kid tore off the gloves and stood up with his hands on his hips.

"Thanks," he said, and sprinted up the stairs.

Aside from working out, there was homework, which, thank God, would end as soon as he graduated. He was no Einstein, but he was no dummy either, and he got his homework out of the way as fast as he could. Some days he'd even knock it out before he practiced. But most times he did it after dinner. And he could do it anywhere: at the kitchen table, on the toilet, in the middle of the living room, even on the front stoop.

Frankie was a different story. He was top of his class, so when he told their parents he needed quiet to study, they made sure everything was as calm as you could get in Brooklyn. If Alfie was practicing when this happened, they asked him to stop. The radio went off. The windows were closed, even on a hot day. Talking was out. If you wanted a glass of milk, you'd better tiptoe to the kitchen. Even then, if Frankie thought it was too noisy, he would announce that he was going to their grandparents' house, where he could have four rooms to himself and they were happy to have him sit and study all day. He would be a good student, like his mother, except he would use what he learned.

His grandfather's house was the best on the block, custom built. All red brick, with his initials, "RP," for Ruggiero Pallone, in black brick on the wall above a sunken driveway and again above the steps to the covered porch. The house was set back from the avenue and had a big garden surrounded by a brick and wrought iron fence. The garden was as big as the house, and had stone walkways, all kinds of flowers, and a grape arbor, where every day his grandfather sat with his pipe and glass of wine, reading *Il Progresso* cover to cover. If you were sitting with him while he read, now and then he would slap the paper with the back of his hand and say to the air, "Ah, *vedi qui!* You see! You see!" When Frankie was over, the old man left him alone to study, but he seemed to hope that Alfie would learn the construction business and take over for him someday. Some nights, especially when his mother insisted that he visit, Alfie would walk down the block and find his grandfather alone in his workshop. The old man was tall and thin, lean and straight as a board. Even when he was cutting wood, he wore black slacks and a dress shirt, usually short-sleeved. He was sixty-something, but his hair hadn't gone gray. He'd be standing over a project, looking through his black-framed work glasses, frowning. He frowned most of the time, including when he watched Alfie try out a technique that he was supposed to have learned. Even if he got something right, Alfie could forget praise. You didn't get praise for what you were supposed to do. You got grunts, like work was all instinct.

The workshop was inside the garage which no car had ever entered. Instead it was a shrine to carpentry. His grandfather had finished the walls and put up beautiful oak moldings and a platform with a pot-bellied stove, two arm chairs, a little table, and a Victrola stand. The second chair had appeared later—just for Alfie, so he could sit there taking instruction and advice. It reminded him of a confessional, except you listened more than you talked.

One warm night Grandpa Ruggiero was in an especially good mood, whistling away like nobody's business, hunched over a long piece of maple. When he saw Alfie walk in, he lowered his glasses and waved him over to the work bench.

"I want you to see. Look here. When you take the planer, you take her *così.* You slip her on the wood with two hands. You slip, you slip, you slip."

Did his grandfather sound this ridiculous in Italian?

"Make sure she eat the wood. Then you push, you push. You try."

The planer was a relic, probably something from the old country, but it peeled off perfect strips of wood.

"You go the whole piece."

Alfie shaved the length of the board, worrying a little more with each push about leveling the cuts. Was he pushing too hard? Was he keeping the planer straight? Was the front down too far? Was there some secret he was supposed to know by blood? His grandfather put a hand on Alfie's arm and stopped him, then bent over the plank and ran his palm along the surface. He was still frowning, but his eyes were full of light.

"Bravo! I see you take your time. And now we join the wood. You know how many ways to join?"

Old Ruggiero held up ten fingers, then another five, and for the next hour and a half he walked Alfie through everything from butt joints to dovetails. How do you figure the strength of a joint? In what directions can a joint move? How do you know what pieces to join? How is a door different from a table, and a table different from a chest of drawers? When do you need glue? If you were going to run the business, you had to know what every carpenter and trades-man under you knew, which his grandfather had known from the time he was Alfie's age. If you knew the mysteries, you could build the world that people saw. So what if Alfie was more interested in the world they couldn't see?

Done with his lesson, the old fogey dropped an opera record on the Victrola spindle, sat down by the pot-bellied stove, and offered his grandson a pipe carved in the shape of a mermaid. Alfie smoked cigarettes, but never around the family. It didn't matter that his father smoked four packs of Luckies a day. For Alfie, smoking around the rest of the family felt like a crime. Everything did, because of Adeline. More and more, thinking about her meant stealing from his family. After Alfie refused the pipe, his grandfather made a show of pulling a black pouch of tobacco from a small figure eight-shaped cabinet, pinching a clump of reddish-brown shreds, packing them into the bar-rel with his fingers like he was playing a flute, then sliding open a box of wooden matches and flicking a stick across the strike board with a pop of his wrist. He took a few puffs and blew a cloud of smoke that filled the entire workshop. The routine reminded Alfie of a magic show.

His grandfather rested the pipe on an ashtray and reached over to pat Alfie's arm.

"I know what you think."

Alfie shrugged his shoulders, playing dumb.

"It's okay. You don't love all the time to work with wood. Me neither, I don't love this work with wood. Not all the time. But it's okay. You make money."

He lifted the pipe and took a few rapid-fire puffs.

"You have a girl, no?"

"I guess."

"Sure. You think maybe *We gonna get married.*"

"I don't know, Grandpa."

Alfie looked at the joined wood laid out on the bench and thought of his mother and father, how they got hitched. They said they'd met at a dance somewhere in the Catskills, at a big hotel his uncle owned. A cousin who worked there had brought his father with him to the dance, where he spotted his mother. They liked each other right off. Why? Because they felt like family? Because they liked each other's looks? Because it was spring? How old were they? Sixteen? Seventeen? Most days now they ignored each other. Once in a while they yelled, and once in a while they danced around the living room. They were victims. Or inmates. If you knew somebody a long time before you got together, was that better? Alfie hoped so.

"You have money, you get the girl you want."

It would be like shopping, and what you picked out and paid for, you might get to keep.

Alfie's grandmother was the only person Alfie knew who could make his grandfather smile. As far as you could tell, they were happy. She smiled at her husband and teased him. If she had the chance, she got him worked up about little things—how late the mailman came or how you couldn't get a good loaf of bread these days. She knew how to handle him. In return, he bought her nice coats and theater tickets and trips to Cuba. They weren't lovey-dovey, but at their age what good would it do them?

When Alfie's father smoked a cigarette on the porch, looking across the train ditch at the gardens, he looked about as happy as a fella could be. Was it because of Alfie's mother? You never knew. He might've been thinking about Rome, about the country, where he belonged. Maybe he was thinking about another woman. It didn't matter. If you had a few minutes to think, you were free for that little bit of time, and later you could remember what it felt like to have that peace and then look forward to the next time you could think for yourself.

"Grandpa, I like the work."

"Maybe."

"I just wanna try something else."

His grandfather got up and walked over to a tall cabinet in the corner. From inside the cabinet he took a big cloth bag with a drawstring at the top. He sat down again, and set the bag on his lap.

"I know," he said, loosening the drawstring.

He reached into the bag and grabbed the neck of an instrument Alfie recognized as a mandolin. The body was some exotic wood, orange maybe. Inlaid mother-of-pearl dotted the neck and ringed the sound hole. The tuning keys looked like little pieces of blue marble. The thick lacquer gave the whole thing the look of a painting.

"You know who make this?"

Alfie pointed his finger at the old man.

"That's right. Long time ago. In Italy. I think then I'm gonna make for people to play. I like the work. Nice. Neat. You stay inside when it gets cold. And you know people gonna like. When your mother start to play, I make her beautiful violin."

The aria playing on the Victrola built to a crescendo, then quieted down again.

"You know why I don't make no more? Because I like to eat, and your grandmother like to shop. *E' gabi*?"

He handed the mandolin to Alfie.

Maybe he didn't give his grandfather enough credit. Maybe, like Adeline, the old man understood. But what about Alfie's parents?

If he told them he didn't want to work for the company, they'd tell him he should've done better in school. And what would his answer be? Music? They might still let him live in his room, but if they did, he'd have to hear every day how he was wasting his life, especially with Frankie getting straight A's. Even his mother, musician that she was, wouldn't go for it. So he might have to live with his grandparents, and do a little side work for his grandfather. Which wouldn't be bad. He could be there when Adeline came to visit. The rest of the time, he'd have some peace. The old folks liked time to themselves. They wouldn't ask him too many questions. Maybe his grandmother would make Alfie fix things around the house once in a while or sit with them while she and his grandfather watched professional wrestling on the television. Alfie had seen the act.

"Look, Rugge'! He's pulling back his fingers. Where's the referee?"

"Somabitch!" his grandfather would yell, saluting the screen with the back of his hand.

After a few matches, the old man would get so tired from yelling, he'd excuse himself and go upstairs.

"Finally," she'd say, and go to the kitchen, to the stash of Lorna Doones she wasn't supposed to eat. She'd tell Alfie to take the box while she made the demitasse. And in front of the television they'd sit, as if he were the younger version of her husband, and they'd eat cookies and watch an old movie until one of them passed out on the sofa.

(1955)

A guy named Carmine owned the Oak Inn. Alfie's drummer, Sammy, was Carmine's nephew. Sammy had played Carmine a reel-to-reel recording of "Aces Wild," the Johnny Ace tune, with Alfie running the horn licks on guitar, throwing in muted chords when he backed off for the piano. That was enough. That and a promise that some of the set would be radio songs—"Earth Angel," "Only You," like that.

The gig was on a Thursday night. Adeline had promised to come down after her last class at NYU. Lately, Alfie only saw her at Sunday dinners, the times she bothered to turn up. When she missed, Aunt Lena would act nervous and apologize. Uncle Enzo, on the other hand, would make excuses for his daughter, now that she'd gone to college against his will. At the last dinner, before anyone could notice she wasn't there, he announced, "My daughta, she always gotta study." And then added, turning to Alfie: "You study, you have a good life." Then he took off his Coke-bottle glasses, cleaned them with his dinner napkin and sat still as a nun, dressed to the nines, looking satisfied with himself, waiting for the *antipast'*. Alfie could never get away with missing these dinners. The one time he did—a Sunday he slept into the afternoon and decided to ignore his mother's knock on the bedroom door—you'd have thought he'd stabbed his grandmother in the neck with a fork. On the job that week his grandfather walked by him a hundred times without saying a word. The following Sunday his grandmother had the maid bring out soup for everybody except him. She claimed she'd forgotten how many people were at the table. This was a woman who counted her silverware whenever she washed it. Even his mother, who could do without the dinners, let him have it.

"Show some respect, Alfie."

"C'mon, Ma, I'm not the only one who missed."

"Don't worry about that. Worry about yourself."

A trap. They expected him to be there because he was always there, and they expected him to stay because he never said he was leaving. Adeline and Frankie each had one foot out the door, but Alfie would have to keep up what the old people started, marry a nice girl who could cook, and find a place to live close by. Every time he sat down at his grandmother's table, his *agita* got a little worse. So why did he go? *Why?* Because every time he sat there on the red velvet seat of the big hand-carved dining room chair, thinking it would be the last time, Adeline made an appearance in her Sunday dress and hugged him, and it was all over. He'd forgive her and forgive himself. What sin could there be? His cousin was the song you heard all your life and never got tired of hearing. Why should a priest get to say what you should want, what you shouldn't want? What did priests know about love?

Tonight, Adeline was showing up just for him. Nobody would be looking over their shoulders. The gig would end, and they'd be alone in Manhattan. Ladies and gentlemen, the moment you've all been waiting for. Alfie sat down on a bench against the back wall of the bar. He pulled out his Les Paul, plugged it into a beat-up amplifier near the bandstand, and played the first few chords of "Sweet Adeline." The bartender, the only other soul in the dark room, clapped a few times, then turned on the television above the bar. It was fight night. Marciano had a big match in a few weeks, and people were talking about it non-stop. At least people in Brooklyn were. Alfie watched a Gillette Razor ad that showed Pee Wee Reese and Roy Campanella shaving together. When they finally got their faces smooth, Alfie put his guitar back in its case, set it on a table near the stage, and lay down on the bench. It had been a chilly day for April, and damp. If he weren't so nervous, he would've fallen right to sleep. Instead, he turned on his side and watched people walk by the bar's plate glass window. A few of them were opening umbrellas. He closed his eyes and thought through his own version of a prayer. When he finished, the door opened: Sammy, lugging his kit. Sammy was a nice kid from the neighborhood. Everybody called him "The Mexican" because of his dark skin and the thin mustache he was always trying to grow. He was the one who put the band together, a strange thing for a drummer to do. But he was like that, always scheming. He looked over the empty room.

"You think this was a good idea?"

Alfie nodded.

"We can say we played the city."

As they set up, a few customers walked in, most of them young, most of the fellas wearing jeans and black sweaters, most of the girls wearing snug striped pants and tight black shirts, almost all of them wearing scarves and hats that sat cockeyed on their heads. They talked loud and seemed not to notice anybody but themselves. A few minutes later, Tommy and George walked in and hooked up the organ and amplifiers. Carmine had promised them a microphone. If he was lying, it would be a night of instrumentals. Either way, the fat bastard still wasn't here. The bartender put on some jazz, which Alfie recognized: Charlie Parker. It was maybe a month ago he'd died, and they were playing his music everywhere. Alfie could understand. It bent time the way you would bend a note. Maybe Alfie could be that good, good enough to get tributes when his time came. For now, it was this room.

By 7:30 the place was full: a dark sea of people, heads bobbing like little waves, and corkscrews of cigarette smoke spinning to the tin ceiling. The band in their chinos and bright checked shirts stood out like racehorses on a city street. Sammy rapped his snare a few times, George tapped out a few chords on the keyboard, and Tommy tuned the bass. Alfie sat on the stool, still nervous, watching the door, waiting. A tall, slim, sickly-looking fella in a black vest, with a v-shaped beard on his chin to match his v-shaped face, waltzed over.

"Hey, Dad, you cats gonna lay it down?"

Alfie rattled the B-string with his pick and shot the goon a one-eyed stare.

"We're playin' some songs."

"Crazy. What's your bag?"

Alfie held the stare, and the thin man stammered out a follow-up.

"I mean, you know, like, what do you play?"

"Rhythm and blues, rock and roll," Alfie mumbled, looking down at the fretboard. He strummed a set of D-flat chords—6ths, major 7ths, 9ths, 13ths, diminisheds, augmenteds—stuff that sounded like it might be jazz and might get the Bohemian off his back.

"All right. Far out."

The string bean shriveled back into the haze.

Between the smoke and the fog on the windows, Alfie couldn't see the sidewalk, which made the waiting worse. His watch said it was a little past eight. Any minute Carmine would show up and tell them to start. The rest of the band stood on their marks like wax statues. Alfie lit a cigarette and took a few long drags. As he watched the door, he tapped his foot to the melody already in his head. Then the door opened. There, instead of Carmine, stood a good-looking guy of about 30, in a red and black hunting jacket, wavy brown hair, built like a wrestler. As he stepped into the room, he raised his hand in salute. Alfie was surprised when half the room raised their hands back to him. A voice boomed out of the shadows.

"Dean!"

Dean weaved around tables, gripping a notebook in one hand held high over his head, slapping outstretched hands with the other.

"Mad, mad!" he yelled so everybody could hear.

Finally, as the shooting star disappeared into smoke, Carmine arrived and jogged to the bandstand, pretending to huff and puff as he did, a hand on his big belly.

"Fellas, I'm sorry. Things, you know."

Alfie shrugged.

Sammy cleared his throat.

"Got a mic, Carmine?"

"Oh, Jesus, yeah. Wait here."

From what Alfie could see, there was no rush. The Bohemians were busy drinking, smoking, yakking. Every once in a while, one jumped up to make a point that you couldn't quite hear. The whole scene was a stage where voices were louder and smells—smoke, booze, sweat—were stronger, and every little thing you did might set someone off like a Roman candle, until pretty soon you'd have a chain reaction and the whole stage would catch fire. If you had any kind of feeling, you had to have it all the way. Alfie didn't know what to do about it, so he played another chord, and before he could play a second, the red and black hunting jacket was standing in front of him. Dean extended a hand.

"Brother."

Alfie shook the hand.

"Brother, Brother, Brother. Watcha gonna play? Some voodoo? Some metrical magic?"

He plucked one of Alfie's loose guitar strings.

"The strings from which we all dangle. We, the puppets of cosmic energy, and you, Maestro, the master."

Was this clown kidding or was he just busting Alfie's balls?

"You gonna turn us on to the *prana*, Dad?"

Alfie ignored him and played another chord.

"That's what I'm talking about, Man. Energy, energy."

Dean took a pull on his butt and blew a smoke cloud over Alfie's head like he was expecting him to do a rain dance.

"En-er-GY!" he shouted, snapping fingers to his own beat.

Alfie's eyes drifted to the door behind him. Still no Adeline. How could you settle your head? Start by getting rid of any lingering jackasses. He tapped Dean's arm.

"What do you want to hear?"

Dean shut his eyes, still sucking on his cigarette, until a thought arrived.

"Surprise. Can you do that? Surprise me?"

Alfie's wink sent the king back to his fan club, who clapped him on the back as he danced his way through their ranks. Sammy rapped his snare again. George thumped a bass line. The front door swung open. And there was Adeline. Alfie hardly recognized her. She wore a long black raincoat, open, and under it a tight black-and-white sweater, tight black pants, and on her face cat's-eye glasses. At her side was a tall man in a gray double-breasted overcoat and a wool fedora, a get-up like his uncles wore. He had to be at least fifteen years older. The couple waved, and Alfie pointed them to the table with his guitar case on it. After settling in, the man walked to the bar, and Adeline waved to Alfie again. Alfie didn't want to smile, but couldn't help himself. To keep from looking like a mook, he turned to the band. Sammy had a suggestion.

"I'm thinkin' all instrumentals."

"Isn't Carmine gonna care?"

Sammy chuckled.

"My uncle can't even find a mic, the fat fuck."

Alfie didn't care either. He always heard lines of music better without voices over the top. And he'd have the lead. Of course, some songs didn't feel the same without words, but that made it easier to stay cool. Now here was Carmine, giving him a thumbs-up, setting up a mic off to the side. Sammy shrugged. He had his uncle pegged.

Another rap on the snare, and here was Adeline's escort.

"Ted," the man said, extending the hand that wasn't holding a tumbler of scotch.

Alfie shook it.

"Alfie."

"Your cousin can't stop talking about you. She thinks you're a real talent."

A regular scout.

Ted took a step toward him and leaned over.

"She has excellent taste."

Alfie turned away from the spicy smell of Ted's cologne.

"Yeah."

Ted took a step back.

"Well, will you have some time after the show?"

"Should. Yeah."

Ted nodded and scrunched his face, so his long, pointy nose almost touched his chin. As Alfie watched him stride back to Adeline's table, Adeline watched Ted the way a believer would stare at the crucifix in church. Where was her head? Why did people like what they liked? How many of these Bohemians really liked jazz? How many had the records at home? Versus how many just liked wearing these clothes and feeling hip? Did Adeline like a man in a tweed jacket? If she did, was it because this character favored the look? Or because she read somewhere that smart fellas wore tweed? She liked to read. Why? What was so great about reading? When you were reading, what were you doing? You were following what other people did. Which was great if you were learning how they built a form or wired a box or how they attacked a piece of music, but what if they were only eating breakfast or taking a walk in the park? Shouldn't you just eat your own breakfast or take your own walk? Then, if you wanted to think about it, you could sit on your front stoop and think about it. No books necessary. Ted pulled a pipe from his jacket and started packing it. He was probably a writer. Jesus. Why was Adeline studying English? He thought of her father, his rotten English. She said she wanted to work in publishing, but Alfie wasn't sure what that meant. What kind of work would she do? Did she know?

Carmine came to the mic, grinning like an awkward kid. Time to stop thinking.

"Ladies, gentlemen, all the way from across the river, The Lonesome Boys."

Sammy called the first tune: "Mystery Train." Tommy walked in the bass, while George on keys laid down the chords. Alfie gave the long notes just enough tremolo. He thought about how good it was to control a melody, like when you knew somebody loved you. What that must feel like. What Adeline had probably known from the time they'd met. Maybe why she kept his hopes up.

The solo came, and Alfie felt his hands heavier now, hammering the strings, sharpening the tune like grinding a knife blade.

"Gone, Man, gone!" a woman's voice called out.

Alfie slid back to the rhythm, doubling George, following Sammy's sticks. He was swaying now, moving the room. Shoulders in black slid side to side through the smoke. Carmine's palm pounded the bar, and old Dean shot to his feet, clapping and stomping like a country preacher. The melody bubbled, but Adeline's arms draped Ted's shoulders as she searched his profile for something she needed. Only a few people near the stage could have heard when, against his will and plan, the lyrics started coming from Alfie's mouth.

"Train, train. Comin' on down the line …"

As he sang the guitar lapsed into lazy phrases. The crowd slowed. Adeline and Ted kissed in a darkness that couldn't be dark enough, until the song finally pulled into silence. Then the room erupted. Dean ran to the stage and patted Alfie's shoulder, shook hands with every member of the band, and did a raggedy jig to nothing and jogged back out of sight. Sammy pigeoned his head to the ghost of another beat. Alfie caught the energy. He plucked a solitary note, then a second. A cymbal crashed. Then in came George, banging out boogie-woogie. He was solid with the rhythm, and they were off like no tomorrow. Alfie ate up the melody and soloed, then let others take it, one by one, and by the time they brought it back to him, the crowd were on their feet. Carmine wide-eyed him from the bar. If the Bohemians wanted wild times, here they were. Alfie leapt back into the line, diving as deep as he could, making runs all over the fretboard. Here it was. No, there. He ground out something close to the bass line, popping the pick and stinging the strings up near the bridge. It was all he could do, all you could want. It brought Adeline out of her seat, shaking her hips the way you knew they could move but couldn't believe until you saw: curves in a long road. Ted stood in place, rocking just a little from foot to foot, a spectator used to seeing those hips move. Now the closing lick, settling old scores. A triple stop, then an explosion of applause and stomps.

With every song Adeline and the room moved faster, as Alfie fell deeper inside himself. He followed the runs into "Cupid's

Boogie," "Sixty-Minute Man," down "Lost Highway." Breathed new life into "Earth Angel." Flew into "I Played the Fool" and landed hard in "Fool's Paradise." In the brown haze, dancers leaned on one another to save themselves. At tables the faces of saints rested in cradles of hands. Alfie glissed notes, as Adeline let Ted kiss her neck. As his hand disappeared under their table. As she tilted back her head, mouth open, lips to heaven or hell. Anything you wanted and everything you couldn't have.

The band still had a couple of bullets in the chamber, but Carmine was flashing them the one-and-done sign. Alfie took a deep breath and called a final tune. If he'd had a mic, he might've talked the lyrics like Luke the Drifter. Instead he strummed a long intro while the other three boys found their way. When the time was right, he let the guitar tell the story, raising his eyes to a collective trance of calm expressions and mouthed lyrics. Most of these people must have come from other places, maybe when their high school girlfriends or boyfriends dumped them, or maybe when their families started to tell them all the things they weren't supposed to be. They could've come from farms, miles from the nearest neighbor, or from second-rate towns like Rome, where they went to the local theater and watched pictures about New York City and dreamed of the skyline. Or maybe that was a load of malarkey and most of them were just city kids who needed New York to be something special, because *they* needed to be something special. Maybe he was one of these kids. Some of them might have mothers like his, who wished for another way, who wanted their children to live a different kind of life. Some of them might have fathers who were alcoholics, mean ones who beat their wives and kids. Maybe some of them were singled out for thinking too much, in places where most people sweated through their days. Alfie looked down at his own hands on the guitar and wondered if this counted as work. When he looked up again, he saw one blank face after another. Were they happier in a place where everyone knew what it was to be lost? Would he be happier there? The strum had answers, but to no particular questions.

When the song ended, Adeline was sitting alone, Ted's coat on
the seat beside her. Alfie laid down his guitar and descended from
the stage. A lot of the Bohemians got to their feet, clapping for him,
finger-whistling praise. Adeline smiled as if everything were fine,
even though he felt like he might as well be dead. He wanted her
to cry and say she was sorry. But what kind of dope was he? Would
she think for a minute that bringing a date here was doing wrong?
Doing *him* wrong?

"You're wonderful."

Alfie rubbed the back of his head as he moved Ted's coat and
sat down.

"You think so?"

"Really, I knew you were good, but I had no idea you were this
good. God, if I had that kind of talent …"

"You do."

She smiled again, but this time as though she felt sorry for him.
Still, he forced the compliment.

"You're smart. The smartest one in the family. No. You know
what? You're smart all by yourself."

She rolled her eyes, but when they came to rest, Alfie looked
deep into them and thought he saw something he recognized. The
fear the preacher had shown him in the woods. Without warning,
Ted was back, his face appearing out of nowhere, behind Adeline,
who dropped her eyes and made a show of pulling her chair closer
to Ted's, taking his hand.

"Alfie, I wanted very badly for you to meet Ted."

Alfie tried to look friendly, but knew he probably looked like he
could kill somebody.

"Your cousin loves you."

If he was giving the opening, Alfie was taking it.

"I love her, too."

"You two must have a terrific family."

The two cousins shared a chuckle.

"I'll bet the conversations are great. Judging from Adeline, you
must talk about everything under the sun."

Alfie shifted in his seat.

"Well, Adeline and me don't see each other too much."

"Ah, but she tells me about the big family dinners."

Everybody needed a story.

"Yeah, those."

Adeline jumped in, talking fast.

"Ted and I discuss our families all the time. His is much differ-ent, of course. He's from Ohio. A lot of his family are lawyers and doctors. And some are professors, like him."

"Professor?"

Ted cleared his throat, and Alfie, all of a sudden, felt his own go dry. As he was excusing himself to get a drink, Carmine approached the table and shook Alfie's hand.

"You guys knocked the place on its keister. When can you play again?"

"Ask Sammy. He's the boss?"

"My nephew? He might think he is, but he's not who they're gonna come to see."

Carmine turned to Adeline.

"This your girl?"

Like somebody smothering you with your own pillow.

"Excuse me," Alfie said, getting to his feet.

"Wait, where you goin'?"

"Get a drink."

"You kiddin'? Stay here. It's on me."

Carmine pushed Alfie down in his chair.

"I'm comin' right back."

Alfie stared at the stage and the smoke that hung in gray bands over it. It gathered near the lights and floated toward him, stinging his eyes, overwhelming him with the smells of his grandfather's shop, his father's clothes, the pleasures of a hundred strangers. He felt his chest tighten, then saw Carmine standing over him, holding a double shot and a chaser.

"And another round whenever you're ready."

"Well," Ted said, "it was a treat to hear you play, and just to be out."

Adeline latched onto his arm like they were walking down a red carpet. Alfie threw back his drinks. A professor? What made him better? If Alfie made it big, he could have millions of people listening to him. Then what would she think?

"Ted advises a lot of student clubs."

Ted was ready for his cue.

"There's so much going on right now, the meetings last for hours. For instance, this news about the polio vaccine is tremendous. It'll mean a great deal to a lot of families. Between that and the new school construction programs, there may be some hope for the future. If the human race has a future, of course."

Alfie's grandmother had mentioned something about polio at last week's dinner, but Alfie had gotten up to use the bathroom, and when he got back they were on to something else. Between the job and practicing, he didn't have time to read the papers. Most of the news he got, he got from Sunday dinners. Most of that news was political, which, to tell the truth, didn't much interest him. So whatever it was with polio, Alfie didn't want to hear it right now. But he'd listen, for Adeline's sake, so long as Ted didn't get on to politics.

"Look at Austria now. The Soviets seem ready to grant their independence."

Carmine. Thank God for Carmine.

"Another round. Here you go."

Boom and boom: Alfie did the shot and the chaser quick as he could.

"Hey, looka that. The kid's thirsty. 'Nother round comin' up."

The voices in the bar sounded ten times louder. Everybody was stage-talking now.

Ted.

"They're a threat. Naturally, they're a threat, but I think Eisenhower and his gang overestimate them in some ways and underestimate them in others. The Russians aren't stupid. This is a nation that produced Peter the Great, Pushkin, Tchaikovsky. In the end they'll be reasonable. We need to look beyond the current hostility and the old way of thinking about war. Churchill's resigning, and there's a new guard and a new mentality forming."

By now a few Bohemians had overheard the conversation and were gathering around. Ted swiveled his long head both ways, taking in the crowd.

"Just look around the room. All this ferment is terribly exciting."

Bohemians weren't exciting, but Adeline was looking at Ted now like she was Saint Theresa in that famous sculpture. Their grandmother kept a replica of it on top of her piano.

"The real trouble will be in Asia. It seems inevitable."

He looked down at the table and paused, like he was telling a little kid that his favorite uncle was dead.

"The communists in China don't show any restraint at all, and our friend Chiang isn't much better. And we support him in the name of containment. The idea of containing an idea is ludicrous."

Ted should go scratch his ass. In fact, if Ted were ever to step out of line with Adeline, Alfie would have to deck him.

"People are worried about the Soviets in Afghanistan, but if I were a younger man, I'd worry about fighting the Chinese. I'd worry about Taiwan. I'd worry about Vietnam."

The next round arrived just in time. Alfie belted it back quick as the last.

"Alfie, if I were you, with your talent, I wouldn't allow myself to fight in another Korea. But there's so much trouble now that it seems we'll never be rid of the draft. You must think about it often."

What was wrong with this *cidrul*? Who worried about getting drafted? A few uncles had been in the war, but they never talked about it. And his friends who were in the service made it sound like fun. Target practice, crawling under barbed wire, obstacles courses, cherry pie in the mess hall. If you were in with your friends, it was like camp. So, if they called you up, you went.

"Anyway, I suppose Italians are far better musicians than they are warriors. Alfie, you're the living proof."

Adeline didn't bat an eye. What the hell was wrong with her? Her father was Italian—a fascist, no less. Uncle Enzo should only be here now. The old S.O.B. could run down the list of Italian patriots, starting with Garibaldi, which was the only one, to be honest, anybody else could ever remember. But, c'mon, if Ted didn't mind insulting Italians in public, what was the jackass saying to Adeline when nobody was around? Alfie could lay him out right here, but then he'd never work the joint again. And what would she think of him? She was refined. Still, you couldn't just eat shit.

Alfie stood up and raised a shot glass in Ted's face.

"Here's to Mussolini."

He slammed the glass down, kissed Adeline on the cheek, grabbed his case and jacket, and strode out the door and into the Greenwich Village night.

So long, Asshole. How was it possible? Was life ever fair? A bozo like that, and she's in love. An egghead. A Yucatán pinhead, his father would call him. It made you want to give up. Leave. So Alfie would go. And where would he go? It didn't matter. A pinhead like old Ted could talk and talk and get paid for it, while Alfie was breaking his ass to play for a room like that one. He should take his guitar and go. But where? Figure that one out. He was a little dizzy. A ride would clear his head. He took the subway home, dropped off his gear, and an hour after leaving the club was on his bike, headed east on the Belt Parkway.

His father had driven them out to Jones Beach, on Long Island, the summer after they'd moved to Brooklyn. It was the last year of the Indian Village there. Maybe his parents got interested in Indians when they were living in Rome, where everybody liked to talk about Indians this and Indians that, even though you couldn't find an Indian if your life depended on it. The Iroquois were a big topic of conversation, but the Indians at the Indian Village were supposed to be Plains Indians. How they wound up on the beach, who knew? An Indian woman named Rosebud Yellow Robe told them a lot about how tribes lived, about how they believed in spirits and how they never stopped moving. Alfie decided to head for where the village used to be. He was wearing a black leather jacket, like Brando wore. In the part of the movie Alfie could remember Brando rode off with the girl. But could Alfie really get away like that? His mother had heard the bike start up. She had to. And she was probably worrying. She probably woke his father up to tell him she was worried. The old man might be driving around on a wild goose chase through Brooklyn right now.

Alfie was riding alone in the middle of nowhere. It was late and getting colder. The wind was picking up, which just made him want to ride faster down the empty parkway and let his mind unfurl as slowly as a piece of crumpled paper. He rode an invisible tunnel under low bridges, through stretches so dark you imagined the sun could never have touched them. Once in a while the moonlight bled a lifeline through the clouds. At the sharp turn around Hempstead Lake, he mistook a horse path for a lane and almost wrapped himself around an oak tree. After that he slowed down a little. Soon he saw signs for the beach. The salt air hit him as he turned south onto another parkway. He wished Adeline were there, her arms around his waist, her body pressed against his. All her warmth, all their spirit, the sins of the flesh like Holy Communion. The two of them could keep going and find some town far enough away that the family couldn't reach them.

On a night like this the cops didn't bother with traffic. They'd rather park their cruisers and sip their coffee in peace. You owned the roads and everything you could see. Alfie crossed over a causeway and looked back across the bay at small waves lit by house lights along the shore. The exits on this last highway went to different parts of Jones Beach: the West End, the theater, the boardwalk. Every exit was blocked with a wooden barricade, all the way to the tower at the traffic circle. Alfie rounded it and came back to where the Indian Village must have been. He parked his bike on the shoulder and loped over a sand dune. The waves boomed, as a few drops of cold rain started to fall. On the other side of the dune, yellow street lamps x-rayed the rain's assault on a miniature golf course. Imagine him and Adeline there on a summer day. He'd smack his ball over the divider between holes, maybe knock some poor kid's ball into the bushes, and she'd laugh. He wished he could hear that laughter or at least not feel so goddamn cold. The wind was cutting through his jacket. He turned away from the waves, his legs suddenly heavy and his head throbbing. Then a strange thought made him smile. If the Indians were still here, he'd go see the medicine man.

Was life really so bad? He was playing, knockin' 'em dead, on his way. And Adeline was watching. He could see her whenever he wanted. Playing regular, he could live anywhere he wanted and be happy. Even if she'd convinced herself to love a pinhead, Alfie knew that sooner or later she'd come to her senses. Many times he'd caught his cousin looking at him the same way he looked at her. He wasn't imagining. They could do it. They could go. If anybody cared, they could work it out with the Church.

What a jerk he'd been to run. The first thing he'd do after he woke up tomorrow, he'd go see her and apologize. Get up early and see her. He kick-started the Harley, and tried to forget how she didn't care when he told her what kind of bike it was. Should he be surprised? What kind of girls knew about bikes? He revved the engine. Only one girl he knew gave a shit about his bike, a girl named Michelle. A real piece of ass. Not completely right in the head, but so what? You didn't marry a girl like that. You married a girl like Adeline. And what kind of girl was Adeline? A nice girl. A girl with class and brains. Prettier than Michelle, too. In a different way. So what if he didn't know everything about Adeline? If they knew everything about each other at this age, what would they talk about for the rest of their lives?

He listened to the waves. Relentless. A monster coming to rip you apart. A beautiful monster. If you had to explain the sound of waves, could you? Could you explain why blues songs never got old? He pulled slowly onto the parkway toward the traffic circle. The rain was falling harder now. Better to get back before it really came down. Maybe he could find an all-night diner in one of the towns. As he swung around the circle toward the bay, Alfie thought he heard a car behind him. He pulled to the right. As soon as he got over, he spotted the car coming out of nowhere, the wrong way around the circle, straight at him. He turned hard as he could onto the shoulder, but the bike jackknifed. For a second he was flying, the pavement and bay all one black sheet. He threw his arms out to break the fall, then hit the asphalt sideways and heard the pop. His wrist had bent backward underneath him. He tried to find his breath and get up, but couldn't move, couldn't do anything but watch red tail lights burning through the darkness, mean as the cold and the pain.

(1956)

Frankie looked like a baby giraffe. His neck, long as his arms, sprouted from his short-sleeved black polo shirt, propping up his oversized head. Clown feet stuck out of his black pants. The rest of him was a rail. And he was always looking at the sky, whistling. Here he was now, poking his head through the open window, grinning at Alfie, who couldn't contain himself.

"Get in, ya geep."

Frankie smacked the car door. Crouching down, he clasped his hands in front of him and grinned.

"How's the wrist?"

Alfie nodded, gritted his teeth, and forced a smile. Frankie knew exactly shit, but he was a nice kid. He went to church with their mother. But what really made him nice was even when you knew he wanted to say something to people who were wrong or stupid, he kept his mouth shut. He let them talk and gave them the once-over when they weren't looking. Once he'd taken all the notes he needed in his head, he said goodbye. And people loved him. He never argued—not with his friends during stickball games, not with his parents at dinner. Only with his brother. Maybe he didn't mean it, but he had a knack for bringing Alfie down. Lately it was the only direction.

"I'm better now, Brother," Alfie answered, rolling up his white shirt sleeves and flexing his biceps.

He shifted the Studebaker into drive and shot the car into 14th Avenue traffic. When Frankie cast him a worried look, he eased off the pedal. The El track faded eastward as they rolled south. At the corner of 65th Street, his brother sat still as a stone, looking straight ahead, grinning. Alfie elbowed him.

"You're too quiet, and you're smiling too much."

Frankie came to life, rubbing his palms together.

"High school's over in two weeks. I'm free."

Since the accident, Alfie wished he could be in school again. He missed the way it marked time. Every day now was going by the same, just colder or warmer. The streets of Brooklyn went from dark gray to light gray and back again. Would he care if one day he didn't wake up?

They stopped at a light and Alfie looked Frankie over. The *gibook* was wearing a rumpled fedora he must have pulled from his waistband.

"Who are you supposed to be, Father Flanagan?"

"It's my hat."

"Since when?"

"Since I bought it. Like you bought your car."

He faced Alfie, as if he were about to ask the most important question in the world.

"You like the car?"

Alfie didn't answer. Instead he pictured the wreck of his bike and the fella in the ambulance who kept telling him he'd be all right. The light changed, and Frankie moved on from his question.

"Now leaving Blythebourne," Frankie announced. "That's what they used to call Boro Park."

Alfie gunned the car across 65th Street, into the less familiar but still friendly territory of Bensonhurst.

"Bensonhurst-By-The-Sea."

"What are you talkin' about?"

"That's what these neighborhoods used to be called. Though 'By-The-Sea' meant more Bath Beach. It was a resort for people in Manhattan."

Who knew? But, really, who cared? Brooklyn was full of names that didn't make sense.

"We're in Dyker Heights."

"That's because of the Van Dykes. They were the Dutch family that drained the meadow."

The way his brother told stories was enough to make you sick.

"What meadow?"

"C'mon," Frankie said, like a teacher, "you remember what Rome was like. Everything starts out as country. Dyker Heights was a big meadow. Almost like a marsh. The Van Dykes drained it. With dykes."

"Sure. What else?"

"Nothing else. That's it."

They were miles apart, he and his brother. You could tell Frankie that the Studebaker ran on a special kind of gas you had to order straight from the factory, and he'd believe you, even after he saw you pump gas at the corner station. Not because he was stupid. He was just a *cidrul* that way.

"Anyway, you're free," Alfie said flat-toned. "I'm happy for you, Brother."

"Free for a while."

A left onto 73rd Street, where a couple of old Italians sat sprawled on folding chairs in front of the corner social club. Alfie recognized their faces from the job site. Union "delegates" who gave his grandfather trouble. Whenever they showed up, the old coot got that look that said, "I need this like I need a second asshole." Then he'd curse in Italian. "*Vigliacc'!*"

"It means they are cowards," Grandpa Ruggiero told him. "Nothing is worse than to be a coward."

They might be cowards, but they were gangsters too, and they specialized in busting balls and, if they had to, heads. Alfie avoided them at all costs. If he let them get to him, he'd be more like his grandfather, the sap with the face that said you could do everything right and still be punished.

Frankie noticed the turn.

"Why we heading this way? I thought we were going to Bay Ridge?"

Alfie sniffled and rubbed his chin.

"No, we are. We're just taking the scenic route. New Utrecht. 86th Street. You never know. We might see something."

They drove exactly one block on New Utrecht, under the elevated train, before Alfie made a quick right onto 74th Street.

"Where you going now?"

"I forgot. I'm out of cigarettes. I can pick up a pack on 15th Avenue."

Frankie eyeballed him.

"There's a million stores on New Utrecht."

"Yeah, but the parking."

"The parking, c'mon. Isn't this Adeline's block? Sure it is. I was just here the other day."

"Why were you here?"

"She asked me to come by. She was having guy trouble, she said. Every once in a while she calls me to come over and talk."

"Talk? She should have girlfriends for that. Plus, she's older than you."

"So what? She's my cousin. She says I'm wise."

Alfie looked again at his brother in the fedora.

"Wise?"

How much did Frankie know about her?

"Anyway, I'm still going down this way for butts."

Alfie slowed the car as they passed by Adeline's, a detached house with a brick porch. He pulled to the curb in front of the five-and-ten and got out. Too bad Adeline wasn't on the porch, though maybe it wouldn't be such a hot idea to see her with Frankie here. Sometimes he just needed a glimpse of her from a distance, even through a window. But Uncle Enzo's car was gone, which meant they must be in the country. A few years back the old greaseball had bought another house way out on Long Island. Only once did he invite the rest of the family. It was a warm Saturday, a year ago. After dinner, Adeline asked him to walk with her on the beach. She was wearing a summer dress. The wind off the Sound fluttered the dress above her thighs.

Back in the car, Frankie was staring down 15th Avenue like he wanted to annihilate it.

"It's funny how all the stores are the same."

Alfie lit a cigarette and blew smoke out the window.

"What do you mean?"

"Every few blocks: a drug store, a hardware store, a five-and-ten, a pork store, a deli, a pizzeria, a pastry shop. Always the same. Why would people want that?"

A breeze filled the car with the smell of pizza. Alfie took another drag and felt his stomach roll. He flicked the still-burning cigarette out the window.

"What can I tell ya? People need things, and they like to eat."

"But don't you feel sometimes like you need something different?"

Work, home, dinner, pick at the guitar, take a date to the movies, and then, for a big exotic night out, go to the Chinks and then Jan's for a sundae. Without gigs he was sinking into a bottomless pit of shit. Even his father took trips upstate. Alfie was living the worst of his parents' life. Why did his brother have to rub salt?

"What? You want a French restaurant? A museum? How about the Museum of Pizza? Or better yet, the Museum of *Gabagool'*."

"No, c'mon. I'm just saying, I wonder why no one here ever tries anything new. Don't they look around? We live in New York."

Alfie snorted.

"No, we don't. We live in Brooklyn."

Sunset crowned the west end of 86th Street. Over the harbor the sky was turning pinkish-orange under bands of thin purple clouds. A sky like they'd see when their father took them fishing after supper. He'd get up from the table and head straight downstairs, which meant they should get the poles and get in the car. They'd pick good spots on the bulkhead, throw in their lines, and watch the dying light put on its show over Far Rockaway. Lately, the sky scared Alfie. When he thought about the ocean, he thought about jumping in and swimming out until the waves got high enough so he'd lose sight of land. When he went under, the dark blue would flood the islands of Alfie's two futures: one, a place where he walked barefoot in the sand as waves lapped the rhythm of whatever song he played for a line of happy people, led by Adeline, who walked behind him toward the sunset; the other, the mouth of a cave, where he hid himself behind a single tree bending in the wind that blew in dark clouds, one lower than the next.

For now, he had his own idea for something new, and he had his brother.

"You remember that book, *Buffalo Bill and the Pony Express*?"

Frankie laughed.

"Sure. I remember the cover. The cowboy riding away from the Indians, with the arrow flying over his head. That why you're speeding up?"

"You remember the story?"

Frankie stuck his head out the open window and watched the dying sun, until the wind blew his hat into the back seat. Then he turned again to Alfie.

"Yeah, Buffalo Bill as an Army scout. I remember him killing Indians."

"He did, but the important thing was he was a kid and yet he was the only one who could spy on the enemy. And he did it alone. Think of the chances he took."

"Who was the enemy? Remind me."

"The rebels. The southerners."

Frankie laughed again.

"What's funny?"

"Now the Army's full of southerners."

"What difference does it make? Listen. The rebels killed Buffalo Bill's father because he was against slavery. Bill didn't know what to do, so he joined the Army to figure it out."

Trouble always seemed to start with colored people. Just like Rome, except nobody ever took Buffalo Bill away. He stayed there in Kansas and fixed things. And you could see how he helped free the slaves. Alfie had nothing against the colored people he knew (not many), but outside of music what good were they?

The Studebaker crawled along the edge of Dyker Park.

"I was thinking of joining the Army," Alfie announced.

Frankie tilted his head, like a dog hearing a broken whistle.

"Yeah," Alfie said, "I think I wanna join."

Frankie twisted his mouth.

"Brother, I don't know if anyone told you, but soldiers don't get to play much guitar."

Alfie banged his wrist against the steering wheel.

"I can't play much guitar as it is."

"Yeah, but when the wrist heals, you will."

Alfie rolled his wrist in the air. The bones clicked loud enough to be heard. He could use it okay—shoot a gun, hold a hammer, work out, probably pass the Army physical—but picking the guitar the way he wanted to?

"It's not coming back."

"Give it time."

"It's over a year, and I don't think I can go another year like this. I have to try something else, so I thought you might want to join up with me."

Frankie folded his arms.

"I just got done telling you I'm free."

"Yeah, though technically you'd be fighting for freedom."

"Fighting who? Fighting where?"

"You never know. There's Russia, China, Israel. Anything can happen. And you might get to see the world."

Frankie's fingers brushed an invisible fly from his forearm.

"Maybe, but I'm no fighter."

He reached back and grabbed his stray hat from the back seat, reset it on his head, then rolled up his window as they came to a stop at the corner of 7th Avenue.

Alfie couldn't say exactly why, but having the kid with him during basic training would make it a hundred times easier. He felt selfish thinking about his brother this way, but he needed strength. He dreaded working, eating, sitting in his chair, listening to the radio, and doing it all over again, going through all the motions.

None of it put ideas in his head or words in his mouth that he could use to talk to Adeline or anybody else who might help him. And if Alfie disappeared and Frankie didn't, what else would she tell his brother? What other ways could Frankie get between them?

The light changed, and Alfie hit the gas. A second later Frankie cranked the window down again as he yelled "Wait!" He called to somebody on the sidewalk. Whoever it was, his brother had a knack for distracting himself from a tough conversation.

"Oh, Sal! Sal! ... Alfie, pull over a minute."

"It's an intersection."

Frankie pointed to the corner.

"Over there, by the Esso."

Alfie pulled into the gas station and tried to remember their jingle from the ads, which always showed people driving down big highways, usually out west. Imagine the sunshine on your face, cowboy music coming through the speakers.

"Howdy, Pahdnah!"

The voice belonged to a thin kid about his brother's age. All you saw was shoulders and a head, he was that short. When Alfie cut the ignition, the kid stepped back, to take in their car. He wore black-rimmed sunglasses and a black porkpie hat.

"I dig the wheels. Crazy, Man."

A Bohemian, or a type who thought he was. Either way, he had one hell of a Brooklyn accent, the kind he and Frankie never quite got. Bohemians were supposed to talk a certain way that Alfie couldn't put his finger on. But then Bohemian could mean a lot of things. There was "La Boheme," which of course his mother played over and over, and thought was great, even though the characters were poor and cold, and she cried every time the girl died. Imagine Adeline dying in a beautiful dress. Buried. Gone. What would it feel like to see her buried? To be buried yourself?

"Sal," Frankie said, "my brother Alfie."

Sal looked in.

"Cool caahh."

Alfie gave him a two-finger salute.

Sal smiled and bobbed his head like a boob, until Frankie broke his rhythm.

"So what are you doing all the way down here? I thought they called you 'Sal Bath Beach'."

Sal fidgeted with the brim of his hat.

"No, no, they don't call me that no more. No, c'mon."

"Anyway, what's up?"

Making a show of it, Sal nodded toward Bay Ridge.

"On my way dat way, ovah deah. Gonna meet some Poly Prep cats down at Hinsch's."

Frankie winked at Alfie, then returned to questioning Sal.

"Egg creams?"

Sal dropped his eyes, but Frankie slapped his arm playfully.

"If you want, Sal, next week I'm going over to Café Reggio, in Greenwich Village? I know a few people there. I can come get you. Maybe your friends wanna come too."

Sal smiled again.

Alfie studied his brother.

"Yeah, yeah, that's hip," Sal said, taking a step away. "So where are youse … I mean, where are you cats headin'? What's the scene?"

Frankie leaned back in his seat and pushed his hat down over his eyes.

"It's hard to say. But c'mon, we'll drop you at Hinsch's."

From Hinsch's the brothers drove south, as the moonrise over Staten Island flooded the Verrazano Narrows with pale light. At the end of 4th Avenue, they parked in front of a dingy coffee shop that was actually called The Narrows. Alfie reached into the pocket of his dungarees for coins to buy them both a cup of coffee. They sat at the counter. Alfie kept himself busy staring at the pretty waitress who served them. When Frankie got bored enough, he proposed a walk near the water. Across Shore Road they followed a flight of stairs down to a terraced park. Moonlight turned the canopy of thin leaves above them silver. The sound of cars on the parkway and the sight of the water in the distance relaxed Alfie. Forget Adeline. Forget everything. They walked a good half-mile without saying a word. When they reached the handball courts, Frankie stopped.

"Wait here a minute."

Alfie turned his palms to the dark blue sky.

"What? You wanna practice?"

"I have an idea."

Frankie opened the chain-link gate and walked to the high white wall between two courts. Handball was perfect for the city that way. One thin slab of concrete gave you a game on either side. If you had two good players in each game, you might get twenty or thirty people watching them. An event out of nothing. From his pocket Frankie pulled what looked in the sickly light like a rock, and started drawing on the wall. Alfie looked over his shoulder, down the half-lit paths.

"What the hell are you doing? What if a cop comes? You wanna spend the night at the station house? Worse, you wanna hear your mother?"

Frankie stopped and smiled, then went right back to work.

Alfie shrugged. "Have it your way."

He checked the paths one more time, then walked over to the newborn mural. Frankie was drawing it in charcoal, so it was hard to make out in the dim light.

"What is it?"

"It's abstract. In a way."

"It looks a little abstract."

Like a comic book bomb blast, but also like a face. The blast or the face had sticks around it, maybe trees, maybe with burning leaves. Alfie took a few steps to his right. What did Frankie see? What did he say when he talked to Adeline? How would his brother like it if Alfie smashed his face into the white wall? Now Frankie was furiously scraping the concrete with a coal nugget in either hand. He himself could have been standing inside the painting: a dark figure against the background of moonlit water flowing through the Narrows.

"It's based on something I saw in Rome."

"What? Rome, New York? Where in Rome would you see something like this?"

Frankie stopped what he was doing.

"In my head. In a dream. I was a kid. I didn't know what I was seeing, but I never forgot it. Every year since then I try to draw whatever it was, but I never get it right."

He went on scraping.

"But I'm getting closer to this first image. I think being outside helps, so I try it outside whenever I can. That's why I carry the coal around."

He scraped a streak from the bottom of the mural to the top.

"Being with you is helping too. I think you're in it."

Frankie held the lump of coal up to his brother's face and squinted one eye.

"Hold still a minute."

"Get outta here!"

That was enough art for one night, enough bullshit. Alfie needed to hear some music. He started back to the car.

"Wait, wait."

When Frankie's footsteps caught up, Alfie stopped.

"You finished now?" he asked, not turning around.

"Finished? No, I'm never finished. But tomorrow whoever plays here gets a free show with their handball game."

"You think that's fair?"

Alfie's legs and chest were burning. He was the blazing tree.

Frankie looked confused.

"What are you talkin' about?"

"You go and write on a wall that other people have to use?"

Frankie chuckled.

"You're kiddin' me, right?"

Alfie started walking back to the car, cursing under his breath loud enough for Frankie to hear. Frankie followed behind him, lips zipped. To need somebody else this way made Alfie want to choke. Especially someone who might be stabbing him in the back. Brother or no brother. The plan was to need only one person at a time. You did the rest on your own. That was freedom. Doing whatever you wanted whether it hurt other people or not, that was something else.

A black car turned off Shore Road and rumbled down 4th Avenue, slowing almost to a stop as it passed Alfie leaning against the door of the Studebaker. He lit a cigarette, taking a pull that drew the fiery ring halfway down the stick. Everybody wanted to peg you. They could all go take a flying shit. His brother too. Frankie was still shaking his head as he crossed the avenue. He looked Alfie up and down.

"Who are you, James Dean?"

Alfie didn't smile.

"If I was, at least I'd be in the movies and not in some nobody's dream."

"Actually, you'd be dead."

They got in the car. Alfie ignored his brother and tuned the dial until he found Bo Diddley. The night was darker now. Only a few apartments still glowed, and the street light above him was a bright mouth blowing smoke into space. Alfie wanted to knock out its teeth, pull all the secrets he didn't know from its throat. Instead he turned up the radio. To be in a club. To be on stage. Alfie rapped the steering wheel in time with the beat. Bo Diddley. The preacher had once told his father that a man they knew wasn't worth diddly. He could've been talking about Alfie. Where was the poor preacher now?

"Where are we going?" Frankie asked.

Alfie said nothing and hit the gas.

Coal.

"What were you doing back there?"

"Making art."

"You call that art?"

Frankie rolled down his window and took a deep breath.

"I'm gonna go to art school."

"What do you mean 'art school'?"

"I'm gonna study painting. I want to paint."

His brother was supposed to be an architect, go to City College. Now he was going to art school and palling around with a girl cousin.

Bo Diddley gave way to Elvis Presley. A number Alfie had seen on television.

"You hear me?"

"I heard you," Alfie answered, slamming the car to a stop. "You think that's a good idea?"

Frankie tried to hold back a smile.

"Probably not, but I'm doing it anyway."

"The light's changing. Where do you want to go?"

"Ebbets Field."

"Some people never grow up."

Alfie watched the road and ground his teeth.

"Ebbets Field, comin' up."

He headed toward Ocean Parkway.

"Listen, Alfie …"

"It's like a shrine now, right?"

"What?"

"Ebbets Field."

"I just feel like seeing it," Frankie said. "Home of the World Champions."

Baseball was a waste of time. The usual. So was a nostalgia tour. Nothing new there, like Frankie himself said. Like family.

At the next light, Alfie turned the car around.

"Where are we going now?"

"I got another idea."

They drove up the other side of Prospect Park, picking up speed as they went.

"What's the matter, Brother?" Frankie asked. "I thought you'd be happy for me."

"I am happy for you."

"Coulda fooled me."

Alfie ignored him until they reached the end of the park. The lighted arch on Grand Army Plaza rose up like a temple. The Studebaker rolled to a stop.

Alfie tried thinking of ways to make his brother feel bad.

"Tell me about the arch, Brother."

Frankie sighed.

"No, c'mon. You like to talk. I know you know something about it."

He drummed his fingers on the dashboard.

"No, go ahead. I always wondered."

Frankie rubbed his eyes and forced a yawn.

"All right. It's a Civil War monument. To the Defenders of the Union. The city built it in 1895."

"Took them a while."

"It wasn't like World War II."

"What's that mean?"

"It means Americans had to kill other Americans."

No matter how much of an asshole Frankie might be, he made good points. Whatever he said, people were inclined to believe, just by the way he said it. A friend like that would help a lot in a place like the Army.

"Frankie, listen. We can join the Reserves. You do your training, and then it's just a weekend a month. You'll still be free. You'll get money for art school. Which I don't see your father paying for. And you won't have to get drafted."

Frankie smirked.

"Nobody's drafting me."

Again, Alfie wanted to hit him, but more he wanted to tell him how sick he felt being in Brooklyn, like he was sinking. His brother must have seen the desperation on his face.

"Listen, Brother. Joining the Army's a big thing. I have my own plans, but I'll think about it. Okay?"

He was still smirking, but his voice sounded serious. Maybe he was just putting Alfie off, but you had to give him the benefit of the doubt. Alfie leaned his head back onto the headrest and looked out at the arch. Behind it a few stars were sparkling over the apartment buildings across the plaza. Grant a wish. They drove through the park to Bedford Avenue, and parked near the main gate of Ebbets Field, so Frankie could gawk for a while. Alfie watched his brother. How far were they really from being kids? He remembered how easily he could impress Frankie: tie a knot, smack a stickball, scare away a bully. And how in the bedroom they shared Frankie would ask him to talk until he fell asleep. Alfie started the car and drove them back toward Atlantic Avenue. Frankie lowered his fedora over his eyes and spoke.

"What did the doctors say?"

"About what? My hand? As far as they're concerned, it's healed. But it's not healed all the way."

He strained to splay his fingers.

"At least you still got your looks."

"With this nose?"

"Brother, we don't have small noses. It's like everybody in Brooklyn's in a biggest-nose contest. You have nothing to worry about. You're my brother, so you're a good-lookin' guy."

"Yeah, who thinks so?" Alfie asked, as they passed some colored girls walking toward the El.

"I bet one of those girls right there would take you."

His brother wasn't kidding, but Alfie couldn't think about something like that. Sure, there were plenty of nice-lookin' colored girls, but all he had to do was imagine the lemon-sucking look on his mother's face, and what big spoon or ladle she might throw at him. His father, of course, wouldn't care. He'd caught the old man sneaking looks at colored women. But God forbid a colored girl-friend came to visit Alfie on his lunch break, the fellas on the site would break his chops for weeks. All day long it would be, "Hey, Honey. Hey, Sugar. Can I fix you some chitlins?" That kind of crap.

"Maybe you need to go out more."

"I go out," Alfie answered without feeling. "I'm out now."

"Wait." Frankie made believe he was dialing a phone. "Let me call *The Daily News*. I can see the headline: 'Baliato Goes Out: Colored Chicks Go Wild!'"

"You're an asshole."

Earning the title seemed to make Frankie happy. He made a show of putting his legs up on the dashboard and his hands behind his head. Alfie tried to fight the idea that his brother really was an asshole.

"What do you know about girls? You're never with a girl, except Adeline."

Frankie's grin straightened out. He brushed the legs of his dungarees like they were dirty.

"Girls are trouble," he said, sitting up straight again.

"You sound like your mother."

Frankie paused before he answered, then made a sound like he was spitting a seed out of his mouth.

"I do? Look what one girl's doing to you."

"I don't have a girl."

"Sure you do. The wrong one."

His brother had some balls, especially considering his little chit-chat sessions.

"You're a real asshole."

"Yeah, you already said."

The whole conversation reminded Alfie of a story that a kid in the neighborhood once told him. Something about Frankie. Something you didn't want to hear. The kid who told him was a weasel, so Alfie didn't believe it. But now his brother was really pressing his buttons. If he wanted to act this way, Alfie would teach him a lesson. He started the car, peeled into the traffic circle, and flew up Flatbush Avenue toward the city. Crossing the Manhattan Bridge, Alfie almost backed off and changed the plan, but then Manhattan's buildings were standing there like a flashy crowd looking down their noses. The haze hung around their necks like fur collars. Beyond them were miles of lights like strings of pearls running out to Jersey. And beyond that was darkness he felt like he might never understand. Frankie must have really thought who he was. And did he think Alfie was some kind of boob? The kid didn't know the first thing about Alfie's life off the block, the places he knew, the little clubs in Downtown Brooklyn and the things he saw there. Alfie thought about the musicians. What they wanted. What they'd taught him. Most of them decided to play rock and roll because they had to. But it was jazz they really loved. They talked about 52nd Street like it had been paradise. Jazz was all right, and maybe Alfie would've ended up playing it, too, if things hadn't gone the other way. So forget it. Tonight he could kill two birds with one stone: go visit one of jazz's graveyards and show his smart-ass of a brother something about life.

When they hit Manhattan, he headed uptown, to the Club Samoa. It was one of the few clubs left on 52nd. The Somoa, the Pigalle, and Flamingo were on one side, what you might call the tropical side. The Moulin Rouge, the Harem, the Ha-Ha, and Jimmy Ryan's were on the other. Ryan's was the only one where music was still the thing. The rest of the places survived as strip joints. The Somoa meant something to Alfie. An older drummer had taken him there, and there he'd gotten his first professional hand job. He parked the car on 6th Avenue, and the brothers walked around the corner. A few steps from the club's door, Alfie heard footsteps behind them. His father had taught him how to throw a punch. You didn't like to do it, but if some *germoke* was coming after you, what choice did you have? He turned with his fist cocked, and saw a big, goofy face, all nose and teeth, floating on a bear's body. Whoever this character was, he was wearing what looked like a bus driver's cap.

"Whoa! Whoa there, big fella. I didn't mean to startle you. Harry Marcus, at your service."

Frankie shrugged his shoulders and craned his neck to take in the club's marquee. It rose straight over their heads, up the brick facade of a dilapidated tenement building.

"Let me get the door for youse gentlemen."

Alfie raised his eyebrows.

"You're the doorman here?"

"For the whole block. They call me the Mayor, except I take tips."

He smacked Alfie's chest lightly with the back of his hand.

"Ya hear me?"

The brothers shot each other quick smiles.

"C'mon," Harry said, "I'm joking around. Though maybe the Mayor takes tips, too. Who knows? Anyway, I thought youse two were movie stars."

Alfie shook his head and laughed. This place hadn't seen a movie star since the Forties.

"I knew it! No, wait, let me guess. You're on Broadway."

Frankie, who was trying to look inside the club through a dark window, answered, "Not quite."

"It's all right. You're still important customers. Ya understand? C'mon in. C'mon. Before they tear the place down."

Harry pulled the door open, and a bass drum beat its way onto the sidewalk. Alfie dug out a quarter and handed it to their guide, who slipped the coin into his pocket.

"So you're not movie stars. So what? You're all right. You're young. Have a good time, gents. The girls are waitin' for ya."

Frankie shook his head.

Inside the club the first thing you noticed was the bandstand, which looked more like a walk-in closet, about eight feet wide, closed in by three paneled half-walls. The fans of a fake potted palm by the window reached out over the slightly raised platform. A crammed-in quartet was pumping out "Sing, Sing, Sing," sweating through their dress shirts. They were playing to a handful of customers up front, most of them older fellas throwing back drinks and shouting at each other over the licks. Behind them the club was a bamboo-lined tunnel. The bar had a South Pacific theme, with tiki torches and tribal masks hanging on the walls over the liquor bottles. Alfie waved Frankie toward a table in the half-light on the opposite side of the room. They ordered two draft beers from a nervous girl in a hula skirt. The girl looked at Frankie, smiled, and averted her eyes.

Good. He'd fix his brother yet.

When the drinks arrived, Alfie paid the waitress with a five spot, and lit a cigarette. Frankie leaned back against the wall and forced a smile like a dim flashlight through the thick smoke. Finally, the music stopped. A worn-out emcee in a sharkskin suit shambled to the microphone. His voice was deep and rough, all phony enthusiasm.

"Gentlemen, now for the moment you've all been waiting for. Please welcome the sophisticated lady of the high seas, the woman who can board any ship, the dame who'll steal your treasure chest, the lovely and dangerous Miss Cherry England."

The emcee clapped like a drill sergeant as he backed into the shadows. A boom of the bass drum cued Cherry, who sauntered onto the floor in front of the little stage. She wore a pirate hat with skull and crossbones. Around her waist was wrapped a matching Jolly Roger. Skull-shaped pasties covered her nipples. From each one hung a tiny parrot pendant. She made the birds hop with every shake of her shoulders and hips, as the band launched into "Sophisticated Lady." Alfie took a drag on his cigarette like it was all he had left in the world, serious as a monk. Frankie, on the other hand, the mook, looked like he was about to bust out laughing. Alfie frowned and signaled for him to pay attention as Cherry worked her way through the tables. When she finally stood gyrating in front of theirs, Frankie stopped laughing. Before he could do anything about it, she'd taken a seat on his knee. He looked like he wanted to throw up. She caught his expression and moved on to Alfie. Six inches in front of him, she sank lower and lower. She was old for a stripper. By the looks of her neck, maybe forty. But the beauty of her face surprised him. Her eyes were sea green, her nose was perfect, symmetrical, and her lips were like red pillows. Her cheek, which she rubbed on his, was smooth as a baby's. But there was something in the way she looked at him that said no one was ever pulling a fast one. If she weren't a stripper, you could marry a girl like that.

Alfie listened to the saxophone as Cherry stared into his eyes. He'd heard the song a hundred times but couldn't remember the lyrics. One line maybe. A flame that flickered. But what the hell did it matter? She had her hands on his thighs now, leaning in. Her lips stopped an inch from his, then her head veered to the left and she whispered in his ear, before rising and drifting toward the stage. Alfie stared at her long and hard, feeling the ash from his cigarette drop onto his knuckles like a hot mosquito. He closed his eyes, expecting his brother to be at his shoulder any second.

"You want me to tell you what she said?" he'd say.

And Frankie would nod and take a sip of beer.

And Alfie would say, "You really need to know?"

And Frankie would give him a rap on the arm.

And Alfie would pull his brother close and tell him.

"She said, 'How'd you like me to walk your plank?'"

But the question never came. When Alfie opened his eyes, Frankie had his back turned and was taking a big swig from his glass. Without looking at Alfie, he stood up and headed for the door. Alfie grabbed him before he got there. The bouncer noticed.

"Problem, fellas?"

"No, we're okay. I'm just talking with my brother."

The big man nodded and left them alone. The place didn't have a million paying customers. Frankie sat down again and exhaled like he'd just run five miles. Alfie could imagine what he was think-ing: The whole thing was wrong. What were they doing here? His friends would never go to the burlesque. That's what their father and uncles did. These were new times. Plus, by now their mother and father were worried. Alfie was still studying his brother's face when a bongo drum kicked in. The drummer on the bandstand squeezed the bongos between his knees. The emcee appeared, scanned the small crowd, and with a quick flourish of his arm, an-nounced, "Mulaa Mulaa!"

A dark-skinned girl danced into view. She wore a grass skirt, bikini top, lei upon lei, and a palm-leaf headdress. She might be from the South Pacific or she might just be a dark Italian passing for an islander. Either way, she knew her moves. With each step or hip shake, a bongo sounded, a slow rhythm at first, then faster and faster as she stepped and shimmied around the room. Before long every inch of her body was quivering as the drummer banged his skins. Her skirt hissed like a snake. Whenever it seemed like she couldn't move any faster, she did, and as she did, she began to sidle her way between tables, brushing her backside against the nearest mark.

Almost through his second beer, Alfie was just the spit short of drooling. Mulaa played to his leer, lingering in front of him, adding all kinds of twists and shuffles to her routine. Alfie couldn't help imagining Adeline moving like this, wearing almost nothing. He inhaled deep, to catch the scent of perfumed sweat, then tilted back his head, Adeline hovering above him like an obscene angel. And wasn't it obscene to think of her this way? What if he touched her? He didn't believe in Hell necessarily, so maybe he'd get away with Purgatory? And what about Heaven? If she made you happy, what other reward did you need? Frankie was eyeing him now, probably judging him. Could his brother live with him and Adeline being together? Or would he try to make Alfie feel bad about it for the rest of his life? Maybe Frankie wouldn't mind if he could paint them together: Alfie and Adeline on a bed, all his weight on top of her, the two of them locked in a kiss, pulling at each other's clothes. In a dirty room lit dim yellow. Maybe with flames at the bottom of the bed.

Alfie reached out to touch the hula girl and sent her rolling like a wave in Frankie's direction. Before Frankie could make a move, she was on top of him, still grinding, as the drummer's hands flew. The beat slowed to a steady thump. Mulaa shook until her skirt dropped to the floor. Down to a red g-string, she settled onto Frankie's lap, still rotating her hips and smiling at the other men in the room as she slid her hand under the table and along his thigh. He looked to his brother for rescue, but Alfie just took another sip of beer and lost himself again in a dream he saw swirling somewhere in the patterns of colored light on the ceiling. Frankie grabbed Mulaa's hand and pushed it away. She rose, her body springing to life with the quickening of the bongos. Catching the exchange, Alfie thought of his brother when he was little, asleep next to him, hugging his baseball glove like a Teddy bear. Alfie stood up. Outside the front window, a couple of drunks were staggering down the sidewalk, one holding the other up, the character who'd greeted them following right behind. If Alfie really fell, would his brother help him up? He drained the rest of his beer and felt it run down his throat like thin blood. All his sympathy drained away with it. He stepped to the bar where Cherry England in a silk robe sat taking a break. He sat next to her, slid his glass to the bartender, and whispered something in her ear that made her smile. When he stood up, Frankie was on his way out again. Alfie headed him off.

"You leavin'?"

"Looking for you."

"Here I am."

He grabbed Frankie's arm and pulled him to the bar.

"And here's my friend."

When Cherry England spoke, she had an honest-to-God English accent.

"Lovely to meet you," she said, taking Alfie by the forearm and coaxing him toward the back of the room.

Frankie stopped.

"What's this?"

Alfie faced his brother like they were two prizefighters.

"A private show. You first."

Frankie tried to answer through his teeth, so Cherry wouldn't hear.

"I don't want a private show."

"Sure you do."

As Frankie tried again to beg off, Alfie grinned like a monster. To hell with art school. Alfie could tell his brother what happened when you dreamt too big or you ignored what was right in front of you. Frankie should be thankful, but here he was acting like Alfie meant to stab him.

"I feel sick, Brother," Frankie said.

Alfie furrowed his forehead.

"I do. I'm sorry. Something I ate."

Before Alfie could stop him, Frankie bolted out the door, his white shirt glowing in the artificial light of 52nd Street. Alfie trailed him to the car, catching up with him near Rockefeller Center. He felt himself going soft again.

"You cost me a lot of money, you know that?"

Frankie didn't answer. When they got in the car, he slammed his door shut and slouched down in his seat. Even in profile he had a look on his face that said the price of fighting him was he got to judge you.

"You said you wanted something different."

Not a muscle in Frankie's body moved.

"Let's go," he said, his voice dead.

"Go where?"

"It's your tour of the city."

It was late already, but Alfie didn't care. Nothing had happened. Nothing had changed. Nothing would change. He could at least have spent the night with Michelle, getting some action that he didn't have to buy. He saw himself now, creeping up her mother's driveway. He'd throw a pebble at her window, and she'd come to the side door. They'd make out on the couch, because they could. Her mother was hard of hearing and she slept like a rock. At least that's what Michelle told him. Sometimes Alfie couldn't help thinking it was an arrangement Michelle and her mother had. His own mother would ask what kind of girl this was. And if she answered her own question, she'd say, "American" or "*putann'.*"

Or he could just be home, sleeping. His grandfather expected him at the site tomorrow, early, so he could start learning how to read blueprints. The old crow wasn't getting any younger. In a few years, Alfie would have to step in. Maybe someday he'd be planning buildings on Broadway. They were going up everywhere lately. Every few blocks you could look behind green plywood walls and see old office buildings halfway taken down or stripped to the steel. It was a little indecent looking through the old brick facades at the exposed girders, like seeing your great-aunts in their underwear. A building had a body, and a lot of guys had suffered to bring it to life, and before too long it would be dead, just like most of those laborers who built it were dead, like his grandfather would be soon. Then it would be his job to bring more buildings to life, and then, maybe while he was still alive, somebody else would come along and tear them down. So really what good was it, any of it? All of these names on plaques on the site walls? All of the sweat that would go into making something new? Maybe that's why the ironworkers could take their lives in their hands and walk those beams like they were walking on curbs. If they fell, what difference did it make? Their wives and kids would suffer, but at least they'd get insurance checks. No matter what his grandfather wanted, Alfie knew deep down he'd never run anything. Definitely not in Brooklyn. He looked at his brother and at the rosary that Alfie didn't quite understand why he'd hung from his rearview mirror. Up Rome, after the beating his father took, the old man looked like he might die. When he was laid up in bed, bruised and bandaged, Alfie asked what he could bring him.

"A cigar, a jug of wine, and a deck of cards."

And maybe that was why you put up with it all—school, a job, rules—so you could light a cigar once in a while or get drunk and touch a woman like Adeline, or at least dream about touching a woman like Adeline while you touched a woman like Michelle or Cherry. Or maybe you did it just to see walls go up and come down.

Downtown, in the Village, most of the buildings were ancient, but you knew nobody was in a hurry to get rid of them. When they got there, Alfie pulled over near Sheridan Square. Frankie was watching him, but Alfie turned the other way and looked across 6th Avenue. The few trees were thick with leaves, and the sky above them, above the buildings, was clear and full of stars that struggled to show themselves through the man-made light. It was late, but people still thronged the sidewalks. Couples walked arm in arm, and a lot of other people wandered alone, staring into the store-fronts, watching the couples as they passed. You could only guess what café or club they'd come from, answering only to themselves and not hurting anybody. You had to be a little scared of that free-dom, but then you had to like the order of the scene, the way it resembled a postcard.

Frankie mumbled something, and Alfie shook off the thoughts filling his head.

"What?"

"I said, we should've come here in the first place."

The last thing his brother needed to do now was complain.

"Yeah, why?"

"What's that supposed to mean?"

"Look, Frank ..."

"No, you think just because I don't want some woman our mother's age to touch me, I have a problem."

"I thought I was doing you a favor. Besides, now you know what it feels like."

Frankie looked hard at him.

"What are you talking about?"

"You know why I don't see you? Because you always make me feel like something's wrong with me. But maybe it's not true. Maybe something's wrong with *you*."

Alfie realized he was starting to yell and that the windows were down, and that a few people walking by were staring at them. In his side mirror he spotted a squad car crawling down the avenue. The last thing he needed was a night in jail. His eyes followed the cruiser until it turned onto a side street. There were rules. Alfie would have to show up at a regular job and sit around at Sunday dinner for the next forty years, getting fatter by the year. And his brother would get away scot-free. He'd move to Manhattan or wherever-the-hell-else painters lived, and paint every day. Do what he loved. Would he ever come back to Brooklyn and sit on a porch and smoke cigars or drink beer? The only sure-fire thing with him was to take in a ball game. And their mother had always made sure Frankie got to go. From when they first moved to Brooklyn, she'd ask their grandfather for a little extra money, even lie and say that it was for clothes. And then she'd let Frankie say he was too sick to go to school. And off to Ebbets Field they'd go. No doubt about it, the kid had always had it easy. And from now on when he saw Alfie, would Frankie The Artist be slumming it?

"You weren't doing me any favors tonight," Frankie said.

Alfie's brother was beginning to feel like a stranger, which made him an enemy.

"Yeah, I guess fellas like you don't go in for strippers."

If Alfie had punched him, Frankie couldn't have looked more hurt. But fuck him.

"Fuck you," Frankie almost whispered.

A cruel calm settled into Alfie's voice.

"Hey, if you don't like women, you don't like women."

Frankie's face was bright red, and he clenched his fists so you could see the knots of scrawny muscle in his thin arms. He got out of the car and slammed the door again, then leaned into the window, almost spitting at his brother.

"At least I don't want to fuck my cousin."

Now Alfie wanted to punch him. But what would their mother say?

"You're out of line."

Alfie could feel the tightness in his neck, the blood rushing to his head. He squeezed the wheel over and over like he was strangling it. His words came flat and hateful.

"Fuckin' fairy."

In the dirty light of the streetlamp, Frankie stood with his arms folded, almost hugging himself, like a sick angel. He looked like he might cry, but Alfie couldn't get himself to care. Whatever else Frankie was, he would never be his friend. He'd only ever be good for making Alfie feel more alone and useless than he already was. Alfie started the car, and Frankie opened his mouth to say something, but before he had the chance, Alfie had stuck his head out the driver's-side window, to watch for traffic as he pulled away, deaf to everything but the sound of horns that echoed down the avenue.

(1958)

Junction City was a shithole. Anybody in town who wasn't Army was either colored or poor or both. Downtown was all right—a few nice limestone buildings and a couple of joints that served good burgers and fries—but after dark the hookers and dope addicts took the place over. Any decent person you saw at night had come down from the base. Some Fridays or Saturdays, instead of joining the other grunts in some *schifazz'* bar, for a change of pace Alfie would drive to the prairie, where you could look out for miles and see nothing but a gulf of grass. If there had ever been houses or people, they'd been drowned in green and brown waves. Once in a while a few wild turkeys or prairie dogs wandered by. Country as country could be, but a whole different kind of country from Rome. There, you had the hills around you. People were meant to live in a valley like that. The prairie didn't seem like a place where people were supposed to live. The Indians camped by the rivers to hunt buffalo, but then they moved. The Indians in New York mostly stayed put, at least until the white men showed up.

Whenever Alfie went to the prairie he brought his guitar. Instead of hunting he strummed and sang into the wind, which never seemed to stop blowing. Even with his bum hand, the music felt pure, because he was singing to himself. Or to someone who he knew couldn't hear him. His voice bent in the breeze like another blade of tall grass, and he lived like a day without a name. In fact he got through most of his days here anonymous. It was why he'd joined, wasn't it? To dive and come up somewhere else, somebody else. Now he was a pair of fatigues and a serial number. At least he'd learned a few things. He could cook a little. He could wire telephone poles. He could type well enough to finish a letter in ten minutes. If he had a girl, he had her for a few hours, or days, or weeks if she wasn't the ordinary farmer's daughter. Not like the fellas who went overseas. They came back with German or Jap wives. Instead of a wife, Alfie had a problem. He kept his problem on the table next to his bed: a picture of Michelle in her petal pushers and a tight blouse. Most of the time he turned the frame face down on the table. He felt weak when he thought about her and the whole situation back home. It made him feel like an invalid. No way to climb out of the hole he'd dug.

To stay here was one answer, but in the long run it would only work if he could go to sleep in the grass and wake up without a conscience and with the history of Kansas locked in his brain and the keys to a family farmhouse in his pocket, and a name like some of the local boys had: Wiley or Anderson or Happ. He wouldn't mind that. If a new life ate you up, that wouldn't be as terrible as your old life doing it. Either way, at least he'd get so old that he'd want everything to end. And then what? If you went to Heaven, whatever you did there never ended? What if it was something you were supposed to love but didn't, like drinking anisette? Maybe that's why joining the Army hadn't scared him. Either you'd get out or you'd die fighting somewhere you didn't know. An end. But now he knew what his life had to be. Michelle had sealed it.

Before her, he'd even thought of becoming a priest. Maybe a monk. No more chasing after dreams. He could take care of trees and animals, and no matter what he did, it would be all right. And monks learned how to cook. His brother might have something there. Frankie had switched to cooking school, and he loved it, their mother told him. Alfie could live with the monks and write to his brother, and his brother could tell him what was going on in the world. They could exchange recipes. But who was he kidding? How long could he last that way? A few days in he'd be thinking about banging Michelle in all the different places and all the different ways they'd done it. He'd think about how he pumped her full of anger. He'd empty all his worst thoughts into his piece-of-ass girlfriend in the most degrading ways he could think of. Throw her on the bed and ram her so hard her head would slam against the headboard until chips of plaster fell down inside the wall; fling her up against the stove and fuck her from behind, right there in her mother's kitchen; tear a hole in the crotch of her petal pushers and force her down on his cock in a photo booth at Coney Island. Monk? The monks were either crazy or fairies or they did or thought about doing all the rotten things he and everybody else did, only behind stone walls way out in the country somewhere. When you were out on the prairie, you didn't have to hide, and ninety-nine times out of a hundred nobody was trying to find you. You didn't have to go looking for God in the dark or for some other excuse to run away.

It was a nice August day, cooler than usual. Maneuvers had ended a week before. A lot of the boys in his squad were headed to a cabin on the Republican River. Heyen, a local kid whose family owned the place, had promised to get some girls to meet them there. To Alfie it sounded like a mess. He sat down on his cot and tuned his guitar. The top string wouldn't come in. He plucked it a little harder each time, until it snapped. What now? He put the guitar down and got up to stretch. Right where he'd been sitting was a letter the postal grunt must have thrown there and that Alfie had missed. As soon as he recognized the handwriting on the envelope, he felt butterflies. He tore it open and read. Adeline would be in Kansas this weekend. Her husband Ted, the asshole professor, was offered a good job at Kansas State, over in Manhattan.

Jesus.

Some of the fellas in his section talked about Manhattan. About the college girls and the nice downtown with the brick sidewalks.

He finished reading the letter. Adeline and Ted were renting a house in Manhattan, near a place called Aggieville. Maybe he knew the place. Maybe he could come and help them get settled in. Ted had a bad back. They could go out to dinner. He could get to know

Ted better. Adeline would be "eternally grateful." Alfie picked up
his guitar again and strummed the same three chords on the bottom strings, until his hand got tired.

The next morning, Saturday, he got in his car and drove along
the Kansas River. The sky was pure blue. Johnny Cash was singing
"I Guess Things Happen That Way." For once the wind was light, so
he rolled the window down and cruised with an elbow in the breeze
and a hand gripping the roof. From the road the prairie was monot-
onous, until Manhattan came into view like a limestone mirage. He
was driving into a make-believe town in the middle of nowhere, to
see someone who'd already disappeared. It was "The Wizard of Oz"
without the yellow brick road.

On Manhattan's main street, which had the strange name of
Poyntz Avenue, Alfie stopped in a little five-and-ten next to a theater marquee. When he asked for Aggieville, the clerk made a face.

"Down the college."

He sized up Alfie and his uniform.

"Don't know what you wanna go there for."

Alfie bought a candy bar and drove the half-mile downtown,
where he found a few blocks' worth of stores and restaurants. Not
much to see, but clean. The store windows were spotless and reflected the sunlight onto the new whitish-gray sidewalks. Could
they make Brooklyn new like this? Could you bury a whole city
and start over? Alfie stayed in the car and drove toward Adeline's
house, a few blocks away, on a street with another strange name,
Bertrand. On the way there he drove by the campus. It looked like
an estate with different miniature castles all over the grounds. His
father had always said farmers had fortunes hidden in their mat-
tresses. Down Bertrand a few blocks he found the house, #830, a
craftsman bungalow, a kind of plan he favored. He thought about
Adeline getting up on a Saturday morning, lounging in her robe
on a comfortable couch, with her cup of coffee, in her big living
room, looking out the front windows. He could imagine their legs
touching through thin cotton. But instead here was Ted on the
porch, holding the edge of his hand to his forehead like he was

having a hard time seeing Alfie's car, then making a big show of saluting and jogging down the steps in his chinos and short-sleeve shirt.

"Hello, soldier! You're a sight for sore eyes. And a sore back."

He gave Alfie an awkward hug. They were the same height, but Ted felt like a rag doll in Alfie's arms.

"Forgive me. I never know how to greet a new cousin."

The word "cousin" sounded strange out of Ted's mouth. He was waiting for Alfie to say something, until he couldn't wait any longer.

"Adeline's in the house. Having a drink. It's been a long few days."

As far as Alfie knew, she'd never been much of a drinker, especially not in the afternoon.

"Are you hungry? Was it a long drive?"

Alfie fingered the candy bar in his pocket.

"I could eat."

Ted led him into the wide vestibule, where he started talking about the potential for an apartment upstairs. As Alfie looked around, he lost track of what the goof was saying. Adeline's presence fogged the air. Ted had made her a ghost, and Alfie imagined her haunting the upstairs bedrooms, appearing in windows and hallways, fading from sight. Then through the thick, warped glass panes of old French doors her outline appeared, blurry and distorted, unreal. Her light sweater melted around her shoulders, as her long arm and delicate hand raised a highball glass to her lips. She lay back on a print couch set in the middle of the room. In the soft light from the window, she was striking a pose. She was more beautiful than she'd been in Brooklyn, her hair pulled back, so you could follow the contour of her graceful neck—like the porcelain profile on their grandmother's cameo—down to her shoulders. The new lines in her forehead and tight curves of her cheeks formed a face that knew more of the world than the last time he'd seen her. She was a woman, something Alfie still didn't understand but could recognize. Her head turned slowly toward him, and for a few seconds her eyes were question marks. Finally, her lips parted and she rose from the couch, first walking, then almost running toward him, as he pulled open the door. He'd hugged her plenty of times, but never like this. She clung to him. The same way Michelle would wrap around him when they finished. Like she was anchoring him to a spot. Like she wanted time to stop. It made him want to be alone forever. But this was Adeline, all of her seeping into him like a drug. Then he felt Ted's finger tapping his shoulder, and remembered watching his mother and father dance, imagined someone else trying to cut in. Ted literally put a hand between them and pushed Adeline a few inches back. Alfie tried to read her expression, but her head was down.

"Sorry. Your cousin forgets herself."

Adeline stepped back.

"Dear, do we have any food in the house?"

She looked into Alfie's eyes. Hadn't she been expecting him?

"I'll see."

As she walked away, Ted elbowed Alfie as though they were buddies in a bar.

"Great, Sweetheart," he called after her, cupping a hand next to his thin-lipped mouth. "Just nothing too complicated. You're not much of a chef."

This was the crap Ted's kind pulled. Alfie wore a uniform and didn't go to college, so he must be a caveman. If Ted bossed his wife around, said nasty things to her, he would make himself just like Alfie, a tough guy. Adeline came back a few minutes later with a plate full of Ritz crackers and slices of cheddar cheese. She also held up a second glass of Scotch, which Alfie politely refused. She handed the glass to Ted and sat down on the couch. Ted looked right through her, annoyed, his face crimped.

"Darling, that's rude. Let's show your cousin the digs."

He rested a thin arm on Alfie's broad shoulders and laughed close to Alfie's face, cigarettes on his breath. Alfie put his arm around Ted's back. If this were a wrestling match, he would fling him into the turnbuckle and launch him out of the ring. Instead he pushed him away.

"You know, Ted, I think I want to take a little walk first, maybe catch up with my cousin. That be okay?"

Alfie could feel his lip curling as he spoke. And he got the reaction he wanted. Ted looked stunned, like the rebels in Cuba might look if the U.S. Army showed up for their hostages. Since he'd been in the service, Alfie had learned a few things about the world, about current events. He had more time to read the newspapers and less time for fellas like Ted. Still, this stiff was Adeline's husband, so the best thing was to keep a distance.

"Okay?" he repeated.

Ted nodded, took a moment to study his glass of Scotch, then knocked half of it back. Alfie grabbed Adeline's hand and lifted her from the couch. She followed him to the sidewalk. He couldn't remember a single other time she'd followed him. Any time they were alone she was the one who led, who talked, who set the agenda. The way she walked too was different. He'd always thought she had a royal walk. Nothing sappy, but elegant. Like a pretty Queen Elizabeth, with longer arms and legs. Now her shoulders slumped, and she walked with her head down, like she was dragging herself.

"I like your neighborhood."

Adeline took a deep breath and stretched her arms over her head. The locust and sycamore trees were thick, so the street seemed half woods, half civilization. Adeline took another deep breath.

"Do you really?"

"Sure. Reminds me of Long Island."

"Without the ocean."

"Remember Long Island?" he asked.

She said nothing.

Through the canopy of leaves he could make out the small hills rising behind the houses. Alfie looked around, waiting for her to talk, but then had to prop up the conversation by himself.

"At least you have hills."

She laughed.

"You were always kind."

He didn't remember anyone else ever describing him that way.

She went on, perking up.

"They're making the college into a university."

"Oh, yeah?"

"That's why Ted took the job. A big opportunity. He talks a lot about how the whole country needs great minds, not just New York or Boston or Chicago. Ever since Arkansas he worries about integration."

Alfie didn't want to hear it, and Adeline caught him looking away.

"He thinks he can make a difference."

Alfie spit a quick laugh.

"What? In Kansas?"

"'Bleeding Kansas,' he calls it."

Alfie had read about it. He didn't want to argue. Adeline was sensitive. But if either of them knew the place, it was him.

"That was a hundred years ago. Most of the col ... the negroes here, they're in the Army. The rest of them live in Junction City, and who bothers them?"

"Ted thinks we need to help them integrate, everywhere."

Alfie hadn't really cared much about it either way. The colored soldiers were different. It was hard to imagine walking out on your porch and waving across the driveway to one. Besides, any time he'd seen white and colored people together in the civilian world, it meant trouble. Let them live their own lives.

"And what do you think?" he asked.

Adeline halted.

"What?" he asked.

She shook her head and rubbed her nose.

"What?"

"According to Ted, I don't think at all."

Alfie could picture the *cidrul* saying it, with his Scotch and the pipe Alfie would like to ram up his tight ass.

"You're the smartest girl I know."

Adeline turned and walked a step ahead, then turned a corner toward a big hill. She stripped a few leaves off a locust branch as she passed it, then tore the leaves into little pieces with her white-painted fingernails.

"Well, I don't know much—not about integration or Alaska or unions or the Middle East or the Soviets. And if I'm so smart, how did I wind up here?"

She took hold of his arm.

"I'm sorry to bother you with my business."

"No, it's all right. I'm not sure why I'm here either."

He faced her now, squeezing her shoulders before he could think to stop himself.

"You're twice as smart as that guy could ever be."

She shrugged.

"Believe me, I'm not. They're going to make him a dean, maybe the head of the university someday."

Alfie said nothing.

"It's been a hard year, and now we have to start everything over again."

Alfie cocked his head.

"I never saw you drink like that before."

Adeline started walking away, almost trotting, like she was double-timing. After half a block she slowed enough for him to catch up. When he did, he heard her speak through clenched teeth.

"That's my business, too."

She turned on him.

"You know, you're lucky you're in the Army. At least you know what you're doing."

All Alfie had done was run to a blank space. Had she followed him on purpose? Did she whisper something about Kansas in her husband's ear? And what about Ted? Running the asshole down wouldn't do him or her any favors. He could hear his father's voice. *Just keep it to yourself.* Until you can't.

"Well, you're here. I'm here, too. I guess we make the best of it."

"What's the best?" she said, stopping again, red-faced.

Alfie looked up the hill.

"If I knew that, I'd be smarter than both of you."

He hugged her with one arm. Her body softened.

"C'mon."

At the top of the hill they found a park and a path leading to an overlook. Below them was a big "Manhattan" sign set in boulders on the hillside. They sat on a wooden bench, and Adeline crossed her legs and stretched an arm behind Alfie. She was almost horizontal. Alfie followed the line of her body toward the view of prairie beyond the town. A few low hills marred the horizon.

"I'd love to move to California," she said. "I'd like to write novels and screenplays. Ted thinks I'm a good writer. So do other people."

"How come you never showed me what you write?"

She looked at him like she was trying to recognize his face.

"I didn't think you'd be interested."

She might be right, but how the hell did she know? Did he look like that much of a dope?

"You were so involved with music, why would you care?"

She was sincere. You could tell by the way her lips went straight after she spoke. But Alfie couldn't help but think that she was also acting. She'd always been dramatic, like she understood that whatever was happening at that moment, in her world, was the most important thing. Did she really understand who he was or who he could have been?

The sun was getting hotter. He could feel the sweat beading on the back of his neck.

"Give me some credit."

She put her arms around him and nestled her head on his shoulder, the way a real girlfriend might.

"Do you want to see my writing?"

He lolled his head and smiled.

"Sure. They give us plenty of time to read."

The first gray cloud of the day cast a shadow on the hillside. Alfie welcomed the shade. They lay back, watching more clouds gather in the distance. She could say she liked California, but he knew she wasn't going anywhere. She'd be here, and so would he, at least for a while. When she shifted, he pulled her closer. She didn't resist. Alfie watched the slow movement of the river below as it followed its course through the endless land around it. Blood didn't have to mean chains. Those kinds of chains were weightless as clouds, Adeline's breath on his cheek. He turned to face her, and when their lips touched they both let them melt into a single form. No pushing to a kiss or pulling away to loneliness. All they could say hummed through stilled flesh as their eyes played a hundred small twitches and rolls that were all and only possibility. They had inherited what they couldn't touch. When the sun flamed up again, Adeline released herself and sighed. Alfie watched her as in profile she closed her eyes in the returning sunlight. After a few minutes of perfect quiet, they stood up arm in arm, and she led him down the path, her body like a girl's again. She walked with more energy than before. Alfie watched her, feeling that wherever she was, he could be at ease, that life didn't have to be a battle. You just had to work out the terms of a peace and make it last.

Halfway down the hill Adeline took his hand and squeezed it.

"What will you do when you get out?"

"I don't know."

She smiled weakly.

"Honestly, what will you do?"

When he thought about what he could do, the ideas whirled around themselves like a tornado.

"If I knew where home was, I'd say I have to go home."

"What do you mean?"

Like it or not, he'd be a father soon. He could tell her, and maybe she wouldn't bat an eye. If she could come this far with him, maybe she could go further. But then maybe she'd never look at him the same.

"I'm just talking. I get low sometimes, you know?"

She reached up and he felt her hand sweep across his hair, cradling his head.

"I know. Me too."

Here at the end of the path, at the edge of Manhattan's streets, they hugged again, just beyond the view of families starting their weekends, cooking, mowing lawns, playing ball, getting ready for a day in town or a drive to see their relatives. As close as she pulled him, as much as he wanted to touch Adeline everywhere, lead her to a bedroom and find his way back to love, he imagined a hundred pairs of eyes on them, each one a way of seeing what he felt as nothing but wrong. He kept holding her, but loosened his grip, allowing space between them. As they walked hand in hand onto the first neighborhood street, Alfie couldn't help thinking about Ted. Anybody who could have her and complain about it, what made a guy like that tick? For that matter, what made Adeline tick? He wished her father were here, so he could see what he'd done to her. Uncle Enzo had always been high and mighty, and that's the kind of man his daughter expected. When they reached her house, Adeline let go and put her hands in her pockets. She stood for a minute like a young girl waiting for her mother to call her inside.

"I think I need a rest."

She trotted up the front steps. Alfie followed in her wake, and when he entered the living room found Ted stationed at a small desk in the corner.

"You're back," he called, without turning from his work.

Adeline took off her shoes.

"I'm going to the bedroom for a rest."

"That's fine, dear. I've sent out for food. I assume your cousin's hungry."

Alfie said nothing and sat down on the couch. Adeline disappeared. For a full minute Ted didn't bother turning around. But what did you expect? Alfie peeked down the hallway and saw the bedroom door closed, then walked over next to Ted's desk. The schmuck finally looked up and gestured for him to sit in a wing chair a few feet away. Like Alfie was being interviewed. Ted started to say something, but Alfie interrupted him.

"Ted, you know my cousin is a great girl, right?"

Ted began to say something, and Alfie remembered what the C.O.s were always telling them about keeping your cool in all circumstances. Whatever circumstance this was, Alfie was trying hard to follow their advice.

"Listen, Ted."

He leaned in and laid a heavy hand on the desk. Ted's thin face tightened.

Defuse the situation.

"Let me say this: I'm happy for you. Congratulations on coming here."

Alfie paused for effect. Out the window he saw a young couple walking a German Shepherd. A little boy, maybe five or six, followed them on a scooter.

"It's not New York, but it's all right."

"We like it fine so far," Ted said, relaxing.

"Glad to hear it."

Alfie rapped his knuckles on the desk.

"You think Adeline likes it?" he asked.

"It seems so."

"Good," Alfie said, moving his hand from the desk to Ted's arm. "Because she's a great girl. So you have to watch how you talk to her. You have to treat her a certain way."

Ted's face contracted again.

"If you're saying ..."

"You're a smart fella, Ted."

Alfie heard himself sounding like a union delegate on a construction site, and he was happy about it. Not that it was right, but sometimes things weren't right.

"I'm just saying I don't want to hear anything I don't want to hear. You understand?"

"Alfie, if this is a threat ..."

Alfie stared at Ted until he flinched and looked away. The asshole would tell Adeline all about their little talk, and Alfie would be the bad guy. Or maybe she'd like it. Maybe she'd know she wasn't alone.

"Ted, you didn't hear a threat from me. We're just talking. Like cousins."

Alfie turned his head slowly toward the bedroom hallway.
"I love my cousins, Ted."

Ted took a deep breath and pushed his chair back from the desk.
"Alfie, is there something else you'd like to say?"

Alfie pursed his lips. The terms of peace.

"No. Just tell Adeline I had to get back to base. I'll come again soon."

Anyone good, anything good, you had to keep close. You could talk all you wanted about the world, but you could only know what was in front of you. On his way home he'd take a detour to the prairie, to remind himself of what was good. Then he'd drive back through Junction City, to remind himself how miserable people could be.

(1962)

When his mother set the pot of rigatoni on the table, Alfie exhaled. At least something today had gone right. But his father grumbled. The old man preferred rotini or spaghetts. Alfie didn't care. His mother looked proud as she ladled one scoop of macaroni after another into her first son's oversized bowl. Her other son, her pride and joy, had flown the coop, and Alfie was the consolation prize. He couldn't escape her attention now if he wanted to. She had to know what he was going through. When Michelle wasn't looking, he smiled a thank you. He didn't like his wife to see him happy with his mother. It was better to complain about what a pain-in-the-ass she was, so Michelle didn't feel like she was the only one Alfie ever criticized. Michelle was busy smoothing a napkin in her lap, over and over, like it mattered that it was wrinkled. Next she moved to smoothing the ridiculous outfit she had on, a pink number like Jackie Kennedy wore, complete with the pill box hat she'd set down on the counter—here, in his mother's tiny kitchen. Too much television. Too much time in the house. The whole situation made Alfie feel bad for their daughter. Neither of them was cut out to take care of her. Maybe the different ways they couldn't handle it balanced out and the kid would grow up normal. Alfie's father had never said word one about his marriage, but whenever Michelle opened her mouth, he gave her that sideways grin to signal, politely, that he could never listen to anybody who talked like a Gatling gun. His mother, on the other hand, didn't have a problem saying what was on her mind, though she was usually smart enough to talk to Michelle through Alfie.

"Does your wife want more macaroni? If not, I'll put the pot back on the stove. Sometimes she likes a lot, sometimes she doesn't. I'm never sure."

On purpose or not, Michelle was too distracted with her outfit to catch the full drift, but she finally looked up as her mother-in-law was putting the finishing touches on her comment.

"Oh, no, that's fine, Mom."

And then the fatal mistake Alfie could always count on her to make.

"I had a chocolate bar before we came up."

Alfie's mother picked up the pot and took it away. His father dropped his head and coughed a rough cough into a closed fist. Once he started hacking, he couldn't stop, and had to excuse himself from the table and shuffle to the little bathroom off the kitchen. The sound of his father spitting into the toilet stopped Alfie's appetite cold. But that was his life these days. Nothing was what you wanted it to be. His mother, as good as she was, always hit him with the wrong question at these exact moments.

"How's your job, Alfie?"

"Okay, Ma. You know. Job's a job."

Could he even argue with her that he wasn't wasting his time? Selling encyclopedias door to door? You might as well be selling coal. Before that he'd worked at Western Union, in the mailroom, because his friend Snooky had an in. Before that he'd apprenticed to a sign engraver. Before that he'd worked the door at a local bar until he decided he couldn't look at one more drunk without wanting to punch him out. Everything led to a dead end, but at least it didn't lead to a desk. The thought of staring at a blotter all day made Alfie sick to his stomach. He shook the image from his head and shoveled a few ziti into his mouth. He believed, like a lot of Italians did, that good gravy gave you energy, so whenever his mother made it, he'd eat, even when he wasn't hungry. Tonight, he'd go down the basement, put the radio on, and work out. The one hour a day that was his.

"Excuse me, Ladies and Gentlemen," his father said as he sat back down. "Hadda clear out the ol' galoozala."

The old man was getting older fast: he talked more slowly, he walked like he was pulling a cart behind him, and, the way he did tonight, coughed like he was choking on a pit. Did his mother notice? Did she care?

"No one wants to hear about it, Matty. Mind your manners."

His father stabbed two ziti with his fork and saluted his mother with them.

"That's my girl," he said, stuffing the ziti between his yellowed teeth.

Michelle laughed like he'd made a funny joke. Alfie's mother glared at her.

"So, Dear, how's your mother?"

His mother knew how to go for the throat. Michelle's mother, the alcoholic, was her jugular—her mother and her blond hair. Which was a little less than blond unless she kept it dyed. Michelle lowered her fork and primped her platinum bouffant.

"Same as the last time you asked, Mom."

His mother had never actually given his wife permission to call her Mom or Penny, as though, granddaughter or no granddaughter, she didn't expect her to stick around. His wife was no good at reading signs, although in this case she might be intentionally ignoring one.

"And how's Jennifer? We hardly see her."

Alfie didn't wonder why Michelle hated spending time with his mother, but he did wonder how he'd allowed this all to happen, how he'd taken the easiest road, marrying Michelle and moving into the apartment downstairs. If not the easiest road, the one his mistakes led him down. When Alfie and Michelle had to admit that she was pregnant, they got married at Borough Hall and started dealing with the questions, such as where they might live. His grandfather settled that problem by telling the tenants downstairs from his parents to leave. Their kid—no kid anymore—had been shooting pigeons with a BB gun and telling the young girls on the block how he wanted to pluck their eyebrows. His grandfather couldn't have it, so off they went, and in came Alfie with his ready-made family. You could say it was good to be close to your family, especially your parents, and in a lot of ways you'd be right. But a lot of those ways had never mattered much to Alfie, and even less after the accident, and less still after Adeline left. How much could you smile and tell everybody you loved them? How much gravy could you eat? How many times a day could you see your father sweeping the driveway and ask him how he felt? How often could you tell your wife to stop yelling and screaming because your parents might hear? And could he blame Michelle, the mother of his child? She was as miserable being here as he was. Still, he blamed her.

When they finished eating, Alfie's mother cleared the plates and his father stretched out his arms to exaggerate a yawn.

"I don't know what it is, Pen, but one glass of wine puts me down like a lame horse."

His mother came back from the sink, wringing a *mappine*'s neck.

"You're a broken-down old horse, all right. Look at him, Alfie. You'd think he was a hundred years old."

Alfie pretended to size his father up, thinking, as he did, about how, after last Sunday's dinner, he'd wandered into his parents' bedroom, hoping to find a pack of cigarettes in his father's nightstand, and instead found a set of rosary beads and next to it a ragged matchbook from The Savoy, a restaurant in Rome that Alfie recalled but where his mother and father had never taken them. Not things he would have expected his father to keep.

Out of his reverie, Alfie remarked, "He's not young."

The old man pushed his chair from the table, stood up, patted Alfie on the back, kissed Michelle on the cheek, and wandered into the living room. Alfie and Michelle followed him and retrieved Jennifer from the bedroom where Alfie used to practice guitar. She'd fallen asleep before dinner. Her grandmother wasn't happy about

her absence, but she wrapped some macaroni for the little girl to eat
later. Alfie carried his daughter down the creaky, linoleum-covered
stairs to their apartment. She was three years old, blond like her
mother, but a lot quieter. She was also a reason to work a crummy
job and a reason to come home. He held his daughter close as he
bent down to lay her small body on an unmade bed, then pulled the
paint-entombed bedroom door behind him closed as it would go.
From the other bedroom he heard the sound of two shoes dropping
to the floor. Michelle was already undressing, a site that, in spite of
himself, he never wanted to miss. She would stand in front of the
mirror and twist her lean, shapely body in all directions as she took
out her earrings and undid her necklace and bra. Then she would
slide the bra down the length of her arms until her breasts peek-a-
booed in the mirror. As he walked to the threshold, Alfie knew how,
at that point, all his energy would concentrate itself in his balls.
When she caught him watching, she would slide her thumb inside
the elastic of her panties and work them over her hips until they
fell to the floor. Then she would come to him, and all the worries
and fears of the world would fall away. This time she'd only slid the
bra to her elbows. Then, to his surprise, she raised her arms and let
the bra slide back in place. From the top of her bureau she picked
up two envelopes and without saying a word turned and held them
out to him.

"From who?"

She didn't answer.

The first was a personal letter with the return address of 304
Chestnut Street, San Francisco, CA.

She stood in front of him, arms folded.

"I know who it's from."

"My cousin. So what?"

He hadn't seen his cousin in four years. What anybody had
known about her then, about him and her, didn't matter anymore.

"No one ever hears from her. Why's she writing to you?"

Alfie folded the letters in half, shoved them in his pocket, and
swiped his hand across his mouth, like he'd seen Jackie Gleason

do a hundred times. A flush spread from Michelle's face, down her neck, to her shoulders and chest. Her lips quivered. He wasn't used to her crying. Yelling? Arguing? Sure. But she wasn't a crier. It was something besides her looks that he liked about her. She didn't just sit back and take guff. She gave as good as she got, even if with him she never exactly won.

"What the hell do I know?"

He put his hand in his pocket and ran his fingertips over the edges of the envelopes.

"What's wrong, Michelle? What's your problem now?"

"I think you're the one with the problem."

Alfie put one hand over his heart.

"Me? I'm having a nice day, not saying a word. But it's like every day. All I hear from you is complaints. This is wrong, that's wrong, I'm a piece of shit. If I'm such a piece of shit, what am I doing here?"

His glanced toward the other bedroom, then fixed his eyes again on Michelle's face. Too made up. Too tight all the time. Never enough smiles.

"Alfie, you don't talk to me all day unless you want something."

She looked down at her body and stomped to the closet, where she found a robe that she put on as though somebody were ringing the doorbell and she had to answer.

"I get the feeling sometimes you don't even like me."

Now the tears were welling in the corners of her eyes, and he felt like a true *strunz'*. He let his shoulders go limp, then, with more effort than it should take to apologize to a wife, he took her hand and began stroking it.

"Michelle, c'mon. Look at me."

He caressed her shoulders under the pique fabric of the robe.

"I love you," he lied.

"Then say something nice to me sometime, Alfie."

"You look beautiful."

"Something else. Talk about me the way you talk about your cousin."

Did he talk that much about Adeline?

"What the hell do I know about my cousin? She's on the other side of the world. I talk about my brother, too. We were kids together. You know how it is."

But he was pretty sure she didn't know. Her father had died in the war, and she'd always been alone with her mother. No sisters or brothers, and maybe one friend he could name. She was all his. He rubbed her arms, and she drew away from him.

"What was the other letter?"

"From New York Life, I think," she said, undressing again, then getting into her nightgown. "I don't read your mail. But I can't help seeing the addresses."

He reached into his pocket and inspected the second envelope. "Yup."

New York Life all right. He'd seen the listing in the want ads, and remembered how his cousin Jimmy had worked there. He'd decided to stop at their building and apply, because if he had to be stuck selling things, he should at least make enough money to get them out of here.

"What does it say?" Michelle asked as she knotted the sash of her robe and sat on the bed.

"They want to interview me."

She stood up and looked over his shoulder, then popped up in front of him, grinning. It was a desperate grin, but a willing one.

"You think I should go?"

She said nothing, but reached her arms around his neck and kissed him, gently at first, then harder, until he dropped the letter on the floor.

"Close the door," she said, as her robe fell open.

An hour later Alfie got up, put his pants on, like he was going to work, picked up the letter from New York Life and went and sat at the secretary desk in a back room off the kitchen. A heavy moon hung over the house behind theirs, an orange face in the sky. Its light through the window made the tiny, cold space feel warm. In a town like Rome, you'd call it a harvest moon. In Brooklyn it was a moon like in "The Honeymooners," a skyline moon. The theme song played in Alfie's head as he opened the desktop and took out another letter that had come a few days before.

Dear Police Officer Candidate:

We welcome you to our ranks.

Your decision to join the New York City Police Department will forever change who you are. Every man who wears the NYPD uniform takes an oath to support and defend the laws, and citizens, of the city and state of New York. We take pride in ensuring the safety of the American public in our great city.

You will be part of New York's Finest. You will be a part of what makes New York City the capital of the world. In the weeks and months to follow you will be undergoing examinations and training as part of your candidate processing. Every officer has undergone the process which you are entering, and I am confident that, with hard work and persistence, you will become the next member of New York's Finest.

Sincerely,

Michael J. Murphy, *Commissioner*
New York City Police Department

He set the letter down next to the one from New York Life and leaned back in the rickety chair, arms behind his head. A life insurance company or the police department. Two ends of the same business. Gambling on life or trying to protect it. If you sold insurance, you were in business for real, working on commission, with no limit to how little or how much money you could make. In a few years, you might know enough to open your own brokerage.

You could rake it in, as long as you were ruthless, not too soft about what people needed versus what you were selling them. He had to admit, too, that the thought of making happy couples—most of them had to be happier than him and Michelle—pay him a kind of tax for their happiness made him a little happier. You'd knock on a door and a nice-looking wife would answer while her happy husband was washing up after dinner. Or during the day you might meet the happy wife by herself. As a cop, naturally, you followed more rules. Maybe you bent them when they were in your way, but basically you were in the Army, except with better food. In theory, you were helping people, stopping a husband from killing his wife or a wife from losing her kid or even making the local store owners feel safer. They respected the uniform. Alfie remembered what that was like. And a lot of his cousins were cops. When he thought about them, how they were, it was hard to picture them helping strangers. Still, he'd seen good cops in the neighborhood, even in Manhattan.

He folded up both letters and pushed them to the side of the desk, then pulled Adeline's letter from his pocket. The sound of boys harmonizing on a corner floated on the night air. Alfie opened the envelope, and a strange perfume filled the room. Like spices you might use for cooking. As he unfolded the letter, a few dried red flower petals fluttered to the desktop. He read the return address again, the words "San Francisco." The Yankees were playing the Giants in the World Series. Everybody was talking about it. Even his mother was talking about it. Probably because Frankie was talking about it. The rare times Alfie saw his brother these days, he always brought up baseball. You'd think his type wouldn't care for it anymore, once he grew up and all. The Series seemed like it had been going on for a while, so San Francisco must have been giving them a hard time. He remembered reading that a couple of games had gotten postponed. The last game was supposed to be on Tuesday. It was in San Francisco, but you knew the Yankees would win. They always won. Still, it was hard to feel bad for the Giants. They'd left New York for San Francisco, and San Francisco had Adeline.

Alfie started reading by moonlight. Adeline was in a place called North Beach. You didn't picture a beach in San Francisco. She said he would love it: all kinds of music and food and people. She liked people, his cousin. Good for her. She had a little apartment with a roommate. Out her kitchen window she could see San Francisco Bay. And Alcatraz. They were closing Alcatraz. That was good, she said. It was inhumane. Every day she and her roommate watched boats come and go from the island. She wondered where they would take the prisoners. Alfie liked the idea of her in an old kitchen, sitting there with her coffee, looking out the window at a strange city's morning light. Not that she was lonely. She said she had plenty of friends, a lot of writers and artists. Alfie wanted to like that idea too, but he couldn't help rolling his eyes. She had started smoking, and she hoped that didn't disappoint him. Why should he care? Who didn't smoke? When you were married to a woman like Michelle, you needed to smoke.

Adeline also said that San Francisco wasn't like New York. People were freer. She called it the "Pacific spirit." Alfie tried to imagine the color of the water there. He knew they had mountains right on the ocean. It didn't sound bad. The thing was she wanted him to visit. She'd show him everything: The Golden Gate Bridge, North Beach, Chinatown. Did she remember that they had bridges and Chinatown in New York too? She loved her friends, but she needed to see his face, and she couldn't come back east for a while. She didn't say why. The bottom line was she wanted him to come.

He picked up the letter, then walked to the bedroom where Michelle was still asleep with the blankets wrapped around her like a shroud. She was nothing more than a shadow in the eerie half-glow of the room. The yellow light dimmed to gray as clouds crowded the picture window near the closet. A haze hung in the air, a curtain that Alfie was afraid to peek behind. He backed out of the room and found himself frozen in the middle of this apartment. He thought of Rome and the preacher and his father and the sensation of everything around you moving while you were standing still, like being strapped inside a rocket on its way to outer space, a rocket

that would keep going until it reached the nothing you had to become. A noise from the street, maybe a garbage can falling over,
snapped him out of it. He went to Jennifer's bedroom and opened
the door. Her sleeping body was turned away from the moonlight.
Her bare arms squeezed a Teddy bear with wide white eyes that
made him look like he was suffocating. His wife had forgotten to
close the blinds. He looked out the front window and saw a sea of
city lights floating in the darkness above the train ditch. He closed
the blind, then kissed his daughter's forehead and went to sit on
the couch. As his eyelids drooped, he emptied his mind into the
black air. Soon it filled with the sound of waves crashing against the
rocks of Alcatraz. The Golden Gate Bridge soared over the water.
He pictured the ocean beyond it. He opened Adeline's letter again
and held it in front of him. A draft slipped in through the old living
room window sill. Winter would be here before they knew it. The
moonlight broke through the clouds, streaming in, and Alfie lifted
the letter to its pale rays.

(1963)

The plane would have to land in the ocean, because the land belonged to the mountains. These were the mountains in John Wayne movies, brown and dry, but without the wide-open spaces. No Crested Buttes. No Red Rivers. One of his aunt's movie magazines said that John Wayne actually grew up in Los Angeles, and that his real name was Marion. He even played football for USC. You could imagine him on the bench or on the beach. Maybe he surfed, like the Beach Boys. Alfie pictured him instead in his full cowboy outfit, riding over one mountain after another, all the way to the sand. He could see the Duke guiding his horse straight into the salt water, turning around in the saddle to take in the scenery until the only thing left of him was a ten-gallon hat bobbing in the waves.

The plane wobbled and shook as it flew over open water and banked hard to the left. For a few seconds Alfie's window faced straight down. The whitecaps danced a regular pattern. Watching them from this angle gave Alfie the heebie-jeebies. He held onto his armrests as though, in case of a crash, they would keep the ground from grinding his bones to dust. Not even his time on Army transports had made him comfortable in a plane. The older woman next to him smirked. She wore a hat with a feather tucked in the band, as if to say flying was natural. Then, as the plane came level again, an honest-to-God city rose from the dark blue water. It stood at the end of a thumb of land, and if you looked beyond it, you could see another smaller city across a huge bay. Off to one side Alfie spotted the Golden Gate Bridge, then Alcatraz. What else should he look for? The ground was a cradle of ridges and currents. Trees on the hilltops looked prehistoric. You half-expected to spot a pterodactyl in the sky, and you did spot their cousins, pelicans, splashing down in shallows where the first ugly fish might've crawled onto land. You were stepping out of time, into a different world. In New York, decades settled themselves in the grime on brick buildings' façades and in concrete gutters, and the closest thing to a dinosaur was a pigeon. Ever since Kansas, he'd locked himself into that sooty landscape like a new fossil.

The cab from the airport was orange and black. It shot Alfie along a highway wider than any two back home. The freeway ran between the bay and the last line of hills before the ocean. It ran past a bridge that cut an island in half on its way across the bay, then ended in a downtown street. The ups and the downs of the streets took him through a business district and a Chinatown and along a wide avenue to Chestnut Street. An uphill run of Chestnut angle-sliced the base of Adeline's plaster-faced house like a hypotenuse. At its angle with one wall was a small door made of wood that could have come from the deck of a schooner, if it hadn't been painted a coral color you'd expect to see on a tropical island. The address was marked in black spray paint. Alfie stepped out of the cab and dropped his duffel bag—a relic from Army days—on the sloped sidewalk, then knocked at the coral door, which rattled in its rickety frame. He stood with his hands in his pockets, one leg a foot up the hill from the other, trying to get his bearings. He waited and whistled "My Darling Clementine." The melody echoed down the empty block and drew his eyes to the high horizon at its end. Before he could knock again, the latch clicked, the door swung open, and a beautiful, tall, brown-haired woman ducked into the doorway. When she saw Alfie, she took a step back and leaned against a wall, a hand on her hip.

"You have to be Alfie. Addy said you might be late."

She stared him down, an honest-to-God Mona Lisa with a body like a Venus wrapped in a tight black skirt and sweater, long hair pulled back with a black band, legs in black stockings, and feet in open black shoes that Alfie could picture by the side of a bed. In half-light she could be Sophia Loren. Alfie hadn't come all this way to gawk at another girl, but he did, and she acted like she expected him to, until she finally extended a hand.

"I'm Viv. And you look dead on the vine. Follow me."

Alfie humped his duffel through the door and stepped into the dim hallway, his head scraping the ceiling as he walked. He passed a doorway here and another there, but couldn't see into the darkened rooms. They were in some sort of a basement. Up ahead weak light from a tiny back window outlined his guide's curves as she climbed a flight of stairs. Alfie marched after her, then climbed, fumbling with his bag as he emerged into a kitchen that looked a hundred years old. In the middle of the room, on a scarred wooden table, were a dented coffee pot and two scuffed cups. On the back wall was a sink with a window above it and next to it a windowed door that gave onto a small back porch and stairs that led down to whatever yard or alley you had in the back of a San Francisco house. Through the window Alfie could see the bay. In the foreground he recognized Fisherman's Wharf, and beyond it, in the middle of the waves, Alcatraz. While he took it all in, his guide walked around him, making a big show of looking him up and down.

"Have a seat."

He took the one facing the window and set his bag on the painted wood floor.

"Do you mind?"

"You're a guest. And you're family. Cousin, n'est ce pas?"

"Cousin."

"Addy said you didn't say much, but that you're good people." Viv pulled out a cigarette. "And your picture doesn't do you justice."

Alfie patted his pockets for a lighter. Before he could find one, she walked to the stove and bent over the flame, giving Alfie a backside close-up.

"Do you like wine?" she asked, spinning on her heel, sending a vapor trail over his head.

"Sure."

Who the hell was she that he should be nervous? She sounded like an actress. He couldn't make out the accent. Not exactly like the cabbie or the people at the airport. Not like Kansas either. A little more southern. She sat down with her legs almost touching his. She arched her neck and blew a ring of smoke straight up toward the bare light bulb on the ceiling, so that the bulb looked like a tiny planet.

"Every cat gets different kicks."

She smiled and stared at him until he felt even more uncomfortable.

"Where's Adeline?"

"Out. Back in an hour or two. She had a little business."

His cousin knew he was coming, no? But maybe it was better this way. You couldn't just fly across the country and jump into what was about to happen, whatever it was. He needed a few minutes to ask himself questions he knew that he couldn't answer. Outside the window a heavy mist was filling the sky and blanketing the bay.

"You said you have wine?"

Viv smiled.

"Is that a request?"

She picked up an open bottle and a clean coffee cup from the countertop.

"Hope you don't mind?"

As she poured, his eyes rode the length of her.

"A woman like you pouring me wine, why would I mind?"

Who did he think he was, acting like this in his cousin's house? But to hell with it. He was free. This little bit of time would disappear as soon as he saw Adeline.

Viv poured two glasses, then stretched out in her chair like she was alone, talking to the wall.

"A woman like me. Hmmm."

He knew a few women like her back in New York. Liberated types who would tell you exactly where you could go.

"Addy never mentioned her cousin being everything plus?"

"Come again."

She exaggerated a sigh.

"You're handsome."

He felt his face flush as he took another sip. Viv pointed at him with her cigarette.

"Well, Addy didn't tell you she had a doll for a roommate, did she? You're supposed to say something like that. Tell me you wouldn't mind taking me out for a nice dinner while you're here."

Alfie finished his wine.

"Okay. We'll all go to dinner."

Viv snuffed out her butt in one of the cups.

"You're not exactly hip, are you?"

"Not exactly."

The wine's acid bit the back of his throat.

"How do you get your kicks then? I bet Addy wouldn't mind my asking."

"I don't get kicks."

She shot him a side eye.

"Everybody gets kicks. If you say you don't, then I'll just have to guess at your bag. I'll bet I can guess."

Viv's fingers drummed the tabletop as she examined him. It was the sound of raindrops on his bedroom window as he woke up next to her and reached for a bare shoulder before he could remember who she was.

"Speaking of your bag," she said, a twang poking through the fake way she tried to talk, "what's in here?"

She stretched her leg under the table, snagged the strap of his duffel with her foot, and dragged it close to her chair. When Alfie saw her reaching for the zipper, he instinctively reached down as if to stop her, then caught himself. A quick shock of surprise set her jaw, before her face melted into a nonchalant smile.

"Easy, Cowboy. This isn't a shakedown."

She locked eyes with him, opening her lips ever so slightly as she reached again for the zipper, this time pulling it slowly along the bag's teeth and pulling apart its folds, revealing a week's worth

of clothes folded as neatly as Alfie could manage after Michelle had
lost her mind and emptied his bureau drawers onto the bedroom
floor. Now he wanted her to look. Viv felt around inside until her
hand came up holding the only luxury he'd brought along, a Marine
Band harmonica he'd bought just a few days before. He still hadn't
taken it out of the box.

"Addy said you could play."

"Guitar. Used to."

"May I?"

Alfie nodded.

She dug out the harmonica and blew a few dissonant squeaks
and buzzes, then laid it on the table.

"Can you blow?"

"I doubt it."

She got up, poured herself some wine, then sat down again.

"You're a riddle, Jim."

She leaned back in her chair again, keeping her eyes fixed on
him. He thought seriously about grabbing and kissing her right
there, maybe up against the sink, maybe pulling up her skirt and
running his hands down the length of her stockings. Except for the
talk, how would she be different from the girls in Upstate bars, the
ones he and his cousins escorted to parking lots or little clearings
in the woods? The only difference was this one would buy her own
drinks.

"Let me show you around the pad."

Viv could be the one who taught him to get out more, to get
past a point where he could tell himself he was doing the right
thing by staying with Michelle. She'd let him go lower than low,
burn himself up, so that he'd be all new for Adeline. Once he saw
Viv's bedroom, he'd never see the inside of his own apartment again.
Goodbye to the dilapidated kitchen and the worn furniture and the
cracks in the walls and dingy moldings and the stuck windows and
the views of the train ditch across the street. Goodbye to the sound
of his mother's voice coming through the ceiling, and goodbye to
all her remarks and all his father's sad looks when he left for work

in the morning, plodding down the stoop steps like he had lead
weights hanging from his neck. Goodbye to what he'd become. As
long as he could say he'd been devoted to somebody, he could fake
most of the rest of life, like he used to play a few songs he didn't
feel so he could get to the tune that lifted him. If he went with Viv
now, he'd have nothing left but himself, and he'd be able to go to
Adeline with all his sins on his shoulders, and give her a chance to
say, "Nothing you ever did wrong matters now." But as Viv took his
hand, he could hear his daughter's voice asking questions about the
people who passed and the stores and the cars along 65th Street
and all the things that children would eventually forget were once a
mystery. He didn't feel guilty exactly, but responsible. He could live
with the idea that she would be sad or disappointed once he was
gone, but when he saw it as giving up, the thought scared him. If
you could leave your own kid behind, what else could you do?

Viv led him first to the apartment's small living room, which
looked more like his grandfather's workshop than a parlor. In a
back corner was a desk covered with notebooks. The desk faced a
big bay window. The midday light poured through the window onto
a long, rough wooden table coated with splotches of dried plaster
and covered with small, half-finished statues that shared the surface
with ash trays and dirty rags. In the other corner was an old-fashioned cabinet radio, and along the wall between the radio and the
window was a battered leather couch. The only other items were a
few straight-backed wooden chairs scattered around the room.

Adeline wasn't a sculptor, so Alfie had his opening.

"What are you working on?"

Viv looked at the long table, then at Alfie, like she'd swallowed
five canaries.

"It's a series. Do you know what that is?"

Did she take him for a *cidrul*?

Alfie clenched his teeth.

"Well, I know it's not like the World Series, so, let me guess, it
must be a bunch of statues."

She raised her chin.

"Sculptures, you mean."

"Yeah, those things on the table."

The Brooklyn minority of Alfie's accent was taking over his voice, as it sometimes did when he lost patience.

"What's the one near the end? It looks like a fish standing up on its dorsal fins."

Viv's chin fell to her chest.

"If I didn't know better, I'd say you were good and elevated."

She walked over and petted the figure's head.

"This is Kenneth. He was the granddaddy of the San Francisco scene. He was a poet, but really more of a prophet."

She traced the line of the figure's shoulder and arm with her index finger.

"He's got a haiku inscribed on his arm. Addy and I wrote it together, and a friend of ours translated it into Japanese characters."

"She knew him?"

"Who?

"The prophet."

"You could say he had her under his wing."

Alfie saw Ted's smug face, and felt what he'd felt around Ted, being a fish out of water, a fish on hind legs. Viv pulled down on the edges of her sweater, bringing her torso into sharper relief.

"I like sculpture."

"Come here," she said, "I'll show you the one that's turning out the best."

She brushed past him and stood behind the smallest figure on the table.

"This is Maria. She's a fierce poet. From New York, like you."

"Adeline knows her?"

Viv kept her eyes on the statue.

"She does. Unfortunately, they don't dig each other. Maria was jungled up with Kenneth before Addy made the scene, and there was friction. In fact, I had to pretend this little princess here was somebody else we know."

She winked at Alfie.

"But that's our secret."

She pointed to the figure's head.

"Look here. This is the beginning of her mouth."

Alfie made out an indented circle.

"A fierce mouth. When it's finished, you'll see her teeth. She'll be making a proclamation. She's been doing that ever since she got together with this super-hip Negro writer, Jonathan. He was all the rage until he went back east."

When she said this, she watched him, maybe for a change in his expression, which he wasn't going to give her. Viv smiled again.

"Touch it."

Alfie pressed the figure's back. The clay was a little firmer than he'd expected. Then Viv's hand was on his shoulder, her face a few inches from his.

"Would you like to see the rest of it?"

Alfie shrugged.

"The place, I mean."

As they crossed in front of the bay window, the sound of keys dropping on a table echoed from the kitchen.

Viv stopped and puckered her lips in a fake pout.

"Viv?"

The voice in the kitchen rose from better days, but the face that came into view had left those days behind. It was Adeline's all right, but thinner and harder at the edges. The full lips were a straight line. The face seemed surprised that he was there. She'd asked him to come, and now she was seeing him as a memory. Adeline lowered the two bags she was holding and took a few slow steps toward Alfie, then hugged him like she was afraid he would break. She tilted her face up toward his. A few creases under the eyes, a few marks on the skin that he remembered as a clear sky at sunrise. Viv touched Alfie's and Adeline's arms at the same time, then backed away toward the bedrooms and disappeared. Adeline looked ready to cry, or maybe Alfie was seeing more in her blankness than he should.

"I'm sorry. You know, sorry I wasn't here when you got in."

"No, I should've called when I got to the airport."

Could he tell her that to call would've been to spoil his escape? Once he'd shut the apartment door behind him in Brooklyn, he'd needed to be on his own, or at least pretend he was.

"I'm sorry," she repeated. "I had things to take care of this week. I fell behind."

He absolved her with a wave of the hand.

"It may not look it right now, but I couldn't be happier you're here. And later on I want to show you around. Right now, though— I'm sorry—I think I need a nap. Is that okay? I mean, are you hungry? Did Viv feed you?"

"Not exactly, but I'm not hungry."

He hugged her again, this time holding her. Her limp body felt like a mistake, but maybe he wasn't being fair. People got tired.

"Take a nap," he whispered in her ear, watching the bottom of her straight black dress dangle just above the floor as she left him alone with the unfinished figurines.

The apartment was quiet and the sky overcast enough for Alfie to fall asleep on the old couch. He slept for an hour before a strange sound woke him. A foghorn. He remembered walking on the concrete pier with his father and Frankie, and he felt the urge to walk now. On Adeline's desk, he found a pen and paper, and wrote a note to say he was taking a little stroll. He took the harmonica from the kitchen table. At the corner of Grant Avenue, he pulled it from his pocket. The mid-weekday sidewalks were empty, the neighborhood all private houses. He lifted the instrument to his lips and blew a single thin note. It didn't sound bad, so he let his mouth cover more of the openings and blew what passed for a chord. To the right the avenue rose higher. Alfie followed it, running a scale as best he could. At the corner of the next block he picked up the melody of a Ray Charles tune he liked. It was in F, but he managed in B-flat.

D ... D ... C ... Bb ... A ... *I've made up my mind.*

Across the street a small green sign read "Coit Tower," with an arrow pointing to Alfie's left. He followed a second sign up another hill. No matter where you walked, you were going uphill. At least the effort suited the blues. When you loved somebody, you were always climbing a hill, never knowing what you'd find at the top. Sure enough, Lombard Street dead-ended. Alfie walked to the guardrail that marked its end. He surveyed a different part of the bay, the part with the gray bridge that ran from San Francisco straight through a rocky island in the middle and on to Oakland. To his right a young couple held hands and took in the view for a moment, before walking a path to a winding road that started up another hill, this one steeper than the last. Alfie followed them. He passed houses to the right and pine woods to the left. A few hundred feet along he could see through a break in the trees to the base of a white tower. He followed the road as it curved up and around to an even better view of the water, which, it occurred to him, was everywhere. If you lived here, you couldn't avoid beauty. But would you start to ignore it after a while? Hate it? If the whole place was a fairy tale, what right did people have to think they could live in it?

The road was lined with trees you didn't see in New York: strange pines with whitish bark and huge needles, and smaller trees with glossy leaves that looked like overgrown magnolias, and vines thicker than his grandmother's arms. Then all of sudden came a chorus of squawks from the tops of the trees. Alfie strained his eyes in the weird gray light that was poking through the clouds, and at the very top of one tree he could make out a green and yellow bird with red markings. Pretty soon a few more flew above the branches and started another racket. Parrots. He decided that once upon a time there must have been pirates here, too. He could picture the pirate ships anchored in the bay, the pirates coming ashore to drink and sneak up this way, on the lookout for their next set of victims.

When he reached the parking lot around the last bend, a few tourists were pointing binoculars or cameras in different directions.

Behind them was the tower, a wide white cylinder like the Leaning Tower of Pisa, except perfectly plumb. Alfie stepped inside and bought a ticket at the window, where the clerk handed him a little pamphlet with information about the tower. A woman named Coit had left money to build it, to honor the city's firefighters. In her day she followed the firemen to fires, and even dressed like a fireman sometimes. There were worse hobbies.

The tower was built during the Depression, and the first-floor walls were covered with murals, commissioned to give artists work. Alfie's shoulders went slack as another melody ran through his head and his fingers dotted an invisible fretboard to capture it. If only he could paint. One painting called "Leaders of California Life" showed a cowboy, a farmer, a surveyor, and a steelworker. They were standing still, as though they'd already done whatever they had to do. The real action was in the paintings of workers: "Industries of California," "California Industrial Scenes," "Agriculture and Industry," "City Life." There were workers at power plants and steelworks and garment factories and print shops and bakeries and on docks and platforms and street corners and down manholes and up telephone poles and in firehouses and police precincts and me-chanics' garages and grocery stores. They all looked like giants, a quarter the size of the buildings. They stoked fires, turned cranks, hauled bundles, swung hammers, kneaded dough, poured milk into vats, poked, cut, measured, stitched, and sometimes read and ate lunch like the world was depending on them eating fast so they could get right back to work again. Most of the workers were men, but a lot of them were women, and even more of them were negroes or Mexicans or Chinamen or some other shade of brown or red or yellow. They worked together, and everything they did mattered. They were a city, more important than its buildings or even the ocean around it. Alfie was almost thirty and when he was out sell-ing insurance, it felt like he worked alone or at least worked only for himself.

He bought a ticket to the top of the tower and found the ele-vator. The friendly operator talked non-stop as he ushered people in. He told them how the place was built out of three nesting, reinforced concrete cylinders, the kind his grandfather's company used for the New York sewer lines. Here, somehow, they were beautiful and they'd probably last hundreds of years unless another big earthquake or bomb hit, a thought that disturbed Alfie as the elevator rumbled to a stop. He exhaled when the door opened onto a room with a staircase leading up to the open deck. The small alcoves around the perimeter were lined with windows that reminded Alfie of church. Only a few other people were on the deck, so Alfie could go from alcove to alcove, taking in a different view each time: the city, with its hills; the mountains across the bay in one direction; the mountains across the bay in another direction; the other city across the bay; the islands in the middle; Alcatraz; the Golden Gate Bridge; the ocean. Sure, you could stay here and feel like you never lived anywhere else, or if you had lived anywhere else, feel like you'd been missing something. But what if everybody felt that way? Where would that leave the rest of the world? What about the people who had to stay behind in places like Brooklyn and Upstate New York, who were keeping a kind of faith that a lot of times gave Alfie a headache? He inhaled the salt air and closed his eyes.

Satisfied, he took the elevator to the ground floor, left the tower, and followed a different route down a long flight of wooden stairs and through a different neighborhood, eventually finding his way back to Chestnut Street. By the time he got there, the sun had broken through the clouds, so that he felt warm for the first time since he'd touched down. Even going downhill he was sweating through his chinos and button-down shirt, the traveling clothes he still hadn't changed. When he reached Adeline's house, the dwarf front door was half open. He knocked, and when no one answered, he walked down the dark hallway and up to the kitchen, where he found Adeline and Viv having lunch, talking and giggling like best friends in high school. If Adeline had ever had a friend like that in Brooklyn, Alfie had never heard about her. The two friends didn't notice him on the staircase at first, so Alfie stopped near the top, to listen as they went on like *chiacchierones*. Viv's voice was the louder of the two.

"Whatever you do, don't give him bright disease. I mean, do you really know that he's not a square?"

Too late. He must have breathed heavy, because Viv leaned over and spotted him.

"Look here. The Great Explorer's back. Where you been, Daddy-O?"

Alfie and Adeline exchanged gentle smiles.

"The tower."

"Would you look at this, Addy, he's sightseeing without us. Diggin' the scene."

As Alfie stepped fully into the room, Viv winked at him, then at Adeline.

"Next time, Darlin', let me show you the ropes."

Adeline rolled her eyes, rose to her feet, and took Alfie's arm.

"I think it's time to split," she said, accenting the final word for Viv's benefit, he thought, and leading him back to the staircase. "Unless you're tired."

"Tired? No. I could walk all day."

Alfie looked over his shoulder at Viv, to say a polite goodbye. With her long fingers she waved him a secretive toodaloo.

The afternoon sun slipped up the slope of the street and out of sight. Adeline squinted in its dying face, like she was listening for something it whispered. She said nothing as they walked first down Chestnut, then over to a crazy block that zig-zagged its way uphill. Down-going cars followed the street's sharp elbows at toy speed. Side by side, Alfie and Adeline walked past pink and white wedged gardens, into the orange sunlight that bathed the hill's crest from the west. Chimes tinkled in the wind, and when they reached the top of the block, a cable car was pulling to a stop. They jumped on, and Adeline paid the fare before Alfie could reach into his pocket. He gestured an objection, which she shrugged off, pocketing change from the conductor. They held onto the overhead straps as the car jerked, then rumbled downhill toward the bay. She leaned into him, her head on his chest like he was a public pillow. The cable car slowed as the slope flattened. The smell of chocolate filled the air. Adeline nodded toward a red brick building across from the end of the line.

"Candy factory. Run by Italians. There are more of us here than you'd think."

The car came to a turn-around, across from the factory on one side and open land skirting the bay on the other. Adeline walked Alfie toward a pier in the distance. A ribbon of stone steps gave walkers access to a strip of sand and clusters of half-submerged rocks. No one had even a toe in the water, but some people were sitting on the steps, with their shoes off, like they wished they could wade. The walkway ran a good half-mile out to a concrete pier that curled away from a hilltop battery like a cutlass. Alfie and Adeline found a spot near the end of the pier and sat on its edge. Their feet dangled a few feet above the black water as they faced Alcatraz. In the distance, gleams of dying sunlight lit the burnt orange of the Golden Gate as it towered over whitecaps. If they drove across and kept going, where would they end up? Alfie pictured the bay from the new Alfred Hitchcock movie he'd taken Michelle to see before he left. He'd told himself he wouldn't forget about his wife, until he saw the actress in the movie and thought about Adeline. Then he didn't care anymore whether or not Michelle knew he was lying about an old Army buddy in California who needed his help. Why not let her know the real reason? She deserved what she got for how she made him live. Naturally, he hadn't told Adeline any of this. He studied her face as she stared into the water. She had her own problems. The bay breeze blew her hair across her eyes like a veil. It blew warm and cool at the same time, like it was sweeping back and forth across centuries.

"This is a good spot."

She brushed her hair to one side and nodded.

"A lot's happened, Alfie. To me, I mean."

"You're not the only one."

Her eyes followed a seagull gliding to a soft landing on the water. She spoke now like she was talking to herself.

"I meant that my life here is something I didn't expect. You know, you don't ever really know what to expect when you go someplace new."

"Probably not."

"No, and a lot of things have happened. I've done a lot of things I'd guess you wouldn't expect. Or maybe back in Brooklyn no one would have expected me to do. I don't know."

And how bad could they be compared to what he was doing?

"I don't know why I want to tell you these things. I feel as though I owe you an explanation."

Alfie touched her arm, and she laid a hand on his.

"I came out here to be free and to write. I think you know that. But it was harder than I thought, not least of all because I was alone. Have you ever been all alone?"

The question caught Alfie by surprise. So did the answer. He lived with Michelle and Jennifer. Before that with his mother and father. Unless you could call living in a barracks living alone, the answer was no.

"It's not what you'd think it is. It's nice, I suppose, to have your own space, to eat what you want, and come and go as you please. But eventually, you know, you need someone to talk to. When I first got here, I stayed in a little hotel near the Fillmore, the negro section of town. I was able to get up and write for a few hours in quiet. Do you know what real quiet is like?"

Winter nights in Rome and the howl of wind racking the walls of their little house. So quiet for so long that a train's horn twenty miles away was a gunshot.

"I loved it, but then I'd feel lonely. I'd have to leave and find a café. Which wasn't hard. In that part of town, there were plenty of beatniks looking for places to sit—they hate it when you call them that, by the way, 'beatniks,' so you're better off calling them 'artists,' even if they don't make art, which most of them don't. Or just don't call them anything. Anyway, I would sit in this one café at the edge of Japantown, and I'd take notes and look at the people who came and went and wonder where they'd all come from. Some of them drawled a little, like Viv, and some sounded like they came from Brooklyn. And I found out that if I just sat there and stared into space, someone would talk to me. When they did, I couldn't have been happier. Whatever they said, no matter how vacuous it might be, I was happy to hear a voice. Some of them talked about the government and all the terrible things it was doing. Some of them talked about the books they were writing or their paintings. And some just rattled on about family members like I'd known them for years. At first I thought, you know, what a bunch of gasbags. But then my money started to run out, and what they said started to make more sense. If I wanted to write half the day and sit in public the other half, I'd have to make a choice: be like them or get a job."

The word "job" struck a sour note in Alfie's ears. Adeline pulled a pack of cigarettes from a big pocket on the front of her dress. He gestured for a bum, and she handed him the pack and a book of matches from a place called The Cellar. They both lit up and puffed miniature clouds over the dark water.

"You know my father. If he could see me now, right? But I'm his daughter, so I had to get a job no matter how far away the old bastard was. So I took a job right there in my favorite café, and eventually one of those nice young men who sat down with me said he knew a girl who needed a roommate. And suddenly ..."

She waved her arm in the air like Bette Davis.

"... my loneliness was gone."

Adeline coughed out a hard laugh and tapped a cone of ash into the bay. She slipped the pack of cigarettes back into her pocket and, like she'd found something lost, pulled out a tiny book with a flame on the cover. Alfie couldn't make out the title. She thumbed through it and smirked, then read a few lines.

> I stand in the dark light in the dark
> street
> and look up at my window, I was
> born there.
> The lights are on; other people are
> moving about.

"I can't help feeling that way sometimes. I know you understand."

Alfie smiled as she dropped the book back into her pocket.

"Was that a poem?"

"Part of one."

He nodded and smiled again. Whatever he said now might tell her that he didn't understand or that he didn't understand the same things she understood.

"I feel alone, Alfie, and when you feel alone sometimes you act strangely. I won't lie to you. I've done some things you probably couldn't imagine."

What did she think he'd been imagining?

"For one thing, I've smoked lots of dope and taken lots of pills that didn't come from doctors."

Was he supposed to be her priest?

"Look, Adeline, between clubs and the Army …"

"I was naked on stage. Can you believe that? Your Aunt Lena's daughter up there in lights for everybody to see. Of course, only about a couple of dozen people ever saw that particular play."

She fumbled with her hair, then finally tied it into a sloppy bun.

"Not that the play was bad, but no one with money for theater tickets is hanging around North Beach. Although that's not quite true either. I don't know. Maybe the nudity kept some people away. Or maybe the threat of raids. The cops here like raids."

She looked through him, then went on.

"I was trying something new, and I wasn't quite myself. That was just after Jonathan and I split up. Did I mention him? Probably not. Another thing you might not have expected. Jonathan is a negro writer."

She paused for his response. He took another drag and withheld comment.

"Anyway, I liked him, but he wanted too much from me, and no, not that kind of too much, but to move in with him and give up all my time, and, like I said before, I was enjoying my freedom. And then, too, he didn't like some of my habits."

She looked away, through the fog creeping in, disguising the waves.

"Alfie, I don't want to lie to you."

To lie, you had to think you were answering somebody's questions. He didn't come here to ask questions, but the more she said, the more he wanted to ask, and the more he wanted to ask, the more he hated himself for coming here. He didn't like that the thought of her with some black Bohemian upset him. He tried to think of his father and the preacher, about the colored girls along Prospect Park, but their faces became a single face that might as well have belonged to an alien. His cousins and friends from the neighborhood were sitting next to him now like evil spirits, eavesdropping, frowning, whispering terrible things about Adeline.

"The real problem, though—you'll either hate me for putting it this way or dig exactly what I mean—wasn't Jonathan or smoking dope or being naked in public. The real problem was not getting it right. It was failing, you know. After all the time I spent waiting to get to a place like this, I was failing. I couldn't write the way I wanted. But you know how we Italians are, hard-headed. So I tried different kinds of writing, longer poems and the beginnings of a novel. Still, I found myself getting frustrated, like I had something to say but didn't know what it was. So I started reading at the clubs, and once in a while somebody would praise me. Every now and then a hotshot kid writer, usually a few years younger, would ask me to have a drink, which meant a drink and maybe something else, and before I knew it I'd been out with half the men in the room. Which, believe me, didn't make me too popular with the other gals. Viv at least stuck up for me, but it was tough, and sometimes when I'd get up to read, some of these chicks would actually hiss. It got so bad that the emcees would have to tell them to cool it, they were giving the place a bad vibe. Things went on like that until I got so mad that I started writing and reading these rants that just told everybody in the room to go fu...you know. People loved it. They stopped giving me grief, which was good, except that now I was like the scene's mascot. I was the slightly older woman that every other woman in the room could watch and think to themselves, 'I'll never end up like her.' But I still needed to be around other people. And enough people on the scene are like me. They believe in the artist's cliché." She gulped and sighed and looked at Alfie like she was waiting for him to finish her thought.

"The cliché?"

She bugged out her eyes and spun her hands in a way that reminded him of her mother.

"That you have to suffer for your art."

Alfie wanted to laugh, and to tell her off. How stupid could you be? Suffering would always find you.

"I wouldn't know anymore."

Adeline dropped her eyes, then pushed herself back from the pier's edge.

"Anyway, I'll take you to a reading tomorrow. You can be my audience. Though I guess you just were."

The showerhead spat in Alfie's face. The water was hot one second, cold the next. He was about to run a bath in the tiny tub when a knock came on the bathroom door.

"Are you decent?"

"In the shower."

The door creaked open, and a blast of hot water hit Alfie between the shoulder blades.

"*Puttana diavolo!*"

Adeline laughed.

"There's a trick, you know."

"No kidding."

"Don't move."

Adeline's arm snaked inside the curtain and grabbed the faucet.

"Push the handle in a little when you turn it."

The water cooled, and the arm retreated.

"Do you mind if I sit and talk?"

"Why would I mind?"

The toilet cover dropped with a clack.

"It's been hard not seeing you," she said, as though it hadn't occurred to her before.

What should he say?

"I've often wondered whether or not you'd like it here."

"I don't know yet."

Her lemony shampoo stung his eyes like no tomorrow.

"There are so many great things about San Francisco. The scenery is beautiful, of course, but there's so much art in the air. I wish you were here for the arts festival next month. It's at the museum, right near the Presidio. You'd love it."

Alfie blinked his eyes furiously until he could concentrate on what Adeline was saying.

"You know, it's funny to think of all the museums and galleries in New York that we never saw. People here talk about them all the time like they're cathedrals in France. I had to come to California to learn what New York City had to offer. Our families just never took us. Why do you think that is?"

Alfie thought of his father in a museum, any museum, on a bench in the middle of a big room, watching all the people file in and out and wondering why they cared. Why did anybody care? Alfie was only 29, but he suspected that life wouldn't get any better. Imagine you're in your fifties or your sixties, or older even, and every day you're thinking, "Boy, am I lucky." Or are you?

"If I told you they were busy, would you believe it?"

A cabinet door squeaked open.

"I'm not blaming them, though I guess I am."

"Listen, if my mother had her way, she would've taken me and Frankie to a museum every week. And we probably would've fought her tooth and nail. She talks about you sometimes, my mother."

The cabinet door squeaked closed.

"She talks about how beautiful you are and how much your parents miss you."

"She must mean how much my mother misses me."

"Your mother comes over every week or so. Your father too sometimes. But mainly your mother. And they sit in the kitchen and talk. A lot of complaining."

"What else would they do? They're stuck there."

Adeline practically spit the words. But why? Didn't they send her to NYU? Didn't they let her do what she wanted? What did she expect? In the old country her father was an engineer—which he let everybody know—but here he sold clothes. He had money, sure, but he was miserable. He gives his daughter everything, then she's gone. He probably did nothing but piss and moan to Aunt Lena. Alfie squeezed the bar of soap he was holding.

"You got something against Brooklyn?"

Silence. Then a drawer groaned open.

"I bought all of these toiletries for your visit. Now I can't find them. I'm sure that soap in there is too feminine for you."

Alfie put the bar to his nose.

"I even bought nice shaving cream. Of course I hid it from myself. It's here somewhere."

She rifled noisily through the drawer, coming up with the prize, which she placed inside the curtain.

"I want to travel more, Alfie, so I'll have to get better at keeping track of things. I've been thinking about joining the Peace Corps. Did I mention that?"

The water was getting hot again.

"Uh-uh."

"I think I'd be great in the Peace Corps. Do you ever get the feeling you need to help people?"

God was supposed to help those …

"Did you ever think of joining the Peace Corps?"

Alfie snorted, then pretended he was clearing his throat.

"Never occurred to me."

Some people said it was a spy program, which wouldn't be bad.

"I think about it all the time. It would be wonderful to go to South America."

What did she know about South America?

"Bolivia, for example. Oh, look, I found your shampoo too."

Her hand, holding the bottle, made a return appearance inside the curtain.

"Next time."

She was all over the place. All over the country. All over the world. Who did she think she was? She had all the freedom you could want, but it was flowing through the drain guard into a sewer. As she left the bathroom, she told him to put on his dungarees—which she made a show out of calling "jeans," like he should follow her lead—and whatever tee shirt he might have with him, preferably a black one. They were going to Grant Avenue, where, she said, the action was. To a bagel shop.

By the time they reached the bagel shop, a good half-mile up the avenue, Alfie was sweating again, and hungry. The shop, it turned out, was a hole in the wall with dingy paneling and dingier little wooden tables. With Adeline on his arm, Alfie approached the counter.

"Do you have poppy seed?"

The thin drink of water at the register shot him a nasty smile and spoke to Adeline.

"Is he kidding?"

She elbowed Alfie and laughed.

"Sorry, they don't actually serve bagels."

He pretended to be only slightly annoyed.

"I had my heart set on a bagel. Isn't this a bagel shop?"

The clerk smirked.

"The Harmony Bagel Shop. We emphasize harmony."

He ignored them again, scratched his beard, picked up an empty glass, held it to sunlight from the dirty window, blew on it, and wiped it with a towel. Like he was in a saloon. Adeline looked in Alfie's eyes and probably knew he wanted to choke the twerp with his towel.

"How about a roast beef on sourdough?" she asked him.

"Sure."

The clerk put down his towel and handed Adeline a ticket.

"Comin' up. I'll call your lady when it's ready."

Adeline's expression hinted that she wouldn't mind choking the little punk herself. They shared a laugh, then found a table against a long wall and watched as one after another scraggly customer wandered in off the street.

"I come here to write sometimes."

Alfie looked around the crowded room.

"How?"

"Too much quiet can be as bad as not enough."

Alfie didn't answer.

"I listen to what people say, for ideas."

She stirred her coffee until the center spun like a whirlpool.

"This isn't the stuff I read at the clubs. This is for me. These are the stories I want to tell, now that I have stories to tell. The books I want to publish, so people can all wonder about the source. Do you ever wonder about that, the source of people's stories?"

"I used to. I don't have time anymore. I'm a salesman. I hear too many stories."

"There's no such thing. That's all we have."

And what about the ones she hadn't told him? He was about to ask, when a voice in the doorway filled the bagel shop. A man's voice, high-pitched and gravelly, from the mouth of a muscular little character with straight black hair that hung down over his eyes. He looked like Moe from the Three Stooges. The accent was pure New York.

"Getta outta heah, ya bum! Randy, how do you let these friggin' Philistines clog up your doorway?"

Adeline smiled.

"That's Emile Barbarata. Believe it or not, he's an original Beat."

Barbarata ape-walked to their table.

"Look at this *faccia bell*," he said, grinning like a fiend. "And who's this Lancelot, darling?"

Adeline squeezed his hand.

"This is Alfredo Baliato."

Barbarata yanked Alfie out of his chair and bear-hugged him.

"Beautiful. We're all *famiglia*. Not like these *murte fams* blocking the door."

"Alfie's a wonderful guitarist."

"Was."

"He's modest, too."

Barbarata turned his gaze toward Adeline.

"So, sweetheart, I heard Bergman was supposed to come down today. I guess you heard the same."

"A little birdie."

"Ha! A homing pigeon! And look, here comes Daddy Pigeon himself."

Barbarata pointed to a light-skinned colored fella, who was singing lines without a melody as he came through the door.

"Whoooooose starry dynamo? Whoooose ragged claws? I tell you, and I tell you, and you sell me and you sell me, and we wonder when the whimper comes. Why, haalooo!"

He quick-timed it to their table, stopped dead, and stood straight as an arrow in front of Barbarata like he was waiting to salute him. When Barbarata stood up, the negro spoke in a fake bass.

"Does the President know you're here, soldier?"

"No, Ya Honah, he doesn't."

"Does the Governor know you're loose, fellow traveler?"

"I don't think so, Ya Highness."

"Does the world know its soul is on fire?"

Barbarata cupped a hand to the side of his mouth.

"I'll guess we'll have to ask it, ya bozo."

The performer bent low to kiss Adeline's hand while he kept one eye on Alfie.

"This, *mon ami*, is what they say a negro wants."

Adeline caught the spark in Alfie's eyes.

"You gentlemen need an introduction."

"I'm nobody, certainly no gentleman," the negro said, extending a hand, "Who are you? No, really, all that jive aside, the name is Ronald, but only my mother and the government call me that. I prefer the abbreviation of my slave name. Whose acquaintance do I now have the pleasure of consummating?"

He studied Alfie's face. Of the colored he'd met, only the preacher had looked at him like that. Alfie shook his hand.

"I sense a kindred," Ronald said. "Call me Ron. Unless they order you not to."

"Alfie."

"You must be Addy's beau."

"Not exactly."

"Yeah, they all say that. They all know that this here is my girl."

He wrapped an arm around her waist and winked.

"I mean that in the New Orleans way, you know. Nothing to fear, here. I can tell by how she looks at you that a paltry brother like myself is wise not to bother competing. Besides, what's competition ever done for any of us?"

"Speak for yourself," Barbarata answered. "Competition's what made us great, and by 'us' I mean poets, and it's what'll show the world that when all you pretenders are dead and buried, they'll still be reading my stuff."

"You see what I mean, *mesdames et messieurs*," Ron said to no one. "I can't compete."

He drew a slip of paper from his shirt pocket.

"But I can recite."

He tore up the slip of paper.

"And so I sing a song of love or something like it."

He raised his voice so the room full of customers could hear.

"If you can pardon me, good people. If you can bear with me, if you can listen, if you can bear it, I announce to you and to all the good pedestrians and motorists of Columbus Avenue and to all the tribes of this great bay and the many nations present and expunged, that we claim this site for proclamation. For God and Emile know what we must do.

"So I begin with this song of love, written by a new friend, through me, for a Madonna from the East."

Ron cleared his throat.

> Begin from the East, you comet's tail
> trailing dust of slums behind. Begin
> your circle in dusty devils.
> At the lip of its gyre her lips
> like volcanos kiss time
> from its molten core. Your heart
> is fluid as tides arriving
> when she leaves, leaving
> when you arrive. Has she turned
> from you because your face dissolves.
> You both know liquid echo
> like the sum of vibrations.

Ron hovered, humming in the middle of the room. A few of the Bohemians hummed along like back-up singers while the rest of them nodded their approval before turning back to their tables of friends. The hummers hung on his next breath.

> She waits at the edge of the West
> to cast herself in, but in a mystery
> she spins inside, Cumaean Sybil
> sharing secrets with the final king.
> She didn't plan on digging him,
> but this is fate whose loopy melody
> we're jazzing in the starkest night
> that almost feels like a rectitude of day.

Ron pretended to collapse from the effort, staggering in a circle until a few followers engulfed him in hugs, guided him back to Alfie's table, and slid a chair under his thin frame. Three of his lackeys eased him down, two men and a woman. The woman patted his arm.

"The Ancestor of the Beat."

The shorter of the two men rested his head on Ron's shoulder.

"The Original Beat."

The taller man, a little older than the others, who looked like Wyatt Earp, mustache and all, rolled his eyes, but you could see by the way he watched Ron that if anybody tried to touch him, Wyatt would break him in half.

The young woman floated between Alfie and Adeline.

"I'm sorry. I'm Sunny Joy."

Alfie and Adeline shook her hand. Barbarata waved her off.

"She's a pain in the ass."

"And you're a grumpy old man."

Barbarata shrugged his shoulders and made an Italian hand gesture Alfie had seen a thousand times.

"What are you talkin' about, old? I'm thirty-three."

"Like I said, grumpy old man. I prefer the youngbloods."

Barbarata scowled.

"Sure you do. That's why you follow this *azupep'* around like a bitch in heat."

Sunny slapped him on the back of his head, and grabbed the younger of Ron's helpers by the arm. Her voice became the Song of the South.

"How dare you question my honor, Sir?"

She turned to the young man she'd grabbed.

"Defend me, Benjamin."

Benjamin took off his glasses and slid them into his shirt pocket. He stood gangly and slightly stooped in a worn pullover and dungarees, and spoke in bursts.

"This woman is pure. This woman, this woman, this woman … a meadow after rain. She's pure mist. Her own artist. Artiste, if you will. Emile speaks without just cause. Unjust Barbarata."

"Go ahead," Barbarata growled, "exact your pound of scalp, you wild Indians."

"Baaaaarbarattttaa! Baaaaarbaratttaa!"

Ron had come back to life.

"Every day is your baaaaarrr mitzvaahhh. Great gift of a barbarian."

He swiveled his head around to take in their half-standing, half-sitting little party.

"If y'all want to gift your art to the world, you will need me. You shall see. But first I need a few minutes to recover from your assault and from the delirium I feel pulsing from that man right there."

He pointed to Alfie, who was enjoying the back and forth.

"He's come all the way from the East, from … where now?"

"Brooklyn."

"From Brooklyn. Brooklyn? Well, all right. From Brooklyn, and we can help him see the truth of our city. Who here can reveal that truth?"

"The truth is disappearing," Barbarata said.

Adeline nodded, but Sunny Joy objected.

"What are you talking about? This is the truth. Look at Ron. For that matter, look at you, Barbarata. No one's telling you how to live, that you have to fit in and come home from work every day and take off your shoes and socks and watch television until you fall asleep on the couch."

Barbarata smirked.

"That doesn't sound half bad."

"Not for you, maybe," she said, "but imagine how that would be for your wife."

"I have a poem about that, you know."

"Great, but she should have a poem, a lot of them, and she should recite when she wants to."

Mischief lit Barbarata's eyes.

"She does. She's an English teacher."

Barbarata slapped his knee, got up and slapped Ron's knee, then returned to his seat and let a serious expression settle over his doughy features.

"See, Albert," he said, tapping Alfie's arm.

"Alfie," Adeline corrected.

"See, Brooklyn, here's why I gotta split the scene. Conscience doth make cowards of us all, doth it not? Plus my friends are all fled, and they're all more famous than me, except for Ron here, which is why I hold him in such high esteem."

Ron cocked his head and winked at Emile.

"You, Sir, are something like a gentleman."

Then he winked at everyone else.

"A gentleman in that you have never had to work a real day in your life, and for that, I salute you. The world owns fools aplenty."

Alfie could see what they both wanted. He wanted the same. The same way his uncles and cousins wanted to be rich and wanted to be more American than the Americans. But if they were rich, or if they were famous artists, what would they have left to say? If Alfie hadn't wrecked himself, had made it, had discovered single lines and licks that would've lived in people's heads, how long would it have been before he got bored? But that was a stupid thought. Music had as many notes as Adeline had ways to look at him. If he could get tired of what he wanted more than anything, what else could he want? Wanting beat having. But how much wanting?

"Do you ever get tired of hearing yourselves talk?"

The question came from Adeline, whose annoyance seemed to lift Barbarata's spirits.

"The lady speaks. Questions, even. A question I dare not answer. Ronald?"

"I too must remain as silent as the waters in which many have drowned."

"See, that's why you're not famous. We all know exactly what you mean. Remember," Barbarata advised his small audience, "to be honest, you have to be misunderstood."

He emptied his coffee cup.

"But what the hell do I know? I'm going. I'm lighting out."

He looked at Wyatt Earp, whose actual name Alfie still didn't know.

"Cowboy, where's my horse?"

"Barbarata," Ron yelled after him, "what about the reading?"

Barbarata surveyed the roomful of hipsters.

"They can all read my books!"

He stood up, rapped on the table, turned, walked out the door, and vanished into the twilight traffic.

"Well," Ron said, "the greatest gift is to be forgotten. Somebody said that, but I forget who."

Wyatt Earp, Sunny Joy and Benjamin all pulled up chairs, as if on cue, to join a discussion led now by a single instructor. Wyatt sat next to Alfie and shook his hand.

"Alfie, I'm J.P."

For some reason the introduction made Alfie more comfortable, and he put a hand over Adeline's as she spoke again.

"J.P.'s a native, one of the few on the scene."

"Born and raised in Noe Valley."

"Alfie, J.P. must like you. It usually takes a few days before he says a single word to anybody new."

J.P. turned to her.

"Didn't take me long to talk to you. I must've been just out of the service."

"Service?"

The question held a little more surprise in it than Alfie knew was polite.

"Marines. We're not all derelicts here."

Ron interrupted.

"In fact, I think most of us have seen the other side from the inside, sometimes from the bowels, the black bowels. This town at least gives the impression of not being Jonah's whale."

J.P. returned the interruption.

"San Francisco was a whaling town."

"Back when my people were whackin' cane," Ron added.

"I thought your people lived in the City of New Orleans. Isn't that what you like to say, 'The City of New Orleans'?"

"You heard of plantations? Not everybody was a house negro, Mr. Diggins."

J.P. smiled, leaned back in his chair, and stroked his mustache. The table went silent.

"Marines?" Alfie asked.

"Thundering Third, Camp Pendleton. You serve?"

"I was regular Army. Fort Riley, Kansas."

The two shook hands again, and Adeline shot Alfie a worried look.

"Yeah, you have the look about you. If you don't mind my saying."

Alfie shook his head. Sunny Joy sang a tune.

"Tell it … to the Marines!"

Ron suddenly sounded defensive.

"We're all veterans of something. This is the place you come after you've started to see truth."

"The truth," Benjamin said. "What is truth? One truth. A truth. Truth. Behind all of this, maybe somewhere one great sage knows THE TRUTH. I'm trying to find him. If it's a him."

Adeline made a dismissive sound.

"You can all talk about truth. I still haven't met him. It, I mean. I came here to live."

Ron didn't miss the beat.

"And live you have!"

Alfie felt Adeline's hand squeeze his.

"See," said J.P., "that's the trouble. Folks came here and started to think that for some reason San Francisco was a place to escape reality. Like the place doesn't have a reality of its own. Look around. They're tearing down all the old buildings and putting up towers. And who's living in those towers. Anybody here? You think North Beach is safe? You think even negros in the Fillmore will be able to stay there?"

"This negro ain't goin' nowhere."

"Ronald, I have no doubt they'll leave you alone. I think they respect you in a roundabout way. And I respect anybody who can come to a new place and really live there."

He saluted Adeline and talked about the beauty of San Francisco Bay, and the independence of its people, and that being reason enough to defend it. And who, Alfie wondered, had he himself ever actually defended? A cousin in an Upstate bar fight? He'd never fought any real enemy in the Army. And did he even fight for the block? When he was a kid he never had to, and now, who cared? If they blew the whole block up and moved his mother and father and Michelle and the kids to some town in New Jersey, would it make any difference? Why not be free to go where you wanted? He could come here. This could be his place too.

"A free country," Ron said. "You are free as the hamster in the glass cage, so spin that wheel."

"Speaking of which," J.P. said, "were you out yelling at cars today?"

"Well, Sir, I don't recall exactly, Sir, but, yes, I may have spoken my piece to a motorist or two just this morning."

"Well, then, isn't it about the time of day that Bigoweenie rolls by? And shouldn't you visit the powder room?"

"Now that you mention it, I do feel a sudden urge."

Ron disappeared into the back of the café, and Alfie asked the inevitable question.

"Bigoweenie?"

Sunny Joy made up another tune.

"Big Bad Bigoweenie, the nastiest man west of Alameany."

Benjamin gave the short answer.

"He's a cop."

"He's name is actually Biagini," Adeline explained. "He lives to harass anyone he thinks might be a quote, unquote, beatnik, but especially Ron. He thinks Ron's a nuisance. Which I suppose he is."

"Like the time he put the red dye in the machines at the laundromat," Sunny said.

Adeline's voice sounded annoyed now.

"He's one of these Italians out here who's defending his turf. And he hates to see a negro with a white woman or even with a white friend. The Italians here have always hated us, even though some of us are Italian. We're more of a "them" to them. They see themselves as Americans now, and we're communists."

This last comment made J.P. laugh.

"Man, I hate communists. Even the pretty ones. But she's right. And no offense, but some of these Sicilian fellas, especially the cops, if they could put all the so-called beatniks in a single room and blow 'em sky high, I believe they would. The funny part is that in my neighborhood people always liked to say how the Italians were good for nothing but food, and even that stank to heaven."

Generations of non-Sicilian Italians spoke through Alfie.

"No offense at all. Adeline's the only pure Sicilian here."

She slapped Alfie's hand, then covered it with hers, turning again to J.P.

"I wonder if any of these Cretins knows about Gramsci? Italy's given the world some great communists."

Maybe Adeline belonged here, or worse, maybe she belonged someplace he couldn't. Could he have a friend named Sunny Joy? Could he have a beer with a *cidrul* like Benjamin? J.P. was all right, but how long would he put up with this bunch? For a minute Alfie felt hopeless, until he thought about his friends in Brooklyn. In other words, about nobody. If he could come home to the same apartment as Adeline, the people who'd bother him would be exactly nobody. She could teach him what she knew. Or he could learn on his own and teach her something, whatever it might be. If they had a kid ...

"Well," J.P. said, "I hate to break up all this talk of communism, but I heard a rumor about this girl from Texas singing at the Coffee Gallery. Benjamin, that'd be your neck of the woods, but maybe surfing in L.A. washed the Texas right out of you."

The first line of the Texas girl's "Leavin' This Mornin'" hit Alfie like a plains-bound freight train. Her strum drove the wheels and her voice blared bright and high. They stood close to the stage, and he could see himself standing at her shoulder, the both of them wailing inside a boxcar with the big doors flung wide open, playing to an audience lined up along the rails for miles. Not that she was some kind of beauty, and not that she could ever be his girl, and not that her voice was sweet, but something about her and something about that voice told the world that even if it was hard, if you did all the things you told yourself you'd do just as soon as you got the chance, you could live.

J.P. tapped his foot and bobbed his head. Sunny Joy and Benjamin made an odd pair, dancing near the corner of the stage, drawing a smirk from the singer. Adeline stuck close to Alfie's side, watching him, like she might be wondering if seeing a performance like this would make him sad. Maybe a few years ago it would have, but now it was just good music. Or was she just jealous? He locked arms with her and walked her to a table in the back. She smiled and stared into his eyes. After a second number, J.P. joined them, and the three ordered beers. They sat quiet and listened. The singer wrung the blood from every song. The way she sang "Bourgeois Blues," you'd've thought she was a man and colored. The way Alfie felt now, like he couldn't stop and couldn't go, he could imagine singing the song himself, imagine himself being colored. But why would he want to be? When the singer took up another tune, Adeline leaned her head on Alfie's shoulder and wrapped her two hands around his biceps. She looked into space as the song went on, avoiding his eyes until the music stopped. Was she waiting for him to say something? If that's what she wanted, he could say something, but that something was still forming in his mind, like a speech he'd memorized a long time ago and never had the chance to deliver. He'd have to dig it up word by word until it made sense again. But the words had changed.

The singer ended her set with a version of "Black Mountain Blues." He pulled his hands completely away from Adeline and rested his head in his palms. How could a woman that young know that much? He felt the urge to get closer to her, to touch her for just a second, so some magic might help him do what he had to. As she thanked the audience, Alfie rose to his feet and nodded to her. She lifted her guitar in salute and strode off stage. Adeline twisted her mouth and spoke only to J.P., who seemed also in awe.

"She is somethin'."

"I suppose," Adeline said, as the applause died. "If you like the country-gal type."

J.P. grunted, and Adeline made a proposition.

"How about we head to Loudmouth Night?"

J.P. looked from Adeline to Alfie.

"You want to tell him what it is?"

Adeline twisted her mouth again.

"No, that would ruin the surprise."

She led the group out and down the street to a big corner bar with a wood panel-framed and tinted front window. Inside, a long-haired priest stood in a slapdash pulpit on a balcony above the audience. A dark-haired woman in a party dress handed him a wooden crate with the word "SOAP" painted on it in red. The priest lifted the box over his head and the audience called out, "Amen."

"Our former virgin, Mary, will now call the first reverend of the evening."

"You," she said. "Father."

The priest brushed back his gray hair like a movie actress granting an interview.

"Of course. How could I forget?"

He rested his hands on the podium and glared at the audience from on high.

"I want to talk to all of you."

"Preach!" a shaggy beatnik standing next to Alfie yelled.

"I say I want to speak to all of you about the language you have so used and abused in memory of my bygone friends. You must hear yourselves speaking a language you claim to be your own, which indeed you know has sprung forth from the lips of men and women whom I will not call your betters, but your elders. So many of those expressions you would say are hip are only formerly so. How can it be that you wallow in phrases such as 'The Outside World' when the world has come to us? The world is inside. Inside this city and inside us, and it may be a poison introduced by the government or men on the moon or your own mothers and fathers, but we have drunk deep of this poison. And you must believe a man of the cloth when he speaks to you about poisoning and about the common language of the common man. What do you call them? Still call them? Oh, yes. Squares. The language of the squares. Are you squares, my children?"

"NOOOO!"

"Children, in the blessed names of Duncan and Ginsberg and Kerouac and all the faithful departed Californios, are you part of the machine that gave us The Bomb?"

"NOOOO!"

"Alas, my children, I disbelieve you. Do I see rockets in your pockets?"

"NOOOO!"

"Do I see so-called beatniks in the place of true beatitude and rhythm?"

"NOOOO!"

"Let me see then what you are!"

The priest leaned half his body over the railing and scanned the crowd with beady eyes, then leaned back and pounded the podium.

"I have seen the light you have seen, that signal that called you from many corners of Squaresville and entered you and in doing so became the artifact of cool, which you brought here with you like a treasure to live upon as you wander these streets and enter these halls and discover that many of the poets and prophets are already gone."

The crowd booed.

"I heard they're coming back," somebody yelled.

"That may be. They do get around. Perhaps then I am judging too harshly, and of course only one being is qualified to judge and he sits at the right hand of Buddha."

The priest did a double-take at his own vestments, and laughter racked the room. It broke a spell that had overtaken Alfie. He started to observe the faces around him, including Adeline's, their twisted grins and snorts. They were demons, everywhere.

"I have seen you all, and seen the light, and I will tell you what you are!"

"Tell us! Preach!"

"You are paying customers!"

"Hooray!" J.P. hollered, raising a glass of Scotch.

"And to you, my good people, I cede the floor. But before I do I must remind you that anyone attempting to read a poem here will be cast into flame. But there will be no talk of the flame when this man speaks, for he is Mister Barney Gargle."

A short man, youthful and flabby, wearing a top hat, waddled up the stairs and mounted the soapbox. He smoked a cigar and talked out of the side of his mouth. He grumbled as much as talked.

"Cats and chicks, our troubles are over. Our troubles are over. And I'll tell ya. Can I tell ya? I'll tell ya the solution. I have the solution. In fact, it is a solution. And the solution is here."

He lifted a mug of suds.

"The solution is here. The solution is beer. But you'll say to yourself, 'Here is beer, so what?' Here, yes. Here's your beer. But, really, it's *my* beer. I paid for it, and you can't have it. But what if there were one place in San Fran where anybody could walk up and get a beer for free. How would you dig that then, my brothers and sisters?"

The crowd cheered.

"Here's what I say. I say free beer for everybody!"

Another cheer.

"I say we need a public supply, in a place everybody knows. A place where everybody knows to go. A place everybody can see from anywhere. So there's just one place I'm thinking of. Just one place. And that place is the Tower. The Coit Tower. Our beloved tower. That's the place for our fountain. A beautiful fountain. A beautiful fountain of beer! Ya hear?"

More hooting and hollering.

"But you might say, 'Barney, there's no fountain at the Tower. What are you talking about, a fountain at the Tower?' And I'm saying to you, Man, the Tower is a fountain. We can make it a fountain. It just takes a little American ingenuity. A little ingenuity. A little bit of tubing. With tubing we can do it. We'll run tubing to the top and shoot the beer up, and it'll come down like rain on the beautiful cats and chicks of this fair, fair city. You'll catch it in buckets. I promise you that. I promise you that. I promise."

Barney bounced off the soapbox and raised a hand in triumph as he joined the crowd, which was moving now, bubbling like a pot of boiling water. Every second a new face bobbed past, but not Adeline's. He searched the room and caught a glimpse of her by the bar. She was tipping back a drink, next to some skinny malink, whose little round glasses looked like they were fused to his nose. Alfie huffed.

"She'll come back."

J.P.'s heavy arm fell across his shoulders.

"She has plenty of friends here. She's a sociable gal. Tell me again. How do you know her?"

The answer didn't have to be a lie exactly.

"We grew up in the same neighborhood. Our families were close."

"Good to keep up ties. I wish I could've done that with my old gang, but they all went the other way. Never questioned anything."

Is that what made a beatnik, questions? Everybody had questions, but not everybody needed to ask them out loud. J.P. lit a cigarette and offered one that Alfie refused.

"Anyway, if she's your gal or will be, she's a good one. Much more than a doll."

"I know."

"Glad. She deserves good treatment, and she hasn't exactly been getting it from these gin mill cowboys around here."

The priest's voice rang from the pulpit again.

"My people, I mentioned before the blessed names of the great ones who once graced this altar. Now I bring to the altar two young men who are doing all they can to help us remember them, doing their damnedest to channel their beautiful souls. Those beautiful souls, these souls, this duo also from the east, Finkelman and Fourier."

A loud boo diluted the applause. To Alfie's surprise, it came from J.P. himself, hands circling his mouth, letting loose like a foghorn. When he ran out of air, he grabbed Alfie and spoke in his ear.

"These two make me want to re-enlist."

Finkelman's thin, straight black hair escaped his bowler hat in every direction, and he wore a tight vest over a striped shirt. He was a cross between Charlie Chaplin and Emmett Kelly. Fourier wore a ponytail and a long dark brown beard. His hair looked like it weighed more than he did. He dressed like an accountant: short-sleeve, button-down shirt, chinos, and loafers. In one hand he held an unlit pipe, in the other, a notebook. Finkelman reached over and flipped the notebook open.

"Here," he shouted at Fourier. "Start right here."

Fourier arched his back and spoke.

"Consumerism is consuming the young people of America."

"Oh, America," Finkelman whined, "when will you give your young consumers peace?"

He raised an index finger in the air and was about to say more when Fourier interrupted.

"Do you want me to answer?"

Finkelman acted bothered.

"Answer what?"

"Well, the question you just asked."

"My question?"

"Your question."

"But, listen, Jack, that was just my jive."

"Your jive?"

"My means to an end. You could say my modus operandi?"

"Do we need a modus operandi?"

"I believe we do, and I can tell you and this whole audience why. Because we are talking about bread, the getting and spending of bread on bread we'll never eat. Oh, America!"

J.P. launched another vicious boo, this one so long and loud that Finkelman and Fourier had to acknowledge the source. As soon as he got their attention, he unloaded.

"You two remind me of a couple of fellas used to come here a while back. You know who I mean?"

A woman with blond hair down to her waist stepped in front of J.P. and poked him in the chest.

"Why can't you get off their case? They're just here to speak."

The club door opened with a squeal, and a breeze blew across the room. J.P. sidestepped the woman and kept up the assault.

"If we're ever gonna get somewhere, we need to get past 1956. What do you say, Gents?"

Fourier surveyed the audience for the source of J.P.'s voice.

"Hey, whoever you think you are, you should know that 1963 is just another number for the powers-that-be, rhyming, I think, with Kenn-eh-dee, to put up in lights, to say things aren't what they always make them out to be, unless we say no. Say no to 1963!"

How could anyone winging it like this believe even half of his own bullshit? When people said words had power, Alfie always thought they meant power over other people, but words had even more power over the people who spoke them. And maybe that went for the people who wrote them. And maybe Adeline believed too much of what she wrote, whatever that was. Why hadn't she ever shown it to him? Did people like these dirty queers on the stage understand any better than he did? Suddenly, Alfie felt ashamed of the words in his head. His own brother was queer. Did it bother him a little? Sure. But it wasn't the reason they didn't get along. Other things about his brother got on his nerves, mostly that Frankie was getting away with something Alfie couldn't. Like whatever he did was all right. That's the way these two clowns on stage struck Alfie, too, like what they said had no consequences, and they knew it.

"It's a shame you have to listen to these folks while you're on vacation."

J.P.'s voice snapped Alfie out of his haze. The big man was looking down into the cloudy glass that held the last of his drink. Alfie answered absent-mindedly.

"I'm not here on vacation."

J.P. gave him a funny look, like he should explain himself. But what could Alfie say? You couldn't call chasing someone across the country a vacation. He wouldn't go back home and feel refreshed, would he? He'd go back home and feel … what?

"More like an adventure, I suppose," J.P. said.

Alfie pointed at him.

"That's it. Guilty."

"No need to feel guilty, Friend. We all need it. Hell, that's why I joined up with Uncle Sam."

Alfie couldn't remember anymore why he'd joined. Fort Riley was just Adeline now, just like Brooklyn had been Adeline, just like San Francisco would be Adeline. All different versions of her. If he wasn't careful, the whole country and then the world would be Adeline. Adeline in the trees. Adeline in the clouds. Adeline in the grass. Adeline in the waves. He could sing to her and hear the echo for the rest of his life. Her breath would follow him like the smoke that swallowed him as the night wore on. She'd be everywhere at once and no two places at the same time. The thought of her name all over the map made him dizzy. He could use a drink, and was about to hit the bar, where he could still see the outline of her shoulders and hair, and next to her still the malink in the black sweater and dark glasses. Alfie was headed toward the skinny void when the door of the place slammed open with a crash. A brawny cop in blues filled the entrance. He could've been Ernest Borgnine's brother. The same shitty grin. Friendly and frightening. But this Borgnine had a prizefighter's shape. His raised arm didn't taper. He shuffled side to side, like he couldn't wait to bust out of his corner. He was about to take charge and he knew it. Boom went his voice.

"This, ladies and ladies, as you know, is a raid."

J.P. put an arm around Alfie's shoulder.

"You have such happenings back in Brooklyn?"

Alfie had seen plenty of police action, but raids seemed like something from his father's day.

"That behemoth in the doorway is Biagini. He enjoys social order, and, well, he thinks what we're up to here doesn't qualify. It might be best if we found another exit."

J.P. strode toward the back, but Alfie was distracted by the sight of Adeline. The malink had her by the arm and was pushing open a metal door to the side street, literally dragging her out. Alfie bolted toward them, knocking people over as he ran through wisps of smoke. He grabbed Adeline's other arm as she was about to disappear. He expected to see tears, but she turned to him with a hard face.

"Let me go."

Alfie relaxed his grip.

"Who's the asshole?"

"Not now. Let me go."

She grunted, twisting away from the malink, who made a move to grab her again until he saw Alfie looming. She reached over and lifted Alfie's hand, then planted a stillborn kiss on his cheek.

"Trust me," she said. "I'll be back."

On the narrow sidewalk outside the bar, people brushed past, most of them younger than Alfie, laughing, waving cigarettes, acting like the city had been built just for them. A stream of headlights lit the avenue and the twisted trees with white bark and sheeny leaves that lined the sidewalk. They shielded walkers from a dark dome of night sky that chilled the air. Alfie hadn't expected the cold. Shivering slightly, he started in the direction of Adeline's apartment, passing a bookstore with a display that filled its front window. Above the splayed books hung a sign: "All Books in the Window Have Been Censored or Repressed." Yet here they were. And here he was. He hadn't come with the idea of taking Adeline back home. He'd given that up after Kansas. But here he was, and she'd said she'd be back. Normally, if a girl told him something like that, under these circumstances, he'd be gone. Of course, nothing about this whole town seemed normal, except the names of the streets: Columbus, Broadway, Greenwich, Green, Grant, Union, Filbert, Chestnut. Okay, there were a couple of oddballs like Vallejo and Francisco, but they were just normal Spanish names. And then what was normal about the way he lived back home? Or about this little trip? Normally, a man up to something like this might wonder what his wife was thinking. God forgive him, but he gave less than a shit. Michelle's face could be the face of any of these women passing him. As Alfie walked, he began to feel tired. At Union Street, he came to a park. Two white steeples topped the trees. Under the trees people on benches talked low. He spotted an empty bench and sat down. Alone on another bench lit by streetlamp sat an old man, his legs out and shoulders back, like he was waiting for a train to take him to some village in Italy. A brown fedora crowned his huge forehead. His face was craggy as the bark of the tree that spread its gnarled branches behind him. Next to him lay a folded newspaper. As Alfie watched, the old man reached into his shirt pocket and pulled out a piece of Italian bread. He tore an even smaller piece off and tossed it on the path in front of his bench. The night didn't stop a pigeon from swooping out of nowhere and gobbling it up. The old man tore off another piece, threw it, and waited again for a bird. Maybe the old man had waited a long time for the woman he loved, then lost her. Or he'd found out she wasn't what he'd wanted. In Brooklyn, the old Italian men sat together on benches, too, and played bocce or checkers in the park. Their lives revolved around concrete tables. Or they sat at café tables and ate the pastries their wives told them they shouldn't eat. Their wives, if they hadn't already buried their wives, were home cooking or watching their programs or having coffee with their *goomads*, complaining about their husbands. The sound of cathedral bells interrupted Alfie's reverie. They tolled eleven, late for an old man, who must have read Alfie's mind as he smiled, tossed the last of his bread, picked up his newspaper, tipped his cap Alfie's way, and hobbled bow-legged down a park path. Alfie got up and followed him briefly around a semi-circle before losing him in the darkness.

By the time Alfie reached Chestnut Street, he was ready to close his eyes. He trudged uphill, stopping at each cross, to look out at the obscure bay and shadows of mountains in the distance. As he climbed he hoped that the tower would come into view and pull him forward, but it stayed hidden behind other buildings. When he finally reached Adeline's door, he decided to ring first. When nobody answered, he let himself in and collapsed on the old couch.

He dreamt that he was drifting on a raft, drifting out to sea, watching the land, the continent, everything he'd ever known, shrink and disappear. Then he heard thunder, and waves began rolling his raft up toward the red sky and down again into blue canyons. He was holding on for dear life, when beads of sweat on his face tickled him awake. He opened his eyes to Adeline, her face a few inches from his, her thin fingers stroking his cheek.

"I'm back."

She spoke so slowly and softly that she seemed to be trying to remember how to speak at all. Alfie looked at his watch. Just after five. The darkness outside the bay window had faded to gray.

"You are."

"Move over."

She lay down and pressed her body into his. This was the first time he'd held her so close. Her hair smelled like marijuana. He wanted to say something before she fell sleep, but then he started thinking about Viv, about her body and her hands, how she acted like she was in control. She would turn to face him, touch him all over. Her hands would mold him like clay. Should he do the same to Adeline? He rested a hand on her shoulder and resigned himself to keeping still and drifting off. He felt Adeline push her body deeper into the cushion. She pulled his arm over her shoulder and cradled his hand in hers, then whispered, "Tomorrow."

Sunlight and women's voices woke him. He was alone again, cheek stuck to couch leather. The voices rose to a pitch, then went quiet. A few more minutes passed before Adeline appeared in the doorway, fresh as a little girl on Christmas morning. She entered the room, wearing a yellow dress with black polka dots, holding a white sun hat in her hands.

"Get dressed," she told Alfie. "I borrowed a car."

A little while later they were driving an old Ford convertible over the bridge to Oakland. The bay and its cities and towns stretched out in all directions. There was no way to measure the landscape. To get his balance, Alfie stared at Adeline's profile: still perfect, especially when she wore sunglasses and a headscarf. The corner of her smiling mouth was turned up, like her nose, and her cheeks were red in the breeze. Smiling, they sailed into Oakland, passing tall buildings and snaking through tight neighborhoods until they took the exit for Berkeley. Adeline pointed up and down the wide avenue in front of them.

They parked among the downtown brick buildings, which, except for the palm trees around them, looked like they belonged in New York. Adeline led him to a bookstore with an awning the color of her dress.

"This is one of my favorite places."

Alfie read the lettering.

"Print and Mint. Moe's Books."

"Moe's a prize," she said, holding open the door.

How many fellas could one woman have in her life?

Inside the store were more books than you could read in fifty lifetimes. Books on shelves lining the walls from floor to ceiling. Books stacked on tables and under them. Books in the aisles. Books next to the cash register. It made you wonder why anybody would want to spend time writing a book. What were the odds that anybody would read it? You had a better shot with a song. Near the register, a tall, balding man with glasses, wearing a lilac shirt and smoking a cigar, was sliding books onto one of the high shelves. He could have been one of Alfie's uncles. Adeline went up to him and tugged his sleeve. The man turned around with a puss that made you think she'd interrupted his dinner, but when he saw it was Adeline, he smiled.

"Ah, Sweethaahht!"

Yet another New York accent.

Adeline was beaming now.

"What's new, Moe?"

"New? Nothing's ever new. It's the same problems in different packages."

He looked at Alfie.

"Who's this?"

"This is Alfie. He's from Brooklyn, too."

Moe shook Alfie's hand and pulled him in for a hug.

"The sacred borough of my birth."

He reached into his pants pocket and took out a wrapped cigar.

"Can I offer?"

"No, thanks."

"There's so much trouble in the world that, believe me, my friend, you need to drink and smoke a little. Because," he explained, pointing now at Adeline, "you can't run away from trouble. You can try, but it stalks you. I came out here when I quit all the hub-bub of New York. I wanted a nice, quiet life."

He took a few quick puffs.

"Little did I know they argue more here than they did in Brooklyn. And you know what? They're right to do it. They read. They know the problems. And now I shelve books all day."

Moe extended an arm in front of Alfie.

"Look at this elbow. It kills me. Constantly. And it looks like a wire hanger."

Adeline took his wrist and lowered his arm the way a nurse would for her patient.

"You wouldn't have it any other way."

Moe kissed her forehead.

"You see this girl. A true spirit. To the true spirits the world is always happening. Always happening and overwhelming. Everything has a meaning, but the meanings aren't clear. For example, they close Alcatraz. Then you have bombings, strikes, demonstrations down south. The British government is going to hell. We're flying spaceships to Venus. What does it all mean? Where is it taking us?"

He ran to a table near the front and waved them over.

"Look, have you read this yet?"

He held up a book with a plain black cover and a title in bold red letters. The author had a French name Alfie couldn't quite make out.

"*Planet of the Apes*," Adeline read.

She took the book and flipped it over, reading the back cover and looking unimpressed.

"I know, you might say, 'Moe, it's only science fiction.' But I'm telling you, this guy's got it right."

Alfie leaned over Adeline's shoulder and pretended to read the back cover with her. She laid the book back on the table. Moe picked it up and insisted, "Take it."

Adeline hemmed and hawed, but eventually slipped the book into her shoulder bag.

"Okay. Enough of that. You two look like you were having a nice day. Let's change the subject."

"Moe, tell Alfie where you're from in Brooklyn?"

"Brighton Beach, home of the happy Jews. 'Happy why?' you might ask."

He winked at Alfie.

"Who wouldn't be happy with family, everybody's family, around, good food like you never find here, and the ocean on top of it? You could walk to Coney Island. In fact, that's where I got my start, working the booths. My uncle owned a concession."

Moe told the story like he'd been waiting all day to tell it.

"He loved how I handled the customers, and one day he said, 'Kid, why don't you go into acting?' And me, a schmuck, I listened. That's how I got to Broadway, though not exactly Broadway. But I was on stage for a while. A while. And after a while around other actors, I had to admit to myself I was no good. No, what I really had to admit was I had no money and I was cold half the year. Oh, how I hated the winter. Then I read an article about California, and the rest you can guess."

He picked up another book and held it in the air.

"But I'm still a performer, just like you." He pointed to Adeline. "Remember, no matter what they tell you about being genuine and truthful, we're all performers. Shakespeare said it. I'm saying it. All this," he said, surveying the expanse of his store, "is an illusion. Like all the other illusions: locking people up, sending people into government, sending people into space. They send us. We send ourselves."

Adeline took the cue.

"I'm sending myself back to school."

"School? What school? Berkeley? A girl like you?"

"Not this school. A school I'm still searching for. When I find it, Moe, I'll write a book, and you'll sell it. And what do you mean by a girl like me?"

Moe chewed his cigar as he considered the question.

"A girl who seems to know what she wants. Most of the kids around here couldn't tell you what they want for dinner."

She glanced at Alfie.

"What makes you think I know what I want?"

Moe plucked the cigar and held it in front of his face.

"A man like me doesn't know too much, but I do know when a woman knows what she wants."

Adeline smiled a smile that pulled her skin tight as a mask.

"These are impressions I get," Moe explained. "They might be illusions too, of course, but then every illusion is an impression of life. It's my illusion and I want it to help you. Some help, some hurt, these illusions. I don't like the ones that hurt, the ones that mislead, if you know what I mean. That's why the sign over there says 'Toilet,' not 'Bathroom.' No one's bathing in my book store."

Moe's voice fell to a dramatic baritone.

"No one is absolved here."

He walked to the counter and pulled a wrapped sandwich from the space below. He unwrapped it and took a healthy bite, which he sent down with a gulp of coffee from a stained mug. Adeline browsed the tables around the register, while Moe signaled Alfie to join him. He leaned over and half-whispered in the younger man's ear.

"You like this girl?"

Alfie didn't know what to say, so he nodded.

"Sure. If you're lucky, someday you'll walk around complaining about her. I complain about my wife every day."

Moe smiled warmly and pointed down an aisle toward another wall of books.

"Look around. Take one. If you don't find something you like, then you don't like books."

Books had cast a spell on Adeline. They wanted her time and her life. They told her to ignore what was most important. Moe shook his hand, then disappeared into a back room. Alfie let the book offer go and stepped outside. Adeline's sunglasses were already on when she came out and took him by the arm.

"Let's go," she said. "We're heading for the hills."

They drove around the front of a big campus until they reached a gate. Past the gate a road wound its way halfway up the high hill that hemmed the campus in. They parked in a visitors' lot and walked along a treelined path to a small green near a monumental clock tower. From a bench on the green they could see across the bay to San Francisco and the Golden Gate. The sun was high, but it slipped behind the clouds often enough to cool the afternoon. With her hair down now, Adeline looked like a student, as though she belonged here, enjoying a view of the land that was as far as you could get from home. They could find a house in the hills and live here on the edge of a strange world.

"That little island over there is Alameda," she said, pointing, "a military base, and then right across of course is San Fran. And over to the right, across the Golden Gate, that's Marin, which is a place we should go. It's almost like being in Europe. Or at least that's what people here like to say."

Alfie looked one way and then another, nodding his approval. He took her hand, staring at her until she lowered her sunglasses.

"It's beautiful."

"I'm so glad you like it. Maybe you think I'm a little less crazy now."

"I never thought you were crazy."

She took off her glasses and slipped them into her bag.

"About what happened last night."

He touched her arm.

"You don't have to tell me anything. I'm just here to see you."

"I know. I'm thrilled you're here."

Alfie half-chuckled.

"You've been gone a while."

"I know. And sometimes I feel like I'll die alone in California. The people here want the best of you, but they don't seem to have much time for the worst."

Alfie chuckled more deliberately.

"So you need me to hear the worst?"

"No, believe me, plenty of people here know the worst. But there's a difference between knowing and wanting to know."

Her eyes gleamed like her father's. A gleam that said she might know what you were thinking, and that the information she gave you next depended on that intelligence. She didn't want to give you anything you could turn against her, because then you might take something she could never get back. It was the look of someone who was used to striking a bargain.

"There are some beautiful little towns up the coast. You hear the ocean all day, and you feel free, like no one's watching you and you can be exactly who you want to be."

"You like the ocean that much, huh?"

"Come on. You remember how much I liked Long Island, and even Coney Island. Moe calls it the Crown Jewel of the Barbary Coast."

She extended her legs and let her shoes drop to the ground, then rubbed her feet in the grass as though she were trying to bury them.

"San Francisco is wonderful, but it's disappearing. Not actually disappearing. It's slipping away from all those people you met last night. They all went there to get away, but once you're there, away disappears, and they find out that they're back where they started. The world is still watching, except that it doesn't care anymore. Only the other people in the city care, and they're more or less like the people everywhere else: They only care that what you do isn't bothering them."

It bothered Alfie that somebody as smart as Adeline needed to come all the way across the country to find this out. Outside your family—and you couldn't always be sure about them—who could you expect to give a shit?

"I think Jonathan cared about me. Like I said, he saved me, in a certain way."

He wanted to shake her.

"I'll bet you didn't need to be saved."

She leaned forward and plucked a few blades of grass, then tossed them into the wind.

"Don't be so sure."

"Whatever you need," he said, allowing a note of hopelessness to color his voice.

She looked at him as though she wanted to cry, then stood up and took a deep breath.

"This is such a beautiful day. We can swap troubles some other time."

The sun came out full blast again, daring them to keep sitting in the open. They moved to shade, strolling a path flanked by gigantic pine trees. The familiar scent relaxed Alfie. She wasn't asking him to do anything he didn't want to do. Not exactly. They understood each other. They didn't need to speak as they looked out over the hills and listened to each other's breath, holding hands as lightly as they could.

A few hours later they were staring at a black wall. Every wall in the place was black. Everyone around them was wearing black. Some wore black eye make-up, and a lot of them had long, dark hair that glistened in the hard light of naked bulbs suspended from the black ceiling by thin chains. The music surprised Alfie. It was a country version of "Mona Lisa," up-tempo, and it made people jerk around

like they were plugged into the same outlets as the bulbs. Alfie
knew that Adeline could dance, but now she just swayed, her black
dress hugging her body. She was half in the bag before they'd even
left the apartment. By the time he'd gotten dressed and ready, she
and Viv had put away a whole bottle of red and were about to open
another when he appeared and they both said almost like they'd rehearsed it, "Oh, good!" As soon as they'd gotten to the club, Viv had
faded into the darkness, leaving him and Adeline in the middle of
this black room that had no furniture, just what passed for works of
art on pedestals, each of them under a homemade cone light fixture
that mimicked a spotlight. The closest pedestal to them supported
two white ceramic hands, one waving and one giving the finger. As
Alfie walked closer to it, Adeline grabbed his arm.

"Don't touch."

Just as she was scolding him, a man taller than Alfie brushed
past. He stopped for a moment next to the middle finger sculpture, where the spotlight showed he was wearing a black suit with a
yellow tie, his arm draped over a girl who looked a couple of years
underage. He grinned at Alfie through a full beard, then vanished
into the sleek crowd. A few people around him whispered the name
Bobby Dark.

"His joint."

"Great place if he ever opened it."

"Born lazy."

"Slave to the habit."

Bobby had gotten Adeline's attention. Her eyes followed him
and his companion into the recesses of the room.

"You know him?"

Adeline slurred an answer Alfie didn't catch. His father had
taught him to recognize all the shades of drunkenness. At this
point Adeline wasn't completely gone. With a little effort, she could
still focus.

"Everybody knows him. He used his family money to open a
gallery, The Bat."

She leaned sideways and pointed toward the door. "It's next door. And then he opened The Cave, this place. It's more for happenings and little concerts, and on a night like tonight, readings."

"So, a lot of these people, you know them?"

She rolled her eyes around the room.

"A few."

"Why is everybody wearing black?"

She turned to him, scowling, arms folded.

"Don't you remember why? Did you forget about being a musician?"

Alfie didn't answer. The muscles in his neck tightened up, so he had to lean his head back for relief. What did she know about being a musician? Not every musician was Johnny Cash, and it was only a couple of times Alfie could remember playing to an audience all in black. He didn't care too much about it then, so why should he care now? But this scene still annoyed him, like the whole crowd had made a pact to act the same. Some of the couples shared the same eye make-up and wore the exact same clothes. When you saw them walk past, you might think you were seeing double. And here was Adeline, who wanted to tell him about being free, wearing a dress so thin that it looked like one of their great-aunt's funeral veils.

"They wear black, Alfie, because they think the culture we live in is, um, what's the word? ... deadly."

Her voice trailed off as she pronounced the last word.

"Dea-TH-ly," I mean. "They think it's rigid, like a corpse, and it's killing us. And, if you ask me ..."

She seemed to get more drunk as she spoke, even though they hadn't yet reached the bar.

"If you ask me, they're also mourning the loss of their selves, what made them themselves before they stepped away. Away from the mainstream and started looking for something."

This sounded like horseshit, and if he thought she believed it, he would tell her so. Instead, he told her what he now realized he was here to say.

"You can come home with me."

She froze, then looked away,

"I couldn't do that. Not because of you, but you'd be going back to a wife and child. And of course ..."

"I thought Bohemians—excuse me—artists didn't care about that."

The alcohol was wearing off.

"That's a lie. Half of these people are married. Or they will be in a year or two."

Alfie exaggerated another look around the room, then mugged.

"I guess you'll know what color clothes to buy their babies."

Adeline let a snorty laugh slip. He laid his hands on her shoulders.

"Look, I'm not here to tell you what to do. You wouldn't listen to me, anyway."

"That's right," she said, backing away. "But I do want to talk to you about something. It's important, but I just need ..."

"What?"

"I have to see first."

"See what?"

"See to see. I promise you'll understand."

Before he could follow up, the nearest wall started to move.

Adeline recognized Alfie's confusion.

"Bobby built movable walls. They fold, too. He even puts out chalk, so people can write on them."

One wall on the move read "Touch. Don't Touch." Sure, but the why was missing. Then again, the why was always missing. Why were all these little masterpieces meant to shock people? Who were they supposed to be pushing away? The country was in good shape. There was no war. Nothing major. And everybody here looked like they were eating okay. There were problems, sure, but most of the problems that mattered were the ones you made for yourself.

Adeline tugged him along.

"Let's look around. A lot of these installations are new. Here, look."

Alfie read the small placard on the pedestal: "Black Dahlia"

The thing, because it wasn't strictly a painting or a sculpture, hung from the ceiling by a string. It was a police photo of a girl who had been murdered. Her body was cut in two pieces. The focus was on the lower half, which was wearing a black belt. A long bird feather was stuck to one side of the photo. Under it was a black stocking stuffed with condoms, cigarettes, a compact mirror, loose hair, and a pocket knife. The picture itself had nails driven through it, into a piece of wood. Adeline's hand hovered over the photo.

"Who killed her, I wonder?"

Watching Adeline's face go blank, Alfie felt a chill and backed away. Other conversations drifted into earshot.

"Saigon will drag us down."

"*Gone in Saigon,*" someone sang.

"American imperialism at its finest."

"The police state wants vacation property."

"Here's all the vacation I need. Take one. Take a Mickey Mouse."

"I hate Mickey Mouse. How about a Buddha?"

"Whatever melts your butter, Jim."

"I'm melllltting! I'm meeelllllltting!"

"And Hoover is always watching."

Alfie pulled Adeline toward him again.

A voice yelled from the dark.

"We're about to start! On your marks."

Behind them a spotlight popped on, lighting Bobby Dark parked in front of the kind of microphone Sinatra would've used in his younger days.

"Get set. Go, Man, go."

Dark stepped away and a malink, bonier than the one who'd taken Adeline away, appeared at the mic. He stood there, looking over the crowd like he was waiting for them to quiet down, which, when they finally did, cued him. He spoke in bursts.

"The FBI and other forces are coming."

Ten seconds of silence.

"For you and the people you love."

The easy weight of Adeline leaning into him.

"They will try to hunt you down."

Pressing closer.

"The way a hundred years ago they tried."

Murmurs.

"They tried to hunt the Mormons down."

A few giggles.

"They did hunt the Indians down."

Quiet again.

"Because they wouldn't buy in."

A low hum.

"And that is why you should join me."

Silence.

"Join me and join ARF."

More silence, and a trembling from Adeline as she giggled.

"ARF: The Association of Rat Fucks."

A cheer.

"I am a rat fuck."

"Yes, you are!"

"I have sworn myself to the protection of all rats, everyone who society sees as dangerous."

A louder cheer.

"And we are a haven for rat fucks like all of you."

Adeline's voice ran from giddy to hard in one sentence.

"I guess I'm a rat fuck, Alfie. At least in Brooklyn."

She didn't have to swear. But then maybe all women like her swore and he'd have to get used to it. He laid his hand on the small of her back and let it wander lower, hoping she'd notice and hoping she wouldn't. The crowd's yelling died, and she turned her head to look at Alfie's wayward hand and then at Alfie, doing nothing at first about either. Then, her eyes straight ahead, she reached back, stroked his forearm and removed the hand from her backside.

Before Alfie had time to be ashamed, the chief rat fuck popped up in his face.

"This I give unto you."

He handed Alfie a square of paper with a picture of Goofy printed on it.

"What's this?"

The malink moved on without answering, and like magic Viv appeared in his wake.

"If you don't know what that's for, King Bee, give it to me."

She plucked the paper from his fingers and pressed it slowly into the front pocket of her snug dungarees, extending a leg so it brushed Alfie's thigh.

"Something else to show you later."

Adeline watched the little scene as though she and Viv had planned it. He shouldn't think that way, but then he didn't know how or what to think anymore. Viv locked arms with both of them.

"So do tell, kittens, is all of this art? Or are all these Jacks and Jills just stoned beyond redemption?"

She laughed at her own joke, then sashayed away with her arms open to someone she'd spotted at the next pedestal. Alfie side-eyed her figure as she went, wishing he could keep his eyes only on Adeline.

"Ho!"

A little troll at the mic was hollering.

"I say hey-ho!"

"Hey-ho!" the crowd called back.

"Try a cento on for size, like so:
(raising himself on tiptoes)

"And life slips by like a field mouse
that has no language, coursing
beneath the quiet heaven of
your eyes."

(exhaling into the microphone)

"The deepest feeling always shows itself in silence
where nobody gets old and godly and grave.
I don't want to go on as a root and a tomb.
Happy people die whole."

(crouching, then returning to, for what it was worth, full height)

"My lips are now burning and everywhere.
What are all these kissings worth
if thou kiss not me?"

(with mock trembling lips)

"Women know when love is over."

(applause from the women in the room)

"I wanted you, nameless Woman of the South.
no poetic fantasy
but a biological reality
'cause I ain't got nobody
and nobody cares for me."

(curtseying, backing away, goodbye)

He wasn't the only one asking for love or what people called
love. An Italian-looking girl took the mic. She threw her long black
hair over one shoulder, ran her hands over her hips, and spoke loud
and nasally.

"Touch. Do Not Touch.
Leave. Do Not Leave.
Breathe. Do Not Breathe.
Live. Do Not Live.

Here is one thing
you should never do.
Here is one thing
I have done."

She stamped a heavy foot on the plank floor.

"I have seen. I have not seen.
My eyes took on
a life of their own
and my eyes left me.
My eyes were breathing
on their own, then
living on their own,
then, they made a baby
on their own, and this
was a vision, and this
I could name or deny.
This vision led me
around by the nose.
You can see how big
my nose is, as big
as my vision, and so
I see. I do not see
beyond my nose,
but I pretend my vision
sees for me, and that."

The girl lifted her mane back over both shoulders and let it
veil her face as she took a bow and walked off. Adeline nodded as
Bobby Dark reappeared at the mic, spotting her and motioning for
her to come up.
    "Speaking of beautiful, groovy chicks with vision …"
    Adeline sidled her way to the stand. Someone whistled. A male
voice over his shoulder made a remark. Another voice laughed.

"I want to dedicate these little poems—very little, I promise—
to a friend from far away."

She raised her chin toward Alfie and closed her eyes. He heard
sighs. Off to the side Viv was shushing people.

"I also want to thank Ronald."

She visored her eyes with one hand and scanned the room.

"Is he here?"

Somebody yelled the name. Nobody yelled back.

"Either way I want to thank him for printing these in *Wings*."

She tilted back her head.

"The needle pricks me
like a divine thorn cast off
by the dying rose."

A clap from Viv's direction.

"I have offered you
my body..."

Some schmuck in the back couldn't resist.

"Thank you!"

Adeline closed her eyes.

"I have offered you
my body, my leaking blood
to keep you alive.
Blood is the color of sex
and the violence
of forgetting through the veins.
Veins are open doors
we enter to lives we wish
we could call our own."

Adeline's blood was Alfie's blood. She was laying open her veins for
people who would bleed her. A few of these people in the crowd
applauded, but most restarted their conversations as though they'd
barely noticed what she'd said. Alfie got the feeling that most
of them paid attention only to themselves or to the people they
wanted to get in bed. But then he could be thinking about himself,
or, he could convince himself, thinking about himself the way he
used to be. He watched Adeline's face for any sign of the truth. She
stood there stony, until Dark tapped her on the shoulder and led
her away. Alfie watched them as they disappeared through a door
Dark slammed shut behind them. He tried to follow, but the door
was locked. If this character built walls that weren't walls, maybe he
built rooms that weren't rooms. Maybe he was taking Adeline to
his personal sex dungeon. Then they'd come back like nothing happened and it didn't matter. That was probably the Bohemian way.

A half-hour passed, then another. No Adeline. No Viv. Nobody
he knew. Fuck it. Alfie pushed through a forest of dangling cigarettes. Voices around him chattered in a foreign language about
"blastin' crap" and "beatin' the gravel" and "coppin' a bit" and "turnin'
on" and "wiggin' out." The front door was a rumor, until he blew
through a cloud of smoke and onto the sidewalk of a narrow street.
It was packed with Bohemians, white and black, huddled in little
groups or leaning against walls, some walking up and down like
they were on patrol. Alfie dodged his way to the curb, where he
took a deep breath. It was a cool, still night. Cars crawled by, their
windows open or tops down. He needed to walk and clear his mind.
It was a strange neighborhood. He'd have to keep track of his route.
Across the street and down the block was a movie theater. He'd
go that way. The theater was showing an Elvis movie, *It Happened
at the World's Fair*. His father had just started working on one of
the World's Fair pavilions in New York, "The World of Tomorrow."
Alfie walked into the light of the movie marquee and looked at the
poster. It showed a tower that looked like a spaceship. Elvis stood
next to the tower, big as Godzilla, in a gold jacket, playing his guitar and singing. Below that a smaller Elvis was kissing a redhead.

A ribbon across the poster advertised the "hit" song "One Broken Heart for Sale." Even Elvis could lose his touch.

At the corner a blind man, maybe ten years older than Alfie and wearing a filthy black jacket and torn chinos, was reaching out to people as they passed. Two pretty teenage girls approached him.

"What's shakin', Dad?" one of them asked, giggling.

"Young lady, I could use help to get across the street."

The girls kept walking. Alfie grabbed the man's arm.

"This way."

The man thanked him, and they started across, when Alfie noticed a commotion in the middle of the intersection. Traffic was completely stopped. Drivers leaned on their horns. In the middle of it all was a familiar character: Ron, the crazy colored poet. He was dressed in black pants and a white dress shirt, jumping around between cars, holding what looked like flyers, which he waved at the drivers. Three cops were coming towards him from different directions, but he was too caught up in whatever sermon he was giving to notice. When the cops got close, Ron raised his hands high in the air and backed away toward the curb. A cop came running at him full speed. Alfie thought for a second to shout something, maybe that he knew Ron, maybe that he wasn't dangerous, but then didn't he deserve what he was about to get? What right did he have to stop traffic and hold people hostage while he went on about some bullshit he'd made up an hour ago. It was the kind of thing his people liked to pull. Alfie heard the breath leave Ron as the cop tackled him onto the pavement. Now he'd have to get involved, but the blind man was tugging him in the other direction, probably thinking they were about to get run over, pulling him to the corner. When they made it across the street a few shaggy kids were yelling at the cops.

"Pigs!"

"Enemies of the people!"

"Fascists!"

Little drops of spit were flying from their mouths, falling into their pointy beards, glistening in the lamplight.

One of the cops heard and steamrolled toward them. One of the kids yelled "fuck" and they all took off. When he reached Alfie's corner, the cop gave up the chase. He said loud enough for anyone nearby to hear, "Shitheads." Behind him another cop was pulling Ron to his feet. As soon as he was up, the cop punched him and down he went again. The one next to Alfie yelled, "Cut the nigger loose. Let's go." And as fast as the whole show came together, it was over. The cops jumped back into the squad cars and zoomed off. Their sirens spurred the civilian cars along. Soon the intersection was empty. Even the blind man had gone his way. Only Ron was left, sitting on a curb, holding his head in his hands. Alfie considered approaching him, but watched instead as he got up slowly and staggered down the block.

In the sudden quiet, he felt like he'd dropped to earth from another planet. The air, the sounds of music from clubs in the distance, the swoosh of tires as cars glided by: Everything was alien to him. The same white trees that lined Columbus Avenue stood all around like sentries. The buildings, with their rounded bay windows and corniced roofs and overhangs, looked like robots. The street signs, plain black lettering on white squares, floated in the night sky. He was walking through a make-believe city, a place where he didn't exist. Down the block were nothing but little robot houses. Not a shop or a person in sight. Some invisible hand was moving him like a figurine.

Alfie followed Clay Street to a terraced park on a hill. He needed to look out from the highest point and get his bearings. He found the spot in the middle of the park. In one direction stood a row of Victorian houses, out-of-place against the skyline glittering behind them. In the opposite direction were less flashy houses, their windows lit dull yellow. Straight ahead of him, between two mansions, was the open blue-black space of the bay, and behind it, flickering lights dotting mountains in the distance. He bobbed in the darkness, letting all the place names he knew drift past him without catching any. This town and the entire world were anonymous.

He left the summit and wandered the park paths. Young people passed him in pairs and small groups. They dressed like most of the kids he knew in Brooklyn, but these kids acted like something was eating them from the inside, tearing at their skin. They talked the way he remembered his brother doing when the two of them were young, full of energy, trying to find words to release it.

"Bread, Man, it's all about the bread."

"What a gas!"

"Down at my pad."

"Pigs, you dig."

"He was bugged."

"Mad!"

"Throwing babies off of balconies."

They sounded like they were going shopping and losing their minds at the same time. Maybe Adeline was losing hers, and maybe that's why she'd invited him here. She needed a minder, a job that a few years back he would gladly have taken. But she'd gotten him here just to try him out and wasn't even sticking around to see how the audition went. It was criminal. She was a criminal, and so was he.

The downscape of the park path sped Alfie's step. By the time he hit Clay Street again, he was trotting. Something told him to move it. But while he'd been standing still, the street had come back to life. People rolled back and forth like little waves breaking across the sidewalk. He had to wade through them all the way back to Fillmore. Somewhere close by, Adeline was one of these breakers. By now she should have rolled back to the Cave. He'd have to test her, gauge the temperature, move with her until she showed him where she was headed. When he reached the club, Bobby Dark was blocking the doorway, hands in his pockets. Alfie tried to step around him.

"We're closed."

Deep breath.

"I was just here."

"Friend," Bobby said, looking past him, "that may be true. But the facts remain what they are."

Nobody could keep the facts what they were for long, not even somebody the size of this asshole. Alfie could slam the toe of his shoe into the giant's shin, and he'd go down like a ton of shit. But then Alfie wouldn't be a minder. He'd be a reminder to Adeline of what she probably didn't like about him and what, to tell the truth, he should keep to himself. She probably complained to Frankie about it all the time. "'If only your brother' this and 'If only your brother' that." And didn't Alfie deserve the complaints?

"Closed," Dark repeated, still refusing to look at him, as though he were a fly that the big mook didn't have time to swat. Not to hit him would be one more time Alfie just went along with somebody else's program. His mother's or his father's or Michelle's or Adeline's. Or, you could say, God's. You could say to hell with them all, and you could say to hell with God. But the way things were going, he might need God, so Alfie said a prayer for patience. Still, he was ready to lay Dark out, when out of the black hole of an entrance came Viv. She smoothed her sweater and looked him up and down.

"You're late, Mister."

She leaned back, in her clingy outfit, against the building's dirty stucco wall, a racy book cover.

"Late for what?"

"For the shindig, Jim. Your cousin must have all the cats on a string by now."

The word "cousin" got Dark's attention. He leaned in to listen. Viv took Alfie's hand.

"Let's split."

The faces on the streets darkened as they walked. If she was taking him to a negro party, she could forget it. The last thing Alfie needed was to save Adeline or Viv from some juiced-up mameluke. He'd be lucky to get out alive. Viv was leading him to his doom. He thought of taking off, getting a cab and going down to the wharf. The water would calm him, and he could wait for Adeline to make her way home. But soon enough they were seeing more people with black clothes than black skin, until they came to an avenue with a median wide enough to be a park. Small apartment buildings faced the median. In front of one of these a crowd was blocking the sidewalk. A cloud of smoke rose over them, thicker than the mist blowing in from the ocean. Alfie shivered as Viv came to life. She swayed her hips to a bass line sounding from the middle of the crowd, the kind of line that had always struck him as a death march.

"Now this is a scene, Alfie. C'mon."

Viv raised her hands and shimmied into the circle. The crowd's chatter rose to challenge the strum, then ebbed as a singer's voice rose into "House of the Rising Sun." The voice wasn't like the voices Alfie had heard sing the song before. Those were hillbilly voices or black voices, pure sadness and suffering. This was a voice that could've been his brother's: thin, a little whiny, straining to sound rough. Alfie stood outside the circle and looked up to a line of third-floor windows filled with people who wandered in and out of sight like phantoms. One of them stopped to look down at the crowd, then, it seemed to Alfie, to stare at him. The strumming stopped, and Viv was back.

"I want to hear you play."

"No, you don't."

"We'll see."

She strode toward the entrance, and he followed. They climbed a flight of worn marble stairs, slowing down every few steps to slide past one drink of water and then another, one holding a glass of wine, one wearing sunglasses, another lighting a joint and blowing smoke overhead, another talking about "getting enough of the necessary." Like they'd wanted to be actors but had wound up in the wrong part of California. The music started up again as they made it to the third flight. Bongos, each one playing a different beat. If this was a movie, it was a Tarzan movie. Sure enough, when he and Viv found the right apartment and made their way in, the first thing they saw was two half-naked negroes, a man and a woman, doing a kind of rain dance in the middle of the room. They were twisting and bending and gyrating in slow motion, like they understood all the different beats at once. At first they stood apart, but then little by little stepped toward each other until they were pressed together and grinding. Alfie scanned the room for Adeline.

The beats got faster, and soon the two dark bodies were grinding so hard they might as well have been banging right there. Kids, almost all white, watched. One shouted.

"Go, go, go!"

The performance struck Alfie as wrong. He walked past the dancers, who took up a small space in the middle of the smoke-filled room, and led Viv to a corner. Pushed into the corner was a mattress covered with an Indian bedspread. Near the bed was a round coffee table, and between the windows was a grandfather clock. Nothing else. No other furniture here or in the next room. The whole place was half-lit by candles set on shelves hung at different heights on the walls. Light and shadow played on faces. Viv nudged Alfie again.

"Drink?"

They moved to the kitchen, where a single naked bulb exposed years' worth of sauce and coffee splatters on the painted walls. She handed him a paper cup and poured. Alfie put his nose to the sour wine, took one sip, and set the cup on a counter.

"If you had to guess, where is she?"

Viv swirled a mouthful of wine for a few seconds, then swallowed.

"I'd say she's hiding, on the lam, tucked away in a little nook or cranny. She loves crannies."

Viv finished her wine.

"Come to think of it, so do I. You dig a cranny, Hoss? I can show you one."

If Adeline could disappear for a while, why couldn't he?

"I told you I wanted to hear you play."

They left the kitchen together, holding hands, single-filing through the crowd toward the sound of a guitar. In the back bedroom they found the source, a kid who looked Spanish, sitting on the floor under a window, finger-picking a Mexican melody. Alfie knew it but couldn't name it. He nodded to the kid, who stopped playing and waved for them to sit next to him. A thin buck-toothed girl with long blonde hair slid over to make room.

"Hey, Man, what can you play?"

The kid handed Alfie the guitar, and Viv clutched his arm, her mouth just east of his ear. What could he play? He thought of Elvis on the theater marquee and it came to him. "Blue Moon of Kentucky." Elvis did the song fast, so he'd have to do it Bill Monroe style. He strummed the opening chord, slightly out of tune, and felt a little ache in his wrist as he curled it around the neck. He sang the first line of lyrics, and before he could get to the second Viv stopped him.

"You *are* sweet."

What did he do?

"Did Addy tell you or did you do your homework?"

"About the song?"

She slapped his shoulder.

"About me, Slick. I'm a Kentucky girl, born and bred. Bowling Green."

As he started to sing he felt a nibble on the back of his neck. The blond girl joined in with a beautiful harmony. Her voice was part owl, part sparrow. Viv noticed and tried drowning her out, belting like the worst voice in an Appalachian choir. By the time they got to the second verse, she'd slid her hand under the guitar and onto his crotch. When he finished the song, the blond girl hooted and the Mexican kid shook his hand like he was ready to give Alfie a contract. Alfie handed the guitar back to him. Viv had his arm in a vice-lock now and was pulling him up, then pushing him through the smoky room toward the hallway. She found the bathroom and pushed him inside. He stood with his back to her, looking in the mirror, watching her rub his chest like she was a goddess with eight hands. Then the hands drew back, and he saw one of her arms raised above his head while her other arm pulled her sweater over it. A second later, she was undoing his belt. He looked at himself in the mirror and closed his eyes, trying to imagine Adeline. Viv's hand was around his cock now, and for some reason he thought of Adeline and her negro boy-friend. He imagined her doing the same thing with his black pole, then putting it inside her, him stabbing her with it, and Alfie pulled away, then pushed Viv toward the sink and bent her over. He closed his eyes again, hoping for a different vision, but now the negro was doing what Alfie was about to do to Viv, and a word Alfie had often thought was stupid crept into his mind: "nigger." He opened his eyes to shake the word, but when he saw himself in the mirror, it returned in capital letters. If he was one of them, maybe Adeline would want him. There was what you heard about them, for one thing. But what would really attract her would be what he figured attracted her to the black poet: freedom. First, the thought seemed ridiculous. Negroes didn't seem especially free. They came from slaves and, even though he couldn't help thinking that some of them were up to no good and deserved the way white people looked at them, a lot of them still lived that way, in places you'd never want to live, with jobs you wouldn't want to have, eating things you wouldn't necessarily want to eat. One of the Black grunts in the Army would bring back pigs' feet any time he came from a family visit. Why would you eat the feet? Then again, his uncles ate the skin, sautéed no less, not even fried. Still, some negroes seemed freer than anybody he knew. They were the ones who seemed to give less than a shit what anybody else thought: the ones who were loud and sang while they walked down the street and took up enough space for three people. They would never be white and would never be with the program. And it was the program Adeline wanted to escape. To her, Alfie was part of the program. Maybe it was different when he'd played music. Alfie wasn't sure what he'd been then, but once the music went, it was like he'd lost it and settled in for one long nap. He'd jumped into a bunk at Fort Riley and hadn't gotten out since. Whether or not Adeline knew it, he'd been in jail. Maybe she sensed it. Maybe that's how he'd come off in Kansas, too. So she came out here and shacked up with a negro. Did that make her free? Was somebody like Ron free? Whatever Ron was, Alfie wanted no part of it. What Adeline wanted didn't seem like freedom. It seemed like a dream. If you were sleeping, you couldn't be free. Alfie didn't want to be asleep anymore. He wanted to wake them both up, so they could find some other freedom, together. He backed away from Viv, and the sound of her breathing filled the room. The clamor of voices outside died down. Adeline was some-where. Alfie touched Viv lightly on her bare back.

"I'm sorry."

She exhaled, coughed, then laughed softly. As he pulled up his pants, she turned to look at him. He who couldn't possibly be a man. Something so low she couldn't name it. Something no woman in her right mind would want around. Alfie turned away.

"I'm sorry," he said again. "This isn't right."

He wanted to laugh at the idea of anything being right, but instead he opened the door to the hallway. From the front of the apartment came the sound of a woman's voice, almost a familiar voice, yelling.

"It's too much, I tell ya. How's any respectable person supposed to put up with this?"

When he glanced back inside the bathroom, Viv was fixing herself in the mirror, smoothing her hair, acting like she was alone in her own apartment. Her reflection in the mirror smirked at him as if to say she should've known better.

Alfie walked back to the living room, where a short cop was writing something in a notebook. At the front door a woman his mother's age, wearing a house dress and slippers, was arguing with another cop, this one taller, who stood there with his hat pushed up high on his sloping forehead, looking down his long nose at the woman as she pointed her finger around like a gun.

"I want them all thrown out. Tonight. I don't care where they go. My husband is the super here, and these people have been noth-ing but trouble."

She talked like an American, but from her face and gestures you could see she was a *paesana*. Alfie tried to flash in between the warring factions without either noticing, but the *paesana*'s voice fol-lowed him down the stairs.

"Another one! Go ahead. Get out and stay out!"

Outside, Alfie found himself standing between two cops, nei-ther of whom gave him the time of day. A mini-mob was taunting them from a few feet away.

"What do pigs have against parties?"

"Officer, can you help me? Somebody stole my rights."

One cop pulled out a pack of cigarettes and offered a smoke to the other. The cop with the cigarettes caught Alfie's eye and offered him one, too. Alfie signaled no thanks. Then he thought to ask whether or not the cops had seen a young woman in a thin black dress. The answer would be they'd seen a hundred, so he started to walk off, scanning the mob. Before he took two steps, he felt a hand on his shoulder.

"I guess the police and I got here together."

J.P. stood there in his dungarees and Cowboy shirt, like he was at a rodeo. Alfie took a breath.

"You missed the party."

"Not the first one I've missed."

The two men walked slowly down the street. The mist had lifted, and it was chillier than before. The shouting behind them faded. J.P. stopped and looked out over the grassy median.

"I suppose you haven't found her yet. Your cousin, I mean."

Alfie was about to make up an elaborate story about their definition of "cousin," when J.P. cut him off.

"It's all right. I'm not here to judge you. Lot of things about gals you can't control, and that's one of 'em."

"Do you know where I can find her?"

J.P.'s eyes drifted off as he spoke again.

"You know I like her. Got nothing against her at all. But if I were you, I'd get away and go back home. You're not likely to find what you're looking for."

He shook Alfie's hand.

"Guess I'll see you," he said, and headed in the direction of where the sunset would be.

Now the full weight of night lay on Alfie's back. The cool air dried his throat and burned his lungs. His legs ached. He was miles from Adeline's apartment. He wanted to scream her name, but then he'd sound like Marlon Brando or some other Hollywood dope pretending he was important. Get away. Go home. Go. Home. Where?

He lumbered back toward a circled mob, which was widening into the street and onto the median. Kids, most of them just a few years out of high school, were leaning against lamp posts, sitting on curbs, or lying down in the grass, like they were on nighttime recess. One of them eyeballed him as he passed. Was he an undercover cop? Was he lost? Who cared? Most of them were too busy filling the air with bullshit. Beyond the cluster, across the side street, a little group was kneeling on the sidewalk, staring at a woman lying face down in the gutter. Closer in, Alfie could hear her moaning. Her black dress was torn in the back and streaked with dirt. She moaned again and rolled her head to one side. Adeline. One of the people kneeling in front of her turned around. It was the little fucking delinquent malink from Loudmouth Night. Alfie charged and knocked him out of the way, then scooped her up and carried her to the closest stoop. Her eyes were closed, but she was talking.

"It's the first time, the first time, the first last time and the last, last time."

He stroked her cheek and her eyes opened half way.

"It's my man-cousin."

"It's me," he answered.

"Me, me, me, me."

"Can somebody get a doctor?" he yelled.

Nobody moved.

He put his ear to her mouth. The breathing was regular, and she whispered.

"Hero."

Was she making fun of him?

Her eyes opened.

"Did you meet James? James!"

Alfie spun back toward the sidewalk. The malink was rubbing his forehead, getting to his feet, smiling. All a big fucking joke.

"Hey, Brother ..."

Alfie hit him with an overhand right that knocked the skinny bastard backward a good ten feet into a tree. Meanwhile, another beatnik, this one with a triangle beard, came up and laid a hand on

Alfie's shoulder. Without thinking, Alfie launched another right that staggered the punk. The urge to hit one of these *cidruls* again was hard to resist, but by now Adeline had gotten to her feet, swaying and yelling.

"They're my friends, Alfie. Who do you think you are? You think I don't know?"

Kids from all up and down the street were circling the scene.

When he looked at her again, Adeline was wiping tears from her eyes. As he walked toward her, people in his way backed off. He put his hand on her warm cheek, but she slapped it away. She reeked of booze and smoke.

"Leave me," she said, smoothing her dirty dress. "Go home."

The air around him suddenly became a vacuum. He imagined the vacuum lifting him over the city, over the hills and the bay and the mountains, and dropping him, like a rock, back into his life. He closed his eyes, and when he opened them he saw Adeline's face again. She stood a few feet in front of him, more conscious now, shooting him a look that was half ice and half question he knew he couldn't answer. Before he could think of what to say, the second idiot he'd hit walked over and led her toward a parked car. She got in without looking back, and the car pulled away. A few at a time, the crowd disappeared, and before long Alfie was standing alone on an empty sidewalk.

(1963)

L eaning on the rail at the edge of the bay, Alfie wondered if he was doing anybody a favor by being around. Since he'd gotten back, Michelle had only one use for him and otherwise gave him the silent treatment. In return he said nothing about San Francisco. Gangsters called this approach *omertà*. He could tell that his father had questions, but Alfie ignored the old man's sideways looks. Still, everything was changing, constantly, like the color of the water. It was obvious. Everybody could see into him now that he was empty. Michelle, Adeline, even his mother and father had decided to stop throwing their love into the ocean.

Alfie watched iron workers walk the cables of the half-finished bridge to Staten Island. It was a miracle they didn't all jump. Sooner or later somebody would stop loving every last one of them. Everything would change. All over Brooklyn, all over New York, everything was changing. Every day, people he'd seen on the streets of Borough Park for years were vanishing. But the iron workers held on. He'd heard they were Indians from Canada. Every week they drove down to work on the bridge, drank like fish after work, then drove back home for the weekend. They lived by rules that never changed. And still, every now and then, one of them would fall or kill himself on the highway or lose somebody who loved him.

It was Saturday, but he wished he could go to work, so he could stop thinking for a while. For the past few weeks he'd been taking the subway up to Harlem, visiting little mom-and-pop shops, knocking on apartment doors, trying to get through the awkward sales pitch the company made you memorize. All the things you could never anticipate. What would you do if? Whenever he made a sale to one of the negroes, he thought of the preacher, how he almost deserved what Alfie had done to him, because he was trying to sell people on God. Another kind of security that might or might not help them. He stared at the black faces asking questions about premiums, and he wanted to slap them for complaining, for wasting his time when they knew that in the end they would pay, and when they also knew—or at least he did—that in this world their lives weren't worth the paper the policies were printed on. But it was a job, and it got him out of the house and away from Michelle.

Since he'd gotten back, she hadn't let up. She told him she didn't know why she'd married him, and he didn't bother to answer. Even another kid on the way didn't matter. The trip out west made her hate him as much as he could hate her. When he was in the house, he confined himself to the living room. When the bathroom was free, he'd hole up there, reading books on woodcarving, gifts from his grandfather, who was barely hanging on. If not those, then he read the magazines people left behind on subway benches. He kept his stash of these under the couch, where he usually slept: *Life* and *The New Yorker* and a lot of travel magazines. He looked for articles on California and then compared them to other articles on Italy or France or the Caribbean, to prove to himself that California wasn't so great. Otherwise, he played with Jennifer, who was almost five already. When Michelle left her alone with him, Alfie tried to teach her Italian swear words like *"Fat 'n cul'!,"* "Up your ass!" One day when Michelle came home, Jennifer greeted her with *"A fiss' e mamata!",* "Up your mother's crack!" Michelle figured out roughly what it meant and didn't laugh. In fact, she seemed smarter than before. She gave him the dead eye.

"That's lovely, Alfie. It shows the kind of respect you have for women."

Come Monday Alfie followed the usual routine, walking to the Sea Beach line, then changing trains at Times Square. Sometimes he rode the Broadway local to 125th Street, but this morning he got off at 116th and took a nice long walk around the Columbia University campus. It was a few minutes before 9 a.m., a time of morning when students were gathering on the walkways and by the massive doors of the old brick-and-granite classroom buildings. Sparrows were singing in the branches of the cherry trees as he walked under them, as the occasional gaggle of students, most of them boys, talking too loud in one another's faces, passed too close, like he wasn't there. A few kids sat on the steps, around the big statue of a woman in a robe who was sitting on a throne, holding a scepter in her hand and a book in her lap. Like they were all supposed to be Romans. The kids sat around smoking cigarettes, waving them in the air, arguing. When was the last time he'd studied anything? For a while he was reading books about the Old West, and he read books on woodworking, even ordered one on making guitars. Now and then he'd try the Bible, but it bored him shitless. Alfie took a seat on an unoccupied step and read the names inscribed on the cornice of the enormous library building facing him. From his briefcase, he pulled a small notebook that he used for recording customers' questions. He wrote "Thucydides" on a blank page, underlined the name, then slipped the notebook back inside the case. He felt like he'd accomplished something. At least he could lean back for a minute, close his eyes and enjoy the cool morning in a strange place. When the sun began breaking through the clouds, Alfie walked back to Broadway and turned uptown. Tulips were blooming on the median, and the smell of brewing coffee wafted across the wide boulevard. He'd grab a cup from the Chock Full 'O Nuts and walk along Riverside Park. He'd have to move, though. Even negroes expected you to show your face at a certain hour.

Manhattan didn't look so bad from here. The brick buildings were well maintained and not so tall that they made you feel invisible. You had a view of the park and the river. This was a city he could like. The city he hated was Midtown, especially the blocks around Penn Station. Frankie had his restaurant there, and once in a blue moon he'd pass a message through their mother, or worse, he'd called Alfie personally, to invite him to dinner. To tell the truth, he didn't particularly care for his brother's food or for his company. He didn't like the way Frankie talked now, like one of these college kids. Diarrhea of the mouth. And it was all Italy this and Italy that. Sure, it looked and sounded like a nice place to visit, but their family had left it behind for a reason. Maybe Brooklyn wasn't great, but you had to appreciate America. Frankie sometimes sounded like he didn't, even though he made his money here. Some of the negroes Alfie dealt with gave you the same feeling.

"Joshua Harris, Attorney at Law" was embossed in small letters on the plate glass window of the 125th Street storefront. How many colored lawyers could there be in the city? You'd think this Joshua Harris would do a good business here, but the office didn't look like success. Inside was a gigantic metal desk in front of a luan door marked "Private." Against one wall were a few metal folding chairs. Everything looked cheap or borrowed, except for the colored girl behind the big desk, who could've passed for Lena Horne's younger sister. When Alfie approached, the girl lifted her eyes from a book and sized him up. If she couldn't quite figure him, he couldn't blame her. How many white faces could she see in a week up here? On two of the folding chairs sat an older colored couple, their hands folded in their laps. Alfie cleared his throat, and the girl lowered her eyes to her book again.

"Excuse me, Miss. I'm here to see Mister Harris."

The girl looked up again, more slowly this time, laying a bookmark between her pages. She didn't smile.

"Mister Harris is out."

Her voice sounded refined, higher and softer than he expected.

"He should be back after lunch. You're welcome to wait."

Her eyes suggested he have a seat on one of the empty folding chairs. Alfie looked at his watch. Who knew how long a colored lawyer could take for lunch? He scratched the side of his nose and turned to look out the window, as if watching the sidewalk would make Harris suddenly appear. When he turned to the desk again, the girl was watching him, smirking.

"If you like, I can pour you a cup of coffee."

Her smirk broadened into a full smile, and warmth flooded Alfie's cheeks.

"Thank you."

Alfie took a seat and tried to cross his long legs in a businesslike way, but as small as the rickety chair was, he couldn't help feeling a little ridiculous. The girl smiled at him again, then disappeared into the back before reappearing with his cup of coffee. He could see now just how beautiful she was. Tall, figure like a goddess, smooth skin somewhere between peaches and caramel.

"Oh, I'm sorry," she said, handing him the cup, "I didn't ask how you take it."

She was holding back a smile now. Maybe she liked his looks. Maybe life hadn't completely washed him out. He thanked her and watched closely as she floated back behind her metal fortress. He sipped his coffee and looked around for something to read, but the only printed words in sight were in the girl's hands. He closed his eyes and tried to relax. A few minutes later he heard the creaking of folding chairs, and opened his eyes to see the old couple leaving. Another sip of coffee, but by now it was too cold to enjoy. Without meaning to, Alfie cleared his throat again.

"Oh, would you like another cup?"

"No, no, that's all right."

Her face was an invitation.

"I was just wondering, though, about your name."

She raised an eyebrow.

"It's an ordinary name. Nothing unusual, if that's what you were thinking."

"No, I wasn't thinking anything like that. Just curious. It's not a secret, is it?"

She chuckled.

"No. It's Gladys."

"Gladys?"

"See. I told you."

"You're the first, ah, Gladys I ever knew."

"Hmmph. Do you know me?"

Colored girls weren't shy. That was no news. But he should be at least a little careful what he said, no?

"I guess not, but maybe I could."

He didn't know exactly what a colored girl blushing looked like, but he was pretty sure Gladys was blushing, and when she noticed that he noticed, she bowed her head, to compose herself.

"Now, would that be a good idea?"

Alfie scratched his chin and shrugged.

"I don't know. Maybe."

She gave him a long look. More amusement than anger.

"You realize I'm at work?"

Alfie raised his cup of lukewarm coffee and swirled it, watching the tan liquid spin, pretending he might take another sip. He felt a twinge of embarrassment, but that gave way to a strange feeling of freedom. Gladys's being colored meant he could take certain liberties, didn't it?

"You get off work sometime today, don't you?"

"Well, yes, I do."

She smoothed her hair.

"But I expect you'll be long gone by then."

Alfie set his coffee cup on the desk and tried to look at ease.

"Not necessarily."

They exchanged silent looks, until he extended a hand.

"My name's Alfie."

She gave him two fingers.

"Short for?

It felt good to smile, a rarity these days.

"I could tell you over a drink."

Before she could answer, the front door swung open and banged against the wall.

"Say, Gladys, we got some kinda trouble here?"

Alfie had been in enough bar fights to jump at the touch of a man's hand on his back. On instinct, he spun around with his fist cocked. In an instant he felt the impact of a cannon shot to his temple. The room spun as he crumpled against the wall and tried to cover up. A flash of fists flying in the weeds. His father down and bloody in the dry leaves. How the old man rose and how Alfie climbed to his feet, only to hear the hiss of another fist as it connected with the other side of his head, this time driving him through the doorway and onto the sidewalk. Then a woman's voice screaming.

"Carl, stop! Oh, Jesus, please!"

Alfie rolled away from where he fell, only to feel a mule kick to the ribs, then another that felt like it broke his arm. His father again. First rule. Cover your head. Curled in the fetal position, Alfie waited for the flurry of kicks to stop. Ear to concrete he could hear footsteps, louder, toward him, voices shouting.

"White trash motherfucker!"

"You'll kill him. Please, stop! Get away!"

Laughter. Grown men laughing. Negroes. Gladys's face next to his. Concrete. The kind of bed a colored girl got you. But a warm, soft hand on his forehead.

"I'm so sorry, so, so sorry. He's crazy, just crazy."

Laughter again.

Alfie opened his eyes to her beautiful coffee face, but over it a circle of cruel faces, white grins against dark skin on mean display. Everything his cousins would say about *mulagnans*. Kill you soon as look at you. Good for nothing. Alfie couldn't cover the distance between the demon smiles and Gladys's angel face, so he closed his eyes until the voices went quiet. After a long time, he opened them again, to a doughy white medic, who had taken Gladys's place.

"You took some shots," the medic said, reaching up to twist the valve on a tube connected to Alfie's arm.

Alfie turned to move, but Doughboy held him down with a fat palm to his chest. Alfie groaned as he struggled to draw a deep breath.

"At least you're leaving Harlem. I told the driver to take you to Saint Luke's, down near the university."

He hung the IV bag, so it tugged the needle in Alfie's arm.

"Bet you won't be coming back here anytime soon."

(1968)

Michelle's mother was batshit crazy. She practically ran the other way when she saw her grandchildren. Alfie's mother, on the other hand, gave the kids whatever they wanted. She spent hours letting them monkey with her old violin or play with their toys in the middle of her living room. If they acted up, maybe she'd wave the wooden spoon at them and bite her lip until either they laughed or she did. Even his father gave them all the attention they wanted. You had to be amazed, in fact, because the old man could never seem to manage the same for Alfie and Frankie. When they were kids, he worked, came home to sleep for a few hours, then left for his shift at the bar. Inside the house he was practically invisible. Only at the lake or in the woods did he spend a lot of time with them. Then he'd show them how to tie a hook or load a shotgun. You knew that he loved you, that he worried about you, but still sometimes Alfie had secretly wanted something bad to happen to their father before he left for the day. Then maybe he'd stay home and relax. Frankie, on the other hand, didn't seem to care. Their mother's attention was enough for him.

Alfie sat on the couch, pulling on a pair of black socks that would probably turn out to be too thin for the early spring weather. Down the hall a bedroom door creaked open. Jennifer ski-walked out in her foot pyjamas and plopped her little body down next to him.

"Are you going to see Grandpa?"

She was almost ten now, too old to keep in the dark, although, God knew, Michelle tried.

"You're a smart girl."

"Can I come?"

She leaned against him, and he kissed the top of her head.

"Not this time, Sweetheart."

She wrapped her arms around him, knowing the game.

"Why not?"

"Because he just got there. Let him settle in."

She sat back in her spot, a thought furrowing her brow.

"Why are you going, then?"

He straightened his cuffs and didn't look at her.

"Dolly, it's just for a few minutes. That's all the nurses let you have. And only one visitor at a time. They're strict. Like nuns."

"Why don't you like nuns?"

Did she seem more like him or Michelle?

"They're not nuns, these nurses. They know what they're doing."

Alfie believed this to be true. He liked the idea at least that somebody might.

"Come here."

She stood up and hugged him again. He gave her a squeeze, then peeled her off. She shrugged and sighed. As the sound of her mother's footsteps got louder, he kissed her again.

"I love you. I'll be back. But do me a favor while I'm gone."

Jennifer nodded, her straight brown hair falling across her face.

"Please, you and your brother, don't give your mother a hard time."

Michelle usually deserved it when the kids gave her a hard time, the way she snapped at them about every little thing, but he had to keep the peace.

At the hospital, his father's mood surprised him. He acted like he was staying at a resort. When Alfie got to his room, the old man was smiling, holding a pretty nurse's hand. She followed what he was saying like it was the lyrics of her favorite song.

"And did you know how they built the Parachute in Coney Island? Well, they started with ... ah, now, look who came to see if I'm still kickin'. This is my oldest. Alfie, I was just tellin' ..."

Alfie put up his hand, and his father frowned.

"Sometimes my son's grumpy as a porcupine."

The nurse giggled and stole a quick glance Alfie's way. She was a looker. He smiled at her, but let any chance at conversation die. Once she left the room, he leaned over the bed and gave his father a kiss on the cheek.

"I'm not one of your old aunties, Son. Give your father a hug."

Alfie hesitated, knowing he'd feel his father's bones where muscles used to be. As he laid his hands gently on the old man's small shoulders, he heard faint static from the transistor radio on the nightstand. His father didn't seem to give it or the IV sticking out of his arm a second thought. As a cop Alfie had been in his share of hospital rooms. He knew that the room usually held clues to the patient's chances of leaving it alive. You wanted to see a lot of equipment and notes nurses and doctors left for one another. That meant they had hope. His father's room was nearly empty. Not even a chart at the foot of the bed. A dull nausea hit him with the thought of having to watch the old man fade like a warm October day. Every time his father stopped talking or fell asleep, another leaf would fall. He would try to convince the old man that he'd be okay, but he'd be lying, and the last thing he wanted now was to tell more lies. His father's alertness, his Indian summer, meant Alfie would have, if nothing else, a chance to confess the lies he'd already told and the truths he'd left out. The thought of never confessing to him gnawed at Alfie's conscience. He looked at his father, who was holding the transistor to his ear, squinting.

"Dad?"

"Your brother give me this. Can't ever get it to work right."

"Dad?"

"Here, you take it."

Alfie took the radio and studied the dial.

"I was just thinking about something."

His father sighed.

"Well, gotta be more interesting than what I'm hearin' from this tin can."

"About Joe Jefferson."

The old man's face tightened and his eyes went glassy, like he'd spotted Joe coming toward him from a hundred yards away.

"Old Joe," he said. "I ever tell you about Joe's house up Rome?"

Alfie had never thought about the preacher's living arrangements.

"I visited with him right before our last hunting trip."

His father side-eyed him. Did he already know?

"Not to bore you, Son, but I remember that day like it just happened. I still see myself walkin' along the muck. Hated walkin' that road, especially after a day's work. Bad enough we lived on the other side of Dominick Street, smack on top of the copper factory. Smoke and noise all the time, mosquitoes from the canal, and the worst of the snow. My brothers and cousins were all fixed over the Mohawk Street end of things, all close so they could walk down the block and get a drink of water in every other house. And, oh, didn't your mother complain about it, too.

"'All your family's over there,' she'd say, 'and we're outcasts.' Said she felt like we lived closer to her family, and they were all in Brooklyn. She was always pushin' me to move across Dominic Street, but in those days I could barely afford what we had. Anyway, that day the chill was already in the air, and it was gettin' twilight, and there I was headed to Joe Jefferson's, right into the colored neighborhood, though it wasn't so big you'd even call it a neighborhood. I understood the colored fellas had it worse than most, but couldn't the preacher get himself a telephone? Couldn't they all pitch in for one? The war was over. But no dice. And my car was up the shop. So I hoofed it over, and I remember walkin' the train line, lookin' down the tracks, waitin' for the horn. You remember that

New York Central horn? Sounded like God was sending the police. Joe liked to talk about God, like he knew him personally. But that never bothered me. I knew he knew about as much as I did."

Matty cleared his throat, and Alfie automatically poured him a glass of water from the metal pitcher on his nightstand.

"It gets me right in the ol' *gola* sometimes," the old man said, pinching his Adam's apple. "But I was sayin' about Joe, you know, he was a Godly man, no doubt about it. We used to sing 'Wicked Path of Sin' together. But the preaching was his thing, as much for the talk as for Jesus. I run into him once when he was on one of his missions to the train station. I was back from Utica, comin' down the inside stairs, and there's Joe standin' against the wall across from the benches. A couple of older church ladies on either side of him, handin' out Bibles to any face that looked half-ways friendly. Anybody who took the time to take one got that smile. And then when some pretty girl walked by, the smile took Joe over like the Holy Spirit. It was always that way with him, from when we were boys. A smile like he was ready to tell you all his secrets.

"So that evening I'm walkin' by the station, which was sorta empty by then. And it was one of them gray days. Nothing but gray sky all the way down the canal toward Oriskany. I remember thinkin' even the canal looked depressed. Made me feel a little a-scared. Maybe not a-scared so much, but a feeling like you'd have from lyin' on your back and looking up at the stars too long. Like there was something about Rome you weren't supposed to know. Like there was something out north that might be hungry and coming for you. Pretty sure I pulled out my flask along the way. Me and that feelin' sat down for a nip.

"By the time I got past the muck and came up on the colored section, it was almost dark. The James Street Bridge was lit up at night, so I decided to cross into town, except for some reason I stopped in the middle. That canal water was twice as black as the Black River. Just like a mystery. The canal had a million things to say and didn't make a sound. That's why I always preferred the river. It would at least whisper to you, especially come fall. I probably thought that same thing every time I went to see Joe before huntin' season. Damned preacher. Same walk every year, except that year it felt longer."

His father stopped talking and caught Alfie's eye, like he was waiting for him to laugh or make a remark. Alfie kept quiet, wanting the old man to get to the point.

"I never told your mother any of this. She was just lookin' for the excuse to pack up. And what I knew about Brooklyn, it wasn't what I featured. I always thought maybe you felt the same, but I guess it don't matter now."

The old man turned his face away and kept talking.

"Jefferson lived all the way on George Street. Had a gray house hadn't been painted since before the Depression. And it was too small for Joe's family. But that evenin' when Joe answered the door, he was all smiles like always, like God just pulled him out of the wilderness. Still, the house was his opposite. The parlor off the hallway was dim as could be. All the shades were drawn, and his old settee was dusty as death. Next to the chair, I remember, he had just a little dilapidated table for his newspaper, his coffee, and his whiskey; and then he had a rickety old desk for a guest. I can picture Joe sitting back on the couch, grinnin' and smackin' the newspaper with the back of his hand. He loved to talk about the news. I remember he says, 'Matty, Matty, Matty, you don't have to be no genius to see who got this one in the bag.'

"'Watcha mean, Joe?' I says. 'You mean the election?'

"'Ain't you read the papers?' he says.

"So I says, 'Tell the truth, I ain't had a chance. Been walkin' since I got off work.'

"So he flips a page and says, 'Sorry about that, *Amico*.' Because you have to remember, he worked for my uncle so many years, he picked up a few odds and ends of Italian.

"'If I knew you was comin',' he says, 'I'd a made my special coffee. Fresh outta gin, though.'

"And I fibbed a little, told him, 'Honest, Joe, it just hit me to come over.'

"'That's all right.' he says. 'Don't take this up wrong, but you know you're like my brother, 'cept when my brother comes to visit he usually stays a week. Besides, look at this.'

"He snaps open the paper.

"'They think Dewey's gonna run away with it. That's a sad day.'

"So I tell him, I remember, I says, 'Both of 'em's the devils we know.'

"And he's telling me how Truman done colored folks a lotta good so far. Buildin' all these new schools, and his wife's people in Newark sayin' how Truman was giving the kids free lunch. I didn't have the heart to ask if his family might be comin' back. Hadn't been but the summer Shirley took the kids to New York. So I just let him talk. He had that voice was like a tonic. And he went on about Truman and Dewey and colored folks, and then we drank to the workin' man and maybe a gal or two we used to know. And then, naturally, we talked about huntin', about that last trip. It was Joe's idea to take you along."

The old man stopped talking for a breath and a sip of water.

"Lately I been thinkin' about Joe. Be a helluva thing to see him again."

His father's whole face seemed to sag now, his mouth hanging open enough for his yellowed teeth to show. How could Alfie tell him what he knew about that last hunting trip? His father was already a dead man, and a dead man didn't need terrible stories.

The old man wiped his lips and started in again.

"First time I met Joe Jefferson was up at my uncle's hotel. We couldn't been more than fourteen, the both of us. He was workin', cleanin' up with his mother, and they had me back in the kitchen, peelin' whatever there was to peel. I go to use the bathroom, and there's Joe, his hands half in the toilet. Now, my folks never said nothing bad against colored people, so I go right up to Joe and say, 'Scuse me, but I gotta use the bathroom real bad.' And he says, 'Well, that's fine soon's I finish it.' And I says back to him, 'No, I mean I gotta go real bad.' And he says, 'My mama just about kill me if I don't clean this here toilet.' And I says, 'Well, then, give me that brush and I'll do the dirty work.' And he just smiles and hands it over. And from then we was closer than two peas in a pod."

It struck Alfie that he'd never had a single friend like that.

"When we didn't have to work, me and Joe'd go off huntin' and fishin'. And when we weren't doing that, we'd talk about girls. This is a long time before your mother, of course. Ah, women. Joe could charm a baby bird out of the nest. He'd point out a colored girl on the street and say somethin' like, 'Now, look right there, Matty. Ain't that the prettiest thing ever shit between two shoes?' And naturally I knew the girl was colored, but I'd say, 'Sure is, Joe.' And before I could say anything else, he's crossin' the street to talk with her. And I'd be the one taggin' along."

His father paused, a little embarrassed by his part in the story, it seemed to Alfie.

"Then there's the times we pulled each other outta scrapes. Not too many people appreciated seein' me with Joe or Joe with me. One time we was in the colored section of Utica, and a group of colored fellas—maybe six, seven of 'em—told Joe he'd made a big mistake bringing me around. Don't even remember why we went there."

His father took a deep breath, negotiating with the memory.

"But those boys were about to leave me bloody on the side of the road. And what does Joe tell 'em? Well, doesn't he say, 'You know who this here is? This here is the police chief's nephew.' And they look at him funny, but he keeps it up. 'Maybe you ain't tryin' to believe me, but if I was you, I wouldn't take no chance.' And they look at each other, and then they all make sure they tell me how lucky I am I got the police on my side. And then didn't Joe and me laugh ourselves silly on the way home. Most of the sheriffs out that way woulda locked some of my family up on sight. Yeah, if Joe saved me once, he musta done it a dozen times."

The story, or telling it, seemed to tire the old man out. He closed his eyes and sank into his pillow, then into sleep. Alfie thought about calling the nurse, but saw his father's chest moving up and down.

"Dad?"

"You ain't gotta worry, Son," he mumbled, eyes still shut. "I'm still here to bother you. Just too bad, you know, the way things turn out sometimes."

His weak voice sounded the weary note he'd used so many times to keep Alfie and Frankie in line. But the story wasn't over, and his father came back to life, changing tone again, like he was explaining things to himself, almost as though Alfie weren't there.

"We lost touch for a few years, Joe and me, while I was busy gettin' married and raisin' children. Then somethin' strange happened."

The old man shook his head and grinned.

"Harry James and his band come to town. I don't remember how we done it, but your mother and me got tickets, which was tickets to a dinner and the show at the theater. Big buffet dinner down the Savoy. After I get Pen her food, I get up to get my own, and this colored girl is serving me. I'm being polite and talkin' to her. Pretty girl, if I remember. And to be nice, I tell her 'bout the colored folks I know in town, and of course I say Joe Jefferson, and dontcha know Joe's her cousin, so I ask where can I find him. And that was that."

The old man's eyes started to close again, and his head fell slowly to one side. In a minute he was snoring. He'd wake up soon enough, so Alfie pulled a metal guest chair up to the side of the bed and watched him. Asleep, his father looked twenty years older than he was. He'd been aging like a dog since Alfie's trip to San Francisco. How different things were then, when Alfie could still see some light. Once he went on the job, everything got darker by the day: the people he dealt with, the things he saw, and, worst of all, the future. Not to mention life at home, a hell he'd lowered himself into. It was the opposite of relief from the skells he locked up and the other low-lifes he saw on the street, especially the colored ones, who looked at him like they thought the world would be a better place if he dropped dead on the spot. From what Alfie could see, Joe Jefferson was the best of colored people. Most of them weren't worth spit on the sidewalk. The men treated their women like dogs, and their kids like they owed them nothing. Meanwhile Alfie owed everybody everything. He was supposed to keep the *mulagnans* in line, keep peace in the streets, and keep up appearances at home. All so his daughter and son could grow up normal. Except nothing was normal. His wife couldn't stand him. The kids always looked confused, like they didn't know what to do next. And he didn't know what to tell them. When he was home he wanted to be on the street, and when he was on the street he wanted to be home. The only salvation lately was the special unit the lieutenant had decided was perfect for him.

"You got the right attitude, Baliato," he said. "People need order. Nobody goes to church anymore."

Order meant they sent the unit out to bust heads when heads needed busting. Sometimes it was brutal, but Alfie didn't care. Not that he enjoyed it, but he'd learned how to treat the night stick as just another tool. He even learned to twirl it, like you saw in the movies. He convinced himself that it made a kind of music when it hit different parts of a body. The back of the neck was a low G. The shoulders were a solid middle C. The knees were a F. And if you had to whack a hand or an ankle, that was a high B-flat. The best way to take a criminal down was to treat it like a song, a number you knew you'd play for a few minutes with other members of the band. You could pretend the groans were applause.

He wished his father would talk to him, give him some magic advice. He thought of the day he went to see the old man at the World's Fair Grounds. Right after San Francisco. He was 55 then but still working as a laborer. Alfie's company had just transferred him to an office on Queens Boulevard, so he let the old man know he'd come visit him for lunch. It was a sunny day, warm, and Alfie drove with the window down, singing along with the country and western station. When he got there, the old man was sitting on the bumper of his '57 Chevy parked near one of the unfinished World's Fair pavilions. A sign said it would be called "The Better Living

Center." Looking at it then—a big steel skeleton with a bunch of men in suits standing in front of it, holding clipboards—it seemed more like a place to die. All around them, maybe it was a thousand acres, looked like a bomb had hit. Everything was dirt and jalopies and cranes holding chunks of metal in the air over open buildings, and the sound of jackhammers and rivet guns and saws, with showers of sparks shooting up here and there like little smoldering volcanoes. His father was working in hell, but, as usual, it didn't seem to bother him.

"You believe it, Son. Some poor bastard misses a step and falls off the heliport. Right over there, behind us. Ironworker. They're all crazy sonofabitches."

His father poked the crown of a meatball back into the half-loaf of Italian bread that cradled it. Alfie was amazed how much care the old man took with his hero, touching the meatball with at least three fingers, one at a time, to tuck it in. Alfie had brought his own lunch, a tuna sandwich with too much mayonnaise, the way his wife always made it. When he complained about sandwiches or anything else, she flew off the handle and went on about what a bastard he was to her, which was true.

"Go live with your mother, Alfie. Nothing I do is ever right. How about a thank you once in a while?"

By this time, if she was holding a spatula, she was slapping it against her hip, getting ready to throw it at him.

"What do I have to do for you to show me some respect?"

It made him sad and angry with himself that she was right. Basically, he'd ruined both of their lives, and he was too tangled up to do anything about it. Neither of them could raise a kid alone, and she was pregnant again. He was frustrated and ashamed. He would've liked to stop himself from taking it out on his wife, but he couldn't. So many times he'd almost said something like, "Why did you have to be such a piece of ass?" Instead he complained, or worse.

"Who taught you how to cook?"

Then the clincher.

"Maybe if your mother wasn't half a whack ..."

And the spatula would fly. And Michelle would start crying. And he'd either start yelling, to drown her out, or he'd just leave.

It was a relief to be here with his father, just listening to him.

"Rather be on the ground any day of the week. Easy work, if you ask me. But work's work. The thing, Son, is gettin' home. How's your wife doin'? She oughtta be pretty well along."

Alfie swallowed a bite of his sandwich and washed it down with a Pepsi he'd gotten from a machine in front of the Pepsi Pavilion. From there, you could look across the lake and see the edge of Forest Hills. So close he could've walked home.

"Four months this week."

"That somethin'. Your mother's gettin' excited this time around, I can tell you."

Alfie didn't quite believe it. When his mother found out Michelle was pregnant the first time, she'd threatened to ring the doorbell and slap the little *strosh* in her face. But these were the noises men had to make, men like his father, men who liked to work so they could get out of talking about anything too serious or unpleasant. Alfie understood, though it bothered him to see his father working this way. He was almost a true old man, and Alfie's grandfather sent him out here in the sun and the dust, like he was in his prime. Sure, his father was in shape, but you could see he was slowing down. Alfie remembered thinking that his grandfather deserved a kick in the ass.

"How's it going here, Pop?"

"Well, you can see around you. Gonna really be somethin'. The carpenters got their hands full with some of these wild designs, but we're makin' do. When it opens up, we can take the girls. They're sayin' cheap admission for all the workers. Last World's Fair your mother and I never got to go. You and your brother were this high, and we were savin' up money to head to Rome."

His father looked off toward the parkway.

"You wouldn't remember."

Alfie shook his head, and Matty punctuated the memory.

"Good days."

He put his arm around Alfie's shoulder.

"But we're here now, Son, and it's beautiful out. Some days after work I take my pole over the lake there. You'd be surprised some of the bass I get."

Alfie had never thought to fish here. Queens seemed like a place for shopping and sleeping, and that's was all, but Michelle liked it, and that made her just a little easier to live with. Far enough from her mother and from his family. He'd hoped maybe getting married would calm her down, but nothing did. For an hour or two she'd stop worrying about everything under the sun, but then something would remind her, and she'd go on and on, so that even going out for an ice cream she was worried about something. Then all he could think to do was get her to bed, and even then he had to distract her to make that happen. And now they'd have another kid to worry about, and no family near Forest Hills to help. He'd always wondered how his father coped with Brooklyn, and sometimes with his mother. But then his mother was no problem compared to Michelle. And his father never complained about work. In fact, it was always good to hear him talk about it, so Alfie asked, "You like the job?"

"Not bad. Your grandpa's got us set up. Nice little trailer on the cold days. Foreman's not a bad character. Of course the biggest trouble is all the stealin' goes on. Some of these types around here are stealin' the place blind, and the union don't make a peep. Makes you glad they're comin' down on the unions now, making 'em take in colored fellas. Shoulda happened a long time ago. Course they'll find a way to blame 'em for everything that gets stole."

Couldn't his father see that eventually negroes would get their way? If you read the papers, you saw it a little more every day. It wasn't like the days with the preacher. They'd move up, and maybe they deserved to. And what did Alfie deserve? If he told him what had really happened with Joe, would the old man say he understood that Alfie was just a boy? Or would he hold it against him, the biggest disappointment of many disappointments with his number one son? Didn't the old man deserve the truth? Alfie knew how he'd blamed himself for Joe's having to leave Rome. He'd moped around for months. And then, years later, there they were, his father getting older by the hour, working like a dog and not being where he wanted. Alfie could have said something to ease his pain a little.

"Well, Son, no one wants to hear me go on. What about your job? How's that goin'?"

"Which one?"

From the time he got out of the Army until the time he joined the NYPD, Alfie hadn't kept any job for more than a year. Selling insurance, selling encyclopedias, selling real estate. Everything was for sale, and Alfie was no salesman. If you wanted somebody else to buy something, you had to believe in something yourself, or at least convince yourself you believed in something. He couldn't manage it, but he was stuck, and the restlessness ate him alive, especially after he got back from San Francisco. He couldn't leave New York, not for long anyway, and he wouldn't work for his grandfather anymore. That was out. There had to be something else. He could have done something that might remind him of why he was in the world to begin with. Men like his father didn't seem to need that reminder. The old man looked happy even when you knew he was miserable. Alfie needed that spirit. Matty tied up his bootlaces and made his way toward the trailer. Alfie followed him.

"Dad, I have to tell you something."

Alfie's eyes fell on the ugly frame of another building.

"But maybe not here."

Again his father put an arm around him. He studied Alfie's face, searching for what his son was holding back. With his cousins upstate, Alfie had learned how to take a joke. But here, if you kidded with him, it was only 50-50 he'd smile. Or he would take you seriously and argue. You could say he was always thinking about music and the accident and what he'd lost, but to tell the truth, he couldn't remember the time he felt close to anybody but Adeline, and by then not even her. His brother, on the other hand, was all smiles with the family, so his father never seemed to study Frankie the way he studied his first-born.

"Well, Son, if you want, you come by the house after work on Friday. We'll head down to Goombada Minuccia's. Little bit of wine never hurt nobody."

Goombada Minuccia was a real Italian, though you could hardly tell from talking to him. He came over from Italy when he was a boy, and he must've worked hard to lose whatever old-country accent he'd had. To Alfie he sounded like a lifelong Brooklynite. Goombada was around his father's age, a little shorter, with dark hair, thick eyebrows, and a thick nose. He was built like a small bull. The old man called him Goombada, because they both came from the same town, a little village called Laurino, in the mountains south of Naples. Goombada smiled so much that they also called him Happy. Which he was. Partly because he was good-natured and partly because he made his own wine. Since Alfie was a kid, Goombada had had a little cantina set up in his basement: a full bar, two couches facing each other, and a wooden table in the middle of the room underneath a stained-glass light fixture hanging from a heavy gold chain which looked like it belonged in a gambling parlor. The place was designed for shooting the shit.

The old man led him down the driveway to Goombada's door. Inside the cantina, looking like he'd already been there for a week, sat Tony Buongiorno. Tony was a big man, tall as Alfie, but a hundred pounds heavier, and just as cheerful as Goombada, but a little more reserved. Alfie and Matty both shook Tony's hand as they passed him on the way to the bar.

"C'mon. Have a drink. It's a long week."

Goombada poured them two highballs full of his latest red, which tasted to Alfie like a mixture of grass, grape juice and whiskey. His father took a big swig.

"Nice kick."

Goombada's face lit up.

"You betcha. I mean, what are we livin' for?"

They toasted straight-armed, glasses high in the air. The moment made Alfie feel as though he belonged to this older world more than he did to the one he saw around him now. He'd read in the newspapers about the World's Fair and the houses of tomorrow and computers and cars that drove through the air and what it would all mean to the things he took for granted, like familiar voices and the simple things people wanted to do like play guitar or build furniture by hand. If the world was all machines, would people be just like the machines? For years Alfie had felt himself becoming mechanical. But then wasn't his father the same? The old man turned to Goombada.

"How's your wife?"

Goombada faked a surprised expression.

"Goomada? She's wonderful. Upstairs."

They called her Goomada Minni, for Minnie, short for Minerva. Minnie Minuccia. Alfie wasn't sure she was even Italian, but it didn't matter. The name was everything.

"Ah, Minni. She's a real gem."

Tony raised his glass as he said this, and Goombada screwed up his wide face.

"And how would he know?" he said, elbowing Alfie. "He was never married."

The charge made Tony visibly uncomfortable, but he laughed it off, the way everybody expected him to.

"Oh! All I gotta do is look at you to know what it's like, you happy-go-lucky S.O.B.!"

This answer made Goombada laugh so hard that he spilled his wine. He set the dripping glass on the coffee table and sat down. The men went back and forth about the wine's flavor. Alfie tried to be generous.

"This is great, Goombada. I don't get to drink much anymore, with Michelle being pregnant and all."

Goombada looked at him like he had something important to say.

"You should drink more!"

They toasted the idea.

"How is she, your wife?" Goombada asked.

"Okay," Alfie said, making no effort to sound excited.

"I always thought she was a nice girl. All in for you. Right, Matty?"

"Oh, yeah, she never done nothin' but what Alfie wanted."

Alfie could tell that his father almost regretted putting it that way. His parents had been clear enough about how they felt when he got married: no church, baby already on the way, and barely a reception. Not that his father was ever religious, but to them, he could tell, the way he and Michelle had handled it was a sign of disrespect. His mother had talked to Alfie about not knowing the family. His father had never liked to play God like his mother did, but he'd frowned a lot. Since then, they could see through the small effort Alfie made to look happy. They could tell he had no space to breathe. The tone of his father's voice confirmed how he felt, but Alfie wasn't up to defending Michelle. Whatever argument he made, would he believe it himself?

If there was any tension in the room, Goombada ignored it.

"Ah, that's it: a pretty girl, a nice glass of wine, friends. I just wish we had a little *salsicc'*. Usually, Minnie brings some home for me, but today she went to her sister's. What can you do?"

The subject of food got Tony talking.

"My cousin was telling me that in Italy they make all kinds of *prosciutt'*, not just what we get here. They use everything: goat, lamb, you name it."

Goombada pinched together the fingers of his right hand and shook them at Tony.

"But c'mon, excuse me. What about the butcher on Bay Parkway? What's his name?"

"D'Angelo?"

"D'Angelo! Doesn't he make the lamb *prosciutt'*? Ah, believe me, anything they have over there in Italy, you can get here. We're in New York, for Chrissakes."

Alfie looked at his father. He knew how the old man felt about city life. He had friends here, that was true, but he always wanted to be hunting or walking through the woods, or drinking and talking with the men he grew up with, country boys like the preacher. And he wanted to be with his family, all the sisters and cousins who took care of him and remembered him as a handsome devil in a Stutz Bearcat (Alfie had seen the pictures). He never complained in front of Alfie's mother, but everybody could see that he wanted to be back in Rome. Alfie, for one, was glad they got out when they did. He liked the country too, but now he couldn't imagine a life there. No matter how bad things were with Michelle in Queens, they'd be twice as bad upstate, where you were content being a nobody. It made Alfie want to shout, "Three cheers for Brooklyn!" But then what was Brooklyn or Queens or any part of New York doing for Alfie? What good was the city if he couldn't play music or ride his bike through the empty streets? Look where he was.

Goombada was happy with his basement and his shitty wine, but he wasn't finished talking about food.

"Speaking of that, Matty, how's your other boy? He's a cook now, right?"

"Chef."

The word came out of Matty's mouth with such a high tone that Alfie and Goombada looked at each as if to say, "Who's this guy?"

"Big restaurant in the city."

Goombada raised his glass again, and the rest followed.

"*A Salut'!*"

"He's even livin' there now."

"Good for him. What does he cook?"

"Can't say I ever ate much of it? Maybe Alfie can tell ya."

"Snails," Alfie said, in a tone that cut into his father's pride.

Goombada sounded impressed and disgusted at the same time.

"*Ahtso!* Tony, you ever eat snails?"

Tony shook his head and took another sip of wine to wash away the imaginary taste.

"French food. My brother cooks French food now."

"You try it?" Goombada asked.

Alfie hesitated like he had to think about it.

"Not lately. I don't see my brother much these days."

Matty frowned, and they all took another sip. Then somebody knocked on the side door. Goombada frowned.

"Ah, Jeez, now I gotta get up again?"

Alfie jumped to his feet and signaled Goombada to stay put. When he cracked open the door, he looked out and saw nobody there. For a second he thought some kid must be playing a prank. Then he opened the door wider and looked down to see the bald pate of a short old man standing to the side. The old man looked up.

"Who are you?"

"Alfie. Matty's son. Nice to meet you."

"Ah, you don't remember me, do you? Well, I remember you. The newsstand down on New Utrecht and 70th. You remember?"

Alfie gave him a quick nod of recognition.

The old man hit him with a backhand in the middle of the chest.

"That's right. Sonny Malzone," he said, extending to Alfie the hand that had just smacked him.

Before he could shut the door, the character pushed past.

"Oh!" Goombada yelled. "Look what the cat dragged in."

The old man took off his sport coat and sat down in Alfie's seat.

"Cat, your sister's ass! Where's the wine?"

Matty laughed out loud.

"Sonny, good to see ya."

"Matty, I'm dyin' a thirst."

Matty toasted him, taking a pat on the shoulder from Goombada as he walked to the bar.

"Wine, comin' up."

Tony came to life.

"Nectar of the gods."

It didn't matter anymore how terrible the wine was. Alfie needed another glass, to relax. He followed Goombada and set his highball on the bar. Without saying a word, Goombada filled it near the top. Then he filled his own glass, swirled it like a connoisseur, and took a big gulp, following it with a long "Aaahhhh!" He winked at Alfie.

"Hey, Kid, watch this."

He poured another glass and brought it over to Malzone.

"Here you go, Sonny"

As Malzone brought the glass to his lips, Goombada interrupted.

"Ay, you hear what they're gonna do on New Utrecht?"

Goombada winked again at Alfie, and waited—though he didn't have to wait long—for Malzone to react.

"What? What are they doin'?"

"You didn't hear?"

"No, what?"

"Tony, you hear?"

Tony shrugged.

"Matty?"

Malzone looked at all of them, half in a panic.

"What? What are the sonofabitches gonna do now?"

Goombada grinned like a fool and kept it up.

"You're right, Sonny. They're sonofabitches. Especially when they do something like this?"

Malzone put down his glass, looking ready for a fight.

"Those motherless fucks."

"You know what they're doin'?"

Malzone looked around in vain for an answer.

"No. How the hell am I supposed to know?"

Goombada went in for the kill.

"Listen to this."

He cupped his hand around one side of his mouth, announcing it to the world.

"They're diggin' up New Utrecht all the way down to 86th. Gonna take 'em all summer."

A moment of calm. Then Malzone brought his fist down full force on the coffee table, puddling his wine on the veneer.

"Puttana diavolo! Their dirty *whooo-er* mothers should burn in hell! I never seen anything like it. How's a guy supposed to make a buck? They want to kill everybody, the greedy bastids."

Goombada tried to look concerned.

"What are you gonna do?"

"Do?" Malzone answered. "I'll tell you what I'm gonna do. I'm moving to Mexico. It's the mayor and Kennedy and the rest of 'em. They're all crooked."

He slammed his left hand into the crotch of his bent right elbow, the sound reverberating off the basement walls. A perfect Italian salute.

"Up their asses!"

They all laughed and seconded the wish, even Alfie, who was feeling a little better. The old men were a hundred percent occupied with busting each other's balls or reminiscing about the food and the women they'd loved, or arguing about current events that didn't seem to bother them for more than the time it took to curse somebody's family. His father was right in the middle of the conversation, but when Alfie tapped him on the shoulder, he got up with a quick "Excuse me, fellas" and walked up the stairs after his son. They stood in the driveway, lighting cigarettes. Alfie noticed how heavy his father's breathing was, just from the half-flight climb. He wished he could make him young again. If they'd grown up together, what kind of friends would they have been? Now his father seemed annoyed by something, puffing his cigarette and not making eye contact. He finally dropped the butt on the ground and crushed it with the thick sole of his shoe.

"What's wrong between you and your brother?" he asked.

Alfie wondered whether or not his father knew the whole story about Frankie, and if he did, what he thought about it. They started walking.

"Nothing, Dad. I just don't see him."

"Son, your father might not be the sharpest tack in the drawer, but I'm a long ways from stupid."

The 61st Street train ditch greeted them as they turned the corner from 12th Avenue.

"I don't know what to tell you. My brother's in a different world. That's all."

Matty pointed across the ditch.

"Can you see over there?"

Alfie got the point, but let his father talk.

"That's about how far it is from Brooklyn to Manhattan. Do me a favor. Next time you get a coupla hours free, go see your brother. Or tell him come out to Queens. It ain't the middle of nowhere. If you lose touch with him now, you'll regret it. Any regrets I got, Son, they ain't about keeping in touch with family."

Had his father guessed what Alfie wanted to talk about? Might as well come out with it.

"And your wife. It ain't my business, but now you're havin' another baby."

Alfie was relieved. About his wife his father could say whatever he wanted.

"Treat her the right way, Son. You got a family, and it's not getting smaller. You gotta see things different: your brother, your family, your friends, your job. You keep this up, soon you ain't gonna recognize yourself. That's why you gotta have somebody you can talk to. If it ain't your brother, it better be somebody else. For me it was a coupla my cousins and old Joe most of all."

Alfie's hands tightened into fists. Who did his father talk to now? Was it supposed to be him? He showed the old man a nervous smile.

"Yeah, I always wondered what happened to Joe."

The old man shot him a quick glance.

"I had a note from him right after we come to Brooklyn. Didn't I ever tell you?"

Alfie shook his head.

"Gone back to his people."

Alfie stopped walking and laid a hand on his father's shoulder.

"How come you never said nothing to me about what happened?"

Matty squinted.

"No need to. You seen it."

Alfie looked across the train ditch at the line of lights that could have been another civilization. It was the kind of simple, straight answer he should have expected, but the way his father said it made it seem like he was daring Alfie to confess.

"But don't you want to know why it happened?" he asked, searching his father's face for anger, catching instead a look of resignation he knew well.

"Son, if I knew why people think the way they do, I'd be a rich man. I just know most people ain't too sharp. I shoulda known better where I was and who I was dealin' with."

Matty took another cigarette from the pack and reached into his pocket for a match. The cover said "Lucky Strike" and pictured a man in uniform holding out a cigarette like a grenade.

"Things were different then, especially up Rome. I shoulda known they'd come after us. Maybe things are better now, but I can't say as I trust the world that much."

"Pop, listen, I just wish I could've done something."

"What? You were a kid. No offense, but I never met a kid wasn't dumb as they come. So how's a dumb kid supposed to stop the world."

Alfie leaned forward into the chain-link fence that kept people out of the ditch. He closed his eyes long enough to imagine a scene and a day free of everything that had ever happened to him. He opened his eyes and turned to his father again.

"So what I wanted to tell you."

The old man took a long drag. His eyes locked on Alfie and pushed him past the moment.

"I'm thinking once the new baby's settled in, I'm gonna try for the police academy. You think it's a good idea?"

"Well, plenty of your cousins done the same. Pay's alright, I suppose."

Naturally, it was the family reunions that had given Alfie the idea in the first place. When the cousins told stories about being cops, you knew they understood how the world worked, like it was all under control, like they were winning whatever the battle was.

"Michelle won't admit it, but I think she likes the idea, too. And I think I'd make a good cop. What do you think?"

Alfie hoped his father would have an answer that made him think twice, a way out that didn't involve a uniform. His father studied him again.

"If it was a few years ago, Son, I'd say you should go talk to your grandfather, and you come work with me. But now—no offense— you're a little long in the tooth to start at the bottom, which is where he'd put you. That and pretty soon you'd have to do my work for me. So I can't tell you I think it's a good idea or a bad one, you being a cop. It's all right with me, I suppose, so long as you sleep easy."

It had been a long time since Alfie could do that. Across the ditch he saw the outlines of vines in the twilight, and thought of the old men who planted them. They came from the old country and claimed their little plots of land and pretended they had farms. They ate and drank and had kids. They were nobodies, but if they were like his father, they were content to be nobodies. A subway rumbled along the bottom of the ditch. If Alfie couldn't have the one life he wanted, he would have to have different lives. In the twilight his father's age disappeared. When Alfie looked at him now, he saw all the fathers he'd known, all ages, standing shoulder to shoulder in a line-up, and himself in uniform behind a glass partition. "Turn to the right," he'd tell them. "Turn to the left. Now face me."

Alfie woke to the sight of his father's eyes. Twin ponds, each with a brown and black hole at the center, each glazed with a thin, milky mist. The old man had obviously had those eyes on him for a while.

"You look like your brother when you're asleep."

His father's voice sounded like dried leaves blown by the wind. Alfie blinked himself back to life.

"Yeah? Except I'm better looking than him when I'm awake."

The old man liked the joke, and snorted, which brought on a storm of coughs. When he could finally speak agin, he added flatly, "He comes almost every week lately."

Alfie shrugged.

"Yessir, like he's going to church. A coupla months now. Ever since he told us he was moving."

"Moving?"

"Says he's going to Italy with his friend."

Alfie had heard a little bit about the friend. What would his father think if he knew?

"Says he got an offer to cook there."

"Yeah, good for him."

"He didn't tell you?"

"No."

"His only brother, and he ain't told you?"

"Dad, I don't see him. He's too busy."

"Not too busy to come out to Brooklyn now and then."

"I don't live in Brooklyn anymore."

Alfie could feel his lips curling into a frown. He stood up and turned his back to his father's bed.

"Son, can I say something to you?"

The old man's voice gained force.

"I can't tell you and your brother how to get along. That's between men. But I can tell you that it's a good idea to treat your family like friends."

Alfie faced his father again, but said nothing as the old man looked hard at him.

"I'm telling you, Boy, go see your brother before he leaves. You can do that."

His father spoke now like he knew Alfie owed him.

"Don't worry," he said, clasping his father's hand as if they were shaking on a future that Alfie knew neither of them could see. He let go and was about to say he was leaving, when the old man cleared his throat.

"And one more thing I been meanin' to ask you. I know you been busy and you missed the reunion last year. But you do me one favor. If I can't make it this year, you go for me. Tell the cousins I wish I could be there. Have a drink for me. Shoot some skeet. Listen to some of the stories you heard a million times."

Alfie kissed his father's cheek, told him goodnight, and left him to the nurses' mercies.

(1969)

etween the American flags planted all over the property and
the ones flying from antennas on his cousins' parked trucks,
Alfie felt like he was driving into a national cemetery. He
heard shouting but couldn't make out the words. The usual loud-
mouths. He parked and closed the car door as quietly as he could.
Since the Columbia fiasco, where he first had the sick feeling of
hunting another human being, he couldn't stomach too much commotion or too much attention. When he got near the house, he
saw the younger guys huddled around folding tables, playing cards,
swearing. Meanwhile the old uncles and cousins were yelling their
heads off in front of the house, playing *morra*.

Closer in, Alfie heard Uncle Patsy and Cousin Al, both at least
in their sixties now, both wearing windbreakers and fishing hats,
both throwing whatever number of fingers they thought would
get them to the totals in their heads. Patsy's voice sounded like a
blender on high.

"*Cinquaaaayy!*"

No luck.

Al's baritone.

"*Quattroooooh!*"

Nothing.

Patsy again.

"*Sei-eeeee!*"

The old fool danced around like a kid, holding out an open
palm for Al to fill with greenbacks. Alfie smiled, in spite of himself.

Years ago his father had gone back and forth like this with Patsy for an hour. The two men would be so hoarse afterward that they could barely talk. Last year Alfie was just starting to walk again, and his father was already gone. When he called to say he couldn't make it, all he heard back was "Sorry about your old man." He knew his story had gotten around to them, but not a single cousin asked about Alfie's health or about what he was doing. If he guessed right, they were ashamed of him. One year here he'd dusted 23 of 25 clay birds. Only his father had ever done better. And what did it matter now? If some college asshole could break him, drive him off the force, he was letting them all down.

Way back in the old days his cousins had held the reunion at the Red Rooster Hotel in Catskill. That was before Bobby Marchese got caught shooting a pheasant on the front lawn of the church across the street and the police kindly asked them to move their party someplace else. The next year Zed Zamboni volunteered his place. Zed was a distant cousin by marriage. He made a fortune laying marble floors for people who could afford them. With his pile of money he bought a hundred and fifty acres of hill country, built a big ranch house complete with a gigantic stone patio and wraparound porch, and made the rest of the land his personal shooting range and game preserve. The place used to make Alfie feel proud and safe. At least a few days a year, time and everybody but these few men could go to hell. But ever since he'd joined the force, coming here, when he had the will to come at all, hadn't been the same. Still, a promise was a promise, no matter how hard it would be to relax with cousins who couldn't look you in the eye. He didn't want to talk about the old man, and he didn't want to hear the word "sorry." His mind was running a hundred different places where nobody wanted to be. Playing cards was a no-go. Maybe he'd shoot, but with his head not right, what would he hit? And the doctors who were keeping track of him still hadn't okayed drinking. A problem, since most of his cousins were what you might call casual alcoholics.

He greeted the uncles first. They patted him on the shoulder, took his face in their hands and kissed him on both cheeks. Sure, they hadn't asked him what had happened to him, but in their case it was because life had already gotten the best of them. They expected it to happen to you too. One by one they hugged him, looking like they wanted to cry. Instead they told him how much they missed his father, one of their gray gang.

"He was too young, too young."

Next Alfie went over to the card tables. Most of the younger cousins there raised their heads and nodded. Angelo, the cousin he featured least, got up from his folding chair. Angelo was maybe forty now. He'd been a sniper in the Korean War. And like he told everybody he met, with the right bullet and an M-1 he could shoot a guy's eye out at 300 yards. Combat for him was sitting on top of building or a hill, picking off dots on the ground—soldiers, civilians, maybe kids. Did he know what it was to feel a bone snap when you hit it with a baton? To see a woman shivering naked in a corner, bruises all over her face? To hold a child's broken body as he took his last breath and his hands went cold? Angelo was a state trooper, the arrogant kind who gave troopers a bad name, even among other cops. He bragged a lot about telling fellow troopers who took bribes that they were disgracing the uniform. He bragged so much about it that Alfie knew he must be taking bribes himself. Alfie felt sorry for the poor *gibooks* who were shit unlucky enough to have Angelo stop them. A goddamned hero.

"What happened? Did you run into these fuckin' hippies up here? Oh, wait, that was last week. Fuckin' peace and love."

Angelo's breath smelled of beer, anchovy pizza and mildew.

"And your father. I'm sorry."

"Yeah."

"And your mother, at least she's around."

For the first time since the riot, Alfie wanted to hit somebody. Instead, he play-slapped Angelo's cheek and walked past the tables again. This time the cousins ignored him. They were playing draw, throwing back paper cups of beer and red wine, taunting each other like they were enemies.

"You can't play a straight that way, Jerk-off. Look at this fuckin' guy. Does your mother know you play like this?"

Alfie sat on a folding chair away from the crowd, for what felt like an hour, waving off a couple of half-hearted offers to join the game, remembering the first time his father took him and his brother here. Right away, you could see Frankie didn't belong. He was still in cooking school then, living in an apartment in the city. Most of that weekend he'd sat in a corner near the cooler, watching everybody else play cards, play horseshoes, shoot skeet, shoot the shit. He remembered the old man not liking the way Frankie had acted, but not saying anything about it and hardly saying anything at all on the long ride home. Alfie hadn't been too thrilled with his brother, either. What would the cousins think now? Did they know his brother was a queer? Whatever way it was, Frankie had never come back. On the other hand, for a few years Alfie loved it. When one reunion ended, he couldn't wait for the next one. His mother could take the family or leave them, but to his father this reunion, and his family generally, was everything. Coming here was a three-day Sunday dinner, without a woman to nag him and with a chance to shoot till his shoulder was sore. Alfie liked it because you could say what you wanted about anybody else outside the family—who cared about them?—and, if you could take a little ball-busting, you were in the club for life.

Even with his bad wrist, Alfie could still play some simple songs with the old man. He was nothing close to what he'd been, but the two of them could lead the cousins through the standard numbers, mostly from the '20s and '30s. Their repertoire included "Jimmy Brown, the Newsboy," "Dinah," "If You Knew Susie," and some real oldies like "Fifteen Miles on the Erie Canal" and "Bill Bailey, Won't You Please Come Home?"—songs with choruses you could follow when you were half in the bag. It didn't matter that "Bill Bailey" was supposed to be sung by a woman. If there were forty guys there, thirty of them were belting it out at the top of their lungs. During those years Alfie had played cards and been able to talk with his cousins, so long as they talked about things—old family stories, women, food, houses, vacations, kids—only as ways to make smart-aleck remarks or to trigger their rituals. You could always count on what sounded like an argument between two cousins ending this way:

Cousin #1: "You know what?"
Cousin #2: "What?"
Cousin #1: "You're a great man?"
Cousin #2: (waiting for it) "Oh, yeah?"
Cousin #1: "Yeah." (turning to the gallery) "Hey, fellas, this is a great guy right here. He's like a god. Doesn't he deserve a hymn? Give him a hymn. Let's hear it."
Cousins in Unison: "Hiiimmmm. Hiiimmmm. Fuuuuccckk Hiiimmmm!"

Once Alfie became a cop, a game like that seemed stupid, like his cousins were a posse of bored delinquents standing on the corner of the avenue, waiting for something to happen so they could stand up to somebody threatening the neighborhood, or talk about how they would. Sitting apart, Alfie listened closely to what they were saying, especially to the stories. Angelo was going on again about hippies.

"It was like an invasion. Right, Zed? What'd they call it?"

Zed was chewing on a cigar and strangling a beer bottle, one eye on the poker game. He kept the cigar in his mouth while he spat out an answer.

"Woodstock. They were fuckin' everywhere. Giambruzz was coming up the weekend. It took him six hours to get here. Giambruzz, tell 'em."

Giambruzz was a man-mountain, whose mother was one of the goddesses watching over Rome, New York. His father had opened the Circle Bar during the war. Alfie remembered when his old man worked there. It was Giambruzz and Eddie Schiavone who started putting this thing together. As soon as all the younger fellas started to leave Rome and get jobs and get married, they needed a reunion—men only. It let you pretend you were living what could never happen again and maybe never happened at all. Giambruzz walked over to Zed like a drunken bear and pawed his cousin's shoulder. Alfie thought about what might've gone on at Woodstock, about what had happened at Columbia. Since that day, he hadn't been able to listen to music too often. Maybe he should start listening again. He'd heard on the news that the Beatles had another record coming out. But here was Giambruzz.

"I was stuck in traffic on 17, surrounded by all these kids, half of them with no clothes on. Radios blasting. Fuckin' mess. But at least it was raining on and off, and it wasn't hot. I hate the heat. People say they wanna move to Florida. Fuck that. Buncha fuckin' rebels. Everybody down there's half a *mulie*."

He took another long swig of beer. While the rest of the cousins were laughing at the joke, Giambruzz looked over at Alfie as if to say "Go fuck yourself."

"Bet you got a lot of them in New York, eh, Cuz."

Alfie hadn't heard or used the word *"mulie"* since he was on the job. *Mulignan'*. Eggplant. It struck him funny. Eggplants were purple. And all the cousins liked eggplant. Did any of them know why they said it? The muscles in Alfie's arms twitched, and he sat up a little straighter in his chair, looking at Giambruzz now the way he'd looked at the protestors. Normally if a guy looked at Giambruzz like that, it was a fight, but at that particular moment the big fuck didn't care. He was on a roll.

"Anyway, I'm sitting there, so I light up a cigar. And don't you think this fuckin' asshole kid with no shirt on comes up to the car and asks me for a light. I think these kids oughtta get fuckin' jobs, but what do I care about a light? So I pull out the lighter. And then what does he do? He pulls out a joint. And I give him a look and I put the lighter away. Now, mind you, this bullshit festival is on the radar all summer. Every cop and his mother's out. So then the kid starts gettin' fresh, sayin', 'Hey, c'mon, Man, I need a light,' and he's yellin' in my face. Then—you're not gonna fuckin' believe this—he pounds on the door and starts stickin' his arm inside the fuckin' car."

"Oh, shit."

"Yeah, he's reachin' in, so I grab him by his fuckin' scraggly beard with one hand and pull his face down by the steering wheel. Then with the other hand I grab my .45 from the glove compartment and stick in right in his fuckin' face. And he's shakin', ready to shit himself. And I say, 'Look at me, Dickhead,' and I look him right in the eye and I say, 'Walk back over to your fuckin' car right now and don't say a fuckin' word, or I'll blast your goddamn brains all over the road.'"

Half the cousins were still playing cards, barely paying attention, but the other half, the non-degenerate gamblers, were all nodding and laughing, then congratulating Giambruzz on his stand and his story, as the giant stalked over to the cooler, shaking hands along the way, a celebrity. He walked close to Alfie and ripped the tab off a beer can, right next to Alfie's ear. He put his free hand on Alfie's shoulder and squeezed so it hurt, then walked away like Alfie had a disease. Alfie fought the urge to break one of Giambruzz's fingers, because then the rest of them would have a reason to say he should never come back again. They'd get to think who they were. Of the non-card players, only his young cousin Danny, just back from the war, wasn't smiling. Alfie tried to catch his eye, but the kid kept his head down. Did he think his cousins were all morons? Until now Alfie had never paid much attention to how stupid Giambruzz was. So stupid that Alfie decided right there he would never talk to him again. He wondered whether or not his father knew how dumb his cousin was, or whether or not he cared. Maybe it was family and it didn't matter to him. Maybe it shouldn't. And what would his father think about Giambruzz's story? When he sat at the table, the old man made jokes, but he never made himself out to be a tough guy. And the closest he ever came to running people down was warning Alfie and Frankie away from them. Giambruzz never made the list of people to avoid, probably because they hardly saw him.

Once Giambruzz told his story, almost everybody else had something to say. Vinny jumped in first. Vinny was Danny's brother, and he'd also done a couple of tours in Vietnam after playing college baseball somewhere in New Jersey, then dropping out of school. He was smart enough, and the women loved him, but when he wasn't playing cards or dragging the other cousins to the racetrack, his mind and mouth were going a thousand miles a minute. Now he got up from his game and took over. His raspy voice was all bravado.

"Giambruzz, don't talk to me about the fuckin' hippies. A few of my friends from college—not my friends anymore—they're hippies now. I go back and go see this one guy and he tells me to my face I'm a baby-killer. I was a fuckin' radio man, for Chrissakes. I swear I never even had the chance to shoot somebody. Not that I wouldn't."

He raised a glass to the thought and looked straight at Alfie.

Alfie gave him a military salute, then, smirking to let him think he was kidding, gave him an Italian one. Vinny sent him a stupid smile back, sucked his drink down in one shot, and picked up where he left off.

"I know: peace and love, peace and love. I like peace and love. In fact, I love hippie girls because they're always on the pill. Couple of weeks ago, I fucked this hippie girl you wouldn't believe."

Another young cousin took the cue.

"Yeah, and I was banging Jane Fonda the other day."

"No, I'm serious. Billy. You shoulda seen this one. Tits and ass out to here, blond hair, blue eyes. She comes up to me in the store where I was working, and she tells me she wants to buy a shirt for her father, but she doesn't have any money. She says instead of money she can meet me that night for a drink. I meet her at her apartment in town, and that's it. She had all these bottles of Scotch and candles that looked like little wax mountains lined up all along the walls, and enough joints to take down a horse."

"Which you are!" Billy yelled.

"Fuckin'-ay right. I left the next morning, I could barely walk with my dungarees on."

"Did she come back for the shirt?"

"She came a lot, and she didn't have to come back."

"You're a real man."

"Yeah, a real man without a job. I got fired the next day for stealing, which is why I get to work with my big cousin Bobby, paving driveways."

He ran over to Bobby and lifted him off the ground in a bear hug.

"But she was worth every driveway I have to do."

Then a lot of the other cousins told stories about their many bar fights. On the beat in Brooklyn, Alfie was constantly locking guys like them up for drunk and disorderly. Here in the country, they did whatever they wanted, unless the local sheriff happened to be drinking in the same bar a few feet away. Whenever Alfie was with them, there was a fight. It was their entertainment. That and telling stories about fights. Zed did his best to keep the stories coming.

"Louie," he called to a cousin who was pushing sixty and who walked with a limp, "you remember that time at the Idle Hour?"

Louie threw his head back.

"Which one?"

"When your car was boxed in."

They'd all heard the story a dozen times, but it was a good story. In the past Alfie had always liked that as characters in these stories his cousins were never wrong. They were standing up to evil, to a force that took over certain big-mouthed men who weren't part of the family, especially when they were drinking, and especially when they had good-looking women with them.

"Oh, yeah."

Louie turned to the audience.

"I go out to the parking lot and see I can't get out. There's a big Plymouth blocking me. So I go back in and I ask the bartender to ask whose car it is. A few minutes later he tells me the fella's playing pool and I have to wait."

Patsy egged him on.

"I bet you didn't like that."

"No, can't say I did. So I ask the bartender to point him out. And the bartender says to me, 'Listen, I don't need no trouble tonight.'"

Louie winked.

"And I says to him, 'Don't worry. There won't be no trouble.'"

On cue they all chuckled.

"So I go over to this prick at the pool table and I say, 'Excuse me, but your car's out there blocking me in.' And the prick says, 'So?' So I says, 'Well, we got a problem.' And he says, 'You got a problem. I'm shootin' pool.' And I says, 'Well I got a few fellas in here think it's a problem.' And he says, 'That deputy right there don't think it's a problem.' Now, I don't know this, but Patsy and Giambruzz and the other fellas see this going on and while I'm arguin', they go outside. In the meantime I'm getting nowhere, and I wanna take a swing, but I don't wanna spend the night in jail, so I go out to get air."

"To get what?" Zed yelled, breaking Louie's balls.

"Air!"

Louie turned his whole body one way, then the other, like a pear-shaped marionette.

"What'd I say?"

"Air!" they all yelled.

"Anyways, when I get out there, what do I see? All the cousins are standing around the Plymouth, boucin' it up and down. Just then the owner comes out. And he's yellin', 'What the hell are youse doin' to my car?' And don't you think they pick up the whole god-damn thing and move it. While he's watchin'. And he goes runnin' over, lookin' to hit somebody, until Matty tackles him and they all dive on top of him. And they're holding him up in the air, like he's a jolly good asshole. And he's yellin' and screamin', but before he can say too much, they throw him in the dumpster out back. And that's that."

They all clapped, but the few who let their eyes drift over to Alfie or Danny stopped a little sooner. They'd probably miss the joke that he wasn't a cop anymore.

Not to be topped, Zed took the stage and told a story about stealing a fella's girl while he was in the bathroom, and then knock-ing him out with one punch. When he finished, a few more of the cousins took their turns. Pool cues broke over heads, bodies went flying over bars, bottles smashed, windows shattered, lips split open, eyes swelled up, women gave it up in bathrooms and parking lots—with the men who had brought them standing just fifty feet away, and only rarely did a cousin have to go to the hospital for an injury. They were legends, and Alfie had been one of them. His father was always warning him about the dangers of bars, so Alfie would wait for nights when the old man didn't tag along. The cousins liked that Alfie was big, that he looked angry half the time, and that he had a temper. They also knew that he'd boxed in the Army. And Alfie knew himself how hard he could hit. If some jackass deserved it, he didn't think twice about laying him out and trying to go home with his girl. He let himself smile, remembering the times he'd walked out of a bar with one of the cousins holding his arm up in the air, like he was Marciano. Looking back, though, Alfie thought maybe they'd also wanted him to get his face smashed in, so that the women would like him a little less. Most of them were upstaters, and he was a city boy.

"Alfie!"

It was Louie, limping toward him, his hair wild, like a circus clown. All eyes turned to Alfie. Half-frowning faces. Like he was about to testify in a courtroom.

"Alfie, you remember that time in Rosendale? You was—what?—maybe twenty-six, twenty-seven?"

A few heads nodded, remembering a better version of their cousin, one Louie was trying to revive.

"We're out there in some bullshit bar, and there's ten people in the whole place."

The jukebox was playing a tune Alfie liked.

"Some kid—I don't know, he was a little younger than you—is buzzing around all night, like a fly. He's lookin' over our shoulders. Ya know? Right on top of us."

One of the cousins interrupted with a signal.

"How close was he?"

Louie spun around to face the cousin, holding his two index fingers an inch apart.

"This close, I'm telling ya. On top of us. With a dopey grin. And he's sayin' perverted things to us. I didn't even understand some of them."

"No kiddin'!" another cousin called out.

Louie pantomimed a pulled punch.

"Ay, ay! One a youse needs a shot. C'mon. No, Zeddy, you were there, no? C'mon. That kid with the goofy face. He wouldn't let up. So somebody—Charlie, was it you?—somebody says, 'Eh, Alfie, please take care of this kid.'"

Alfie remembered the exact moment, the exact beer he was drinking, the exact red-head whose eye he was trying to catch. And, yeah, the kid's goofy face. He still didn't like the face, but he hated himself now for thinking that way.

"So, Alfie, you remember what you did?"

Fuck you, Louie. And excuse me, Lord, but fuck all of them. For all the things they had no idea about, forgive them. And also fuck them. They made Alfie want to be old as he felt. Ask: Who's that kid in love? Who's that punk who thinks he can play guitar? Who's that soldier? Who's that uniform? It's not me, Lord. Look what I am. Look how I'm nothing.

"You told the kid to come outside, and you kept shoving him toward the door. And you remember what he did, Alfie? Fellas, you remember?"

"Fuckin' kid!" a cousin yelled, so Louie could go on.

"Fuckin' kid keeps comin'. Like he's a wind-up toy or somethin'. And you could see Alfie's face gettin' red."

And they all looked to see if his face was red now, if they could make him be that version of himself again, that pet animal. So fuck them and fuck them and fuck them. And if I say that, my father, do you forgive me? And now do you know everything? Do you know what really happened to the preacher? Do you understand the way your son could be?

"Finally, it's like Alfie can't take it anymore."

They were all smiling, like a stripper had just walked on stage in front of them.

His body one reflex, Alfie stood up and started talking, bullets in his voice.

"So you want to hear how it ends, boys, right?"

They all stopped smiling.

"So I grabbed this goofy kid by his collar."

He looked at Angelo like he'd looked at the kid at Columbia whose arm he'd wrecked, like someone who deserved the pain. He heard his voice getting louder and louder.

"You know what I did, Angelo? You wanna know, dontcha?"

Quiet.

"I hit the kid all I had, right in his fuckin' ribs. Want me to show you?"

Angelo looked like he would piss himself.

"And what did the kid do, Louie? You remember?"

Louie almost whispered, "Sure."

"He went down like a ton a bricks. Remember how he was thrashin' around on the floor? And how everybody in there was ready to jump on me, tellin' me the kid wasn't right in the head? And how they sent for the kid's mother. And how the ambulance came."

He turned to Zed.

"Remember that, Cousin? And remember what you did when all that happened?"

Zed screwed up his face, shrugged, and conceded.

"Tell me, Cuz."

"You didn't know whether to shit, pick your nose, or eat cherries."

Zed waved him off and went for another beer.

"He was half a retard, boys, but I showed 'em who he shouldn't fuck with."

Alfie sat down again and closed his eyes. His cousins' voices were grunts, like you heard when your fist connected with a rib or a cheekbone. Maybe he had always been that animal. All the faces he'd ever hit appeared to him now, suspects in a line-up, with him the criminal. His head was starting to throb. If he'd been drinking, he'd have to throw up. He kept his eyes closed for a long time. When he finally opened them again, he saw right in front of him the big belly of Charlie Baliato, his father's first cousin, another state trooper. He was talking to Alfie, trying to make nice, saying something about the Moon landing. But what Charlie really wanted was to swap cop stories. Since the riot Alfie hadn't talked about the job. Charlie had worked riot detail, and Alfie knew he would start asking questions that Alfie didn't want to answer. Charlie loved being a cop, maybe more than he loved his kids. Which made Alfie think about his own kids and what Michelle might be telling them right now. If Alfie hadn't loved the job exactly, he'd felt like there was something real to it, but that was all over, and maybe so was his marriage. Charlie didn't have those kinds of problems. He didn't seem to have any problems doing whatever he had to do. He'd tell you he did it for his family and for society, and he believed it. Alfie envied him, but he couldn't listen to Charlie's crap anymore. He stood up, patted Charlie's back, and slipped into the darkness behind Zed's house.

Still hot from his story, Alfie welcomed the chilly night air. He buttoned up his sweater and walked to the edge of the woods. A three-quarter Moon lit up the pine tops and a patch of sky above them. A bird his father could've identified called out from a distance. The coyotes would be around too, smelling food, waiting until things got quiet and the dogs disappeared inside, so they could start howling and sniffing around the patio for scraps. A lot of people were scared of coyotes, but Alfie knew the animals were the ones who should be scared. In the backs of their pickup trucks and trunks of their sedans, his blood relatives were hauling an arsenal, enough firepower to wipe out all the coyotes and half the game on Zed's property inside a week. The woods quieted. Alfie inhaled a shot of cold air, then walked to the house.

Maybe he'd eat. Zed's kitchen was small, but it had everything: an old steel sink and a row of pots and pans hanging on hooks above the stone counter; a marble floor; an oversized stove that took up half a wall; and crammed next to it, two huge refrigerators. Alfie opened one of the refrigerators and pulled out a sandwich from the pile of sandwiches he knew would be there. He undid the folded foil and stood at the counter, taking one big bite after another. Why not eat their food? A last meal was the least he deserved. On the counter Alfie noticed something he hadn't seen in years: an Adams Hats matchbook cover. It was preserved inside a small plastic envelope and looked to be from the Forties. He remembered his uncles wearing the Adams pork pies and fedoras. When he was a kid, half of Rome wore fedoras. If you saved enough of these covers and sent them in, you got a free hat in the mail. This one showed one of "Sam Taub's Ring Personalities." His father would've loved it. He'd been crazy for boxing and liked to talk about all the fighters, especially the Italian ones. Alfie picked up the matchbook and read it:

"Probably the only man to win 4 ring titles and almost a 5th."

Salut'!

"His fights were never disappointing, and in fact, those with Kid Chocolate, Barney Ross, Jimmy McLamin, and Lou Amben were sensational."

None of the names rang a bell, but they must have been somebodies.

"You've guessed it. **He's TONY CANZONERI.**"

Alfie wondered if Zed had planned to show this to him: a little message about where they came from. Did Zed remember that smoking had killed Alfie's father? Watching the old man die had made him quit his own habit. Mostly. Alfie slipped the plastic envelope on top of the taller refrigerator, out of sight. Inside the refrigerator he found a door full of Cokes and popped one open. Noise from the card games and music filtered in. The night was still in full swing, but he wasn't going out again. He needed quiet, to be alone and to forget the stories in the air and especially the ones in his head.

"Anybody there?" he called down the hallway.

No answer.

He walked into Zed's living room. The place was a monument to guns and hunting and America. Against one wall was a leather couch, a recliner, and an oversized gun cabinet stocked with twelve and sixteen-gauge shotguns, a 22-caliber rifle, a .270 rifle, an old

Army M-1, and an even older Mauser. At the bottom of the cabinet was a rack of handguns and boxes of ammo. The key was in the lock. Alfie opened it and took out the M-1. He hefted it: a good ten pounds. Zed would never keep it loaded, so Alfie aimed it at the middle star on the flag and pulled the trigger. The gun clicked. He stood it straight up and looked down the barrel. In a firefight you could get off 40, 50 rounds a minute. It was how the Army annihilated the Germans. He rested the gun on his lap and sat back. Mounted animal heads lined the tops of the walls. Zed had gotten so serious about hunting that he would plan his year around exotic trips. He shot antelope, big cats, elk, anything he could stalk. The eyes in their stiff faces were staring at Alfie now. He took a deep breath, then got up and put the gun back in the cabinet, locked it, and put the key on top, out of sight.

On the coffee table were piles of magazines and a few dog-eared books. The magazines were what he expected, all the latest issues of *Field & Stream*, *Sports Afield*, and *Outdoor Life*, plus a few gun catalogs. The books all looked old. He picked up one called *Arms and Ammunition Annual*. The cover showed a hunter wearing an old-fashioned cap and jacket, standing in tall grass, aiming a double-barrel shotgun at the "i" in "Ammunition." Inside was a collection of articles from all the 1952 issues of *Outdoor Life*: "Lightweight Rifles for Big Game," "Wanted: An All-Purpose Bullet," "Jack Rabbits are Big Game-Practice." He tried but couldn't get past the first paragraph of any of them, so he settled for skimming. Some of the titles got right to the point: "Sights for Your Shotgun," "How to Hunt Mule Deer," "Expert Handgun Shooting." Some made shooting sound like dealing with women: "Prettying Up Your Guns" (if you were a bachelor), "Taking Care of Your Gun" (if you were married) or "Birds Can Teach You" (if you'd been through the mill). And some made you think that your life depended on it: "Pressure Can Be Dangerous," "Trajectory and You," "How Not to Miss." Alfie put the book down and picked up another. Pieces of the cover flaked off in his hand. The spine had been reinforced with Scotch Tape, which had yellowed almost to brown.

On the cover was a painting of two fly fisherman, one standing on a rock, one knee-deep in the middle of a river, each of them looking upstream, out of the picture, probably at the fish the one on the rock had hooked. Around the painting were pencil sketches of guns, nets, fish, and game. It was called *The Complete Sportsman's Encyclopedia*. Every page was about making yourself comfortable in the woods. When Alfie was a kid, another cousin had given him *The Book of Woodcraft* and the Boy Scout manual. Those books said that you roughed it so you wouldn't have to disturb nature. This book wanted you to catch or trap or blast anything that got in the way. Almost every page had an illustration. One showed a beaver caught the right way in a trap: underwater, so he drowned. Even the author's name—Buzzacott—made him sound like he would destroy everything he saw. Alfie closed the book as the grandfather clock in the corner struck ten.

A little television would be good right now, he thought. Something funny. But it was already too late for Don Rickles. And no radio around. Feeling cold, Alfie grabbed a crocheted blanket from a wing chair and lay down on the couch. Plenty of nights Michelle made him sleep on the sofa, which wouldn't be so bad except the kids got up in the morning and saw him there. Alfie dozed, but snapped out of it when he heard a noise, somebody else in Zed's living room. He whipped his head around and saw Danny sitting in the wing chair, with a thousand-yard stare, still as death. Alfie tried to get his attention, but it was fixed on the rack of a ten-point buck head hanging over the couch.

"You all right, Cuz?"

The kid didn't answer right away, his gaze falling slow as a parachute, landing finally on Alfie's face.

"You were reading about guns," Danny said.

Alfie considered the coffee table, then Danny's blank expression. "And hunting."

The kid closed his eyes, then popped them open like he'd heard a shot.

"I used to love guns," he said.

Alfie tried to read his cousin's eyes before he answered.

"Me too."

"I mean I could shoot almost anything. Did I say anything?"

Danny fired an imaginary rifle all around the room.

"The funny thing was that in Vietnam I didn't shoot for a long time. My platoon walked forever. For weeks. No V.C. You could hear the artillery and sometimes the bombs, but it was just a long hike. Like they tell you. Like an adventure. Like pretending."

He had always been a handsome kid, but always a little heavy. A likeable kid, though the way he slouched and hardly looked at you when he talked, he acted as if nobody knew he was alive. The Army made him stand up straighter, but it made his face harder, too. His eyes looked glassy, and his lips barely moved when he spoke. Alfie had seen the same look on other vets' faces. Some of them stood on corners all day. Some he had to collar when they beat their wives and kids. Some wound up with toe tags in the morgue.

"I wrote to my girl a lot. You ever meet my girl?" Danny asked.

"No."

"Beautiful girl."

Danny stuck his hand in his pocket. Alfie faked like he was scratching his leg, to get close to his ankle holster. He watched every move the kid made until he saw him pull out a wallet-sized picture and hold it up.

"Smart too. College degree. Here. Look."

Danny wasn't lying. The girl was a cross between Ann-Margret and the Adeline that Alfie remembered from Brooklyn. He held the photo a few seconds too long. Danny snatched it out of his hand, and looked hard into Alfie's eyes.

"I heard what you went through. I'm just like you that way."

If the kid meant they were both half-dead, he was right. Alfie remembered the first day on the job that he'd seen somebody die: an old woman some thug had put in the hospital. Right before her last breath, she mistook Alfie for her son. It made you hate the world. The last couple of years, even before the riot, he'd been having the same nightmare. In part of it he hovered over himself on his deathbed; in another part, he was on the deathbed, thinking of himself setting the house on fire, then floating out into the atmosphere, landing far away, in a strange house, next to Adeline naked on a leather couch, who, without looking at him, in a voice he didn't recognize, asked him over and over, "What do you want?"

"Can I tell you something?" Danny asked.

"Sure."

"I gave her my gun and told her to shoot me."

Alfie knew guys on the job who could talk a pigeon off a ledge.

"You're not like me, Kid."

Danny ignored him and kept talking.

"Since I got back, I can't talk to her. She's showing me curtains, and I'm thinking about the sound of an explosion and then I go deaf and I can't hear her at all. And she's staring at me and asking, 'Are you okay?' What if I told her a story? I have stories I should tell people, but maybe not my girl. What if she's my wife and she knows all these stories and we have kids and she's always worrying what I'm gonna say? Aren't you afraid of that? What if your girl leaves?"

Alfie didn't know much about being alone? He'd always thought that was what he wanted. But the times he'd been alone, he'd been afraid. What do you do if the only voice you hear every night is your own? Maybe that's what happened when you got old? Maybe that's what made you ready to give up and die? What could he say that would help?

"If she loves you, she'll put up with almost anything. That I can tell you."

Danny glanced at him, then scanned the room.

"Is that cabinet locked?"

"Yeah. I tried it."

He'd tackle him and yell for help.

They sat for a minute, silent. Then Danny stood up and walked to a window.

"Can I tell you a story?"

Alfie was exhausted, but he forced himself to listen and watch as closely as he could, like walking a beat on the twelve-to-eight.

"Yeah, of course."

From the patio came chokes of laughter. Danny scratched his cheek with the back of his hand.

"When I deployed to Saigon, a buddy of mine from home was stationed there too. He was in another unit, but we got together. His name was Herm. He married his girl straight out of high school, and they had a little boy named Jack. When we got into Saigon, he bought the kid a jacket. Jacket for Jack."

Danny smiled for the first time, stretching his thin arms over his head as he walked in a circle behind the coffee table.

"This jacket is black silk, and it has tiger patches on the sleeves. What little boy's not gonna love that, right? The whole country of South Vietnam is stitched on the back, with a big "Saigon 1967" over it. Herm's unit was leaving the next morning, and mine was gonna be in the city another week, so he asked could I send it home for him. And I meant to, but we were busy and I didn't get it sent and didn't get it sent, and then a few of days in, word came back that Herm was killed. Done. A rocket hit. Blown to smithereens. No remains, no nothing. One minute he's there, the next he's air."

Danny twirled his finger in front of Alfie's face and yelled, "Woo-hoo!"

Maybe he should get the kid outside, but then he might feel betrayed. No. Stay put. Watch.

"So now I have this jacket. I keep it in the garage, because sometimes I think of the fields there, and the V.C., and the way they disguised themselves like farmers. We called in strikes on the paddies, and an hour later you could walk through and see the burnt bodies with their AKs next to them. You know what we did? We waited for the guns to cool off and then we took them. Good rifles. I know you like rifles. I see the fields and the bodies on the back of the jacket, and I wanna go in the garage and light the jacket and everything on fire, because if the kid wears that jacket, he's wearing death."

He wanted to tell his cousin that they were all wearing the death jacket. He wanted to tell him he was right: a fella as young as him shouldn't have to wear it every day. A young cop or soldier felt like he had that jacket on all the time. But to dwell on it, what good did it do?

The kid was sitting on the wing chair now, far away as the Moon. Alfie slapped his hands on his thighs and stood up.

"C'mon, Danny, let's go get all this crap off our minds. How about a drink?"

He walked to the kitchen door and turned around, waiting for his cousin to follow.

"C'mon, I'm leaving soon. I'll drive you back to the hotel."

Danny stood up like he had arthritis. Alfie walked out the door and went right for Vinny, who hadn't moved from the card game.

"Can I talk to you?"

His tone said, "Right now."

Vinny twisted a cigarette in his ashtray and walked with Alfie to the driveway.

"Your brother Danny."

Vinny was still sober but was almost shouting like he was still in the game.

"Yeah. What? Is he ready to kill himself again?"

Alfie tried not to punch his cousin. This cousin. Any cousin. But Vinny kept talking.

"Before you play psychiatrist, Alfie, let me tell you something about my brother. I bet you think he was always a nice kid. Am I right? You think the war fucked him up, no? Look. War fucks everybody up."

Vinny pulled a pack of cigarettes from his pocket and waved it in the air as he spoke.

"That's what the fuckin' hippies say, right?"

His eyes flitted back and forth across Alfie's face.

"Yeah, it's fucked up. So what? So you fuckin' stay home and play the guitar?"

Alfie clenched his fist inside his pocket. He thought about the university gates, about the cherry blossoms he'd picked up and held in his hand as his squad moved in. What it felt like to squeeze them between his fingers. And Vinny wouldn't shut up.

"You got a brother, dontcha? And what's he doin'?"

Alfie was sure they had their stories about the way his brother was, about how he lived. They talked, because they'd never know the first thing about it.

"Let me tell you something," Vinny said. "My brother was always a fuckin' nut job. Nice kid, my ass. He's cracked. When we were kids, he used to take his food and run to his room, like a rat. And my mother let him do it, because he was 'sensitive,' she said."

He lit a cigarette.

"Fuckin' sensitive. I waited for the day my father would take him outside and beat the shit out of him. But what could he do? His wife. The old man had to get laid, too."

Vinny was standing a few inches from Alfie now, puffing smoke into Alfie's eyes. Piece of shit. Alfie pinched the cigarette and yanked it from Vinny's mouth, then bent it between his fingers. He poked his finger into Vinny's chest.

"Don't be a fuckin' punk."

Vinny jerked his head away and took a step back. He looked more ashamed than scared. Then he gathered himself and took an uncertain half-step toward Alfie, who almost spat in his face.

"Fuckin' hero," Alfie growled. "Let me shake your hand."

He grabbed Vinny's hand and squeezed until his cousin tilted sideways in pain. Then he squeezed a little harder.

"Lot of nut jobs out here, Vinny."

Alfie lifted his cousin's arm and threw it back at him.

"I told your brother I'm takin' him back to the hotel."

Vinny flicked his hand up and down like he was shaking a thermometer, trying to get the feeling back.

"No," he said. "I'll take care of it. Where is he?"

They both searched the patio.

"He was following me. Maybe he never came out."

Vinny walked slowly to the house and disappeared inside.

Without telling anyone else he was leaving, Alfie got in his car. The leg the college kid had broken felt weak now, like the kid's weight was landing on him all over again. The cold vinyl seat didn't help. He started the engine and reached for his bomber jacket, pulled it on, and blew into his hands. Warm it up. Get started. The kids at least would be missing him. He could make Brooklyn and get a few hours' sleep before breakfast. It would be a long ride, but if he managed to stay awake, he'd drive straight through. He could hear raised voices behind him as he rolled down the driveway. Calling or laughing, who cared? The darkness retreated from his headlights. He concentrated on the beams. On the two-lane road to the highway he drove like he was on patrol, crawling along, one eye on the woods for any animal that might jump out and catch him by surprise.

(1973/1972)

The snow had stopped falling the night before, but Alfie knew he'd still have to negotiate the clouds of it that rose from drifts along Route 26. He'd watch carefully for the left at Turin. When he reached the spot, he'd find a patch of ground where he could park his father's '65 Chevelle. As he drove toward the dead middle of Tug Hill, he imagined his father next to him, how he'd be trying to see deep into the woods along the road, and how he might start talking about his favorite hunting grounds and the ways to reach them. Alfie started to say something out loud—as if the old man could hear him—then stopped himself. He took a deep breath, letting his mind wander again as the car rolled through the dead white landscape.

He remembered how, the week before, he'd gone to buy the newspaper, the *New York Times*, which he'd only started reading after he'd left Brooklyn for Rome. It was a brutal afternoon, late January, and he hurried down Dominic Street to the coffee shop. When he got there, he ordered a bowl of soup and unfolded the paper on his table. The early sun was already dying behind low clouds, and flurries were starting to dance outside the window. He rubbed his hands together and read the top headline: *VIETNAM ACCORD IS REACHED; CEASE FIRE BEGINS SATURDAY; P.O.W.'s TO BE FREE IN 60 DAYS*. It occurred to Alfie that he hadn't known peace for at least as long as the war had been on.

After he'd left his miserable marriage and moved in with his mother, she'd asked him every half-hour how he was doing and what he was doing about her grandchildren. She'd seemed to know how he was feeling. He'd seen that expression on her face too many times. When he was young, he'd thought it was just her bad temper. As she grew older, he could see that she was usually angry with the old man, but that when he wasn't watching she looked at him like they were newlyweds but also like she pitied him. Then, when he was talking to her, she looked disgusted again. She knew about anger and disappointment, but also about love. And she could read her own children like dime novels. He'd been back in her house a few months, mostly moping around. Sometimes he'd come to the kitchen for dinner and wouldn't say five words, but one night his mother had come right out with it.

"You never loved her."

It had been an exhausting day, and Alfie was sitting at the table with his head down on his folded arms. His mother was standing at the stove.

"What, Ma? What are you talkin' about?"

"Michelle. I'm not stupid, Son."

"I never thought you were stupid, Ma."

"I kept my mouth shut."

When Alfie was a kid, her voice had filled the house.

"You're not the only one who had a bad marriage, and a bad marriage doesn't give you license."

He raised his head.

"I don't feel like Michelle or anybody else ever gave me, ah, license."

"That's not what I mean. I mean the children."

"What about them? She has them. What am I supposed to do?"

"Alfie, you never leave this house. Go see them. No matter what, you're still their father. Your father and I ... Let's just say he didn't always want to be here, but he was, and I was."

"You telling me you were both miserable?"

"I didn't say that, but a lot of the time it was hard with him. And you're changing the subject. Remember your children."

Alfie turned to his mother with a pleading look.

"Are we gonna eat?"

"Just like your father."

"The man you didn't love."

"I didn't say that either. Of course I loved him, and we both knew what it meant to have children. But he did things, Alfie, that made it hard."

"Like what, Ma? What'd he do?"

"If I didn't say anything all those years, why would I tell you now?"

"What? You're gonna tell me he hit you?"

"Your father never hit me. But there were other things."

"Tell me while we eat."

If she had secrets, especially about the old man, did he want to know them? His mother stood there with one hand on the oven handle and the other holding a wooden spoon like a judge's gavel.

"Okay, you want a story, I'll tell you a story."

Alfie assented with a wave of his fork.

"He wasn't always the nice husband people thought."

She took Alfie's plate and filled it with a chicken cutlet and a heap of mashed potatoes.

"The salad's on the table."

"You gonna sit?"

"I'm sitting."

She sat down without a plate in front of her. She liked to eat while she was cooking, then monitor the family meal. A born director. She laid her hands on the table.

"I'm not sure about the year, but it must have been 1939. Harry James and his orchestra were coming to town. I remember that a fellow from Rome was a member of the orchestra, and they were coming as a favor to him. Your father's cousin Marguerite said that the orchestra had a new Italian singer, a skinny young man who made the girls swoon. The Capitol Theatre was supposed to be packed.

"We'd just moved up to Rome, and the whole time your father had been working so much that we hadn't had a single night out. Not that you could blame him. My family wasn't helping us, and the house on Mill Street didn't come free. And with it being summer and you babies being so active, we couldn't get out. But by then—it must have been October—Matty's aunts knew me a little better and were more willing to watch you boys. Your father's family were basically fine people. If they were poor and if the men drank too much, I couldn't hold that against them. And my family was wrong about Rome. It wasn't depressing at all. It was a quaint town. And it was quiet by the canal. Even with the babies, I could sit and think and play the violin in peace. My parents always had the wrong idea about me. I knew they did, because everyone made a point of telling me how I was the prettiest sister."

His mother watched Alfie out of the corner of her eye, like she was waiting for a remark.

"And everyone talked about how bright we were, my sisters and I. My mother would go on and on. 'Our Penelope could play at Carnegie Hall.' And I suppose I liked the attention, but I didn't like feeling that their hopes—whatever they were—depended on me. I wanted to leave Brooklyn as much as your father did."

Alfie remembered how his parents were supposed to have met through their families. His mother's family had people up Rome, and somehow they knew the Baliatos, and his mother was on a visit, and his father spotted her out one night, and that was that. They got married, and his father, the country boy, agreed to move to Brooklyn. The way things turned out, the old man had to move there twice, to a place he hated, and he had to die there.

"Anyway, the question was how to get Matty out of work for a night. So I dropped hints with the aunts, who, naturally, were married to the uncles, who owned the inns where your father worked. As far as the house on Mill Street was concerned, it was no dream, nothing compared to my father's house, but from the second-floor window I had a good view of the river and the canal. Frankie was happy playing in the little sitting room or in your bedroom; and when you came home from school, you played in the yard with a little friend from the block. It was safe. Yes, the winters were hard.

The aunts liked to tell me how hard they were, and how they let their children leap out of their upstairs windows into the snow. So I thought we'd better step out on the town before the worst of the weather set in.

"The day after I mentioned to the aunts that I'd like to see the show, your father woke up with the news. I remember how he smiled when he told me. 'It's something, Pen,' he said. 'Out of nowhere Uncle Nails tells me to take these tickets. And when I ask him 'What tickets?' he tells me they're for the Capitol, to see Harry James. Of course, I did my best to act surprised. He was so excited. 'We both like Benny Goodman,' he said to me, 'and wasn't he in that outfit?' And his uncle told him to take the night off, a Friday, no less. I can see him now, smoking his cigarette and drinking his coffee, telling me how he'd gotten the tickets from Mr. Vestino, who was hosting a big shindig for the band at the Savoy. When he smiled, your father was a handsome man. His profile was like a hawk's."

She smoothed the tablecloth with the palm of one hand.

"He was coarse sometimes, but I could forgive him. He was good-looking and hardworking, and I knew he loved you."

If by "coarse" she meant the way the old man had talked, Alfie wondered how much that really meant. Around the house his father had been gentle as a rabbit. He saved his moments of anger for the rest of the world. When Alfie was a boy, those moments had terrified him. He'd seen his father beat a man so badly you could barely recognize him. But he'd never hit or so much as yelled at his mother.

"It was raining that day, but then it let up and we took you boys to Delta Lake. The park there was empty, and you could hear the breeze blowing through the leaves. You and your father ran up ahead of me and Frankie. It was always like that with the two of you. But I loved to watch how you both ran along. Nothing made your father happier than having his family in the country. The lake looked like a postcard, and the two of you ..."

She laughed.

"What?"

"I remember thinking that the way you were running, it was like watching two apes in the wild."

Alfie had never thought of his mother as a snob exactly, but now he wondered.

"When Friday finally came, I spent the whole day deciding what to wear and what your father should wear. I made sure to ask Aunt Betsy if I could borrow a couple of her husband's jackets. I laid them out for your father, and we settled on a gray coat with a red tie. The red even matched the seats of our old Packard. I can still picture him dressed to the nines, opening the door for his aunt when she came to babysit. I was so happy we could go in style, because the Savoy always reminded me of a little castle. It had a family crest with the Vestino name over the front door. I don't know if you remember it, but it was right across the bridge on Dominic Street. Really, we could've walked, but we agreed on driving. After the valet took the car, we just stood there on the sidewalk. It was cool that night, so I wore my fur wrap. And the sidewalk was still wet from the rain that day. It reflected all the lights the Vestinos had strung up for the occasion. Even that name, Vestino, it sounded like destiny. I felt like we were meant to be there. When we walked in, Old Man Vestino greeted us at the door. He was a real old Italian."

Now his mother made herself into a performer, doing Vestino's immigrant accent.

"He said, 'Ah, Matty. How'sa you uncle? I don't see him,' and he hugged us. And then he kissed my hand and seemed a little embarrassed by it. You should have seen us then, Alfie, how we looked in the mirror behind that bar. Your father was so dashing in his jacket, and my red dress was just perfect, and my hair done in ringlets the way I liked. I'm not lying to you if I say that some people spun around on their stools to look at us. We stood there drinking our cocktails, and your father pointed out all the Romans. He pointed out the Mayor—Etheridge was his name—and a lot of people your father liked to call 'the Americans.' He couldn't name most of them—just Palmer, the musician who was with Harry

James—but once he got to the Italians in the room, he was like an encyclopedia. There were the Gualtieris, who had the grocery and the bank; and the Falconios, who everybody knew and who had real money; the Mungaris, who owned the Uptown Restaurant; and the Pasqualettis, who ran the Roman Pastry Shop; and there was Coluccio, the construction boss; and the Cicconis, who organized the San Felice Festival; and the Bottinis, who operated the funeral home and, when Matty's father was young, ran their own circus; and Joe Spadafora, who people knew for his newspaper; some of the Volpes, who were everywhere in Rome; the Andronacos, whose store helped a lot of people in East Rome; and the most successful farmers in town, the Giambonas. And I remember I felt guilty that your father's aunts couldn't be there, but I supposed the uncles weren't so interested in any new singer.

"They had a beautiful hot buffet along two walls of the dining room, with a whole line of people—some Italian, some colored—dishing out the food. You never saw such a spread. Like a wedding. They even invented a dish for the occasion: Chicken Harry James. And it seemed so strange to me, all those people in expensive suits and dresses lined up for a buffet, particularly in the Savoy's dining room, which wasn't as elegant as the outside of the building. It was all checkered tablecloths and news clippings on the wall and college pennants. Which was funny, because not too many of the people in that room, at least not the Italians, could've gone to college. Anyway, the line seemed to get longer and longer, so we went back to the bar, and there was Harry James himself coming through the front door, and other men in overcoats, his orchestra. And behind them was the skinny singer. And, would you believe it, when he came in, he looked right at me."

His mother leaned back in her chair.

"I remember those eyes, bright blue, like opals, and I just froze." She took a sip of water.

"And then Old Man Vestino led them right toward us. I swear to you, Alfie, the singer passed so close, he must have felt my breath on his cheek."

She set her hand on his shoulder as if Alfie were the one who needed calming.

"And they walked right past us into the private dining room. The door was closing behind them, and the singer—by then everyone was whispering his name ..."

"Sinatra?"

She nodded.

"He stared right at me and tipped his fedora. Of course, your father was too busy smiling at everyone to notice, and why would I want to tell him?"

Alfie shrugged.

"Eventually we were able to get our food and find seats with an older couple we didn't know. They were talking about the Capitol Theatre. Actually, they were arguing about it. I remember thinking how odd the man looked. His neck and face together looked like a tablespoon."

She smirked.

"He was making the point that no one ever died while performing at the Capitol, because it was built as a movie house. And his wife, who was stocky and bigger than he was, she was insisting that the place had ghosts and that one ghost was a projectionist, and that the ghost would sometimes sit in the balcony or play the organ like they did for silent movies. I suppose I couldn't help myself, so I asked them, 'Is the Capitol really haunted?' And as soon as I asked, your father rolled his eyes. But she sounded so certain, and I was hoping that Rome could be an enchanted place."

A hopeful expression flashed across his mother's face. Alfie had only rarely seen it, and it startled him.

"I wondered if any ghosts would turn up on Mill Street, maybe in our house. My mother liked to say that your ancestors are always with you. Then I thought that some of the ghosts might be Indians or the soldiers at Fort Stanwix. Alfie, I never told anyone this, but whenever I played the violin, I felt in touch with the spirit world, like I could take my bow and poke a hole in heaven."

Alfie resisted the urge to roll his eyes.

"But as I was saying, this couple was arguing about the theater, and then the wife told me the projectionist was the ghost that people claimed to see most often, but that there were others—some of the dancers and the vaudeville performers who played there. By that time, your father had had enough. He got up and went to the buffet table. I remember watching him and thinking he could put anyone at ease. He went down the entire line of serving stations, smiling and joking with all the help. And it was strange. While I was watching, the woman's husband said something to me that I thought was awfully fresh to say in front of his wife. But she just laughed, and I thought that I could never laugh like that if my husband insulted me that way. Then I noticed that my husband was talking with a pretty colored girl, one of the servers. He was practically hanging over her. I can still see her. She was dark, even for a negro, and she had a heart-shaped face and straightened hair. If she hadn't been so dark, I would've told you she came from Arabia. She had those almond eyes, though of course she had a wide nose. And she smiled at your father with those big teeth and lips. It was almost obscene."

She scowled.

"I could understand a man like Matty noticing other women, and them noticing him, but to think of those lips. How could he not see the way they made the girl too different to be with him? I couldn't imagine kissing a colored man. It would be like kissing a ghost. And then he took the girl's hand. In front of all those people he knew. How far would he go when no one was there to see? What kind of a man was he, after all? Who had I married? Whose children was I raising?"

Now Alfie did roll his eyes.

"No, I don't mean I was sorry about you and your brother. but I was so humiliated. I couldn't take it anymore. I stood up and walked toward the exit, and I got as far as the bar, right near the private dining room where Harry James was. The door was open, and a few of the band members were behind a table, smoking and drinking. Frank Sinatra was right in the middle of them. I couldn't help looking in, thinking he was directing the whole thing, the way he was winking and pointing his finger around. Then he looked up with those eyes and caught me staring."

His mother shook her head, as though she didn't believe her own story.

"It's terrible to say, but I imagined the two of us together, far away, maybe on an ocean liner. We would be performing and sitting at the captain's table, drinking a toast. Then we would dance and take a long walk on the deck."

"You wanted to run off with Frank Sinatra?"

She shook her head again and glanced at him.

"It was silly. I knew it was impossible. And then your father finally came looking for me. He was looking high and low, and I still thought how dapper he was in his tuxedo, but how lost. I loved him, Alfie, but for the first time since we met I could imagine not loving him and not being with him. A woman might take him, or else the cigarettes or drinking. Nothing would have surprised me. Men always went before women, anyway. And then he was back, just across the room. He spotted me and looked so relieved. And more than anything I just felt sorry for him."

Alfie sighed and reached for the salad bowl.

"What does it matter now, Ma?"

The question turned his mother's attention back to him. Instead of answering, she watched him shovel salad onto his plate.

"Who is she, Alfie?"

She waited only a few seconds for an answer.

"Don't tell me. I have an idea or two."

"Who?"

She sat down, facing him.

"The woman you want to be with."

"There's no woman."

"Well, then you look like you lost your best friend. And I know your wife wasn't your best friend."

"I gave up on true love a while ago, Ma. What can I tell ya?"

He ate the last of his salad, got up, and kissed her on both cheeks.

"Ma, I'm tired," he said, walking to the staircase, "but I love you."

It was only later, after his mother's stroke, toward the end, that she showed him what she might have known. It was one of those nights when she was watching Lawrence Welk and fell into a trance, like she could see herself there on stage with her violin. Alfie dropped something right in front of the television. When he bent down to pick it up, his eyes met hers. She took his hand and stroked it. And like that the trance wore off. She was an invalid, half of her face paralyzed, but she managed to smile. She was all sweetness and light, like she could already see heaven and had some idea what it was about.

That morning in Rome, when he'd read the headlines about peace, he'd thought about his own situation. Peace was possible. Make peace. Find peace. And how could you find peace when violence was everywhere you looked? His mother had found peace in music, the way he did once. She'd listened to her records, which Alfie played for her, sometimes for hours. He paid his bill and left the coffee shop, stopping a few doors down, to button his coat in front of a pawn shop called The Carrying Place. He appreciated the joke. The Indian name for Rome was now the name of a poor Roman's last resort. In the window he spotted a sixteen-gauge shotgun that looked just like his father's. Alfie had the old man's guns, though he hadn't so much as touched one since his last time at the reunion. It was a sign. He went back to the apartment, found the sixteen-gauge, took it out of its case, and laid it down next to the iron-frame bed. When he went to sleep that night, he thought about how he'd gotten here. He'd only been in Rome—what, two months? He'd needed to get away from Brooklyn, but still be somewhere familiar. So he'd taken a motel room and decided to talk to a few people he still knew on the east side of town. A fella that one of his aunts told him to see said he knew a place for rent, cheap, right on Dominick Street. He could move in right away. It was just a few doors down from Mazzaferro's, around the corner from the old house on Mill

Street. The first time he was alone in the empty parlor, he felt glad the shadows of those days were close.

Every night that week, Alfie slept with the gun by his bed. It made him feel more certain, like he belonged. In Rome he could touch the past without reliving it. He could take a walk to see one of his old aunts, then go back to his routine, which included working the late shift as a security guard at the factory, playing his guitar the best he could, reading the books his mother had left him, taking long walks into town or along the canal, shopping for groceries, buying the newspaper, or eating lunch at the coffee shop. And the guns kept his father close. One night he dreamt he was walking with the old man through the pines and ashes, then across a snow-covered meadow on Tug Hill where they'd always gone for snowshoe rabbits. The sun rose over the Adirondacks in the distance. The air was still, so that every sound echoed. They were standing in the middle of a white clearing, scanning the edge of the woods. When they heard rustling, they raised their shotguns. His father pulled the trigger, and he woke up. Later that day he paid a visit to The Carrying Place and bought an old set of snowshoes, a metal hand-warmer with a red felt cover, and a canteen.

Alfie made the turn off Route 26 and eventually found a place to park the car under a canopy of spruce branches jutting over the road. He strapped on his snowshoes, got the gear and gun from the Chevy's trunk, and started in. He looked for markers—big rocks, openings to a field, old trees—making his way slowly uphill as the wind whistled in his ears. The sun was still below the treetops, but already you could tell how bright the day would be. When he stopped to adjust his sunglasses, a strong gust of wind came up and shoved him forward, so he nearly fell face first into the snow. The sound of the wind through the woods reminded him of his mother's funeral mass. Those high notes on the organ that played that morning, as the mourners, most of them old, walked slowly to the pews. The casket had been closed, but he could see his mother's face the way it was right before she'd passed: so peaceful he could believe she was happy to die and see him move on. When he'd moved back in with her, she'd needed him, and vice-versa. If he wasn't happy, at least he was home. And if she wasn't thrilled with his moping, at least she had one of her sons around. Then she had the stroke, and there they were, the two of them, mostly mute, alone on a block that used to be full of people and a life they used to know.

For a long time, he'd let her think she was a burden, because he'd needed the pity. But he'd also been happy to take care of her. She'd kept him occupied. When he wasn't working his shitty job at Alexander's, he was buying groceries or taking her to the doctor's or out to visit the few relatives left in Brooklyn. Some weekends she'd want to go to church. Any trip involved practically carrying her down the steep stairs and to the car, then lifting her in, and loading the walker into the back seat. Then there was the ordeal of guiding her up the stairs of the church or the front stoop of his aunt's house. He actually preferred going to church, because at least there the priest and the older folks who knew her made a point of saying hello and asking how she was doing. Going to his aunt's was a touchier situation. She was strong, his Aunt Linda, a good woman, and she took care of his Uncle Roger, and Alfie respected her, but he couldn't take how sometimes she would treat his mother like a child. She might be an invalid, but she still had her marbles.

When Alfie would come home complaining about work, she'd make a face that said she felt sorry for him, but also that his life could be worse. She could only slur a couple of words at a time, but she still made sense. His aunt didn't give her a chance to say much of anything. Maybe because she couldn't stand to see her sister, the toughest of the sisters, brought so low. Age was talking, and Aunt Linda didn't want to hear. She still kept herself trim and did her hair like a young girl's and kept up with all the latest celebrities, which she forced Alfie and his mother to watch on the little television set in her kitchen. When they left and settled in the car for the short ride home, his mother would look his way and sigh.

Alfie pulled her mass card from the breast pocket of his hunting jacket and kissed the picture, then slid the card back in. He patted the pocket and quickened the pace. The sun was up now, and its light reflected off the snow field ahead. Stopping to catch his breath, Alfie noticed the icicles hanging from branches all around him, how they held the sunlight but didn't melt. Would anyone care if he froze solid out here and dissolved into the ground when spring came?

The whole time Alfie had lived with his mother, he hadn't talked to Frankie once. His brother made sure he called during the day, when Alfie was at work. After the funeral, in front of their old house, Frankie had come to him with open arms. By his side was a well-dressed fella a few years older. As he released Alfie from a hug, Frankie at least sounded apologetic.

"I miss you, Brother."

Alfie wanted to walk away, buy himself a couple of minutes to calm down, but it was too late.

"How's Italy?"

The anger in his voice made Frankie flinch.

"Did I introduce you to my friend Martino?"

The well-dressed man extended a hand, which Alfie gave a quick shake.

"How's Italy?" Alfie repeated.

"Beautiful?" he answered, as though he were confused by the question.

His brother was trying to speak Alfie's language, whatever he thought that was, which irritated Alfie even more.

"I mean I'm sorry I didn't make it back before. Everything there is crazy. They say the Italians know how to have fun, but all I do is work. And I didn't understand how bad off Mom was."

"You could've called me."

Frankie shook his head and looked down.

"I know, I know," he said, raising his eyes slowly to Alfie's face.

"I guess I was afraid to. I didn't want to see her that way."

"What way?"

"I called her once after the stroke. It was just too much."

Too much for who?

Frankie kept his eyes, a little teary now, on Alfie.

"Anybody in your life?"

"My mother."

Frankie bowed his head again. Alfie put an arm around his brother's back and moved him toward the driveway, away from the klatch of gray-haired relatives and friends. He craned his neck and scratched his chin with a fury that he could see was making Frankie more uncomfortable by the minute.

"If you mean, do I get laid? Yeah, brother. Sometimes when I work till closing, I bang one of the cashiers at the job, usually in a closet. Sometimes in my car. Then sometimes, after that, we go to the diner. Do you ever do that? Fuck in a car? Those Italian cars are kind of small for two grown men."

Frankie shot him a look of disgust, as if he had the right.

"So don't feel bad for me."

Alfie sneered at Martino.

"There are worse things than taking care of your mother."

All he had to do was love his brother. He didn't have to like him. Before Frankie left for Italy, Alfie had gone one last time to his restaurant and told him how much he liked the food. Mostly to please his father. He'd left his brother with a cold hug and a sense that he might never see him again. Now here he was, standing in the driveway where they used to play catch. The old folks, the ones that were left, shuffled past them into the house. His brother looked at him with sad eyes, then spoke again.

"I do feel bad for you, but not because you're here."

Martino walked away, and Frankie moved closer.

"Can I ask you when's the last time you saw your children?"

Alfie laughed.

"You're just like your mother."

Frankie ran his fingers through his thick hair, then smiled a sarcastic smile that had always made Alfie want to knock him on his ass.

"Mom told me that you stopped seeing them, Alfie, so I started checking in, writing letters. And they wrote back. Jennifer wanted to know why you didn't come around."

From his pants pocket Frankie pulled out a pack of foreign cigarettes and lit one.

"I find it funny that I'm in Italy and your daughter wants me to track you down."

The punch his brother had never been able to land. Alfie felt sick to his stomach, but he didn't let on.

"Michelle's bringing the kids over later."

"Is she?"

Alfie glared at Frankie and clenched his fist, as more of the old-timers shuffled by. Suddenly, he felt like he didn't belong there, like his mother hadn't really died, like his brother wasn't really his brother, and all his relatives' faces weren't just old, they were the faces of strangers who'd been fooling him all his life. He wanted to cry, but instead he kissed Frankie hard on the cheek and stalked off. Inside the house, his brother looked his way a couple of times, but Alfie ignored him until he and Martino were waving goodbye from the door.

In the open space of the meadow, Alfie struggled to balance himself on a steep incline. If he leaned forward, he could land his snowshoes flat on the icy crust and stride fast enough so that he wouldn't be frozen stiff by the time he got there. The destination was one of the little gullies made by streams that lined the plateau's belly and quenched its thirst in the warmer months. This was the kind of terrain where he could lie in wait. Without a dog, it was the only way. A little further in he found the gulley he needed, then a good canopy of spruce branches. He brushed away the foot of snow under the branches and, sure enough, found a nice bed of pine needles. It was shadier under the tree, a little colder. He took a small tarpaulin from his pack and laid it down. He could feel heat from the hand-warmer in his pocket. He pulled it out and set it in his lap. For good measure he pulled out his flask of brandy.

For the first time in weeks, he felt his mind moving in a single direction. He lay down and watched a high, wispy cloud float by.

He'd been drifting like that too. For how long? Count the days, count the months, count the years. The numbers were a jagged ladder he could lean against death's wall. The slight breeze through the pines sang with the voices of people he'd never see again. Faces looked down from the branches. Adeline's face spoke to him. His eyelids fluttered. He saw the way she'd looked at him at his mother's wake, almost angry he was there. He'd walked right through that look and right up to her as she stood by herself at the back of the funeral parlor. She looked thinner than she had in San Francisco. Her jaw was harder, almost like her father's, but still beautiful. Her face was a small, white heart, so calm she could be a marble statue. Some strands of her hair, which she wore shoulder length, had gone gray. Her black dress was too flimsy for this time of year. She stood there, rubbing her bare arms, nervous and cold. She extended a hand to him as if it were an effort.

"Alfie."

He thought of kissing the hand, but shook it instead. It was colder than the November air.

"Long time," he said, like a dope.

"Yes."

She was polite and graceful as ever, but her eyes had changed. They moved more slowly, placing people in the scene. They looked at Alfie like the casket behind him was on fire.

"Are you well?" she asked.

"A little grayer."

Alfie thought he saw a flash of sympathy, but then it was gone. She spoke to him like a school marm.

"Aren't you going to ask how I've been?"

All the faces from his past—aunts, uncles, cousins, friends— seemed to watch the two of them standing there, strangers who'd known each other for twenty years.

It was that long ago the first time he was on Tug Hill. He was a teenager, his father a little older than he was now. As soon as the first rabbit came into view, his father fired two quick shots, which sent the unlucky animal sliding into the embankment, dead as a doornail. His father smiled and stepped toward the prize like a conqueror. The rest of the day was one big celebration: a diner in Turin, a bar in Boonville, cigars back at his cousins' house in Rome. A happy day.

He opened his eyes, glad now that he'd taken cover. The sun was knifing the snow like its worst enemy, and from his shelter Alfie could barely follow the stream bed's outline in the glare. He got up gingerly and trudged out from under his tree. The sunlight hit him full force. His head felt fifty degrees warmer than his feet. To get his blood pumping again, he marched back and forth until his legs tired. No sooner did he slide the gun strap off his shoulder then he saw a cloud of powder rise to his left. He leveled the barrel fast as he could and searched the landscape until he saw a blur of off-white against the snow. With no time to set the stock solid, he shot, and felt two lightning strikes into his shoulder. The rabbit squealed and went into a slide. He'd hit it on the crest of a hill, and as it slid it picked up speed, flying up and over another rise. Trying to ignore the pain in his shoulder, Alfie strode as fast as he could in pursuit. At the second crest, he spotted a long, dotted line of blood leading to where the rabbit lay in the open near a stand of small pines. It would be a chore to get him, but if he wanted something to show for the day, he had no choice. He took a tentative step and then a few more down the slope. He got close enough to see that the rabbit was still twitching. If Alfie was lucky, it wouldn't have one last burst of energy and disappear into the trees. He leaned back to keep balance, a little further back with each step. Then it was too late. The slope had gotten too steep, and off Alfie went, sliding over the crust like he was on skis. He slid into another clearing, and just a few yards before a stand of pines, fell on his backside and bounced off a big trunk, skittering another ten feet in the snow before finally coming to a stop. As he sat there sore and shaken, he felt himself sinking down. He was too far from a tree to grab hold of a branch, but he tried not to panic. From here he at least had a good view of the rabbit. Its chest was rising and catching, rising and catching, blood still leaking from wherever he'd hit it. It was dying by itself on a sheet of ice, with sun warming it, maybe fooling it into thinking it had a chance. If Alfie could move, he'd kill the rabbit from where it couldn't see him. But how could he move? His feet were going numb, and his shoulder felt like it was cracked in half. No chance he could lift the shotgun over the snow, which was nearly up to his chest. Just like his father, he would die knowing he was dying. But his father's wants had been simple, and up until the end, even in a place he hated, he'd been able to satisfy most of them. If Alfie got to live a hundred years, he might still be wanting something. How many people died without getting anywhere, and nobody even caring that they existed? Alfie closed his eyes, ready to sleep, thinking again about Adeline.

"Sorry," he said. "How have you been?"

"I'm managing. I still live in California."

Alfie blinked away a memory.

Adeline's dark eyes narrowed.

"My father told me he never wanted to speak to me again. Did you know that? To tell you the truth, part of me wishes my father were dead now, so I could talk to my mother."

She crossed her arms.

"You saw them. They were sitting right over there. She had to wait until he was distracted. Then she looked at me and smiled. That's it. So I have nothing here. From the looks of things, neither do you."

She wiped a tear from her cheek, and when he touched her shoulder, she snapped at him.

"I hated how you left, Alfie. So much was happening, and neither of us understood it. I gave myself permission to hate you for a long time after that."

He wanted to tell her she'd been wrong. But wrong how? Were you wrong if you didn't know what love was? She pulled a handkerchief from her purse and blew her nose. He felt suddenly invisible.

"Still, I don't hate you. I needed you, and I hated that. I never wanted to need anyone, especially not a man, and especially not..."

She dabbed her cheek again. Whatever malice he'd seen in her eyes turned to pity. For him or for herself? He had a hundred things to say, but couldn't manage a single word. She was still standing in front of him, but she was gone. He could play her a hundred songs and she wouldn't care. She spoke again, but her eyes were already looking past him, to places he'd probably never know.

"Sometimes things are nobody's fault."

Things. He was one of these: a negative, a problem. Better solved than thought of. She moved away from the door to let an older woman pass. Alfie didn't recognize the woman, and was still wondering who she might be, when Adeline turned and, without a word, left him standing there. The same goodbye he'd given her, and maybe the best he could have hoped for. But hadn't her voice made him think, just for a minute, that she regretted what hadn't happened?

He opened his eyes again to a blank, white world. She could go to hell. He felt the warm spot now. The hand-warmer. He reached into his jacket, found it, pulled it from its cover, and pushed the hot metal cannister slowly through the snow, working it all around him, until he had enough wiggle room to grab the gun and use the stock for leverage. In a little while, he'd melted and pawed a path to the tree, using the gun as a crutch. He was able to snag a branch with the burlap sack that he'd tied to his belt. Then slowly, painfully, he dragged himself up and onto the surface of the snow. He tightened the straps of his snowshoes and hugged the tree trunk. The pain reminded him of everything gone. On the other side of the pain was an ugly rabbit. Not really a rabbit. A hare. He laughed and took a step down the hill. When he reached the animal, its body was finally still and stiffening up. He picked it up by its long hind legs, then dropped it into the sack, the way he'd seen his father and uncles do so many times. He lifted the sack and stood there in the sun, picturing the old-timers standing in a line across the gulley, with their vests and flannel caps and shotguns cradled in their arms. He could hear them.

"Almost kill yourself for a rabbit? What the hell's wrong with you?"

All the way back to the car they laughed at him.

"I hope you remember where you parked the goddamn thing, you freakin' *moke*, ya."

Alfie's laughter echoed through the woods. By the time he reached the car, the sun was starting to drop. He opened the trunk of his car and threw in the sack and all his equipment. Thin hardwoods poked from the roadside forest like stubble on an old man's face. Not everything was dead. He thought of his uncles again, mostly gone, another one dying every few months, like they were getting bored sitting around a fire, and one by one were calling it a night. Where was his father now? The old man never said much about dying or what he thought happened after you did. If he were alive, he'd say it was a problem he wasn't about to solve. Alfie got in the car and started it up. Steam rose off the hood. He took a deep breath and turned on the radio: "Jambalaya." He could play it in his sleep, but now it sounded like a song he'd never heard before, a strange voice singing, a voice that sounded like a snarl. A rock and roll version. He remembered the first time he'd heard it, picking out the chords, bringing the discovery to his band. Sometime during the second chorus of this version he started to cry. He cried through the rest of the song, then shut the radio and cried some more. Finally, he pulled himself together and thought about Adeline again, beginning with the first time he'd seen her and every time since then that he could remember. It was like what they said happened right before you died, your life flashing before your eyes, except it was her life, or what he knew of it, image after image, word after word, playing out as he watched the sun drop behind the trees.

(1973-1974)

Alfie couldn't breathe. He kicked the top sheet off his legs and sat up. Dust motes blown by the window fan hung in a shaft of sunlight. The weather made the small apartment feel even smaller. The whole summer had been the same, muggy and miserable. He hadn't felt right since May. He should go to the doctor, but at least his appetite was good. He thought about breakfast. There'd be nothing to eat in the kitchen, but he dreaded the idea of going to Gualtieri's at this hour, competing with all the nonnas clogging up the narrow aisles and waving their tickets at the poor old couple behind the counter. They would be yelling, half in Italian, half in English, trying to make eye contact with either Mr. or Mrs. Gualtieri, demanding special treatment. That's how they did it, because that's how they'd done it since he was a kid. Probably the way their mothers and nonnas had done it, too, before and after they got off the boat. On a Saturday afternoon it was fine, but on a weekday morning, when all you wanted was a cup of coffee and a buttered roll, it made you want to stick your fingers in your mouth, whistle, put your hands in the air, gather them around, and tell them all how much better things could be if the world were just a little quieter.

He stopped instead at the coffee shop, then drove to the job. If you could call it a job. Alfie had lost his last job as a security guard when his supervisor decided to make room for his nephew. When his cousin Paulie heard, he found him something else, a job with the city, working on a crew that was restoring something they called "Erie Canal Village," fifteen or so buildings they'd hauled to a single site, to reassemble as a typical nineteenth-century canal town. It would complement the reconstruction of Fort Stanwix and the renovation of downtown Rome. The work was simple enough, but the days seemed longer as the "Autumn in the Village" deadline got closer. All the buildings came from somewhere else. Nothing was authentic. Tourists from everywhere were supposed to flock and fool themselves into believing they were inside history. But most of all it was the locals fooling themselves. Rome was dying. You could see it everywhere. Rome Copper and Brass was running at half-speed. A lot of storefronts were empty. A lot of houses downtown were going to shit, shedding shingles like they had a disease. The same people in cruddy clothes walked up and down Dominic Street all day, looking down dirty alleys, like the jobs they'd lost might be hiding there.

Erie Canal Village wasn't about to bring it all back. But here he was on the site, staring at an old church with a high white clapboard steeple with half its paint peeling off. Another worker, a fella named Creighton, told him it was from a place called Maynard. The church had been founded for men only. So it was strange that the tavern next to it was named for a woman who, Creighton had also told him, was some kind or lawyer or politician. Down the dirt main street from the church was the train depot building, from Ogdensville. It had been built after the canal was already *mezza mort'*. Across from it was a one-room schoolhouse built in the 1850s. And of course they had a general store, in a building that dated from just after the Civil War. The plan there was to stock it with replicas of old-fashioned goods, half of which could probably kill you. The city fathers had decided to build the village on the old canal, a backwater the width of two cars. A new plaque near the bank explained that when the canal was under construction, people called it Clinton's Ditch or Clinton's Folly, and that it took twenty years to finish, and when the railroads came in, twenty years later, its days as a shipping route were numbered. Hundreds of the Irish died digging it, sometimes from accidents, but usually from malaria. Malaria, for Christ's sake. And for what? His own people came here to get away from malaria. The Irish were digging their own graves.

The village was a little ways out of town, on the spot of the old carrying place, where the Indians hauled their canoes up from Wood Creek, so they could carry them to the Mohawk River. Alfie had time before the boss arrived, so he walked along the bank of the old canal, thinking about what he carried with him. What happened to him felt a lot heavier than a canoe, heavy as the history that hung around Romans' necks like a curse, a curse that made them always a little nastier than the people in a small town should be. They liked to talk about all the history, even when it made the days they lived looked small and meaningless. Maybe, to them, covering themselves in history made their local business and local problems seem more important than they were. Not mattering scared them, which is why change scared them. It was a joke, but Alfie got it.

After work, he sprawled on his itchy couch. It was one of those wooly check numbers with thick wooden arms, a hand-me-down from his Aunt Betsy. Now, in the heat, it was torture. Alfie got his one extra bedsheet from the closet and laid it over the cushions. He lay down again and thought about switching on the T.V. for the six o'clock news, but what would be new? Nixon was under the gun, and they were finally bringing the troops home. He closed his eyes and rolled away from the open window. The ringing of the phone made his whole body jerk awake. He rarely got a call. It had to be one of the aunts or cousins. Nobody else knew he was here, and nobody else cared. He blinked his eyes and picked up. For a second he thought the line was dead, but someone was breathing on the other end.

"Hello?"

A voice he recognized started to speak, then stopped. He kept the phone to his ear.

"Alfie, it's me."

The voice was deeper than he remembered.

"Adeline?"

"I'm here."

"Here? Where's here?"

"I'm here, Alfie. At the Rome Station."

He looked out at the hotel across Dominic Street. The sunlight revealed a woman in one of the windows. A guest? A maid?

"Alfie?"

His mind went blank as he heard himself say: "I'll come get you."

Ten minutes later he was stepping through the dust of the station parking lot, craning his neck to see the island platform on top of the canal embankment. More likely she'd be inside the station, sitting on one of the old wooden benches. She'd be wearing black knit pants and a white short-sleeve blouse, a sun hat and sunglasses, like a Fifties movie star. She'd have one small suitcase that would make him wonder how she could've traveled half-way across the country like that. He walked through one of the front vestibules. It was a little past rush hour. A few people were still sitting on the benches. They probably would have come a distance, from Albany at least, or all the way from New York. A few were reading newspapers, a few were staring into space, about to step into the time warp that was Rome.

Twenty-five years ago, the station had seemed grand: the exterior brick work and columns, the benches, the beamed ceilings, big chandeliers, and the two long staircases on the back wall, running to a gallery of ornate windows and the passage to the tracks. It was a golden place, a palace: the light-colored masonry, the patterned floor tiles, the inlaid plaques on the walls. Sometimes he thought his mother had liked going back to New York just so she could pass through. Now, as he scanned the space, searching for Adeline, everything looked gray. Grime covered the bricks, scratches and smudges marred the floor, and years of rising cigarette smoke had turned the white ceiling between the wooden beams nearly black.

He turned his back to the room, and there she was, talking with the ticket clerk by the rounded booth. She was standing in profile, wearing a dress printed with oversized purple and yellow flowers. It was too long an outfit for this heat, but she was chatting away comfortably, like she'd just gotten a job with the railroad, if the railroad were a carnival. Next to her was a valise that had to be four feet long. More like a trunk with a handle. He imagined how many people along the way must have helped her carry it. He stood with his arms folded, watching from far enough away that he could hear only odd words: "California," "family," "sunset." Finally, the clerk disappeared, and she turned toward him. As she smiled she became a much prettier version of his Aunt Lena. She opened her arms and practically fell in his direction, then hugged him like she was hanging on for dear life. When she finally released him, she stood there smiling, lines creeping from the corners of her sweet mouth, and crow's feet from the corners of her eyes.

"I finally admitted to myself how much I've missed you."

It sounded like a movie line, but the way she delivered it, the way she squeezed his hand, he had to believe her.

"Let me take your bag."

He gestured for her to lead the way out. He test-lifted the valise, and decided he could handle it. The P.A. system announced another arriving train. As he surveyed the station again, he felt all at once squeezed by moments, thoughts, mistakes.

On the job site a few days later, Alfie realized that Creighton reminded him of an Old West sheriff, but the more Alfie thought of this fella, who said his first name was D.W., the more he seemed like a barkeep in an Old West saloon. He even had the drawl.

"Creighton, where you from?"

"Wheeling, West Virginia. Eight generations."

He drove one nail after the other, like a machine, into the new door frame of an old shop. Watching him, Alfie thought of his father playing bluegrass guitar.

"You listen to bluegrass, Creighton?"

Creighton groaned as he rose from a crouch, rubbing his small pot belly. He looked like an old beagle who could walk on two legs.

"Back home you couldn't get away from it."

He scratched the top of his head with the claw of his hammer.

"Funny, but I don't listen to much of anything nowadays. Why do you ask?"

"I used to play a little."

Creighton side-eyed him and turned to the door frame again.

"Not much time for playing here. These old gals," he said, waving the hammer at the front of the dilapidated building, "they need more attention than my wife and kids put together. I go huntin' or fishin', and the family takes care of itself. Leave these ladies alone and they start fallin' apart."

Alfie felt a pang of guilt. He'd worked every day since Adeline had arrived. She hadn't said boo about it, but when he left each morning, she stood by the door as he said goodbye, like she was waiting for him to play hooky and take her out. As if in Rome there was something great to see.

"You married, Baliato?"

"Was."

Creighton snorted, like he understood something Alfie wasn't about to tell him. The question made Alfie wonder how long Adeline meant to stay. Did she think this was a permanent arrangement? Since she'd arrived, she hadn't mentioned any plans. Instead, they reminisced about their folks, about life in Brooklyn, about how they'd met. She even brought up his brother, but dropped the subject when Alfie said nothing in response. Otherwise they talked about Rome. Alfie told her about how it had changed. He told her about the park at Delta Lake and about the old Capitol Theater. There was a rumor it was closing, and they should take in a movie there before it did. She said that would be nice. In fact, "nice" was her answer to most things he said, as though she were afraid to say what was really on her mind. If she planned on staying, it couldn't work this way. He wasn't made to walk on eggshells.

Alfie stepped back from the old storefront and took in the sweep of the village such as it was. Against the cloudy sky the buildings showed faces like his old relatives. The slim ones that lined the main strip, all straight lines and big windows, reminded him of his aunts. The single-story post office, with its blue shutters and cloth awning, reminded him of his father. The proud little general store reminded him of his mother, and the even prouder bank reminded him of his Uncle Enzo. They hovered over him, and their interiors were dark with a sadness that hit Alfie like a wave of exhaustion after a big meal. He wanted to take off his toolbelt and go home.

Creighton laid down his hammer and stretched.

"Baliato, I told the old man I'd spruce up the façade of the meeting house. Would you mind helping me out? I could put in a word with him, maybe get you a day off this week."

Alfie didn't feature working up in the air, but a day off was a day off.

"Two ladders around back."

They placed the ladders at opposite ends of the building, then started prying up the clapboard a few inches at a time. Alfie's father had been a master of the claw hammer. He could pull any nail without breaking it, dig out any head that looked lost to the wood forever. "Got this side," Creighton yelled, and Alfie realized he had to make up ground. He moved fast as he could, sliding the claw under each board and pulling until he heard the little scream of the nails giving up their ghosts. With a couple of feet to go, he yanked one board especially hard, cracking it and losing his balance, falling backward. As he fell he managed to grab a rung of the ladder and bring it down sideways on top of him. The grass in front of the meeting house was soft enough, but the ladder clattered down and smashed his knee. Alfie let out a yelp that sent Creighton scrambling down his ladder. Alfie rubbed his eyes and rose slowly to his feet. He could move the knee, but he knew it would stiffen up. He could feel his heartbeat. Creighton lent him a shoulder.

"Looks to me like this might be your day off."

When he got home, Adeline was sitting at the kitchen table, her face turned toward the window. The sight of her brought Alfie back to her apartment in San Francisco, but she wasn't that girl. It wasn't just that she had more wrinkles or gray hair, or that sometimes she wore glasses like she was doing now. Her voice had a new, strange calm to it, and she moved more slowly, like she was taking time to decide on every single action and word. She turned her profile to him, and he thought of Katherine Hepburn. He watched her there as she ran a finger around the edge of a tea cup, until she noticed him.

"You're back early."

He pointed to his knee.

"A little accident."

Before he could take two steps, she was at his side, guiding him to a chair, humming a note of concern.

"Is it swollen? I'll get ice."

She wrapped a few cubes in a dish towel.

"Take off your pants."

"Is that okay?"

She set her hands on her hips. He followed orders, and she knelt in front of him, holding the pack against his knee and smiling. It was something like this that he'd always imagined for himself, the care a woman was supposed to show her man, in a way he could see, in a way that took effort and time away from what she might have wanted to do for herself.

"Is it bad?"

"Only when I move."

She frowned.

"No, I'm kidding. It's okay. I made it up the stairs, didn't I?"

She bowed her head again and pressed the pack against a plum-colored bruise on his kneecap, concentrating the way nurses did.

He flinched, and she looked up.

"Sorry."

"No, please. Thank you."

She smiled again, and for some reason he felt the urge to make her uncomfortable.

"It's a good thing we're not in San Francisco."

She withdrew the ice pack and watched him with narrowing eyes.

"What do you mean?"

He smirked.

"I mean with all those hills."

She nodded, got up, walked to the sink, and shook the ice cubes from the towel.

"Alfie, listen."

She came closer.

"You don't have to say anything."

She took his hand.

"It was ten years ago. We weren't children exactly, but there was so much I didn't understand. I have so many things to tell you, if you want to hear them."

He stood up.

"I'm not a priest."

"I don't need a priest," she said, her eyes now that same darkness where, so many times, he'd wanted to lose himself. She kissed his cheek, again, and then his lips, and then, stepping back, laid her hands on his chest. The lines of her face disappeared in the glow of the late day sun. He kissed her, touching every part of her as if he weren't sure that she was real. He led her to his room, where they undressed and sat next to each other at the edge of the bed. She stroked his cheek. A note of worry filtered back into her voice, which fell to a stage whisper.

"Are we about to do something we shouldn't?"

Alfie leaned back his head and drew a deep breath. He caught his reflection in the cheap wall mirror. He was getting uglier by the day, as his father used to say about himself.

"No," he answered matter-of-factly, lowering her onto his bed.

With every touch he imagined falling through the fog their family had always been. In fact, they had been the weather that dictated most days. They had been the sun that woke you every morning and told you to get on with business. Then they had been a thunderstorm that drove you under a tree where you found bundles of their feelings half-buried in the dirt or else birds they'd set free to fly or starve. They had always been hungry for something they knew

by instinct that their grandparents had given up when they decided
on respectable lives in America. Adeline's breasts were his mother's
longing for her life as a musician. His hands on her waist were his
father's longing for the thin promise of a young man's happiness.
Every time she moaned or cried out, she was singing for another
aunt or uncle who'd spent a life trying to reach the next plateau. In
taking each other, they were letting all these spirits go, saying goodbye to the days that, for those poor souls, always ended in endless
desire. This woman in his arms was more than an idea or a dream.
She was God's first hint to him that life on earth could be sacred too.
She was real and, finally, she was his.

Alfie woke first, just before sunrise. He lay still, gathering strength.
With Michelle the key had been to say nothing more than he
needed to get through a day. With Adeline he would have to give
up all his secrets, exchange past for future. He rolled over, and the
bed springs creaked. She stirred and reached for him, her eyes still
closed. He kissed her forehead.

"Alfie."

He kissed her again, and she cuddled closer, then drew her
balled fists to her chin. He pulled her to his chest, and they lay
that way until the sunlight slowly brought them to consciousness.
"Outside, the first cars of the day were passing on Dominic Street,
and the delivery trucks were unloading at Gualtieri's. Gates clattered open. Voices yelled. For a long time, even after he'd come back,
Alfie had thought of Rome as a dead town, a place to bury himself,
where the only people who would know him would know someone
who didn't exist anymore. He would walk to the canal every day
and stand on the footbridge, watch faces and scenes disappear into
the black water, which was as still as most of the evenings. The site
of his first memories stood a hundred yards away, so this was the
easiest place, the natural place, to let them go. All of them sank into
mud, which during the summer released bubbles to the surface, like
it had eaten and belched up the remains of those memories, so that

they evaporated into nothing that could trouble him. But now it sounded as though the town was coming back to life.

Adeline sat up in bed.

"You never asked me why I came," she said, lacing her fingers into his.

He said nothing.

"I wasn't sure if you didn't care or if you were just being polite." She laughed.

"When we were younger, Alfie, it wasn't exactly like you to be polite all the time, but you had your moments."

She kissed his cheek and anticipated his polite question.

"The truth is that when the time came for me to leave my old life, I thought about you."

Alfie forced a smile, trying to open himself, to say something that would allow her to explain and would allow him not to feel like a patsy.

"How did you know it was time?"

She smoothed the sheet in her lap, working through a thought.

"Life woke me up."

He raised his eyebrows.

"I know that doesn't say much, but give me a chance. I said that I had a lot to tell you."

He took a slow breath.

"Tell me."

She lay back on her pillow.

"When I started having trouble with drugs, I quit my job and I rarely left my room. I was depressed and scared. It got so bad that I practically stopped eating, which was just as well since I had no money. Once or twice I wrote to my mother, to ask her for rent, and I guess she was able to slip the cash past the old man. So I had that. When I was hungry, I relied on the Diggers. They were a kind of charity group. And when I couldn't take it anymore I would go out and find a few friends from the café, who would get me drunk or give me pills. Viv carried me for a while, but then even she couldn't take it anymore, and she moved out. But life surprises you. Right after that I ran into Marvin."

He sighed and lay back next to her, staring at the ceiling. She studied his face, then kept going.

"He was from a wealthy family in Chicago, but he was a self-made Zen master. Twenty years older than me, and he seemed like he knew exactly what he was doing, like he could help me. He had what they used to call a "center for enlightenment." It was on the coast north of town. He found me one night wandering the sidewalk outside a show at the Fillmore. I was completely out of it, and he was kind enough to take me to his house. He and his wife let me stay there, and then they just started to take care of me. And I knew I needed it, so I let them. They nursed me through withdrawl, then convinced me to join the center. You could say that Marvin rescued me."

Alfie squinted and smirked.

"Don't laugh. Yes, it crossed my mind that here was this older man on the make. But Marvin liked to think he was saving people, and he was so pleased with his job of saving me that he wanted me to stay on as his personal assistant. It's not like I had better options. I had my own cabin on the grounds of the center, and a salary. I was making enough money to send my mother little gifts with the organization's return address, so my father wouldn't throw the packages away when he saw them. And I lived at the center. My work was there. I owed Marvin. And, yes, we eventually got involved. His wife stayed in the city, and other than the young people who were passing through, we were usually alone, so I suppose it was inevitable. As inevitable as anything that shouldn't happen between two people."

She smiled.

"I helped him and gave him pleasure, and I felt like I was helping the other guests, if that's what they were. Once in a while he took me back to the city, to see our friends. You might say it was a beautiful life, but it wasn't exactly my life. I was more of an observer than anything else. It might sound ridiculous, but I felt like a kind of vessel for other people's truths. All this energy was pouring into me from all these different lives. I had very little time to myself, but when I was alone I felt the old desire to write, so I wrote in the smallest possible spaces: thoughts, images, haiku, anything that made sense in the moment.

"You'd look at my life from the outside and say I was sober and employed and happy. I was almost happy, anyway. And life could have gone on that way. Until Marvin went out hiking by himself, to the top of his favorite hill, and had a massive heart attack. They found him at the bottom of a canyon. A few weeks after the funeral, his wife announced she was closing the center and going back east. A month later I was out in the street again. For a while I thought about going back home, but then I found out I was pregnant. I'm sure you know what my parents would have thought. And I think I actually felt ashamed of myself."

When Adeline had first gone out to California, Alfie had gotten in his mind a picture of her living in a cottage on top of a hill overlooking the Pacific Ocean. Like Maureen O'Hara in *The Quiet Man,* but without Ireland or John Wayne. She'd keep sheep and wander paths and at night sit at her desk by lantern light and write whatever it was she wrote. He never thought about how she might pay for the cottage. Between her garden and the livestock, she could feed herself. Children had never entered the picture.

"The baby?"

"No."

He could allow her a little silence and forgive her, couldn't he? How could you say which sin among a person's many sins was the one you had to condemn? And did he even believe in sin?

"After that I was able to find a little secretarial job and a little house—it was really more of a shack—near Ocean Beach, and for a few years I lived like that. Until one day Viv asked me to go with her and her husband to Mexico. And it hit me how alone I was in California. I rode the train alone. I walked the beach alone. I sat in the local café alone. I even went to the zoo alone and talked to the animals. I'd given up everything to get there and be a part of what I thought was happening. But I just never made connections like I could make when I first got there. Not for very long, anyway. I had Viv, but she had her life. Everybody else kept slipping away from me."

She stroked his arm.

"And I never got over the way you left, or maybe how I made you leave. It was never right, and I knew it, but I chose to be angry about it. One evening after work, I was walking the beach, looking down the shore at the cliffs and lights, and then out into the ocean, and I understood that you were out there somewhere, and that I needed to find you."

Alfie wondered how true her story was. But then did it matter? She'd come this far.

"I feel like I left everything I loved—most of all my family, and you—for a fantasy. I'm lucky to still have my mother, but I'm not allowed to talk to her."

"Not allowed?"

"I think you know what I mean."

Alfie kept a straight face.

"And then I think of you, and you don't even have your mother and father. And I know how close you were."

"Don't be so sure."

Her hand moved over his chest.

"What do you mean?"

"Put it this way. My mother and father were good to me, but I didn't always see it like that."

She sat up, to look him in the eyes.

"Alfie, you did everything for them."

He raised himself against the headboard.

"Did I ever tell you why we came to Brooklyn? It wasn't because my father loved the city, that's for sure. You want to know why?"

She sold him a puzzled expression.

"There was an incident. A friend of my father's. Colored fella. Reverend. My father's best friend, you want to know the truth. We were hunting and some of the locals here beat him up so bad you could hardly recognize his face. Did a pretty good number on my father too. After that, I don't think they ever saw each other again, my father and the reverend."

"That's horrible."

Alfie nodded.

"But that's not the whole story. As far as my father knew, those fellas who showed up in the woods, they always had it in for him and the preacher, and it was just an unlucky thing they were in the woods that day, too."

Adeline was sitting cross-legged now, facing him.

"But that's not what happened."

Adeline cocked her head.

"It was me. I gave them up."

She opened her mouth to say something, but Alfie cut her off.

"No, I did. The kids at school got wind that my father and the preacher were close, and I never heard the end of it. Nigger this and nigger that."

She screwed up her mouth.

"Excuse me. I don't mean to say that's what I thought. I was fourteen. What did I know?"

Alfie shrugged.

"And their fathers owned the bars in town, and I knew one of them especially had it in for my dad. A gorilla named Bronson. I was so mad that I went up to his bar one day and told him who my father was, and when and where him and the preacher were going hunting, and that they'd be alone. I forgot to mention I'd be there, too."

She bit her lip.

"I don't know why, but I never admitted any of it to my old man."

He closed his eyes.

"Alfie, I don't know what to say."

Her voice was all kindness. It was true, what they said about misery. He exhaled, opened his eyes, and kissed her.

"The next time you want to apologize for something you did, figure you have some competition."

Neither of them ever declared that Adeline should stay, but the next day they bought a second-hand chest-of-drawers. She reorganized the closets and spruced up the kitchen. He built her a simple desk and set up her office in the hallway alcove. On nights when he wasn't too tired, they cooked dinner, all their mothers' dishes—steak pizzaiolo, stuffed shells, chicken francese, spaghetti aglio-olio with bread crumb and anchovies—whatever came up in conversation. The past was a treasure trove of useful knowledge, but it was a place they both knew they couldn't stay for very long. The dead had understood them as different people. Speaking with them would be tempting fate, making a mockery of rules they didn't believe in but still feared. They talked about what was happening in front of them, or what they might want to happen. Their conversations were about Rome and the surrounding towns, their flat world.

Come fall Adeline found a job as a hostess at The Beeches. The place had been the Potter Estate when Alfie was growing up. He remembered his father driving his mother there sometimes, to gawk at the stone mansion and the grounds. Right around the time they left, the Vestinos bought it and turned the mansion into a fancy restaurant for the city's upper crust. Since then a lot of the local Italians had baked themselves into that crust. In front of the restaurant was a statue of the she-wolf that suckled Romulus and Remus. The story was that some huckster from Rome, Italy offered the bronze statue as a gift to the city ("The Copper City"), on the condition that the American Government would fly him and his workers in, so they could install and dedicate it. What nobody realized at first was that this goombah had tried a couple of times to come over illegally, and must have figured that this was his best chance finally to get a visa. The joke was on him, though. The Eisenhower Administration kept him out anyway, because of his deportation record, but let the statue in through a middleman, and here it was. Every time Alfie drove Adeline to work, he parked his car and walked around the smallest public park in town. He admired the realism of the statue. The wolf looked like she'd rip your arm off if you got anywhere near the two little boys crouching down underneath her, sucking her teats. Wood was one thing, but Alfie had trouble comprehending how anybody could make art like this out of a piece of metal. One thing he did understand was that no matter what happened to Rome, the statue would be here for hundreds of years. He liked the idea of the statue outliving all these Romans who were so stuck on the history of the place, which only went back, let's face it, barely two hundred years. And how old was Italy?

From the get-go, the manager of The Beeches, some widower great-nephew of Old Man Vestino, was after Adeline. He told her constantly how she had class and how she should let him show her around Rome. So Alfie made a point, every once in a while, of walking her into the restaurant and shaking the *cidrul*'s hand, talking about Adeline as his fiancé. She seemed to like it when he did that. If marrying her seemed impossible, then the idea of it was even sweeter. Once or twice she and Alfie had dinner there, where they met some of the town mucky-mucks, the people responsible for all the urban renewal. The fake past they were building was just about ready for Autumn in the Village. Once it was finished, Alfie could walk away. Adeline had no interest in seeing the finished product, which made him love her even more. The one time she brought him lunch at the site, she walked quietly with him down the village's three reconstructed streets, thanked him for the tour, and left unimpressed. He wondered, though, how she could feel that way as a writer. If you couldn't write about history, what else was there? On the days she didn't work, he'd come home to find her pens and writing pads rearranged, or a new blank sheet stuck in the typewriter he'd bought for her birthday. She never showed him anything she'd written, but the fact that she was writing, and that he could picture her writing while he was doing whatever shitty job faced him that day, made him happy.

When the canal job ended, Paulie found him a job selling life insurance, something he knew. Maybe it wasn't helping anybody too much, but it wasn't hurting them too much either. The people at the office treated him all right, and they left him mostly alone at his desk. He could sit at his desk and imagine Adeline at hers, concentrating, knitting her brow, trying to come up with another thought, another sentence. It reminded him of playing, picking out melodies on the guitar, finding chord changes that could carry him through the best hours of the day. Maybe he'd play more often for her. If he wasn't what he used to be, who was? Maybe it was only writers and painters who got better with age.

One day during the summer, he came home to find Adeline gone and an open bottle of bourbon on her desk. When Alfie drank, it was a beer or a glass of wine, so either she'd bought the bottle for herself or else had gotten it from work. He screwed on the cap and left it where he'd found it. When she got home an hour later, he pretended he hadn't seen it, and when he went back past the desk, the bottle was gone. Later, she sat down next to him on the couch, where he was flipping through a magazine.

"I went for a walk."

"Oh, yeah?"

"Along the river. There's a trail."

"Nice?"

"Beautiful. I wish I'd have brought a notebook. But I made it worthwhile. I got some bread from Ferlo's."

"That's some walk."

She stood up, and with a flourish gestured to her shorts and tank top.

"I went prepared."

He took her in. Still beautiful, still with a perfect figure. Still the woman of his dreams.

"Maybe I'll walk with you sometime."

She sat down next to him again.

"Maybe," she said, exchanging that thought for another. "I called my mother today."

He leaned back and put his feet up on the coffee table.

"When's the last time you talked to her?"

"I don't know. Months, maybe."

"What did you say?"

Adeline rested her feet next to his.

"Nothing special, I suppose. I just wanted to see how she was."

"And?"

"She's fine."

She paused.

"Really, I just wanted to hear her voice. I wanted to feel con-nected. You know what I mean?"

"Sometimes, yes."

"Do you miss anybody, Alfie? I wonder. It never seems like you do."

He rubbed his chin.

"I miss you when we're not here."

She smiled.

"Present company excluded."

He stroked his chin.

"Sure. My mother and father."

She waited.

"I don't really have any friends I would miss, if that's what you mean. The friends I had, they all have families."

"That's not what I mean. Your children, Alfie, why don't you call them?"

Only Frankie and his mother had ever asked. How could he put it?

"It's my ex-wife. After I left, let's just say she wasn't too keen on me. And I never wanted to go to court and fight. I didn't have it in me then. Michelle didn't want me around. When I lived with my mother, they'd come over. Once a month, maybe. But, I don't know, it felt like I wasn't there."

There was pity in her eyes.

"When we were married, I wanted to do whatever I could do for them, especially for my daughter. But then, you know, after

Columbia everything just drained out of me, a little at a time."

She ran her hand through his hair and kissed his cheek. The alcohol was still on her breath.

"Until you showed up."

She kissed him full on.

"So maybe you understand why I wanted to hear my mother's voice."

He nodded.

"What else did your mother say?"

"That my father wasn't doing so well, and that he still wouldn't talk about me."

He kissed her again.

"They still think I'm in California, Alfie."

"What?"

She thrust out her jaw and flipped her hand, the way the old Italians did.

"How could I tell her?"

He nodded again, then led her to the couch, where they lay down and fell asleep. When they woke two hours later, Alfie's stomach was grumbling. He looked to the kitchen, then at Adeline, who was brushing strands of hair away from her eyes.

"Thank God you got the bread."

Adeline had been drinking all week. Not so much that she was drunk, but enough that she got in the habit of taking walks and then coming back to the apartment and falling asleep on the couch. On Thursday, she was home when he got there, sitting in the kitchen, staring at a bag of onions and a dozen eggs on the counter.

"I went shopping."

"Eggs."

"I thought we'd have a frittata."

"Sounds good."

He set his briefcase down near the door and sat with her.

"I got a little news today," he announced.

Suddenly, she looked concerned, and he understood that news, for her, meant bad news.

"Good news."

She set down her coffee cup.

"Down at work, they booked a cruise on the canal, for every-body in the office."

He laid his hand on hers and smiled.

"I thought you'd like that."

"I do, I do," she said, getting up and carrying her mug to the sink. "Is it soon?"

"Next weekend."

If they'd asked him to come alone, Alfie might've said no.

"Honestly, I've never even had a drink with any of these people."

She lowered her eyes.

"Not even lunch," he added.

She shrugged.

"But most of them are okay. So we'll go?"

"Yes," she said, getting up to open the carton of eggs.

The following Saturday they drove to the landing outside of town. As they waited to board the boat, Alfie introduced Adeline to his co-workers. He admired how charming she was when she social-ized. Alfie did his best to hold up his end, making sure to shake as many hands and kiss as many cheeks as he could. But Adeline was as graceful as the boat itself, a restored number, maybe a hundred years old, painted yellow and red, with "Copper City Cruises" sten-ciled on the side.

They left the dock and chugged upstream toward Oneida Lake. Once the boat traveled a hundred yards beyond the James Street Bridge, there wasn't much to see, just scrubland on both sides. On the other hand, a party like this could blast music and yell their heads off, and only the deer and rabbits would care. Tonight they started off with softer music, oldies like Sinatra and Nat King Cole.

The lower the sun dropped, the more recent the music got. By the time it was setting over the lake, they were playing a new song Alfie had heard and liked, called "Sundown." Whoever ran the operation did the best they could to put on a show.

For the first time since she'd arrived, Adeline and Alfie were drinking together. Sloe gin fizzes. It wasn't as bad a drink as it looked, especially with the hors d'oeuvres—cocktail weenies and potato puffs. Later, they made the rounds on both decks. Alfie's office manager was especially nice to them. He seemed shocked that Alfie could have such a pleasant companion.

"Opposites attract," Alfie said.

For a second, Adeline's smile disappeared. She hooked his arm and pulled him closer, listening to the manager as he talked about how impressed he was with the downtown renovation and the new Fort Stanwix project. There would be lots of opportunities for the company. Alfie could do well for himself. The thought of working in insurance for years on end soured Alfie's stomach, but the idea of having a little more money, maybe a house on the outskirts of town, would keep him in. Adeline would like a house, although they hadn't talked much about buying one. If she didn't complain about the apartment, she didn't seem one hundred percent happy with it either. He'd come to understand that she was used to suffering and pretending that she wasn't.

They moved to one of the topside benches and finished their drinks. Twilight was settling over the lake. The little shore towns were lighting up like weak stars on the dark horizon. Muffled music leaked from below, a remake of the old tune "Mockingbird." Only a few people had come up from the bar, and Adeline felt free to kiss Alfie as if they were necking at a drive-in. She drew away and rested her head on his shoulder.

"It's beautiful."

Alfie thought so, too, but couldn't help thinking that the lake ended somewhere south of Syracuse. That was it. No more adventure. Just more upstate land with its dying towns and its blank-faced people and its winters that ended just when you couldn't take any more cold and snow. He could live within the limits, but the doubt that she could, too, weighed on him. Tonight would be as good as it would get for her here. If she got restless, what would he do? If she didn't, how would he feel about that? He kissed her again, and night fell, and the boat turned back toward Rome.

(1976)

Five days a week he drove across the river and passed the site where the government was finishing up the Fort Stanwix replica. The city was working to get it done for the Bicentennial, and making a big deal that it was the first place where the Continental Army had ever flown the Stars and Stripes. Lately, to kill time, Alfie had been going regularly to the Rome Historical Society. He'd found out that the flag story wasn't exactly true. But that didn't stop the powers that be from demolishing the old American Corners and building this monument that was ugly as sin and that cut off East Rome, what was left of the old Italian section, from the rest of the city. Still, Alfie was curious about how a fort was built, so some days he'd walk the couple of miles to work, circle the site, then sit in the new Veterans' Park, to clear his head.

One April day, on the walk home, Alfie passed St. Peter's Church. His mother had taken him and Frankie there every Sunday, right up until the week they'd left for Brooklyn. He'd never liked going to mass, but he'd always liked the building, and lately he'd been feeling a strange emptiness and been thinking he might give church another try. A few drops of rain were starting to fall, so why not go inside?

It was a Tuesday afternoon and the place was empty. Out of Catholic muscle memory, Alfie blessed himself with Holy Water and knelt in a pew. The interior of the church was impressive: white marble columns and a vaulted ceiling that reminded him of St. Patrick's Cathedral in New York. The altarpiece too was white marble, with a spire that housed a gold crucifix in a marble and glass display case. Above it rose huge stained-glass windows, eight of them in a row. The outer four panes were the gospel writers holding books, pointing fingers as they read; the middle panes showed a single image of the Last Supper, one that you didn't usually see, with some of the apostles already up from the table, like they'd heard enough or they were full and needed a walk. On the wall above the windows was a carved, painted white dove at least a couple of feet long. As he took it all in, Alfie noticed that he was breathing heavy, like his father on his deathbed. Now and then it took all his concentration to pull air into his lungs, and his heart would skip a beat every so often. Saying a prayer couldn't hurt. When he did, Jesus seemed to look right at him from the altar, telling him to settle down. Alfie rested his head on his folded hands and absorbed the quiet, until the sound of his heartbeat faded.

That weekend, he went to the public library, to read more about churches. He discovered that it was the Franciscans who had worked to get the Stations of the Cross installed. It took them a few hundred years from the time they did their original Way of Sorrow in Jerusalem, but they managed it. The Stations in this St. Peter's were all original, from the late 1800s. Alfie went back to the church the following Sunday, and stayed after mass, to walk around and study the images. There were fourteen Stations total, which were basically: Jesus gets the death sentence—He carries his cross— He falls a first time—After he gets up, he runs into Mary—the Romans make Simon of Cyrene (a Libyan Jew of all things) help Jesus carry the cross—Saint Veronica wipes Jesus's face (which, you could understand, was the reason they made her a saint)—He falls again—He meets a few of the local women—He falls a third time—the Romans strip Him naked—they nail Him to the cross and pierce his side (because ...Why? Hanging by spikes through your hands and feet wasn't bad enough?)—He dies—they take Him down—they put Him in his tomb (which you knew wasn't the end, so why not have a station to show why everything he goes through is worth it?).

Sometimes he and Adeline walked downtown together, then back along the canal or up toward The Beeches. Other times they went to the coffee shop on Dominic Street, where she told him about the latest news from work, all the things the important Romans were saying over dinner, and all the ways she did her best to escape the clutches of Vestino's nephew; and she listened to everything he'd discovered about the churches and about Rome's history, without needing to give out as much as she took in. He told her a lot of things he'd never told anybody else, even a few things about Frankie, about his parents, about Michelle and the kids. Nothing he said seemed to shock her, but it was all news. She was family, but how well had she really known any of them, including him? How well had he known her? She listened when he was down, even when she was down herself. She helped him on those days he woke up in a futureless haze.

The year before, he and Adeline had bought a cottage close to the river, and had more space and peace, but it hadn't changed things much. Some days he felt like he could shed his skin like a snake and slither into the current. Some days it was all he could do not to scream. He wondered how anybody could be as calm as Adeline seemed all the time, even when she had bad days. He knew that she drank every day, and that if you drank that often, something had to be wrong. But she never yelled or even picked fights. If she sometimes looked at him like she was disappointed, that was the worst of it. She never once asked for a day alone. If you didn't feel right, you generally wanted the world to leave you alone, and it generally did. Where he liked the world not noticing him, she never minded engaging it. She talked about people at work and people she met on the street like they were friends, which helped him conclude that he was really the one with the problem. Some days the world crushed him. Those were the days his breath was short and his heart pounded. Her being there calmed him and made everything tolerable, even if he wasn't feeling for her the way he had before. When he allowed himself this last thought, he felt guilty—about who she was supposed to be, about her being stuck there with him, and about feeling the way he felt now. No matter how beautiful she still looked or how much she listened, he would get the urge to go to church and confess himself, the way he remembered doing as a kid.

Early one Saturday, Alfie left Adeline asleep and drove to St. Peter's. He sat in a pew near the First Station of the Cross, and every few minutes moved to the next one. The way they made this particular set of stations, each one had a carved wooden image painted so it would contrast with the color of the stained glass. You could see the expressions on all the faces. Even his grandfather couldn't carve like this. When he got to the last Station, a gravelly voice with a kind of Midwestern accent spoke to him.

"Usually it's only the children and the old people."

Alfie turned to see a squat, white-haired priest extending his hand.

"Father D'Alfonso."

"Alfie Baliato," he said sheepishly, and pointed to the wall. "I was admiring the work."

The Father put his hands on his hips and inspected the last two Stations.

"Irish immigrants. You've got to hand it to them."

Alfie had never had much use for priests. He let his eyes drift back up to Christ's tomb.

"I haven't seen you here before," D'Alfonso said.

Alfie was glad for the opening. He could at least look the Father in the eye, even if he had to stretch the truth.

"I just moved back."

"Back?"

"I grew up here. Then my family moved away. To Brooklyn."

The priest's eyes lit up.

"Ah, New York." He paused in reverie. "So what brings you back to Rome?"

"A lot of things, Father."

Alfie didn't like the question, but D'Alfonso's smooth voice and manner put him at ease.

"Well, if you're new, maybe you'd like to join me for lunch sometime. My regular spot is Vescio's. I love the stuffed rigatoni. In fact, how about this week?"

Their lunch was the first of what they agreed would be weekly meetings, usually on Saturdays, usually at Ferlo's, for coffee and pastry. D'Alfonso was a relatively recent arrival himself, but he knew a few of Alfie's family, mainly the women. When he asked about them, Alfie would say just as much as he had to, so that the Father learned it was better to leave the subject be. One Saturday they agreed to meet for dinner at the Savoy. Alfie was coming off a particularly rough night. He'd dreamt of Jennifer and Matthew as little children. They were lost in the woods, calling to him for help. Adeline was trying to push him down a path, yelling at him to find them, but he wouldn't budge. The morning after the dream had been just as bad. He'd had to argue with the mechanic about his car. Then, on his way to the newsstand, he'd gotten caught in the rain, and some schmuck had sped by him through a puddle, soaking his pants. By the time he got to dinner, Alfie had a splitting headache. He sat alone at a table in the back of the dining room, waiting for the priest, who was usually on time but today for some reason was late. When D'Alfonso finally showed up, he made a big production of taking off his raincoat, going on about the cold, and telling Alfie that a nun he hadn't expected to see had been bending his ear for a half-hour. He laid the wet coat over the back of a chair and laid his wet cap on a corner of the table, then shook Alfie's hand and sat down, noticing right away something was wrong.

"You look as though you've been chased by crows."

Before he could help himself, Alfie was confessing.

"One of those days."

He started to tell the priest all that had gone wrong with his day and with Adeline, then thought about how many days had been like this since he'd come back to Rome.

"Most days, Father, I get up and I'm in a good mood. You know?

The birds are singing and I can hear voices in the street, and I'm happy. I love the world. Then I go downstairs, and the first person I see acts like a jerk. Whoever it is. I say hello and they ignore me. So I feel a little less happy. Then maybe somebody cuts me off in the car. And I feel a little worse. Then I argue with a woman at the grocery store. And this goes on and on. And by the end of the day, I hate everybody but the woman in my life. Is that normal?"

D'Alfonso rested his chin on his palm, posing in thought. He gave a quick wave to someone across the dining room, then cleared his throat.

"Son, you've got to learn forgiveness."

The menu in front of Alfie featured a picture of the family who owned the restaurant. He recognized one of them. The man in the middle of the photo was a kid he'd gone to school with. If he remembered right, the kid was a first-class jackass.

"I try, Father, but most days I wind up wanting to scream."

The priest made a sympathetic face.

"I understand, but we have to turn the other cheek. It's difficult to live in the world if you're always angry with it."

Alfie admitted that he was angry and that he'd in fact been back in Rome a few years. He talked about what had brought him back and what kept him here. What he got from the Father wasn't quite advice. The old man listened to Alfie, said he was sorry for whatever he'd gone through, then offered a version of "God has a plan." He couldn't say what the plan was, but they could speculate. After a few weeks of these meetings, Alfie found himself looking forward to each day a little more than the last. He looked forward, too, to seeing D'Alfonso, talking to him, but more to doing whatever good he could do during the week so that he could tell the priest about it on Saturday.

One night, lying in bed, looking out the window through half-opened blinds, Alfie realized that D'Alfonso was a happy man, and that lately he, Alfie, was feeling guilty again about being with his cousin. Their common blood was always present, flowing, leaving traces. He supposed that they loved each other, and they were mostly kind to each other, but he felt that, like him, she was always hiding. Maybe it was God's way of saying it shouldn't be. Maybe the way D'Alfonso lived wasn't so bad. Maybe Alfie could lead a religious life. The next time he saw the Father, he asked what it took to become a priest.

"Well, for one thing, you have to be ordained."

"How does somebody go about doing that?"

D'Alfonso grinned and took a slow sip of his coffee.

"You sure you want to know?"

Alfie waited for an answer. The priest sighed.

"Okay. First thing, you need a degree in philosophy."

"Like a college degree?"

D'Alfonso nodded.

"Then you need another degree in divinity."

"Two degrees?" Alfie scratched his head. "No offense, but with two degrees I could be a doctor."

D'Alfonso blew his thick nose into a tissue he pulled from his coat pocket, and nodded again.

"Usually takes about eight years."

Alfie did the math. He'd be fifty.

"No way around it?"

The priest laughed and ran one hand backwards through his thinning hair.

"Not unless you have connections at the Vatican."

Tiny bells rang and the door of Ferlo's swung open. It was a woman, maybe thirty-five, with a pretty face and a figure that filled out her tight-fitting fall coat. She smiled at Alfie and the priest as she walked to the counter. D'Alfonso saluted her, then returned to the business at hand.

"And of course there'd be none of that."

Alfie rolled his eyes.

"I already have a woman."

D'Alfonso laughed.

"Well, you wouldn't—assuming we're talking about you."

Alfie conceded the point.

"Maybe you should become a monk."

The priest might've been kidding, but Alfie decided right then that he'd look into it. As a priest, he'd have to talk to a million people. Worse than being a cop. But monks lived a quiet life. They played music and wrote and had hobbies. But he'd need to know the whole story.

At the library he researched the different kinds of monks. The Buddhists, naturally, were too far out. Among the Catholics, you had too many orders to count, but the main ones were the Franciscans, the Benedictines, the Dominicans, and the Jesuits. Alfie ruled out the orders where you had to ask for money or where you had to try to convert people. That knocked out all of them except the Benedictines. He liked that each Benedictine monastery was its own little world, and that they were big on silence, work, and reading. It sounded good on the surface, but he had serious questions.

Back at Ferlo's he told D'Alfonso what he'd been up to.

"So you enrolled in your own college," the priest said, not quite laughing, but smirking. He took a big bite of his *pasta ciott'* and tapped a finger on the outside of his coffee cup while he chewed. "And what did you learn?"

"I was reading about what they do, the monks. What their days are like. I like the way they set things up. They keep themselves busy."

The priest grunted.

"What?"

"Nothing. I'm listening. Go on."

"I can picture myself living that life. You know, getting up, praying, cooking. My cooking is nothing to write home about, but I'd learn. And I could do some woodworking. And I already help with the house cleaning."

D'Alfonso twisted his mouth.

"You know you'd be cleaning up after the other monks, too. And once you're there, leaving's not so easy."

Alfie thought about it.

"Father, don't take this wrong, but is either of us leaving here any time soon?"

D'Alfonso took another bite of his pastry, glanced at the bar, and spoke while still looking away.

"Sounds like you've already made up your mind."

Alfie reached into his pocket and pulled out a notepad, the kind he'd used on the job.

"No, not quite. What I read in *St. Benedict's Rules*—do priests read those?"

"We're familiar with them."

"In the *Rules* there are a lot of things I didn't get. Maybe I just didn't understand what they were trying to say. I was hoping you could help me out."

D'Alfonso let his mouth hang open for a second before he said anything.

"I don't know, Alfie. It's been a long time. And this is supposed to be just hypothetical, right? But if you think it'll help you."

He gestured to go ahead, and Alfie opened his notepad.

"Let's start here. It says that the abbot is superior and that the monks are like his sons, and that he has to set an example. First of all, how do you know the abbot's everything he's supposed to be? Because he's the one who's supposed to guide you in all these— what do they call them?—here, these 'labors of obedience.' How do you know he's on the up and up?"

D'Alfonso shrugged.

"And if you don't behave the right way, the abbot can excommunicate you. But what if the abbot just doesn't like you? If you didn't like me, Father, and you made up something to get me excommunicated ..."

The priest clucked.

"You mean if I told the Monsignor that you'd confessed to polygamy or that you'd condemned church teachings? Something like that?"

"I don't know. Maybe worse than that."

"In that case, we'd have to go through a lot of steps, and a lot of people would be involved. The Church is a complex organization. But at an abbey, a monastery, you'd be on your own."

He gave Alfie a meaningful look, which Alfie wanted to ignore.

"So what I see is that I'd have to be obedient."

"And do you think you're up for that?"

A gaggle of kids pushed open the door and slammed it behind them, talking non-stop, so that Alfie had to raise his voice.

"I don't know. I did it in the police department. To a point."

The priest said nothing.

"Other things too. Like the whole thing about respect. One of the Instruments of Good Works is 'To respect all men.' That's a little strange."

"How so?"

"Well," Alfie said as he flipped a page, "because it says here that God doesn't respect people. See: 'For God there is no respect of persons. Only for one reason are we preferred in his sight: if we be found better than others in good works and humility.' Now suppose we have a situation like this: Another monk isn't doing his good works or he's bragging about them. Does that mean I still have to respect him even though God doesn't? I'm not saying I'm like God, but I'm supposed to be doing things the way Jesus did them, and if Jesus is God, then what do I do?"

D'Alfonso said nothing.

"Don't get me wrong, Father. Most of the Instruments of Good Works are good. You can't argue with 'Not to give way to anger' or 'Not to nurse a grudge' or 'To hate no one.' I'm not saying it's easy to follow the ideas, but they're nice goals."

"What the doctor ordered, I'd say," the priest said, looking bored and finishing his coffee.

"But you don't seem too enthused. And tell me if I'm wrong, but I bet it's because of some of these other ones. Or maybe it's just me. What about 'Not to speak useless words or words that move to laughter'? Or 'Not to love much or boisterous laughter'?"

D'Alfonso folded his napkin.

"Let's just say the monks aren't big on jokes. By the way, did I tell you the one about the priest who never lit a candle?"

Alfie was getting annoyed, but then he remembered the way his father would rib him. D'Alfonso read his expression.

"Sorry. Go ahead. I'm listening."

Alfie mumbled thanks, took a sip of coffee, and flipped another page of his notebook.

"This one, Father. This is the one that really gets me: 'To hate one's own will.'"

"Yes, I recall that one. I could see that might be a problem. No offense to you, Alfie, but you don't strike me as the type of guy who likes to be told what to do."

"Who does?"

"Ah, well, I can think of a few, but in general you're right. Not that I'm saying obedience is a bad thing. And I'm not condemning the monks either. Some monks do great work, but you have to be a certain sort for the monastery."

The priest winked.

"Maybe I am. I read what some of the monks wrote, and they say that when you're there you can feel the belief. They all believe in something, the same thing."

"That's the theory."

D'Alfonso adjusted his belt.

"Now, as for drinking, how about a glass of wine? I see a friend behind the bar. Let me go ask him."

The priest strode across the dining room like he owned the place. Other customers waved to him or shook his hand along his way. Alfie fell into deep thought, trying to picture himself going through the monk's day: a lot of prayers—Vigil, Hours, Vespers, Compline—and then all the work. You didn't mind that. But what about doing the same thing day after day? How would that be different from his life now? In the middle of a work day he always felt like he would fall asleep. If he were a monk, how would he keep from falling asleep and showing up late for prayers or, God forbid, for meals? But then the work might be interesting, especially if your life depended on it, so you might not be as bored. Unless it was something you did just for the monastery to make money. How many tchotchkes could you carve? If what Alfie read was true, with the Benedictines he could work on getting his soul in tune with the world and with God, with finding God. Which was, he had to admit, a problem, at least for now. It was easy to believe God was around to punish you, but harder sometimes to see the blessings, if that's what they were. But maybe God was modest, and blessings would always be small. For one thing, he'd have more time to pick up the guitar and try it again, even if he had to play religious songs. But he could adapt some of them. He liked the new version of "Morning Has Broken." And the song by Simon from Simon and Garfunkel, the one about America. So maybe hearing all the hymns, he could write a few of his own. It was all simple chords and strumming. If he just played the tunes and didn't take credit, would the monks mind?

D'Alfonso returned to the table with two glasses full of red wine.

"Compliments of the house," he announced, handing Alfie his. "Chin chin!"

They clinked glasses as the priest took his seat again.

"Alfie, I have to say what I'm about to say, because, you know, one of the things that separates the priests from the monks is we're supposed to give counsel. If you don't mind, I have some counsel. If you're asking me about belief, does that mean you don't believe? Or do you?"

Alfie rested his wine glass on the table and ticked it with his finger.

"Sometimes, Father. That's the best I can do for now, but I'm sure that once I'm in, it'll be easier."

"It's never easy. Don't misunderstand me. Some people do well in a place where everybody's heading in the same direction. But that isn't everybody. One way to be happy and to follow God is to be able to measure your progress. And when you have people going every which way—I know it sounds crazy—but then it's a little easier to see that you're going straight ahead. Does that make sense?"

"Maybe. But it can't be good to be with someone you're supposed to love, and then to feel alone all the time, can it? That's my life."

D'Alfonso spread out his arms. His voice deepened.

"Everyone feels alone. But are we alone? Are you really alone?"

Alfie lolled his head.

"Maybe 'alone' isn't the way to put it. Anyway, monks shouldn't have that problem."

"Neither should husbands."

"Are you discouraging me from becoming a monk? Or do you just want me to get married in your church?"

The priest kept silent.

"It seems like in a monastery you're everybody's brother. Out here I have a blood brother and I don't talk to him at all. Everybody needs company, somebody who understands what they're doing. I'm not sure my girlfriend or anybody out here understands. I'm not even sure I do."

The Father leaned across the table.

"If you're looking for friends, Alfie, there's a reason the monks are allowed to have dogs."

D'Alfonso swirled his wine, then took a last gulp before getting to his feet and putting on his coat.

"The check's taken care of. Let's say you can thank the Lord."

Alfie stood up.

"Sorry, Father."

"For what?"

No one had given Alfie advice in years. He thought of his father's advice, and realized that most of it had been ways of saying "Don't do that."

"I appreciate it."

D'Alfonso patted him on the shoulder, then settled his hat on his wide head and walked into the lightly falling snow.

A week or two later, winter set in and didn't let up for four months. Most weekends the priest was busy or the snow was too heavy to go out much. Alfie passed the time listening to music—a lot of it religious—and playing the guitar. This routine lasted a few weeks, before he dug out some old Hank Williams and Big Joe Turner. With the snow falling outside his window and piling up on the sidewalks, he sang the blues so loud that Adeline must have thought he was losing his mind. If she did, she never let on. Sometimes she listened. Sometimes she tried to sing along. Sometimes she just went into another room. Sometimes he told himself that everybody but Adeline could go to hell. But every once in a while, when he was at the office or on the street, talking to people or just passing them by, he'd think about a line from St. Benedict: "You were looking at the speck in your brother's eye, and you did not see the beam in your own."

If Alfie could never be a priest or a monk, he could also never be Adeline's husband. Even if he could do it legally or get permission from the church, he didn't see it working out. No matter how distant he acted, she never argued with him and never gave up trying to spend time. He was losing respect for her daily, which he sensed she knew. Still, whatever it was he'd held onto all those years was keeping him in place. One day when he was especially low, a Saturday in July, he stayed in bed deep into the afternoon. Adeline was working lunch and early dinner at The Beeches. When she got home from work, she woke him up.

"Let's go to the lake."

"The lake," Alfie repeated, like he was learning a new word.

Had she been drinking? He sniffed the air, studied her, and decided she hadn't.

"We'll drive this time, along the canal, out to Sylvan Beach."

It was unusually warm, and they drove with the windows down. There was still no hint of fall in the late August evening air. By the time they reached Oneida, it was dark and the beach was empty. Even the resort towns turned in early. She led him by the hand to a patch of sand far from the beach house and amusement park, then pulled off her blouse. In the moonlight, in her worn dungaree shorts and bra, she was a cross between a wood nymph and an obscene version of one of the Coca-Cola posters inside his uncle's old gin mill. She took his hands in hers, turning his wrists to the moonlight.

"What's the matter, Alfie?"

"Nothing."

She gave him a long kiss, then looked him in the eyes.

"Something's wrong. Something's been bothering you. You're carrying something around."

Some days he felt like he was carrying his own body in his arms.

"Can't you tell me anything?"

He looked up at the moon, then into her eyes.

"I wish I could, but it's just me, how I am sometimes."

"Are you thinking I should just leave you alone?"

He shook his head. Could he live without Adeline or without the possibility of her?

"Then I'm here to help you. Let me help you the way you helped me."

She stood up, slipped off her shorts, walked to the lake, and eased herself into the flat, black water. The sky was just as black, and the stars descended on the scene as she swam. He imagined that the splashing came from above, as though she were slicing through constellations. She disappeared, then broke the surface a hundred feet out, going straight into a breaststroke, her arms and legs fluttering like giant moths in the blue glow. When she stopped, she stood up chest deep and waved for Alfie to come in. He gave himself up reluctantly, stripping to his boxers and trudging into the water like an eighty-year-old man. When he reached her, she locked him in a hard kiss and stroked the front of his shorts. He stopped her, and took her hand in his, weaving their fingers together.

"We shouldn't have secrets, Alfie."

A few lights lingered on the lakeshore.

"I don't have secrets. I have memories. Like tonight. I look at you and I know tonight'll be one of those memories."

"We're still here, right now."

She took his hand again, her face so soft in the moonlight that you might think she was a half-naked saint. Her hand trembled in a way he'd never noticed. She squeezed harder as he spoke.

"One day I'll have this memory. Did I ever tell you about my favorite memory?"

They knelt in the water, and he held her.

"I was just about to turn eighteen, ready to get out of high school. I remember it was a beautiful day, a Saturday, probably May or June. For some reason, it was quiet in the neighborhood, except for the sound of my brother and his friends playing stickball in the street. That day I was working on a new song, not the kind of song I generally liked, but there was something about it. It was Louie Armstrong. 'A Kiss to Build a Dream On.' You know that one?"

Alfie hummed a few bars, hearing the trumpet blaring over the drums.

"I remember how bright that song made me feel, and the sound of the wind in the trees outside my window. The next time I saw you—it was probably after Sunday dinner—I played it for you under one of those trees. And you stood there, swaying, and I thought you were so beautiful that all I needed to be happy was to kiss you."

He tried to stop his tears, but it was too late. She kissed him again, as though their lives depended on it, until he pulled gently away.

"What about your memories?" he asked.

She pursed her lips.

"I remember the beach where my mother and father had their cottage. The first time they took me there, it was like we discovered America. I miss that feeling."

Her face was intense now. He could see this picture of her on the jacket of her first book, this brilliant woman he was holding back. Her hand was still trembling, and his heart was beating hard. If they grew old together, they would have to watch each other slowly fall apart. No memory or dream could change that.

The next day Adeline announced she had a big dinner planned: Caesar salad, provolone and prosciutto *antipast'*, cavatelli with meat sauce the way his aunt used to make it, and a perfectly cooked roast beef. This was all good news, except for the reason. It was like she was telling him that he was her old family, not her new one, not a life of her own. But she was trying to make him happy, and he owed it to her to do the same. He patted her behind as she stood by the stove.

"I'm going out to the bakery."

"So much food, Alfie. Why?"

"Italian bread, *sfugliadell'* and rainbow cookies."

By the second course, Alfie was almost full. He reached across the table for Adeline's arm.

"They don't even eat this well in Italy."

Her face glowed with gratitude, a look he'd only ever gotten from his mother.

"Thank you."

She moved the macaroni around her dish like she was painting a picture, and spoke without looking up.

"Did you ever think of taking a trip there?"

Alfie leaned back from the table, took a deep breath, and exhaled. If she wanted to go, if they could afford it, he'd take her.

"No."

"Your brother's been in Italy for years. You never thought of visiting him?"

He looked at her as though she ought to know better.

"I know you haven't spoken to him, but maybe you should."

Alfie tore off a piece of Italian bread and stabbed a piece of provolone with his fork.

"I never had the chance. And besides, I don't think he'd be very happy to see me."

"You're wrong."

"No, I'm pretty sure I'm right."

"No, you're not."

He wiped his mouth.

"How do you know?"

She laid her hands flat on the table.

"I talked to him."

"Talked to him? When?"

"I shouldn't say I *talked* to him. I talk to him. We talk. Even before I came, we would talk."

He bowed his head.

"I thought you didn't want secrets."

"I didn't. Still, I knew how you felt. You made that clear. But after yesterday, I thought I should tell you. You're right. No secrets. And he's your brother."

He exhaled again.

"And your father's your father."

She pushed her chair away from the table, and moved to get up.

"I'm sorry," he said, tugging her sleeve. "Please. Sit down. Please. I'm sorry."

If she talked with Frankie, then they talked about him. And what could they be saying? Was he telling her what a terrific brother Alfie had been? Was she telling him how they were living together and sleeping together and how perfect it was? Frankie had always known how Alfie felt about her, and yet it was all right for him to talk behind his brother's back. Still, Alfie didn't need to upset her.

Her lip quivered a little as she spoke.

"Alfie, you can be such a hard man."

He noticed too that her hand was shaking. He took it in both of his.

"I'm sorry. I know. It's not that I don't love my brother, though he hasn't made that easy. When I was down, did he ever say to me, 'Brother, if you need me' or 'Brother, tell me what's going on'? I never heard boo from him, for years. He was out doing exactly what he wanted."

Adeline stood up. Alfie didn't mean to say she was just like that, but maybe he did. Unlike them, he'd never had the chance to come out of hiding. And here they were together, still in hiding, wasting themselves. He got up and held her.

"I love you," she whispered.

"Me too," he answered, as the leftover food grew cold on the stove.

Vestino's great-nephew, Roger, had finally given up on Adeline and found another woman. Her cousins had lived next door to Alfie's family on Mill Street, and he remembered her as a little girl in her Sunday best. Whenever her family showed up at Donnie Silano's house, Donnie would have to stop playing football or street hockey or whatever other game the boys on the block had going. The Silanos were as poor as his family, and even though, like his family, they weren't much for church, Donnie and his cousins were always well dressed. The decorum paid off for Little Monica, who eventually snared herself a Vestino.

Vestino and his future wife invited Adeline and Aflie to a flashy new canal-front steakhouse inside a renovated factory in Utica. The leaves were just starting to turn, and Adeline seemed just as happy about the drive along River Road as about going to dinner with other people. Sometimes it was a chore, but tonight, a Saturday, Alfie felt, if not excited, then at ease. Vestino was no longer a threat. Adeline was all smiles and she'd never looked better. Her black dress flattered her, and her hair, pulled back and held in place by a jeweled black band, made her look like a mature princess. She even carried a little jeweled black purse to match. Alfie wore his one suit and pomaded his hair, which, like his father's, had started to turn silver on the sides. When they got there, they found Roger and Monica at a table near one of the big windows overlooking the canal. Roger ordered a bottle of wine for the table and when it arrived made a toast.

"To Alfie and Adeline, health and happiness."

"Likewise," Alfie countered, keeping his glass aloft.

Monica revealed that her cousin Donnie had moved to Buffalo, where he'd become a big success in business services, whatever that was. Then she turned to Adeline.

"I love your dress."

And the two women were off and running. Alfie and Roger were quiet for a moment, before Roger pointed to the canal.

"Remember how this used to be, Alfie?"

Alfie looked out at the still-empty factories across the water.

"A dump."

"It still is, except for this place. But it won't be for long. There are big plans for this whole stretch. Big plans for Rome, too."

Alfie sipped his wine.

"My family's always been interested in making something of the canal. We had this dream that we'd have restaurants up and down, from Rome to Schenectady."

"My pop used to say the Vestinos always had something going."

Roger raised his glass in an uncertain salute to the idea.

"To tell the truth, I have a piece of this place myself, and if things go right, I'm hoping to buy the majority owner out."

"Your own place in the big city."

Roger eyeballed him.

"That's right."

He poured Alfie more wine.

"So what's your story, if you don't mind my asking?"

"No, that's all right."

"You haven't been back that long."

"Three years?"

"Before that?"

"Different things. I worked a little construction, worked security. I was a cop for a while."

"For a while?"

"Long story."

"So you bounced around?"

Adeline interrupted.

"He's being modest. My cou … Alfie is very talented."

"Really."

Monica jumped in.

"Donnie always used to tell me how strong you were, Alfie."

Alfie shrugged.

"Those days are over."

Roger rested a hand on his shoulder, and Alfie tried to forget his old man's warning about letting people touch you.

"You look pretty strong to me," Roger said, laughing.

Alfie smiled at Monica and waited for Roger to take his hand away.

"Alfie was an incredible musician," Adeline added.

Roger tried to sound impressed.

"Wow. But 'was'? Isn't it once a musician, always a musician?"

"I don't know."

"He could play the guitar like a master."

Alfie dismissed the idea.

"Those days are over, too."

"Too bad," Roger said, sitting back. "I love to have live music on the weekends."

For some reason Adeline kept on.

"I think Alfie could've done anything when he was young."

"Really, how long have you known each other?" Roger asked.

Adeline tried to catch Alfie's eye.

"We were sweethearts years ago."

Monica clapped her hands together and giggled.

"That's so romantic."

Roger again.

"So what happened? Why'd you stop playing?"

Alfie looked at his hands.

"An accident."

"If it weren't for that, Alfie really could've done anything."

Alfie felt the wine rising in his gullet. Who did she think he was now? And why did she have to make things sound so dramatic?

"After I moved away, I thought about him for years."

"That's so sweet," Monica said. "What made you come back to Rome?"

"Oh, I'm not from Rome."

"Then what made you come here?"

"Well, Alfie, naturally. I just had a feeling he needed me."

Meanwhile, Roger was giving Adeline the eye, waiting for his moment.

"You're a good woman, Adeline. I could tell that right away when I met you. Alfie, you're a lucky man. A woman like this behind you can change everything."

The thought of Adeline with Roger made Alfie chuckle loud enough for the table to hear. Adeline's face dropped, but Roger started laughing, too.

"You have a strange sense of humor, Alfie."

Adeline turned to Roger.

"He used to have a good one."

For the first time since San Francisco, Alfie saw the hint of a vindictive grin on her face. He picked up his wine glass, waving it in Adeline's direction.

"Here's to my gal, Roger. You should've seen her when we were young. Did she ever tell you that she was a writer?"

Roger looked surprised, but said nothing.

"That's terrific, Honey," Monica said. "I wish I could do something like that."

"Well," Alfie said, feeling the devil inside, "don't feel bad. I don't think Adeline's written a single thing since she got to Rome."

Adeline looked flustered now, but tried to smile.

"That's not true, Alfie. I just don't show you everything."

"I guess not."

Roger looked away, and Monica fidgeted in her chair.

"But," Alfie went on, "I'll bet you want a glass of wine."

He grabbed the bottle and poured so the wine splashed in her glass and stained the tablecloth.

"Here's to your work!"

Roger and Monica sheepishly raised their glasses, and inside of an hour dinner came to an awkward end.

As soon as Alfie and Adeline got in the car, she turned on him.

"How could you humiliate me that way?"

He matched her anger.

"I could ask you the same question. Or do you just not notice anything outside of what's in your head?"

"What are you talking about, Alfie?"

"What you said, about what I could've been."

"It's true, isn't it? You were so talented. You really could've done anything you wanted."

"And I didn't."

"I didn't say that. You had an accident."

He squeezed the wheel.

"The way you said it didn't sound like that. It sounded more like you were blaming me."

"Of course I wasn't. I thought I was complimenting you, but I'm sorry if you were embarrassed."

"I don't care about those people," he shot back. "Maybe you do."

She crossed her arms.

"Why did you come here if you thought I was such a failure?"

"That's not what I thought, and it's not what I think."

"Then why?"

"You shouldn't have to ask that. Have you ever asked yourself why you wanted me?"

There could never be an answer to that question. There were only short periods when his desire for her hadn't made him miserable. To her, he was an audience, someone to watch and tell her that she was doing the right thing, that she was right.

He was about to say something, when she spoke again.

"There's a poem about a dream deferred. It's about all the bad things that can happen to a good dream. Sometimes I feel like I got in the way of your dream. Or I'm getting in the way of it now."

Did she believe that? He found a gentler tone of voice.

"You're not. You never did. I had a dream, but I didn't have a back-up plan. It's my own fault."

"I love you, Alfie. I didn't come for your dream or my dream. I came for a life, because I thought we could have one."

He took her hand. If you had a life, you might not need a dream, and vice-versa. Some people, maybe most people, weren't meant for dreams.

"I love you, too," he said.

They drove home, undressed without speaking, and made love on the unmade bed.

(1980)

Right after she volunteered to work for the Jimmy Carter campaign, Adeline started writing again. Why anybody would want to work for a peanut farmer Alfie couldn't understand. He was glad, at least, that she was writing. And that she'd stopped drinking. He was less glad that she'd also cut out sex, but eventually it felt like a conclusion they'd both been reaching for a long time. After a couple of months, he stopped asking, and she never offered it again. The same way they never talked about Frankie, even though Alfie knew that she still wrote letters back and forth with him. He didn't need to know what they said. His and Adeline's life was here, and if she wanted to tell his brother about it, what did he care? Something else had changed, though. Adeline was preoccupied. She had trouble sitting still or talking to him for more than five minutes at a time. When he asked her why, she shrugged it off and told him she was just busier than before. Between the campaign and the hours at her desk, she was busy, no question, but there was something else. Maybe he was giving her signals. He was as bored as he'd ever been. The job was the job, and, sure, after work he could always hide in his wood shop. But how many bookcases and side tables could he build? He could play the guitar more often, but the thought of never being very good again depressed him now more than ever.

One of the fellas from work, Bruce, suggested that he join a bocce team at the Galliano Club. The last time he'd played bocce was with his grandfather, on the little court the old man had built in the corner of his yard. It was something old men did, but then it reminded Alfie of the good years at the family reunion. Plus, Bruce was all right. So Alfie agreed. The Galliano Club hosted what they called "The World Series of Bocce" every summer. Leading up to it was a string of tournaments: the Bucky Bartaletti Open, the Fred Franceschini Masters, the Al Ortolano Doubles Challenge, and the final tune-up for the Series, the Facciola Brothers Classic, in June. Bruce had a strong team, and he could see Alfie was a natural athlete. He was optimistic they could go all the way. Alfie liked the competition, but he hadn't foreseen how vicious the veteran players could be. They had no problem knocking your ball to Kingdom Come, even when they had no chance of winning themselves. Some of them did it just to make you look bad. By the end of the second tournament, Alfie almost came to blows with some *cidrul* in a golf cap after he practically overhanded his ball at Alfie's. Lucky for him Bruce jumped in between them, but that was the end of Alfie's bocce career.

Again, Alfie found himself with very little to do, especially in the evenings. He resorted to walking up and down Dominic Street, seeing the same five or six old geezers who were doing the same thing. Alfie was only forty-six. He could still do something. One evening, walking along the canal, he decided to buy a boat. He found an old cabin cruiser for sale in *The Pennysaver*. In a few weeks, he had it seaworthy. After a couple of test runs, he started taking fishing trips up and down the canal. The boat would at least get him through the summer. After that, who knew what would happen?

Adeline had started to take her own morning walks along the canal. Whenever he offered to join her, she'd tell him it was her private ritual. One Saturday she returned from a walk while he was pouring himself a cup of coffee. It was a muggy morning. She had on purple shorts and a tight black tank top. He noticed how long her salt-and-pepper hair had grown, down past her shoulders. Like a hippie. Or a mermaid. A girl's body with a mermaid's curves. He decided to hug her. This time she didn't resist.

"Eighty-five degrees today, they're saying."

She looked only briefly in his eyes.

"It's hot."

"What's going on?" he asked.

She sighed.

"Nothing, Alfie. How many times can you ask me?"

"I know, but you're still not yourself."

"Look," she said, stepping back, "I'm sorry. Something has me in a bind."

"What?"

"I didn't want to worry you. And, honestly, I wasn't sure how you might react. You haven't been so easy to talk to."

She pulled her hair into an unbound ponytail.

"It's just that certain things, certain people never leave you."

Alfie leaned back against the counter, waiting for the goodbye.

"This latest thing, it's not so simple. Not a simple confession and we move on."

She rubbed her arms with both hands as if she were suddenly cold.

"I told you that back in California I got pregnant, and that I ended the pregnancy."

He nodded.

"That wasn't true, at least not the second part."

She blushed and turned to the window, her back to him.

"I have a son."

It surprised Alfie that he immediately imagined the boy sitting at the kitchen table, asking him for a ride to school or to drive the boat on their next fishing trip, arguing with his mother about what he wanted for breakfast.

"What's his name? How old is he?"

She faced him again, squinting as though she were working it out.

"His name is Luke. He's almost sixteen."

"Where is he?"

"I'll tell you, but let's sit down first."

He picked up the old *cafetiera* from the stove and poured more coffee. Adeline pulled her cup closer.

"I tried to raise him by myself, but I couldn't do it. I had no money, and I lived in a terrible place. Then I started drinking again. Viv tried to take him for me, but the state wouldn't allow it."

She raised her mug, hiding a pained expression.

"They took him away. Then I left San Francisco for a while, but Viv didn't give up. She got me to sign guardianship papers, and she and her boyfriend took him in. When I finally came to town again, a little more sober, I was able to get him back, but something was wrong. He wouldn't touch me or look me in the eyes. He would only respond to Viv, and even then he didn't seem normal. He was just a toddler, but I could see I'd never be able to take care of him. I asked Viv if she would take him back. He was still young enough to go with her. So that's what we did. She and her man got married and set up house across the bay, and they raised him.

"They tried their best, but it didn't go well. I was right about him. Before very long they had to send him to an institution. And from there he was in and out. When he was eight, they let him go back with Viv. For a while everything was fine. I would visit and see him, but neither of us told him the truth until about a year later. We thought it would be the best thing, and that it would make him happy to know that he actually had two mothers who loved him."

She clasped her hands together on the table.

"But it was a terrible mistake. It only confused him. Whenever I saw him after that, he would stay quiet and just stare at me. And he was angry. She had trouble keeping him in school. Soon he was back in the institution, and every time Viv saw him, he was worse and worse. I couldn't take it. He was my spitting image, Alfie, and he wanted no part of me. I needed to leave. I felt like my being there was only making things awful for everybody. Then, just a year ago, Viv called to tell me they had a new medication that was helping him, enough so they could send him back to her again.

"He was fine for a few months, but then he started asking about me, talking about me non-stop, telling her he wanted to see me, and then telling me he wanted to pay me back for what I'd done to him. She and her husband told him that I tried to do what was best, but he didn't listen. Then he started to hurt himself and do violent things. He destroyed his room. He tortured one of their pets. He even threatened Viv. And then a few months ago, he stole money from their house and disappeared. He left a note telling them that he'd find me. Viv let me know immediately, and from that day on I couldn't stop worrying. I tried everything to distract myself. And then, a couple of weeks ago, I got a letter from him. Only a few sentences. He knew where I was, and he was on his way to settle things. Still, I thought, it could all be just talk. Then, two days ago he called Viv, to tell her he was close."

It was as though a stranger had told him the story. Alfie rubbed his head, trying to shake thoughts loose.

"I don't know what to do. For all I know, he could still be in California. Or he could be around the corner. Most of the time, I think it's impossible for a boy like that to make his way here. But nothing's impossible."

A switch flipped, and suddenly Alfie was back in uniform, working on a case.

"Do you know what he looks like now?"

"Yes, Viv sent a picture last year. I can show you."

She led him to the bedroom and pulled out a wallet-sized photo from a dresser drawer. Alfie held it under the light. She was right. The kid was her double. A handsome kid, almost pretty. She took the photo back, laid it on the dresser, turned to Alfie and hugged him.

"Do you think he's coming here for me?"

Alfie kissed the top of her head and rubbed her shoulders.

"I doubt it, but if it makes you feel better, we'll get out of here for a while. We'll take the boat. No trail."

He knew her fear. The kind of fear he'd seen as a cop. The fear on the face of the young girl in Sunset Park, whose boyfriend had punched her out. Alfie and his partner told her she could get a restraining order. She said, "Thank you, officers," and wiped some mascara from her cheeks. But her eyes said the bum would be back. Adeline might be that afraid. Or—considering that she hadn't said anything until now—it was possible that she really wanted her son to show up.

He forced a smile.

"We'll head for Buffalo, or maybe Albany?"

She frowned.

"And we can let the police know to look for him."

"You know the cops here. What do you think they'll do if I tell them my own son is hunting me?"

She was right. They'd listen to what she had to say, then give him that little look that said, "Glad I'm not you, Friend." They might say a few words to put her mind at ease, then go back to the station and scarf down a couple of hoagies from Gualtieri's. But he'd put in a call to one or two of the guys he'd worked security with, see what they could find out about the boy.

"Okay, but think about it."

She nodded, then took a brush to her hair and faced the mirror.

"When can we leave?" she asked, unbuckling his belt and pushing him toward the bed.

Behind them the sun was sinking fast as Alfie guided the cabin cruiser past the Oriskany Monument and down to Lock Twenty. He'd called into work and taken a few days off. They could relax. He'd even brought his guitar. Adeline sat on the bow, Indian style, a life-sized figurehead, her eyes closed, head tilted like she and the breeze were old friends. Alfie admired the arch of her back and her strong, thin arms. She'd made her share of mistakes, but she was no three-legged table. As they glided around a bend, he spotted an old towpath, where the original canal ran close. He imagined all the hoggees, the drivers who had lived their lives with mules for companions. He and Adeline were two mules pulling the same boat from opposite sides of the canal, in and out of earshot, one or the other always on the side without a clear path.

"How's about we eat something?" he asked. "The chef's on call."

"Whatever you like," she answered, breathing deeply, watching the orange sunlight play on the black water.

Alfie found a place to tie up near a big maple on the bank. So few boats passed these days that the canal was more of an endless pond than a route to anywhere. He lit, then dimmed a kerosene lamp inside the cabin, and laid foil-wrapped sandwiches, paper plates and white plastic forks on the triangular table. In the yellow haze he uncorked a bottle of red. The wine was the color of a bruise. Alfie set it and a bottle of ginger ale down on the table, then went topside. Cow pastures spread beyond the ghosts of towpaths and lonely roads to the south. In the distance were the evening's first headlights on the New York State Thruway and a line of low, dark hills that marked the boundary of the Mohawk Valley. To the north lay more hills over the dead canals and little rivers that eased down from Lake Ontario and the Adirondacks. So many people had come through here: the Iroquois, the Mohawks, the French, the Dutch, the English, down to the Italians, and now another wave.

As he worked, Alfie thought of an Indian he'd read about, Achawi, who lived back when the Indians were still feared, when they mattered. This particular brave happened to run across the half-breed daughter of a French governor. The daughter lived with another tribe who had come down the warpath from Canada. She had a name like Waneta or Lamoka, something familiar to the Mohawks as "Susan" was to Americans. Achawi was handsome, and could settle things with his words or with his tomahawk. One morning Waneta or Lamoka took her usual bath in a stream near Achawi's camp. She was just coming out of the water, a beautiful girl still wet and wrapped in nothing but a thin robe, when Achawi spotted her. And that was that. Done for. Her father, an old French count, who was in his seventies by then, hadn't much bothered with her before, but when he started fighting Indians, he couldn't leave his daughter with the savages. So what did he do? He sent spies, got her coordinates, and sent an army to hunt Achawi down and get the girl back. Achawi wound up killing most of the soldiers sent to kill him, and escaping with his true love at his side. An impossible story.

He took Adeline's hand and led her to the cabin, where she sat on one of the benches as though it were a church pew, her hands folded and eyes on the wrapped sandwiches. Alfie sat across from her, unwrapped a sandwich, inhaled the scent of fried peppers and onions, and laid the delicacy in front of her, then, as she watched, gently slid a paper plate underneath.

"A fork?" he asked.

She took a bite, and he took the cue to devour his sandwich. When he finished, he wiped his mouth with a napkin, crumpled it up, and shot it at the plastic garbage can by the hatch door. He sat back, arms stretched out on the top of the bench.

"Thank you," she said, wiping a corner of her mouth with her thumb and wrapping up the remainder of her meal.

Alfie watched her as she pressed the foil closed.

"What's on your mind?"

She reached under the table and took his hand.

"I was thinking about Luke when he was six years old."

Alfie stroked her palm.

"I hope he can forgive me."

She touched the back of Alfie's neck, snapping out of her reverie, suddenly smiling.

"Tell me. Where are we going?"

"I thought tomorrow we'd get a hotel room in Utica."

Then he laughed.

"Why is that funny?"

"They used to call it 'Sin City.'"

They slept the night in the cabin, and the next morning locked through and docked in the harbor. Alfie led Adeline up Genessee Street to the old Busy Corner. The whole time she scanned the scene like a detective. Alfie's father had told him all about the town. Corruption, bars (speakeasies before them), gambling,

and—although his father never talked about it—enough prostitutes
to live up to the nickname. Alfie's uncles had run liquor for Legs
Diamond. During Prohibition, even after, pleasure boats cruised
through the Harbor Lock, and celebrities on train tours stopped
in Union Station and put up at the Hotel Utica. A lot of money
trickled down. He remembered the hotel: gold and white lobby,
columns, vaulted ceilings and balconies. His mother once took him
and Frankie there, on a trip to see a show at the Stanley Theater:
Ezio Pinza in *South Pacific*. He remembered it being across the
main drag and down Lafayette. When they reached the spot, they
found the hotel boarded up. An old-timer on the street told them
it had gone bust a few years back. So they'd go further in, away
from the canal and the hub-bub, toward where Alfie remembered
the college and the cemetery, the American part of town. Upstate,
that always meant the well-kept neighborhood, away from the new
breed of skells he saw all around him now, the ones waiting on corners to sell drugs. Mostly blacks, but some whites too, who looked
like they crawled out from under a trailer. They wore wife-beat-
ers, and, if they were white, had haircuts that were short on top
and long in the back. Skellcuts. They went from Section Eight
apartments to check-cashing shops to Off-Track Betting parlors.
They were a world unto themselves. The local lawyers, politicians
and businessmen, in their pinstripes and ties, they were another.
And then you had the immigrants, like you always had, but from
God-knows-where.

A few blocks in, the scene improved: Victorian houses still
in good shape, with wrap-around porches, neat lawns and azalea
bushes. Big maples and spruces dotted front yards. Adeline was enjoying the walk, talking non-stop about the flowers and the houses.
They walked out toward the college, where, Alfie had learned, there
was a hotel for parents visiting kids. Alfie's daughter had gone to a
fancy upstate school. Thank God his ex-wife had remarried a fella
with money. Since then, the wall he'd built between himself and his
children had started to come down. He'd reached out to Jennifer,
and visited her a couple of times on her campus. He'd even called

Matthew. Adeline had encouraged him. So, he could understand if she secretly wanted Luke to show up. Maybe it would be for the best.

About a mile down, he noticed a small sign in front of a big Italianate house: Roseview Bed and Breakfast. If Adeline was worried, this was a perfect place not to be found. But, c'mon, if the kid was looking for his mother at all, was he looking in Utica? They checked in under his name. The woman who registered them, the owner, was a high-strung type. Thin, dyed-blond hair, small features, probably a beauty in her day. She filled out the paperwork like she was writing a summons.

"And this is yours," she said, handing Alfie back his driver's license, then remarking to Adeline, "The picture doesn't do your husband justice."

Adeline forced a smile and shoved Alfie toward the staircase.

"My name's Margie," the woman called after them.

"Oh, sorry," Alfie said, walking back to shake hands. "Pleasure to meet you."

He faked a jog back to Adeline, and this time made a beeline for the stairs. Two steps up he heard Margie's smooth voice again.

"And one more thing. Breakfast is eight-thirty to nine-thirty. Do both of you like eggs?"

Alfie looked at Adeline, who was rolling her eyes.

"Love 'em," he answered. "Anyway you do 'em, that'll be fine."

Their bed faced a window with a view of the college in the distance. Alfie drew the see-through curtain and found a radio station playing the old Louvin Brothers tune "Knoxville Girl." The rest of the day they lounged and slept. Alfie dreamt that a young boy standing on the shore of the canal was calling Adeline "Mrs. Baliato." That night, as they sat in the parlor near the fireplace, he wondered aloud what it would be like to marry her. Where would they do it? Where would the honeymoon be? Who would come to see two old fogies, who happened to be cousins, tie the knot? Maybe his brother would show up? They went back upstairs, made love, and fell asleep in each other's arms. The next morning they woke to the clinks of table-setting. When they got to breakfast, Margie, in floral apron, was taking orders on a pad, and catching up the other guests, a young couple, on the news from the morning's *Utica Observer-Dispatch*.

"Did any of you folks hear what happened in Rome yesterday?"

The young man put down the orange juice he'd been drinking.

"Didn't they, um, find somebody dead?"

"*Murdered*. They found the body in the canal. *Strangled*. Yesterday afternoon, the police are saying … Scrambled, you said?"

"Omelet, please, mushroom and cheese."

Margie took the order as she talked.

"Unbelievable what's happening these days. Not too long ago you could go a year or two up this way without hearing about a killing. And then it was always outside a bar. Now with these drugs, you never know."

People like this tickled Alfie. If they only knew what went on. What had always gone on. He wanted to laugh, but when he looked at Adeline, he saw that her lips were tight and her eyes bright with anxiety. He patted her hand, then said to Margie with deliberate calm, "Two eggs, sunny side up."

He could see that staying in one place would keep Adeline on edge.

"We'll call a cab to the boat," he said, as they mounted the stairs to their room.

It was twenty-five miles to Little Falls. Pretty there.

Back on the boat, Alfie pulled out his guitar and strummed a few minor chords, but no particular song came to mind. He could try writing one. "Little Falls" would be a good title. It was a good beginning. He put the guitar away and took the helm. They reached Lock Seventeen just as the half-moon was rising over the river. The hills crowded together here, and squeezed the valley into a narrow, rocky ribbon, where the darkness fell more quickly than usual and felt more treacherous. Lock Seventeen was the biggest lock on the canal, a good 40-foot lift. And Little Falls was a tourist spot. They would have to sit in line behind a few other boats. Each captain had to give three blasts and wait until the lock operator gave the green light. Then he would take his boat slowly in and hitch to the wall. Once the boat was tied, the operator would let the water in or out from the front of the lock. The boat would rise or fall until it came level with the canal again. Then the captain would untie and shove off. All of which took time. Alfie went below and brought back three cans: two sodas and one insect repellent. It was another muggy night. He flipped on the running lights. Adeline popped open her soda and sat in the passenger chair. Her face looked calm now, but a weird calm, like she was listening to someone Alfie couldn't see. The first boat sounded its horn.

"I want to tell you a story," Adeline said flatly. "About my son."

"I'm listening."

She took a sip of soda and cleared her throat.

"When I used to visit Luke, he would tell me all about what he was doing, the way an adult would describe his job. He read a lot of books, and he had an adult vocabulary. He would tell me how he had invented a game for all the people in the town he was imagining, where every person played a different role, but none of them knew exactly what anyone else was up to. Each time I visited, he would tell me a little more about the town and the people in it. Then one day—this was after we told him who I was to him—I went to his room, and he wouldn't talk. Just stared at me. So I started telling him what I'd been doing that week, how I was fixing up my apartment for him to visit, and how I had just come from work. And he still wouldn't talk. I tried asking him questions about his room and about school, and he kept staring. Then, as I was leaving, he looked straight into my eyes and asked, 'Who are you, really?' Alfie, I had no idea what to say. I'd never felt so afraid of anybody in my life."

She took a swig of soda and looked off across the canal.

"That was the last time I saw him."

The boat in front of them sounded its horn. She finished off her drink, and Alfie took her empty can and threw it in the trash.

"What else could I have done? What should I have said?"

"What could you say?"

Adeline shook her head.

Alfie took a deep breath. She'd always left out some of the truth. Maybe she had to.

She tugged at her hair.

"What kind of mother loses her child?"

The boat in front of them had locked through. Alfie exhaled and blew the horn three times. The lock light turned green, and the metal gates opened with a loud, slow creak. He nudged the throttle forward, glancing at Adeline every few seconds as they slid in. He tied up, sat back in his chair, and leaned across to her. Adeline fixed her eyes on the slowly descending night sky.

"What do I do now?"

"I don't know."

He took her hand.

"You held some rotten cards."

"I dealt myself those cards."

Alfie gripped the steering wheel again.

"I wish you'd've told me before now. Maybe we could've done something?"

She looked at him coldly.

"Like what? We could never afford to do anything. We haven't been anywhere in years."

He sighed.

"I just wonder why you didn't trust me."

"If I didn't trust you, why did I tell you at all?"

"I don't know. Maybe you felt guilty. Then maybe you felt desperate."

Her face fell into a pout. She stood up and disappeared into the cabin. Water drained from the lock. The shoreline and the hills rose above them. When the boat came level with the world again and the gates opened, Alfie laid eyes on the lights of Little Falls to the north and below them the black canal like the entrance to a long tunnel. They moored for the night at an old dock at the edge of town, deep in the shadows. Adeline wouldn't talk, and she slept on the opposite side of the cabin, her toes now and then scraping the top of his head where the bench beds met near the bow. Alfie woke at dawn, went topside quiet as a mouse, and shoved off. They'd make Amsterdam, Schenectady maybe, by nightfall, then get another room. She'd forgive him, and they'd figure out what to do about Luke if he actually showed up in Rome.

Adeline was still asleep when they made Indian Castle, where the canal became the river. The town itself was named for an old Mohawk fort. The Mohawks built their forts from logs, which made it easy for the French to burn them, which is exactly what they did to the one here. The only historic building left was a little church built by an Englishman, Sir William Johnson. Johnson built it for his friend Joseph Brandt, a full-blooded Mohawk. Brandt got a white man's education and even visited the royal court in England. Some books told you he was a great warrior and diplomat, others said he was a savage. Once thing was sure: He could live with Indians, and he could live with whites. He scalped people, and he bowed to the King. As they drifted past lonely old houses in the open country, Alfie remembered some of the horrible scalping stories. Warriors scalped for prestige, and sometimes money, but the worst stories of all were about revenge. Out of revenge, one Indian scalped a man's wife right in front of him, while she was still kicking and screaming. A friend of Johnson's had his men line up and scalp a whole group of Indian women and children while he watched. Just because he'd lost a battle to their tribe. One white man scalped an Indian in a tavern, right after the Indian made the stupid mistake of bragging about scalping the white man's father. It never ended.

Adeline woke up late, came topside for air, glanced at Alfie, then went back inside the cabin.

The rest of the day moved slowly. There was a lot of traffic on the canal, a lot of sights to take in: St. Johnsville, with its line of bright-colored waterside houses; Canajoharie, with its shallow falls; the low Florida hills framing the scene. Alfie kept an eye out especially for the old houses he'd read about. The best ones, he knew, would be up past Fonda, near Fort Johnson. It was almost dinnertime when they hit Tribes Hill. Adeline still wasn't stirring. Alfie tied up and went ashore for food. When he came back a half-hour later, with bread, cold cuts, and fresh peaches, he was surprised to find her lounging in the captain's chair, smiling at him as though they'd just met. He boarded, and she stood up to give him a kiss.

"You're okay?" he asked.

She gave him another long kiss and sat down in the passenger seat. Alfie took the helm and drove the boat a little further on. He anchored in front of one of the old mansions. They ate on the bow. The sun was deep orange now, but still warm. As they ate, Alfie thought he saw a figure moving from window to window in the old house, watching them. Adeline followed his eyes, as he turned to face the river. A half-mile or so further were two islands. She nodded toward them.

"After we eat, would you take me there? I just need to walk and think by myself."

She rubbed his arm.

"I love you," she said.

He nodded, trying not to look as uneasy as he was beginning to feel. After lunch, he guided the boat past a few mansions maybe fifty yards from the river's edge. When they reached the west side of the first island, he steered as close in as he could without running aground. They both looked over the side. The water would only be waist-deep on Adeline, but Alfie didn't trust it.

"How about I come along?"

"No," she said. "I can swim, but I won't even have to. Look how shallow this is. I can walk. You stay here. You can watch me from the boat."

"Have it your way."

"Get out your fishing pole."

Alfie lowered her in, then grabbed a towel from the captain's chair.

"Here. Take this."

In shorts and tee shirt, she made her way, holding the towel above the water as she took slow steps forward. When she reached the shore, she waved and set the towel on the grassy ground under a willow tree. Alfie imagined her standing on a rocky cliff above a different river. The moonlight and wind would reveal her body through a thin nightgown. He scanned the island. No one else around. He grabbed a fishing rod from under the gunwale, and began casting. Now and then he looked up to follow her walking along the shore, but he focused mainly on the silver flash of the lure a foot or two below the surface. Once or twice he could swear he had a bite. He felt a kind of trance coming on. Why should you care about the Lukes of the world? About children you didn't even know? About the right way to react? About who you were or weren't? Anything that mattered would be on the other end of the line.

(1985)

Patsy was simple. You could make it a long way if you were simple and you meant no harm. Some of Alfie's other cousins were gone, including big-mouth Angelo, who'd dropped dead before his fiftieth birthday. Nobody deserved that, but at least Angelo had probably said all he needed to say. Alfie got the family updates from Vinny, who'd called him every summer for the past few years. He wanted Alfie to come back to the reunion. It was mostly younger guys now, a new generation, Vinny said. He was hosting it. Zed Zamboni and Giambruzz both lived in Florida. Things had changed. Alfie could have his own room in the house. No ratty hotel. This year Vinny's timing was good. Alfie had nearly forgotten how to carry his anger.

Vinny's place was near White Lake, on twenty acres, not far from the site of Woodstock. It was the best land he could find close enough to his house in Jersey. Vinny had money now. When Cousin Bobby had run into gambling trouble, Vinny went partners with him, and now he basically owned Bobby's business, which had always been a good one.

"I work, cuz," he said, as they stood in the kitchen. "All the fuckin' time."

He took a swig from his bottle of beer.

"I'm divorced. You knew that. And I gave up gambling a long time ago. So, what do I do? I work. I go to Giants games. I watch TV. Once in a while I come up here. I like the routine."

Vinny had a small beer belly, but if you looked at him from a certain angle, you might think he could still play ball. His hair was only now starting to go gray on the sides, and his eyes and mouth showed just a few small lines. Still, he looked like a guy who didn't know quite what had happened to him.

"I'll show you around."

The bedrooms were on the second floor. Alfie's room was quiet and had a view of the woods and hills in the distance. The first floor had an enormous living room, with enough chairs and couches for half of the fellas at the reunion, and a big kitchen with sliding doors that opened onto a deck the length of the house. Off the deck was a swimming pool, and out beyond that were a horseshoe pit and bocce court. Around the other side of the house was a gravel-lined range for shooting skeet.

Patsy sat on the deck, in a cushioned chair, in baggy shorts and short-sleeve button-down, puffing a stogie and humming to himself until he spotted Alfie.

"Aay-Haaay! Look at you! You look just like your father. God bless ya!"

He kissed Alfie's cheek and gave him a weak hug. He was so small and thin that Alfie was afraid he'd squeeze the old man to death.

"Ah, your father," Patsy moaned, sitting down again.

Alfie nodded and tried to catch his eye, but Patsy drifted off to a song of dead voices. The rest of the gang showed up a few at a time. Most of them, like Vinny said, he didn't know. A few he did. The first one he recognized, barely, was Louie, an old man now, totally bald and with bottle-cap glasses that covered half his face. He sized Alfie up for a moment, said nothing, shook Alfie's hand like it was a piece of cardboard, then joined Patsy on the deck. Bobby stood up next, and seemed happy enough to see him. Then a couple of others. And then Zed and Giambruzz, white-haired and tanned in Hawaiian shirts. They walked right by him, and Vinny made an apologetic face as he followed them through the kitchen. The younger ones, the strangers, all had nice haircuts and expensive summer clothes. Vinny had mentioned that a lot of them worked in the stock market and lived in Jersey, right across the river from Manhattan. They didn't know Alfie from Adam, but they hugged him like he was everybody's favorite. He followed them out. They all sat down in a big circle again, and picked up their threads of conversation. The scene reminded Alfie of his old beat in Brooklyn, watching high school kids in the school yards, except these kids could buy and sell him five times over. Alfie stood outside the circle of chairs and leaned on the deck rail, listening.

"I told him we could get him into high-yields, and he looked at me like I had twelve eyes."

"I didn't want any part of him. He's working for some French assholes. I don't wanna go near them, but the bosses want us to pull in every schmuck we can. Anyway, that's why I sent him to you. I figure, you're an asshole, you can handle him."

"I got him. Don't worry. I'm motivated. We got a big LBO coming up. An energy group from Texas that can't get out of their own way. Arrogant pricks. We met with a few of them last week, and they looked at us like we were Mafiosi. Us. And they're the ones making us all pay a buck-something a gallon."

Even when they were talking about things he'd heard of, Alfie didn't get it. The most muscular of the kids was obviously the leader, the one all the others looked to for their cues. He was no more than 25, but he smoked like an old man, taking long pulls and blowing big clouds of smoke.

"Crazy things happening," he said.

A few of them mumbled "Yeah," nodding.

"Look at this thing with Russia. Reagan's supposed to meet with their President? When's the last time that happened? I thought they were our worst enemies. You know what I mean? I voted for the guy. I hope he's not too old to know what he's doing."

Alfie noticed that the kid had a nasty habit of spitting every minute or so. Right on the deck. Like he owned it.

"World's changing."

How the hell did he know?

"Moslems are hijacking planes, the whole thing with South Africa, Ethiopia, holes in the ozone layer. Like a different world. Even the Mets are good now."

The rest of the group jumped in.

"Gooden, right?"

"Twenty games already."

"He could get elected Mayor."

"The first black mayor of New York."

"You mean with all the *mulies* there, they never had one?"

The big dope's last comment seemed to embarrass the skinniest of the kids, who looked Alfie's way like he hoped he hadn't heard.

"Does it matter he's black? He's the best pitcher in baseball."

The big dope made a production of turning to the skinny kid, twisting up his mouth, then laughing.

"You know what. Joey's right. If he's making money for New York, I couldn't give a shit if he was neon purple."

A stocky kid, dressed like a slob compared to the others, didn't miss a beat.

"Unless he was with your sister."

"Fuck you."

"No, I wouldn't fuck you or your sister, but if she has a friend ..."

The big dope leapt up, grabbed the slob before he could run, lifted him up like sack of flour, and threw him into the pool.

As he sat down, the big dope landed the last jab.

"Fat fuck probably doesn't even like girls."

Then, seeing the smiles, he stood up again, cupped his hands around his mouth, and announced, "AIDS in the pool! AIDS in the pool! Everybody out!"

When the group started talking about Madonna and Michael Jackson and Tears for Fears and Live Aid and a lot of other music Alfie didn't know or didn't care about, he stepped away. As he walked toward the sliding door, he heard them talking low.

"Who was he?"

"Who?"

"The guy over there?"

"I don't know," the big dope's voice said. "Alfie's his name, I think. A cousin or something. My father knew him. Said he was an asshole."

"Seems all right."

"You never know."

As the night went on, Alfie talked with most of the cousins. The old men didn't say much to him, and the young ones, when they found out he'd been a cop in New York, only wanted to talk about that. Alfie told them a few funny stories, but nothing about being a tough guy or a hero. He tried asking them questions instead, and got the full rundown on their girlfriends and fiancés and, if they went to college, where they went to college, and who they worked for, and where they lived, and how they liked it there. But did they have their heads on any straighter than he did at their age?

As usual, everybody at the reunion ate and drank like they'd never stop: cheese and crackers, sandwiches, raw clams, ziti, steaks, sautéed hot peppers with Italian bread, casseroles, salads, pies, ice cream, coffee, and a bottle of wine each. Vinny was on his feet non-stop for hours, catering to all the old men, who settled into their thirty-year-old card games, while the young men settled into newer ones of their own. Alfie sat in where he could, but mostly watched, keeping quiet, feeling comfortably out of place. Vinny was the only one he could have a conversation with, and vice-versa, so Alfie waited. A little after dark, Vinny finally tapped him on the shoulder and led him down the deck stairs to a gravel path that snaked around the side of the house and out to a gazebo near the edge of the property. They sat down, and the host offered his cousin a cigar, then started to peel the cellophane wrapper off another.

"Sorry. I don't really smoke anymore. Got these last minute, just in case. I know they're cheap."

Alfie held his cigar out for a light.

"Here you go, Cuz."

They took first puffs and saluted each other. It was a warm, clear night. The stars seemed to hang low as the clouds, scary and peaceful at the same time, and Alfie wondered whether or not he could live in a place like this, in the middle of nowhere. In Rome people got on his nerves, but he knew at least they were around. Here you had to drive just to see a face. Then again you could pick who you saw and when you saw them. Maybe that's why people lived in separate houses in the first settlements. Even the Indians, most of them, lived in teepees. Man was meant to see only who he wanted to see when he wanted to see them.

"How long you been divorced, Vinny?"

"Seven years."

They took another puff.

"She wasn't a bad girl," Vinny added. "And she was a good mother. My kids are great. My daughter's a genius and my son's a great kid, a hell of an athlete. We're praying for a scholarship. You got kids, don't you?"

Alfie had just seen Matthew a few months back, before he left college for the military. Now he was somewhere in Texas. It had been a little longer since he'd seen Jennifer, who was a lawyer now, a couple of years out of school. Before they left Michelle's house, the kids had wanted no part of him, but he remembered how they used to cling to him when they were small. If he'd have stuck it out with Michelle and screamed at her every day, would they have liked him any better?

"Two of them. They're all right, I think. And what about your brother?"

"Danny's alive. I finally got him into the bug house. Greystone. They take decent care of him there."

Vinny flicked ash into the breeze.

"Once my father was gone, that was it. Every couple of days, like clockwork, my brother would go apeshit and bust up a room in my mother's house. Too much. What could I do? My kids were young. Besides, he'd threaten me too. I think he thought we were all a bunch of gooks, you know, out to get him. That's how he drove his wife away."

The music from the house got louder now.

"Fuckin' kids always have to blast the stereo."

Vinny turned his head and yelled toward the deck.

"Hey, assholes! They can hear you in New Jersey!"

He took a deep breath and another puff.

"So, yeah, my brother. I visit him once a week. I'm the only one who does. I bring him little snacks, *biscotti*. Sometimes I bring him Legos. Shit to keep him busy. He likes the Legos. He builds skylines. Every city he can think of. You wouldn't believe it. Even Saigon. The staff there put a few of them on display. So that's good. Probably keeps him from hangin' himself."

"Sorry."

"Listen, Alfie. What did I know then? I shoulda thanked you. So, thank you."

He patted Alfie's knee a couple of times, and lay back in the chair. The boys' shouts from the deck were almost as loud as the music.

"Listen to them," Vinny said. "What the fuck do they know?"

Alfie laughed.

"Hey, but listen to that."

"What?"

"You know that song?"

Alfie listened closely. He knew it well. Something he'd liked so much when it came out that he'd learned how to play it. Vinny drifted off into the final chorus, deep in thought. He spoke low and flat now, almost in a trance.

"Wow. So many memories. I wish I could hear the whole thing again. Ah, but that's the radio."

Alfie stood up.

"Wait, cuz. Wait a minute."

He walked down the steps and around the front of the house to his car, and reappeared a few minutes later with his guitar case. He pulled out the Gibson his father had bought him for his twenty-first birthday. If he could build a guitar from scratch, he'd build this one. Vinny watched him closely as he turned the pegs and plucked it into tune. The first chord was a G. His strum was a little more syncopated than the radio version. He barred it, then slid down to the B-minor. Then the C and the G again, all the way through the verse. It was a long song, and he'd vary the rhythm with every go-round, but the chorus had to have power, and that was—naturally—G to D to C, G to D to C. He played his way through once, without words.

Vinny followed the rhythm with his index finger. He closed his eyes.

"Reminds me of a lot of things."

He'd been playing since Adeline left, but when he played these days, he generally kept it as quiet as possible. Now, when he came back to the top, he felt like he had to sing out. As he sang the lyrics of "The Weight," the sweet coarseness of his own voice surprised him, like his body had been banking pain and wisdom. Vinny watched his guitar, like he was searching for the real source of the song's beauty.

Alfie strummed the last chord slowly, then lowered the instrument. His cousin tapped its feminine body.

"You never met Evelyn, did you?

Alfie rested his hand on Vinny's shoulder.

"No."

"She was a piece of work. The day I met her—at some little store in Teaneck—this song was playing, and she was waiting in line there, beautiful girl, singin' along with it like she didn't care who was around. So I got her number."

Alfie picked up the guitar again and strummed an A-minor.

"She was my best girl. She loved me. She kept me laughing. She even kept me in line. I remember every minute of that first summer. I drove to her house every single day, and she never let me stay over, and it didn't matter."

"She must've had good sense."

"Fuckin'-aay, right, she did. I don't know what the hell I was thinkin'. Why did I let a girl like that go?"

"Because you're an asshole."

"You're right."

"No, I mean we're all assholes. It's just that some assholes are lucky."

Vinny laughed.

"I wish I could see it that way. I mean, you shoulda known her. It was like wherever she was I felt like everything would be all right."

"What happened?"

Vinny spoke slowly.

"I don't know. I was jealous, I think, though I never said nothing to her, and, you know, lookin' back on it, what reason did I have? She was gonna marry me. But then I started thinking it was too easy. Like I couldn't trust the whole thing. Not so much I couldn't trust her, but the way it was happening so fast. And I'd have to give up this and give up that. And so what did I do? I left her for the first piece of ass that came along, who turned out to be my ex-wife."

Vinny sounded used to his regrets, but Alfie could hardly listen. Maybe his cousin still had a chance at the right woman. Or *a* right woman. What was waiting for him and all the people like him who got what they'd thought they wanted? Alfie was a couple of years away from being an old man. Who could he love? Right now he loved Vinny for being around when they were both young, and for going through some of the same trouble. But what did it mean to love someone in your family the way he'd loved Adeline? Was it the opposite of loving strangers? Alfie picked up the guitar and played one more verse of the song, imagining lyrics that could settle his mind. All at once he felt a kind of panic coming on.

That night he stared for a long time out the bedroom window at the moon. His thoughts wouldn't line up, and he barely slept at all before the sun rose. The next day he went through the motions, trying to distract himself, but missing almost every clay pigeon he shot at, and nearly falling asleep as his cousins told stories around the table. His skin felt itchy, and he couldn't focus, not even to play a hand of cards. After breakfast the next day, he said goodbye and hugged them all, even the old-timers, who didn't necessarily want to be hugged. But they were what he had, so he promised to come back again. As he drove away, he felt like somehow his life was over, like he'd be lucky to see another summer. On the way home, he barely escaped an accident, as one scene from the past after another ran through his head.

Back in Rome he tried to catch a nap, but the old house was a furnace. He got dressed again and walked to the church. When he got there, he was afraid to go inside and pray. He walked around the outside instead, looking at the reverse images of the stained-glass windows. At the last window he made the sign of the cross and walked back through East Rome. When he reached the house, he took his guitar and drove to the park where Adeline used to stroll along the canal. She'd been gone a few years now. At first she'd written him a couple of times a month, letting him know how she'd found her son and was trying to work things out. Then she'd written that things weren't going so well. Her son had rejected her once and for all. She didn't know what to do. Then the letters had stopped coming. He felt numb, like he'd dreamed away ten years of his life. The panic that had taken hold of him at the reunion mixed with that numbness, exhausting him. He picked up his guitar and lay down with it on a hammock the city had strung across a little gazebo. He tried an E-minor to an A-7th. Too heavy. Adeline was more like a rain shower than a storm, so he went to a B-flat arpeggio to a C and a quick F. That was her.

> *Adeline's on the way back home.*
> *Her boy's on the run from himself.*
> *She's gone off to find where his heart is.*
> *She's put all her love on a shelf.*

And just like that she was melody. And the song would go the way he wanted. He'd keep her beauty and her heart and let the rest of her lie in a simple rhythm. If you could take all the thoughts in your head down to a single line, pour everything into one idea, you could change things, change how you felt about them. He laid the guitar on the ground and fell fitfully to sleep.

He woke to a hard hum in purple twilight. As the hum grew louder, a pillow of white billowed up over the canal. The hammock felt like it was floating free over Rome. A shape appeared, moving forward through the magic cloud. Sure enough, it was Jesus, or somebody who looked a lot like him. He held his red robe with the tips of his fingers, and spread the robe apart, to show the faint outline of his heart through a transparent white shirt. His eyes were about to roll back into his head, as if to tell God, "I'm ready." Alfie's Jesus had hair that was red and combed perfectly back. Even his beard was immaculate. Above him another figure started taking shape. It was God as an old man in a full-length white robe. And he had some head of hair on him, too: all white, with a long beard to match. He was floating through the cloud like a bird, with planets and stars floating around him. Alfie tried to reach his hand into the cloud to touch God's hand, though it might be easier to reach Christ's robe. He stretched his arm as far as he could, but the cloud disappeared.

When Alfie came to, his face was soaked. In the corners of his eyes he felt the sting of sweat. His clothes were drenched. What he saw couldn't have been a dream. He barely remembered his dreams anymore, but he remembered this vision perfectly. He needed to do something about it. He drove back to the house and rummaged through his workshop until he found the box of tools his grandfather had given him. Laid out on the floor, they looked like a diorama you might see in a local museum. He set the hammer and chisels aside. The next day he went to Lanzello's and bought the biggest piece of basswood they had. That night, he made a quick drawing of his vision, and without the slightest idea how to carve an image, started chipping at the wood with the smallest chisel he had. Every night he stayed up, carving, until he couldn't keep his eyes open. The important thing was to capture the angles in Christ's face, to give the cloud around that face the actual texture of a cloud. He thought about his next move before he went to sleep each night and as soon as he woke each morning. During the day he read library books about bas relief, the technique and the great examples: the Ghiberti Doors, the Elgin Marbles, hieroglyphics, and thousands of French and German altar carvings. Somehow every move he made with the hammer and chisel got him closer to the picture of Christ in his mind. The signals flowed from his head to his hand in a way they used to with the guitar. It was like God was whispering instructions. By the end of September, he'd finished the piece, even painted the colors the way he remembered them from his dream.

Adeline had told him about the arts center downtown, though he'd never gone with her. He called the number in the phone book, and the woman who answered said they had a gallery dedicated to local artists' work. The next day he drove the Father and Son downtown.

(1987)

I t was an invitation. Alfie read the handwritten note inside the embossed card as he walked from his roadside mailbox to the cottage that was his home and studio. His daughter had beautiful handwriting, like a monk's in a medieval manuscript. She was writing to let him know she'd gotten engaged. She wanted Alfie to meet her fiancé. When he got back inside the cabin, he immediately started looking for his suitcase and preparing for the trip, whistling as he did.

Jennifer had told him that she and the fella were moving into an old house in Ithaca. She'd forgotten to tell him how old a house or how steep a street. The hill had the Chevelle's emergency brake hanging on for dear life. He'd decided at the last minute that instead of driving his new pick-up, he should drive the car his parents had driven, to connect the family past with its future. Over the last couple of years he'd been going along with his own whims. They'd given him a new life. He didn't want to let on to Jennifer, but he'd been to Ithaca just a couple months before, for an exhibition of his carvings at a local gallery. A lot was happening for him, but he wasn't here to talk about himself. Besides, Jennifer's fiancé was a professor. Alfie would be better off listening.

The trunk of the old Chevelle, which he'd pulled in behind the two new cars in his daughter's driveway, squealed when he opened it to lift out their gift. It was heavy, and he labored to carry it up a walkway lined with dark yellow and lavender tulips matching the colors of fresh paint on the house, which otherwise looked like it had been built by settlers. Alfie couldn't decide whether or not that meant his daughter had good taste. He had faith that Jennifer was turning out to be the opposite of her mother. As he pressed the doorbell button, he heard barking. First to greet him at the door was a big dog. It looked like a cream-colored lion. Then Jennifer appeared, holding the dog's collar like she thought he might attack, coaxing friendliness.

"Boris, say hi to Grandpa."

"No one's ever called me that before."

She smiled.

"You might have to get used to it."

He stepped inside and put down the package he was carrying.

"Housewarming gift. Engagement too."

She didn't say he didn't have to. Instead she tore off the wrapping.

"Did you make this?"

He nodded.

"Did you make it for us?"

"Who else?"

She hugged him again and yelled up the stairs, "Carl, come see what my father brought!"

When his daughter finally released him, Alfie had a chance to take the place in. The bordered wood floors were in perfect condition, and the moldings were natural maple, original, perfectly preserved. The walls had been re-plastered, not sheet rocked. The living room ceiling was painted with figures of angels and edged with inlaid wood; the one in the dining room was all hammered tin. The center-hall stairway was five feet wide and had a curved mahogany bannister. The place was designed to make you feel like you were rich. Alfie heard footsteps above him, then a deep voice that carried easily downstairs.

"On my way!"

"Dad, this is beautiful."

She raised herself on the balls of her feet, like she was about to hop.

"We're so glad you're here. I know it's a long trip. Do you need the bathroom? Or a cup of coffee."

"I'm okay."

She looked more like her mother than Alfie had ever wanted to notice. Better for her. She had the same blond hair and the same dimples, and he let himself wonder, what if Michelle hadn't been crazy? What if he hadn't been crazy? They'd be here together, proud of this girl the way only two parents together could be. Could he be that kind of father? And father-in-law? He felt proud enough, and unless this fella was a complete *cidrul*, he'd give them his clear blessing.

He heard footsteps again, this time at the top of the stairs. A tall, thin man in black slacks and gray sport jacket was standing there. At first his head was blocked by the second-floor overhang. When he stepped down, Alfie could see that two things were true: He was a good ten years older than Jennifer, and he was black. Alfie wanted for neither fact to matter. If he could spend a week carving a portrait of Martin Luther King, couldn't he have a nice dinner with a black fella who wanted to marry his daughter? Why not? A black fella had run for President. Alfie didn't feature that particular black fella, but that wasn't the point.

"Mr. Baliato, very nice to meet you."

He had a baritone voice, like Nat King Cole, and shook Alfie's hand with authority.

"Carl McNair."

Carl was lean and muscular. His dark eyes were friendly and calm, and his face broke effortlessly into a smile. He resembled a black actor he liked, the one who was always in Army movies. His daughter moved to Carl's side and slid an arm around his waist.

"Carl, look at this. Dad made it for the house."

Carl took a grand step backward, to take in the bas relief image. "This is incredible."

The carving showed two figures sitting side by side, in matching rocking chairs, holding hands, tilting their heads toward each

other as they looked out. It occurred to him to use the perspective
of someone standing behind them as they looked out on the world
that was theirs and that they wouldn't lose for a long time. The idea
that one of the hands in the carving should be black hadn't occurred
to him. He was embarrassed, but Jennifer saved him.

"Carl, I don't think Dad's ever seen a picture of you."

Alfie could feel his face flush as Carl's chin sank dramatically to
his chest. What did this guy know about him? What had Jennifer
told him? Alfie was almost fifty-three years old. What did he owe
anybody? And what did anybody owe him?

"Carl, I hope you don't take it up wrong."

Carl's smile broadened to a laugh.

"Mr. Baliato, if this were the worst thing about being black, I'd
be a much happier man."

Carl studied the carving again, and pointed to the male figure's
arm.

"We'll just do a little touch up right here."

Alfie smiled, and, without warning Carl, gave him a side hug.
He knew they loved to hug, his people. They were like Italians that
way.

"Dad, c'mon. Come in and sit down. Lunch is ready. We can
hug on the porch."

The porch out back was small, but it gave onto a good-sized
yard lined with laurel and rose bushes. The neighbors' houses were
close, but they were picturesque. No two houses looked the same.
They had eaves and alcoves and porticos over the driveways, and
sunrooms with muntin windows and sundials in yards that were full
of flowers. What was the word for a place like this? Genteel.

Jennifer seated the two men at a glass-top table and brought
out a pasta salad with tortellini, sliced olives, artichoke hearts and
even some cubes of provolone. Next came little sandwiches on
nice Italian bread with seeds: *mozzarell'* with roasted peppers and
mushrooms. Alfie took a bite of his sandwich and wiped his mouth.

"So, Dad, what do you think?"

Alfie surveyed the yard.

"Beautiful."

Carl winked at Jennifer.

"Coming from an artist like you, that's a great compliment."

Alfie laughed and wiped his mouth with a linen napkin.

"Sorry, but I don't think of myself as an artist. Sometimes I'm still driving nails for my grandfather."

"Jennifer tells me you were a police officer too."

Alfie winced.

"It's true. I was a cop. A long time ago."

"I work with a lot of police," Carl said.

"Oh?"

Jennifer filled in the blanks.

"Carl works for a non-profit called the Foundation for Equal Justice."

Alfie had heard the name, but he wasn't sure where.

"We encourage law enforcement and government officials to get together with people in low-income communities."

Black neighborhoods, he meant. Maybe Spanish. And maybe it was good thing, as long as he wasn't one of these rabble-rousers. What did he mean by "get together"? When Alfie was on the job, the politicians liked to make their appearances in "low-income neighborhoods." They especially liked going to the black churches. Alfie himself had drawn a few of those details, where he stood in the back of the church, keeping order. He liked the singing. And he remembered how the preacher could barely get out five words before somebody in the audience interrupted him. They loved to yell, but the church people tried to keep the criminal element in line. Maybe this kid was doing the same thing.

"How does that work exactly?"

Carl looked to Jennifer, to see if telling him would be all right. She nodded.

"Well, Mr. Baliato, I hope you don't take this the wrong way either, but we try to combat police bias and any kind of discriminatory policies the government might think of putting in place. The key is community input."

Carl folded his napkin a few times over, nervously, like he was waiting for Alfie to attack. But really, what did Alfie care? The government did a lot of things wrong, so why should anybody think they'd get things right with the blacks? According to Alfie's old man, Carl's people had always gotten the shit end of the stick.

"Good luck."

"It's really important work, Dad. Carl's worked all over the country: New York, Chicago, Atlanta, Los Angeles. He's been on television."

Carl waved off the explanation.

"And he teaches classes on social justice at Cornell."

"Because I'm part of a good practice in town. My firm negotiates land use between the university and the locals. Some of the laws and ordinances around here go back to the Eighteenth Century."

They were do-gooders, the two of them, saving the world. They would probably get their brains beat in, but at least they were trying. As a little girl, Jennifer would walk around their apartment in bare feet, scolding Alfie for getting home late. No more than four years old. If he complained when Michelle made dinner, she took his side and scolded her mother for being on the phone all day. Alfie's mother had the same kind of mouth, but never in public. She kept up appearances. And where did it get her? A woman could speak her mind now and get away with it. She could even earn a paycheck that way. Carl was a lucky sonofabitch.

Alfie smiled at his daughter.

"Good for you, Honey."

They all sat back and sipped their iced tea, until Carl broke the brief silence.

"Can I ask you a personal question, Mr. Baliato?"

It occurred to Alfie that a black man had never asked him a personal question. Not even on the job. A quick "How are the kids?" didn't count. Outside of cops, he'd only known a few blacks in New York, and things with them hadn't gone too well. In Rome the only one who ever talked to Alfie was the preacher. Years back, when Alfie watched black musicians play, he wondered what it would be like to talk their language and be part of that circle, to have that many secrets and feel that close because you thought the rest of the world was against you. But was his family any different? Did blacks and whites ever tell each other their secrets? Maybe on the football field or in a foxhole. If you didn't look like the next guy, did you have to take a beating with him to trust him?

"Why not? I don't think I have much to hide."

"I promise. It's nothing too terrible. I just wondered whether or not you liked being a police officer. As I said, I've worked with plenty of officers, but I'm usually standing between them and people who have complaints about them. We don't get much private time, if you know what I mean."

Alfie felt now as though Carl might be using him as a kind of adviser. Which meant he was giving him the benefit of the doubt. It was a gesture.

"Carl, it looks like we're about to be family. So I hope you can try to understand my answer, which is that sometimes I liked the job and sometimes I didn't. You like it when you think you're keeping people safe—like keeping a young girl from being beaten up by her boyfriend—you like that."

He glanced at his daughter.

"Or when you catch somebody you know is gonna steal money from other people or, God forbid, shoot people. That's the part that makes you feel like you're doing something. Like you're in the Army. Imagine you're in the Army and you can take out the guy who's trying to blow up your platoon, or else a terrorist before he kills innocent people. Like that. Don't other cops tell you the same thing?"

"They do."

"Well, then you're asking something else. You're asking me if there's anything I didn't like about it."

He shifted his gaze from Carl to his daughter and back again.

"I'm gonna guess my daughter might've told you a couple of things about my career as a cop."

They both nodded.

"Did she tell you about the riot at Columbia?"

"The student uprising?"

"Whatever you want to call it. Sure. Did she tell you I almost got killed?"

Jennifer nodded again.

"It's true. I got lucky. And I'm still not sure what I was doing there. Pardon my French, but who gave a rat's ass if a bunch of rich kids wanted to occupy a building that belonged basically to other rich jackasses?"

Alfie made the Italian hand gesture for "What do you expect?"

"So I didn't like almost getting killed for no good reason, and then having people throw things at me as they carried me to the ambulance. I could've done without that. And do I regret some things? The way I treated some people. To be honest, the way I treated some of your people. I thought I had my reasons. And it wasn't just that. I did a few other things I'm not proud of. You might call those things 'harassment.' Is that the word?"

Carl was listening closely now.

"One of them."

"You could say I had mixed feelings up until the riot. Then I didn't have a choice. I wasn't fit for the job anymore. So maybe I'm not the typical cop, if you're looking for the typical cop answer. One minute I was a hero, at least to the other cops; the next minute I couldn't walk. When I was a hero, I was proud of the uniform. When I was doing things I wasn't proud of, or when I failed, I hated it. It's like a lot of jobs. You can do good or you can do damage, and usually you do both."

He looked hard at Carl, guessing, from his serious expression, that the question in his answer got across.

"If you want a second opinion on how I was back then, Jennifer's mother might have a few things to say."

He could be mad about the years she'd cost him with the kids. At least about that. But it was more his fault than anybody's. He turned to Jennifer, who looked suddenly unhappy.

"How is your mother these days?"

Jennifer didn't hesitate.

"She's in Arizona?"

"Matthew mentioned that. With her boyfriend."

"Yeah, her boyfriend. Ron."

She made air quotation marks with her fingers when she said "boyfriend" and sarcastically drew out the "o" in "Ron."

Carl laughed, though maybe he shouldn't have, and Jennifer went on.

"Did Matthew tell you much about Ron?"

"Not much."

"Oh, O.K., let me fill you in. You know that Mom came into money when Grandma died."

"She got the house?"

"Much more than that. The old woman was hoarding a small fortune. Mom got that and the house, which she sold, to move out to Long Island, where she married Stephen, the rich one. He meant well, but he tried a little too hard to be our father."

Alfie interrupted.

"I should've made more of an effort."

Sadness crept into Jennifer's expression, but she waved off his comment, continuing the story like she'd been waiting to get it out.

"Then, you know, once Matthew and I were out of the house, she got divorced and got a settlement. And then she met Ron. Ron was living with her for a year or so, and eventually he found out how much money she had in the bank, and he convinced her to invest a big chunk of it in a restaurant he wanted to buy out in Arizona. Which of course she did, because good judgment was never her strong point. Then she tells us Ron's still married, but that he promised her he was divorcing his wife."

Carl rolled his eyes on cue.

"I know I sound bitter, but the woman's impossible. I love her, but she's a nightmare. She's like a six-year-old. Thank God for Uncle Frank. When I'm really mad at her, he talks me down."

For a moment Alfie felt like a failure, and part of him wanted to ask for his brother's number, so he could call the Italian branch of the family and tell him to mind his own business. Another part was curious about his brother's life.

"Do you talk with Frank a lot?"

"He calls once a month or so."

"How is he?"

"He's doing well, but I think he misses you."

"What does he say?"

Jennifer put a finger to her lips.

"He asks for you, but then it's more like he reminisces. Sometimes he sounds unhappy."

"Please send him my regards. And look, Sweetheart, let's not talk about your mother in a bad way. She's still your mother."

"Sorry."

Walking over to his fiancée, Carl put an arm around her.

"There's plenty else we can talk about, Mr. Baliato."

He leaned over and spoke into Jennifer's ear, as though he were on stage.

"Should we tell your father our other news?"

Sure. She was pregnant. Big surprise. He hated to think it, but that's the way it was with a lot of these people. The marriage came later, if it came at all. Not that Alfie was all for marriage, but when there were kids involved, a marriage where the husband and wife weren't at each other's throats made a difference. It was too easy to leave when you didn't feel officially tied down. But who was Alfie to talk? And why was he getting worked up? They were getting married. The kid—half black, half white, so really a black kid—would be better off than his own kids had been. They'd live in a nice house in a college town. They'd be smart. They'd go to good schools. And with any luck they wouldn't have a father who left.

"Dad, you're going to have a real grandchild."

Alfie stood up, a serious expression on his face, and strode slowly over to the expectant parents. Carl seemed about to flinch, until Alfie shook his hand and kissed Jennifer on the cheek.

"That's great news. You know, I think I might do better as a grandpa. Great news. So when is the baby due?"

Carl and Jennifer exchanged looks.

"It's not," she said. "There's an agency up in Rochester. As soon as we're married, we'll start the adoption process. If it goes the way it should, by Christmas we'll know our child."

Alfie was disappointed, and he probably didn't hide it well. Why? Did he need his bloodline out there? His blood. His father's blood. His grandfather's blood. If the kid was black, would anyone even know the blood was theirs? When you mixed with darker people, you disappeared. That might be why the Americans in Rome hated the Italians, and why his cousins went out of their way to hate blacks.

Jennifer read him.

"It's a choice. We can give an unwanted child a good life."

Carl joined in.

"Most of these kids are born into bad situations."

So he'd read goodnight stories to his adopted grandchild, mostly likely a black grandchild, and sit with him, if it was a him, at ball games. Or if it was a her, he'd show up at dance recitals, and she'd come running off the stage into his arms. And he could teach the kid about art, maybe a little about music.

"We know it looks like we're rushing, Dad, but we put a lot of thought into it."

Alfie raised his hands and gestured for them both to calm down.

"I understand."

They exchanged raised-eyebrow expressions.

"What? You're surprised? Some of my best friends are adopted."

He mugged, waiting for them to appreciate the joke, then added, "I just have to tell you up front: I never changed a diaper in my life."

Jennifer hugged him, as a light rain began to fall.

"Can you stay for dinner?"

"Why not? Where am I going?"

She kissed him and skipped off into the house.

"Be back in a little bit."

Carl blew Jennifer a kiss and led Alfie to the living room.

"Thank you, Mr. Baliato."

"For what? You're the ones doing the work. I get the instant grandkid."

"I mean that it means a lot to Jennifer that you're happy about what she's doing."

Alfie suppressed a smile.

"Carl, I don't know you, but you seem like a good fella, if you don't mind my saying."

"I don't mind."

Carl glanced at the door.

"If I know Jennifer, I'd say she's not coming right back. Can I get you a beer?"

"No, but thank you. I'm enjoying the tea. And I like the yard in the rain."

"You're an artist," Carl said, nodding and pointing at him.

Alfie leaned back in his chair.

"You keep telling me."

"Word gets around."

Alfie flashed him a kind smile.

"When did you start carving?"

"A couple of years ago. I started with a picture of Jesus in a cloud."

"Why Jesus?"

"Ah," Alfie said, raising his index finger, trying to decide how much he could share. "I'm not sure. I don't think I'm much of a Christian."

Carl nodded, it seemed to Alfie, automatically.

"Are you really interested in my carving?"

"You might find it hard to believe, but when I was in school in New York, I spent a lot of my spare time in museums and galleries. I even paint a little."

Alfie leaned forward, resting his hands on his knees.

"Well, all right, if you want to know. I started with the mass cards for my mother and father's funeral. One was the Virgin Mary with open arms. For that one I inscribed the passage that was on the back of the card, 'Blessed are they that mourn.' The other one was Jesus standing on a cliff overlooking Jerusalem, with his head in his hands. I let that one speak for itself. Then I took a trip to the art museum in Albany, and I found this beautiful painting, 'The Finding of Moses.' It showed a bunch of women finding Moses in the bulrushes. I didn't like the perspective, though, so I boiled it down to a close-up of Moses in the basket with just the women's hands hovering over him."

"Moses?"

"Sure. Everybody likes Moses. And then I did George Washington. Not because I particularly liked him, but because I saw a great painting of him standing with the British general who surrendered to him. I did FDR too, but that one was funny, because I got inspired by a picture of a pipe with his face carved into it. So, of course, I carved him smoking a pipe. Then I saw another picture in a magazine, Frank Sinatra with Mia Farrow, so I did one of the two of them together, where he's whispering in her ear. If you ever saw him sing ... Did you?"

Carl shook his head no.

"He has this habit: Between songs he walks around the bandstand and whispers to the band. I always wondered how they felt about that, or how Mia Farrow would have felt about him whispering in her ear in public. So that was interesting, plus my mother always liked Sinatra. Then I did another politician, if you want to call him that: Martin Luther King. Then after that I did one of the 1970 Knicks."

Carl tilted his head.

"No, c'mon. I'm not saying the Knicks are on King's level. I just liked how they played as a team. That was when I first started watching basketball, when I was taking care of my mother. They were something. So I did one of all their heads coming out of one body."

Alfie waited for Carl's reaction, which was just to keep watching and listening.

"Sometimes you make an image and you don't know why. I did a knock-off of a poster for Woodstock, and if you talked to me back when Woodstock was happening, I wasn't too happy about it. But when I saw the poster, it meant something. Could be I'm getting soft."

The rain had stopped now. Alfie sat back, breathed in the fresh air, and drank his iced tea. He took Carl's silence to mean he should keep talking.

"But you know my favorite one of all?"

"What's that?"

"I did one of Indians standing on Manhattan Island, watching Hudson's boat sail into New York harbor. I put one big Indian right in the middle of the group. His mouth is open. He looks stunned. Hudson's boat was a big ship with three tall masts. To the Indian it must've looked like a UFO. Can you imagine what was going through his mind? What else was out there that his tribe had never thought of? So I made sure I showed the boat in the distance, but then behind it, the open ocean, as bright as I could make it."

Carl pointed a finger and winked at Alfie.

"You know, Mr. Baliato, Jennifer didn't give you enough credit."

"I'm not sure I deserve much."

"Well, I'm feeling lucky to meet you."

Was he serious?

"Carl, it's mutual."

"Honestly, I didn't know what to expect. But you've been a pleasant surprise."

Serious or not, he had balls. He'd make a good politician. Alfie hoped he didn't wind up getting shot.

"You too."

Outside a fog was settling over the yard.

"So what are you working on now?"

"I'm going back to music."

"Playing your guitar?"

"I always play a little. Maybe someday you can talk me into playing for you. But, no, I'm doing some carvings of musicians. When they're off the stage. When they're down and out. Do you know about Hank Williams?"

"I've heard of him."

"Ever hear how he died?"

"Did he overdose? Something like that."

"Not exactly. Liquor, morphine, but not an overdose. Died in the backseat of a car."

Carl shook his head.

"Damn."

Alfie lifted his chin, trying to hear some of the old tunes in his head.

"He was my favorite. Talent beyond belief. I loved him, but I also hated him for throwing it away. He was twenty-nine years old. So I wanted to capture him at that last moment, you know, when he's still himself, right before he's gonna slip away. I'm figuring out how to frame him. And the others. I was stuck for a while, but then I saw this painting by Audubon, the one who drew all the birds. It was a sketch of rats that he made after he got permission to go shoot rats on the waterfront, to study their bodies. In his drawing the rats are alive, all huddled together, sharing whatever food they stole, living it up. But they're underground. It sounds weird, but that helped me understand these great musicians. I got this idea that they have to live a kind of life most people can't see."

"Mr. Baliato …"

"All right, listen, I just told you my life story, so call me Alfie."

"Where do you show your work, Alfie?"

"Here and there. Little galleries in Rome, Utica, Syracuse, even a couple up in Saratoga."

"Why not New York?"

Alfie chuckled.

"You know what I know about New York, Carl? To do anything in New York, you gotta know people."

Carl flashed a grin.

"Mr. Baliato, Alfie, I spend half my time getting the media to pay attention to folks with stories to tell. I know some people. How about the three of us take a little trip to New York?"

Jennifer reappeared at the door.

"Who's going to New York?"

"Your husband has plans for me."

She beamed at Carl.

"Like what?"

"Says he's gonna make me famous."

She wiped her hands on her apron.

"Is that what you want?"

Alfie looked out again at the fog and the sun trying to peek through it. He could tell them what the doctor had said about his heart, but why make them worry. If he was careful, he might live long enough to take his grandchild to the center of the world.

(1989)

I taly.

It was one thing to be here as a *Merigan'* tourist from Nebraska. It was another to be here as an Italian New Yorker and a sculptor, what people were calling Alfie these days. The place felt like a land of artists. Just on the cab ride from the station he'd seen more public statues and fountains than he could count. He was so excited that when he stepped from the lobby of the Jolly Hotel Siena into the June sun, he needed to take a long, deep breath and close his eyes to regain his balance. When he opened them, he saw a few tiny cars fly past in the white light. Beyond the cars were tall trees, surrounded by solid buildings, most of them yellow stucco, crenellated, with red tile roofs; a few of them more modern, made of granite or concrete, drab, rising a story or two higher than the older yellow buildings. It wasn't exactly postcard Italy, but the strangeness of the scene made him feel like a young man again. He forgot himself, and practically jogged across the street and into the park, where gravel covered a lot of the ground and divided the space into small clusters of cedars, pines and magnolias. Near each cluster was a park bench. On most of the benches sat older people speaking Italian; on a few others sat people speaking English, German, Japanese, and languages Alfie couldn't recognize.

Frankie owned a restaurant around the corner. The Trattoria Newyorchese, the New Yorker Restaurant. He imagined his brother sitting here in the park, reading his morning paper. Would you want to grow old in a place like this? To have a life, how many friends would you need to make? Frankie had invited Alfie here, he said, to make peace. Alfie had come to do that, and, let's face it, to see the sites, to study some of the sculpture, to eat the food, while he still could.

Alfie wandered toward the other end of the triangular park. Old men with their hands tucked behind their backs strolled by, as young women herded their small children in different directions. It was Monday afternoon, but the park was crowded. Maybe Italians saw more of each other than Americans did, appreciated seeing people on the street in a way most Americans had forgotten. It reminded him of the old neighborhood in Brooklyn. Maybe he could belong. Straight ahead of him, at the tip of the narrow triangle, Alfie spotted an odd-looking fountain. When he got closer, he saw it was a semi-circle. In the center, behind the water, was a small island covered with pebbles. A three-foot-tall statue of the Virgin Mary stood in the middle. The water flowed behind the island, into and out of a tunnel. Swimming in the water were two enormous swans, out of proportion to their home. Still, they looked content, once in a while swimming close to each other, touching necks and bills. The thought that they wouldn't live forever made Alfie want to cry, but then they were beautiful.

The air was heavy, but at least the sun was beginning to sink. Alfie made his way back to the hotel, where, after washing up and unpacking, he went down to the lobby and waited for his brother. The lobby was nothing special. Its best feature was a small rotunda surrounded by heavy, circular, white columns that tried and failed to look colossal. In front of some of the columns were a few leather couches. Alfie sat down and watched nicely dressed people walk in and out the front door and down the main hallway. He remembered how it was to be a cop. People would always recognize the uniform, but it was one in a million they would recognize your face. Twenty years ago now. It was over fifteen since he and Frankie had last seen each other. Would his brother even recognize him? He hadn't let himself get fat, but he was all gray, and his face had turned into a caricature of his younger self. Plus, he was a little stooped from leaning over the carving table. Life was treating him well, but it might not look that way.

A few minutes passed, and Alfie felt the urge to stretch his legs. He stood up and walked slowly around the rotunda until he came to a rack of brochures for local attractions. He picked out one that read "*Il Male Che È Nell'Uomo*," "The Evil Inside of Men." It was an ad for the The Museum of Medieval Criminology and the Inquisition. A second brochure advertised the The Museum of Torture: Instruments of Torture and Capital Punishment. Both museums were in San Gimignano, a town which, Alfie had read, was best known for its stone towers. Medieval families built these towers as part of their houses, to outdo one another. He'd read that Siena had had similar towers, until they started to deteriorate and drop bricks on people's heads. The Italians could live with all this history. No matter how beautiful or ugly or dangerous it was, it didn't drive them crazy. The museums charged 10,000 lire, around six dollars, for admission. Alfie pulled two bills from his wallet: 5,000 lire and 1,000 lire notes. On the first was Bellini, a musician; on the second was Montessori, a teacher. If Italians had to remind themselves of evil and torture, at least they would do it with music and education. Alfie slid the brochures back into the rack.

Uncle Enzo had always said that nothing worked in Italy until Mussolini came to power. Maybe that was true, but to look at them, you'd think the Italians had always had a system. The cabbie, the people in the park, the people on the street, the people here in the lobby: They seemed to know exactly where they were in the grand scheme, and they seemed content with their positions. In Brooklyn, and sometimes even up Rome, people were always trying to get somewhere else. Once upon a time, Frankie had been one of those people, but now, as he walked into the lobby, he looked right at home. Here he was, in khaki pants, a light-blue short-sleeved shirt, and sunglasses. His hair was mostly gray, but he had a dapper haircut, like you'd see on a page from a men's magazine hung on a barbershop wall. His head was still too big for his skinny body, but he was somehow better looking than he used to be. He walked like a young man, waving to the concierge as he passed the front desk. When he spotted Alfie, he stopped dead and took off his sunglasses, then smiled and walked toward his brother with open arms.

"You know, I used to have a brother who looked something like you."

"You look happy."

Frankie's voice sounded an octave lower than he remembered.

"Shouldn't I be? And look at you."

"Yeah, I'm old."

Frankie scoffed.

"Old? C'mon. You look good. Are you settled in here? Comfortable?"

Alfie realized that he felt proud of his brother.

"How could I not? It's beautiful here. And I'm all set up in the room."

"*Sistemato.*"

"What does that mean?"

"That you're all set up."

Frankie smiled and locked arms with Alfie.

"Let's go. We'll take a little walk. I'll show you around, if that's all right."

"Perfect. You kiddin'?"

They walked into the salmon-tinted late-afternoon sunlight and along the outside of the park.

"This park here is called La Lizza, which means something like 'The Arena.' Did you go in?"

"Yes."

"Did you see Romeo and Juliet?"

Alfie flashed the hands-together Italian gesture for "What do I know?"

"Were they there?"

"That's what they call the swans."

"I saw them. Beautiful."

"It's funny," Frankie said. "I guess the Italians think that for any couple that powerful to live in such close quarters, they have to be legendary."

They turned a corner and came face to face with a stone fortress.

"This is the *fortezza*. Only about four hundred years old, which is young for Siena."

The high, burnt orange walls were ugly, but even these were decorated with a few faces sculpted right into them. The faces looked like dogs, and must have been meant to seem ferocious: It was art meant to win wars.

"C'mon, let's take a walk inside. They serve wine, and there's a promenade."

The promenade ran around the top of the fortress, and had a 360-degree view: on one side, miles and miles of low, rolling hills with cypress trees and vineyards; and on the other, the black-and-white cathedral, brick churches, cream-colored towers and brown tile roofs of the city. They walked along one of the tree-lined paths near the fortress wall, and sat down on a bench overlooking the hills. Frankie admired the view as he spoke, without a trace of blame in his voice.

"I was pretty sure I'd never see you again."

Alfie nodded.

"Yeah. I didn't exactly expect an invitation."

"I'm sorry, Brother, that this didn't happen years ago. I don't know why. I was too wrapped up in things here, and I needed to stay away. You understand?"

"Yes. I do."

"And for a while you literally disappeared."

Alfie surveyed the hills.

"I tried."

"And I didn't know how you felt about me."

Alfie held up a hand.

"Things change. A lot of things. I didn't know whether I was comin' or goin'."

Frankie's face suddenly changed, like Alfie had reminded him of something he didn't want to think about.

"You all right?"

Frankie looked into his brother's eyes for a second, then turned back to the view.

"Yeah. I was just thinking about Mom. I wanted to be there."

"She knew how you felt."

"Yeah, maybe."

"Believe me, she was proud of you. Never said a single bad thing about you, or about the way you lived, or where. Nothing."

Frankie looked angry for a minute, then relieved. Alfie laid a hand on his shoulder.

"What else do you have to show me?"

The two brothers left the fortress and strolled down an avenue built on an aqueduct above a soccer stadium in the gulley between the city and its outskirts. Next they passed a piazza flanked on one side by a gigantic, plain brick church. They followed an alley around one side of the church and into the city's tight maze of narrow brick-and-cobblestone streets. Behind and below the church was a building that looked like a miniature castle with three vaulted openings at ground level, like three empty eye sockets.

"This is the *Fonte Branda*. Dante wrote about it. At one time the whole town depended on it. This first opening here led to the drinking fountain. The second one was a fountain where they washed their animals. And the third one was a public toilet."

Now Frankie looked happy again, hopping around like a tour guide, and Alfie noticed you could hardly hear any upstate or Brooklyn in his voice. He would always be the educated one. Never mind that Alfie already knew a lot of the history. What if they'd both been bookworms years ago? How close would they have been? So close that they'd get together every week to talk about the news? So close that they'd confess all their fears and failures?

"It doesn't sound great, but in the Thirteenth Century, this place was highfalutin. The bad thing is a lot of the plumbing in Siena hasn't improved since then."

Frankie spoke nervously. He was fifty-something years old, but Alfie could see the teenager in him, the restlessness. Something was bothering him. He led Alfie a little more quickly down a wider street called the Via Fontebranda, then onto a smaller street that took them to the front of a cathedral.

"*Ecco*," Frankie said, waving his arm in front of the façade, "*Il Duomo.*"

The cathedral was all stripes of black and white marble, like the builders were trying to make a statement about good and evil.

"I know you were never too religious," Frankie said.

Alfie shrugged his shoulders.

"Who's religious when they're young?"

Frankie gazed at the dozens of statues of saints and angels filling the façade.

"Are you religious now?"

Alfie thought about it.

"There's gotta be something else, but I doubt priests know what it is."

Frankie forced a smile.

"I think the church is closed for the day. Besides, the inside's too gloomy."

"Tomorrow, maybe."

It was almost twilight, and Frankie led him quickly through the alleyways, through people pushing past one another to make it home for dinner. In Alfie's condition, it was a chore to keep up, but he didn't want to complain. Now and then he heard the sound of a motorbike's engine somewhere in the crowd, or a voice yelling something in Italian he could almost understand. The sounds energized him. As they stepped into a huge brick piazza shaped like a clamshell, Alfie felt stronger.

"*The Piazza del Campo,*" Frankie said, leading his brother around the tables of an outdoor café. "Dates from the middle of the Fourteenth Century. If you look at the whole thing, you see it's divided into nine sections, because the city then was ruled by a council of nine. The *Palazzo Publico,* that building across the way, and the *Torre del Mangia,* right next to it, are even older."

"Why *Mangia?*"

"The tower was built to have a mechanical bell-ringer, like a primitive robot. And the human bell-ringer who lost his job was known as Mangiaguadagni, which means roughly "big-time spender," because he liked to throw his money around. So the people associated his name with the tower, and it stuck. Maybe because the Sienese have always liked throwing their money around."

It struck Alfie that Frankie had never grown up. He was the same Arista kid he'd always been, except now he had a whole other country to study and a job that allowed him to do it. He wanted badly to tell Frankie that he'd learned, studied, lived a lot since the last time they were together. Then, like it was coming from above, Johnny Cash's voice filled the piazza. Alfie traced it to the speakers in another café, where people were just sitting down to dinner. In front of the tables, on the brick pavement, which sloped downward toward the *Palazzo* and tower, were groups of young people, probably college students, sitting on the ground and talking, fading into two dimensions as the dusk fell. Everyone and everything here wanted to be made into art. Johnny Cash sang again. The kids were all different shades—many of them, it seemed, from Italy, but a lot from other places. They were studying, learning Italian, having the times they would always remember when they went back to their countries and their towns. But would that make their lives better or easier than Alfie's? If they made it to his age, what would they be doing?

"You must've heard about the *Palio*."

"I read about it."

"So you know about the *contrade*."

"A little."

"They were like social clubs that started after Siena's glory days. Probably because they had to make their own glory days."

Brooklyn Day. Parades down Flatbush Avenue.

"They wanted spectacle, you know. So they revived this dead tradition of the *palii*, these big horse races that used to be run in a straight line through some of the city gates. All the nobility sent their best horses for those races: the Medicis, the Borgias, all of them. They shipped their horses all the way here. Like the Derby. It really was the sport of kings, or princes at least."

This part Alfie didn't know, so he paid closer attention.

"They figured the best way to make it a spectacle would be to put it in the town square and dress the whole place up. And nobody dresses up a place like Italians. I know it looks drab now, but you should see it at *Palio* time. They fill the whole piazza with dirt, and they drape huge banners down the facades of these old buildings, and the riders wear incredible costumes, and there are trumpeters all lined up along here. The horses aren't those great thoroughbreds the kings had, but it doesn't matter. They use whatever horses are available. The races have a winner, but it's really whatever horse and rider don't fall or crash into the walls. It's packed with people. But even during the rest of the year, this is the city's heart." Frankie still liked to impress, and he still couldn't hide his feelings. The more he said, the more you could see he needed to talk, to avoid whatever was really on his mind. Alfie tried to keep up.

"What about the Guelphs and Ghibellines?"

Frankie laughed.

"You read about them too?"

"Sure. Which one do you think I'd be?" Alfie asked.

"At one time I would've said no doubt you're a Ghibelline. Now, I don't know."

"I don't know, either, but I think I learned a little bit about recognizing the wrong side. Nobody wants to be the Nazis or whoever they were in Siena."

The two brothers stood there for a moment, taking in the scene. Frankie couldn't look him in the eye. Maybe if Alfie put him more at ease.

"Frank. Thank you. For inviting me. It means a lot."

Again, Frankie looked upset. Alfie laid a hand on his brother's shoulder.

"Is there a place we can sit and talk?"

Frankie led him toward the *Palazzo*.

"We can do that while we eat. There's a place right back there that has the best food in the city. You ever eat wild boar?"

"Did we have boar in New York?"

Frankie loosened up again.

"We should've. Tonight you're having the boar. If you don't mind."

They took a table in the alleyway behind the *Palazzo*. The waiter brought menus printed on two sheets of legal paper.

Frankie raised his sunglasses and held the menu in front of his face like a shield.

"Frank, can I say something?"

The tone of Alfie's voice brought the menu wall down. Frankie focused intently on Alfie's face. Alfie rested his napkin on his lap and met his brother's gaze.

"I want to apologize for the way I used to be."

Frankie smoothed his napkin on the table, and smiled.

"I should apologize, too. I wasn't fair to you, and I got caught up in my career. Which reminds me to congratulate you on yours. Aunt Margaret—I can't believe she's still alive—she sent me clippings about your exhibitions and all the work you're doing with students, and it's wonderful. You've become another person in some ways. I can see it. But then, to be honest, I feel like I'm the one who hasn't changed, and I'm a little embarrassed. I'm still doing the same thing I've been doing for twenty-five years, only in a foreign country."

"This place doesn't seem so foreign."

Frankie tapped a finger on the menu.

"Maybe you're right about that, but I've been cooking and living with the same man for a long time. And, don't get me wrong, it's a fabulous life, but I was feeling lazy, like I'd lost a lot, especially my family. This all sounds like a big cliché, right? Sorry if it does. But certain things happen that remind you of what should be obvious."

"Certain things."

Frankie's expression turned serious again, and he was about to speak when the waiter came to take their orders.

They ordered and Frankie took a bigger gulp of wine, then slid the glass toward the middle of the table.

"Alfie, this is the best day I've had in years. That's the truth. The other part of the truth is that I have something for you, but I can't give it to you until you're ready to leave. Fair enough?"

"It's fair, if I can do the same."

The brothers shook hands like they did as kids, then clinked wine glasses and talked through a three-course meal. As they ate the alley grew darker and spotlights illuminated the piazza. After the meal, they walked back through the stone canyons and into the quiet night of open space outside the central city. Frankie's apartment was close to the hotel, and he promised to be up and ready bright and early, so they could start their tour of Tuscany.

In Florence it was Alfie who led his brother from one museum, one gallery, one church to the next, snapping hundreds of photos and taking notes. Frankie led the rest of the way, through cities Alfie expected and cities Alfie never knew existed but that were home to sculptures and paintings better than anything he could have imagined. Gallery owners liked to tell you there was nothing like your work, which, if you weren't careful, could leave you with the idea that art could change the world. A few times a century maybe they were right. Italy reminded you what art really was, a way of life, and how insignificant you were but still how important you could be for a brief time in a small place.

They ate at all the restaurants on Frankie's long list, and sat in all the beautiful spots Frankie might have sat in before, by himself or with his partner, staring at the sunset and wishing that his brother, or his mother and father, could see them. Their last night in Siena, they ate dinner at Frankie's place—a long, narrow restaurant with sponge-painted walls, tile-top tables, and chandeliers Frankie had collected from all over Europe. It was a slow Tuesday, and by ten o'clock they had the dining room to themselves. Alfie, Frankie, and Martino finished the *panna cotta* Frankie had made special, then nibbled on slices of *panforte*, a kind of fruit cake that was so rubbery Alfie had to dunk it in his espresso when he thought Frankie and Martino weren't looking. After Martino heard all he could probably stand about their week of touring, he stood up.

"Pardon me," he said in a heavy accent. "I'm so tired, and I work tomorrow."

He hugged Frankie and Alfie, then whistled his way out the door. Frankie smiled warmly at his brother.

"I'm glad you and Martino get along. He's a good man."

"I can see that."

Alfie could see too that he and Frankie were the brothers they'd never been. They were equals now. They could talk about art. They could talk about what was happening in the world, everything that looked like a revolution, even about the ways America had changed since Frankie had left. They could reminisce about Brooklyn and Rome, and remember the dead and even some of the living, without dwelling on their losses. Alfie could imagine himself in a studio here, in one of those old buildings in the middle of town, or out here in the newer old buildings, looking down on the little park or on the fortress, history in sight every minute of every day. Then he thought of his cottage back in Rome and the nothingness of the hills there and the quiet of walking along the canal, with just the trees on the banks to keep you company. It was funny how much people were like figures in a picture. Some were meant to be in the center, some at the edges. Alfie's place, like everybody's, depended on the scene. In Siena you could see Frankie sitting at a sidewalk table, holding his glass of wine, wearing sunglasses, the city over his shoulder. He fit as the center of attention. Here Alfie would be a small figure in the background, wandering the streets lame.

Frankie clinked Alfie's glass. Now he seemed nervous again.

"So we have this deal. Did you bring your end of the bargain?"

Alfie reached down next to his chair and pulled a flat, square, gift-wrapped package from a plastic bag. He waggled it in the air. Frankie walked into the coat closet and came back holding a smaller bundle wrapped in newspaper. As Frankie laid the bundle on the table, a terrible thought entered Alfie's head: What if his brother was dying?

"I have something to tell you."

Alfie gripped the sides of his chair and braced himself as Frankie began to speak.

"The last time I saw you, brother, you were in terrible pain. I never wanted to see you like that again. And I'll be honest, I was worried when I invited you that you'd still be that way. No, you don't have to say anything. I can see you're not that way anymore. Whatever it means for a human being to make it, you've made it. And I couldn't be happier for you. So what I have for you isn't something I want to give you, but it's a promise I made."

They both stared at the bundle in a silence Alfie finally broke.

"Do I have to guess?"

"Of course not. It was meant for you to have."

He drew a loud breath.

"It's from Adeline."

Alfie had painted over her memory with a single color, so that the features, the expressions, the eyes that had glowed for him so many times had disappeared behind a trompe l'oeil veil. Now he could see through the veil, and all the details—her movements, the sound of her voice, the touch of her hand and brush of her lips—were a powerful current, and for a moment he felt that current carrying his soul away. He grabbed the stem of his wine glass, to anchor himself.

"She was here?"

"She lived here."

Alfie tried not to look as shaken as he felt. Frankie kept talking.

"Well, not here exactly. She lived in a small town between here and Florence. For several years, in fact. She'd become a novelist, and had a couple of books out. I have them somewhere. And she translated other writers. She never used her Italian with us, but she spoke pretty well. Did you know that? Uncle Enzo taught her a lot. I couldn't keep up with her."

"When did you see her last?"

"A few months ago?"

"How was she?"

Frankie pressed his lips together.

"She wasn't doing well, but she wanted you to have this."

Frankie handed Alfie the newspaper-wrapped package, which Alfie turned over in his hands as though it were a holy relic. He laid it on the table in front of him and felt his chest tighten.

His brother looked him in the eye, his expression both fearful and brave.

"She's dead, Alfie. Multiple sclerosis, mini-strokes, other problems I didn't quite understand when a friend of hers tried to explain."

Frankie drummed his fingers on the table.

"She didn't tell me she was that sick. Or maybe she didn't know."

Alfie had tried and failed a thousand times to erase her. Knowing she was out there had helped him to do whatever came next. His work woke him up in the morning, but she, what she'd meant to him, was the actual dawn. It was fair enough to live with her that way, but this new knowledge didn't seem fair.

"Alfie, I have to apologize."

Alfie blinked, to steady the room.

"For what?"

"Of all the people in the family, I should have understood."

"I don't understand."

"I should've understood you don't get to choose who you love."

"I didn't choose her. That's the problem."

"Alfie, listen. I've been thinking a lot about this, and maybe you could stay for a while. We can find you a nice place."

Both hands on the package, Alfie exhaled.

"I love you, Brother."

He reached across the table and squeezed Frankie's hand, trying to get a hold of himself.

"I wish I could stay. But I'm not very healthy. My heart needs a lot of attention these days. And there's a woman back in Rome. I don't love her right now, but who knows?"

Frankie nodded, and Alfie ended the discussion.

"I need to be home."

He lifted Adeline's package off the table.

"Look at this," he said, tears welling in his eyes. "This is what's left."

Frankie embraced him.

"Can we open these tomorrow?" Alfie said, feeling his legs go weak.

The next morning, Martino answered Alfie's knock, said hello and goodbye, and left for work. Alfie's gift to Frankie lay unopened on a coffee table.

Frankie appeared from the kitchen and handed Alfie a cup of American coffee.

"You all right?"

Alfie sat down on the couch and looked out of a floor-to-ceiling window onto the sun-drenched park.

"I will be."

Frankie picked up the package.

"Should I open it now?"

"No."

"No?"

"It'll be better if I'm not here."

Frankie shrugged.

"Did you open yours?"

"No. I need to get home first."

"You won't reconsider staying?"

"No. But don't get me wrong. In another life—that's what they say, right?—in another life, maybe another time, I could. But not this one. Though I do plan on seeing you again in this one."

The brothers talked about all the things they still had to do in Italy and might do in New York, until the time came to call a cab and kiss each other goodbye. On the ride to the train, Alfie imagined that Adeline would be glad he'd come. She'd have wanted him to take her home. He patted the bundle in his lap. By now Frankie would have unwrapped his gift: a carving of their childhood home on Mill Street. A woman stood at the front door, and a man stood in the front yard while two children raced past him. The landscape was monochrome, bluish-gray, in low relief, while the house and people were painted brilliant colors, almost leaping from the frame. If Alfie were completely honest, the scene would have been different: a view of the father and eldest son in their bright hunting clothes, loading the car, seen from over the shoulders of the mother and younger boy. Behind them the sky would be painted the color of forgetting.

The smell of Brooklyn. The smell of relatives. The smell of ten thousand meals cooked on an old stove. The smell of peeling linoleum. The smell of a bathroom right off the kitchen. The smell of an entrance hallway that hadn't been painted in years. The smell of slip covers on fabric couches. The smell of the street wanting in. They were in Alfie's blood, and he didn't mind them. The smells overpowered the smell of mint from the mug of tea Aunt Margaret had brought him. She apologized for being out of coffee, but he'd decided to come last minute, and it was hard for her to get to the grocery.

He'd come straight from the airport, stopping only to call his aunt and give her an hour's warning. She sat him in a wing chair stationed by the front bay window, which had a view of a little park off the Gowanus Expressway and, in the distance, the Verrazano Bridge. Alfie sat there, his fingers gripping the arms of the chair as he looked down in his lap at the thin brown box and crumpled pieces of Italian newspaper Adeline had used to wrap it. He sipped his weak tea and took another look at the distant bridge, then lifted the lid off the box. Inside was a stack of typed pages with a top page, a title page, that read "The Familiar Sun."

Now the smell was getting to Alfie. He almost gagged as he noticed the layer of dust covering his ancient aunt's coffee table and credenza. For a moment he had to concentrate on his breathing. He stood up and called into the kitchen.

"Aunt Margaret, I'm going for a walk."

Her voice answered, thin as a bird's.

"All right. Don't get overheated."

The sun drifted in and out of the clouds, as Alfie walked along 65th Street. A bead of sweat slid down his neck. By the time he reached Regina Pacis Church, he was dying for a drink. It took most of his strength to pull open the heavy church door. Inside the vestibule he dipped two fingers into the Holy Water font and crossed himself. The organ was playing low, a hymn he knew. The church was empty, except for a young man in a robe appearing and disappearing behind the altar. Alfie chose a pew near the back, set

the box down next to him, and found himself whispering the first
words of a Hail, Mary. He sat back, opened the box, and started
reading Adeline's story.

Every few pages, he stopped to catch his breath and look
around the church, to see if anyone had come in and noticed him.
He stopped reading before he reached the end of the story. He
imagined his beautiful love in her white dress, sitting a few rows up,
waiting for Uncle Enzo to talk to Aunt Lena, so she could sneak a
quick look over her shoulder in his direction. It wasn't fair that with
art the artist could be dead and still make you feel what the dead
couldn't any longer. After all these years, after everything, Alfie still
hadn't mastered pain. He could only hide it in gouges and brush-
strokes, dress it up in beauty, like Adeline had done. She'd had a
vision and passed it along, given it to him as a gift he was only
meant to keep for as long as he needed it.

From the church Alfie walked to 62nd Street, along the old
Guinea gardens at the edge of the train ditch, the first boundary
of his family's life here. It used to be a canyon, but now it was a
gutter, small and pathetic. It was the best the city could do to bury
the noise of the trains that carried people from their little houses in
the furthest-flung sections of Brooklyn to the center of the universe
and back. When he was a kid, neighbors from across the ditch, usually old folks, would bring his family bags of tomatoes and *scarol'*,
and his mother would send him back across the way with the dishes
she'd made from their generosity. The whole neighborhood ran on
a system of gifts. Adeline's gift belonged here.

The greens and tomatoes and peppers and onions and zucchini
were all coming into leaf, and the vines on the chain link fence behind them were a wall of foliage as he neared 12th Avenue. At the
corner he spotted the red and black brickwork of his grandfather's
house on 61st Street. The trees in his garden were taller now than
the house, which he used to think of as a castle. He crossed the
street and walked over to the low wall surrounding his grandfather's
garden, staring at the spot under the grape arbor where the old
S.O.B. would read the newspaper. Leaning for a moment on the

wall, he held the cardboard box with Adeline's story in his hands as though he were holding a baby. Sixty-First Street was deserted and lined with cars that had seen better days. He walked into the street, still cradling the pages. Where 12th Avenue ran to the ditch, the city had put up a dead-end sign and a brick wall behind it. The wall was as high as Alfie's chest. He laid the box on top of it, opened it, lifted out the story, then removed the clip that held its pages together. The wind was kicking up, and he struggled to hold on to the sheets of paper as he shuffled them. His eyes found a sentence that broke his heart, then another that made him laugh or remember what it was to live without horizon. As he scanned page after page, the words became meaningless shapes twirling across white fields and taking on the beauty of her voice in the air, in his ear, in the world as she might have wanted it to be. The wind was stiff now, whipping bits of street trash into tiny whirlwinds. Alfie could feel an invisible hand opening his fingers, until the pages, one by one, flew from him into the emptiness.

Acknowledgements

I began to imagine this novel thirty years ago. Since then many people have contributed to its development. I will try to name them all, but probably I will fail. So, with apologies to everyone who's escaped my memory, I wish to thank the following folks and organizations:

For their constant support, inspiration, and the many, many stories, my parents, George Guida and the late Mary Guida. For their loan of time and energy, Denise Scannell-Guida, my patient wife, Bradley Guida, our clever son, and Paulette Scaglione Peters and Bob Peters, my generous and kind in-laws. For their love and memory, my paternal grandparents, Ruggiero "George" Guida and Antoinette "Nettie" Patelli Guida; my uncles, Peter and Ralph Guida, my aunts, Florence Guida and Diana LaVita; cousins Arnold and Madeleine Bascetta Mohnblatt, Paul Elia, Jr., John Ruscito, and the late Larry and Rose Belcastro. For their mentorship and friendship, the late Robert Viscusi, Anthony Valerio, and Maria Mazziotti Gillan For their editorial contributions, Michael Mirolla, Scott Walker, Adam Berlin, Jeffrey Heiman, Joanna Clapps Herman, John Domini and Fred Gardaphé. For his tutelage in the culture of New York, the late Morris Dickstein. For their literary bonhomie, Joseph Bathanti, Bob Holman, Antonio D'Alfonso, Peter Carravetta, Michael Graves and Richard Patterson. For their knowledge and help with research, former mayor of Rome, New York, the late Joseph Fusco, the late artist Sal DeRosa and his son Steve DeRosa. For their friendship and advice on language and literary license, Monique Ferrell and Julian Williams. For their friendship and support, Chris Cesare, Dan Brodnitz, Gerry LaFemina, Mercedes Hettich, Bob Timm, Christine Timm,

Annette Saddik, James Berger, Joey Nicoletti, Mike Fiorito, Anthony Tamburri, Nancy Caronia, the late Vittoria repetto, the late Gil Fagiani, Maria Lisella, Rene Fressola, Tina Struss, Lee Kostrinsky, Pamela Ouellette, Fred Misurella, Ellen Nerenberg, John Paul Russo, Marisa LaBozzetta, Annie Lanzilotto, Esther Goodman, Mark Noonan, Joseph Fasano, Nicole Alioto, Salome Farraro, Allie Oliver-Burns, Bill Waterhouse, Sonja Olbert, Darlene Bentley, Cee Williams, Chuck Joy, Sean Thomas Dougherty, Scott Williams, Jasmine Willis, and Jan Beatty. For the fellowships and the fellowship, the Research Foundation of CUNY, New York City College of Technology, the John D. Calandra Institute, the Italian American Studies Association, and the Italian American Writers Association. And for publishing excerpts of *The Uniform*, *J Journal* and *River River*.

About the Author

GEORGE GUIDA's previous books include a novel, *Posts from Suburbia*, a collection of short fiction, *The Pope Stories and Other Tales of Troubled Times*, five volumes of poetry, and two collections of critical essays. He teaches at New York City College of Technology, and curates the Finger Lakes Arts Series.